SECRETS
of
HARMONY
GROVE

MINDY STARNS
CLARK

HARVEST HOUSE PUBLISHERS

EUGENE, OREGON

The author is represented by MacGregor Literary.

Cover by Dugan Design Group, Bloomington, Minnesota

Cover photos © iStockphoto / parema, DelmasLehman; Fotolia / varnadoe5

This is a work of fiction. Names, characters, places, and incidents are products of the author's imagination or are used fictitiously. Any resemblance to actual persons, living or dead, or to events or locales, is entirely coincidental.

SECRETS OF HARMONY GROVE
Copyright © 2010 by Mindy Starns Clark
Published by Harvest House Publishers
Eugene, Oregon 97402
www.harvesthousepublishers.com

Library of Congress Cataloging-in-Publication Data
Clark, Mindy Starns.
Secrets of Harmony Grove / Mindy Starns Clark.
    p. cm.
ISBN 978-0-7369-2625-6 (pbk.)
1. Single women—Fiction. 2. Amish—Fiction. 3. Lancaster County (Pa.)—Fiction. 4. Bed and breakfast accommodations—Fiction. I. Title.
PS3603.L366S43 2010
813'.6—dc22
                                                                        2010024019

Printed in the United States of America

10 11 12 13 14 15 16 17 / DP-SK / 10 9 8 7 6 5 4 3 2 1

❧

With love and endless thanks to
Ned and Marie Scannell.
Your friendship and hospitality
help make my books a reality.

❧

ACKNOWLEDGMENTS

Many thanks to:

My Amazing Dream Team: My sweet husband, John,
and our precious daughters, Emily and Lauren

Kim Moore and all of the wonderful folks at Harvest House Publishers

Vanessa Thompson, Alex Cummings, Kendell Weiland, and Shari Weber

Chip MacGregor at MacGregor Literary

Erik Wesner

Kay Justus, Julie Koehn, Chuck Pease, Guy Anhorn,
Patricia B. Smith, and Ricky Alford

The Pennsylvania Game Commission

Ned and Marie Scannell, Paul and Amy Cummings, and Gail Anderson

Our FVCN Small Group

The Lower Providence Branch of the Montgomery County Library system

The Upper Shores Branch of the Ocean County Library system

The Mennonite Information Center of Lancaster, Pennsylvania

ChiLibris and Sisters in Crime

The wonderful members of CONSENSUS, my online advisory council

Harmony Grove
Lancaster County, PA

ONE

A large yellow Post-it Note clung to my office door, its message scrawled out in letters big enough to read from several feet away: *Sienna, Ric and Jon need to see you in Ric's office the minute you get in!!!* The note had been jotted in the familiar, artsy style of one of my copywriters, with multiple exclamation points added for emphasis. Obviously, my recent admonitions to her about nuance, subtlety, and the importance of avoiding overkill in her writing hadn't taken. Then again, maybe we could make an exception just this once. It really was a multiple-exclamation-point kind of day!

Juggling briefcase and laptop, I managed to open my office door and turn on the light before setting both in the nearest chair. I had flown from Philly to Boston first thing Monday morning, and now that I was back just a few days later, I couldn't help but grin as I thought about all I had managed to accomplish in such a short time. Judging by the exuberant note on the door, I had a feeling that news of my success in Boston had preceded my return. I had only been working here at Buzz for three weeks, but I had caught on right away that my bosses were very big on congratulating themselves. No doubt, I was being summoned by them now so they could hear the whole play-by-play directly from me and take credit for their cleverness in bringing me on board in the first place.

It would have been nice to share a quick cheer with my creative team first before heading to Ric's office, but at the moment it looked as though none of them were around. Their desks were all empty; their cubicles quiet. Wondering where they could be, I made my way through the hall, suddenly realizing how empty and still the entire place was. Since the day I started at Buzz, it had been a constant beehive of activity, no pun intended. Now, however, all was oddly quiet, with more than half the staff simply missing. The few employees I passed as I headed down the hall didn't even look up or acknowledge me. Of course, I hadn't really been working here long enough to understand the rhythm of the office yet. Maybe something was different about Wednesday afternoons. Perhaps everyone went on flex time or worked from home.

Then again, I thought, there could be one other possible explanation. Maybe everyone *was* here but they were hiding in Ric's office, waiting to throw me a surprise party! Considering the size of the ad campaign I'd just landed, a celebration would certainly be in order. If that's what was really going on, I was pleased and flattered that they had thought of it—as long as it didn't drag on for too long. Now that Empower had green-lit our basic concepts, it was time for the real work to begin. With only a week to deliver on the next phase, my team and I didn't have much time to spare on frivolities.

As I approached the glass-and-mahogany desk of Ric's ridiculously gorgeous assistant, I was embarrassed to hear my stomach rumble. I hadn't taken the time to grab lunch between the airport and the office, and now I was starving. I could only hope that the festivities would include real food and not just a cake. If someone had thought to bring in little sandwiches or even a fruit platter, I was going to be one happy partygoer.

Pausing at the desk to wait for the woman to get off of the phone, I tugged again at my sleeve, glancing down to make sure it was covering my scars, and tried to keep my face expressionless. Just because I had figured out the party plans ahead of time didn't mean I needed to ruin their surprise.

I could tell she was wrapping up her conversation, and as I continued to wait I tried to remember her name, but all I could recall was that it had something to do with a hotel. What was it? Sheraton? Hyatt? Neither sounded right. I knew it would come to me sooner or later. One by one, I was determined to learn the names of everyone who worked here.

Whatever her name was, she was so beautiful that as I stood there waiting for her to finish her call, I couldn't help but compare my looks to hers.

Though I wasn't exactly unattractive, I was far more cute than pretty, with flyaway auburn hair that never wanted to behave, a heart-shaped face sprinkled with freckles, and youthful features that made me look a good ten years younger than I actually was. I always tried to make up for that with a very professional, grown-up wardrobe, but sometimes even that wasn't enough. Standing there next to this beauty queen, I felt like slinking away to the loser section and not even trying.

Finally, she hung up the phone and turned toward me, the expression on her face surprisingly glacial.

"You're *finally* here," she said, as if I had rudely and willfully kept a roomful of people waiting.

At first I thought she was kidding, but when I realized she wasn't, I couldn't imagine where her attitude had come from. My flight hadn't landed until 1:30 and I had come straight here from the airport. Besides, how could I be blamed for showing up late when I hadn't even known that people were waiting for me in the first place?

Before I could decide how to reply, she was on her feet and walking to Ric's office door, moving more smoothly and gracefully in four-inch heels than most women did in flats. She rapped once, opened it slightly, and leaned in to say something I couldn't quite hear. Then, after a moment, she stepped back and gestured for me to go on in myself. As I did, I decided that just for her icy disdain, her piece of cake would be the smallest one, without much icing. Then again, I realized, women who looked like her didn't eat cake. They just stood close and smelled it.

I told myself to act nonchalant as I swung the door wide and stepped inside. As soon as I did, though, my pretense evaporated. No group of excited coworkers was waiting to yell "Surprise!" This was no party at all. Instead, sitting inside the sleek, cavernous office/conference room were simply Ric and Jon, the brothers who owned the company.

"Thank you, Shiloh," Ric said as I stepped inside and she shut the door behind me.

Shiloh. That was it, of course, same as the hotel chain I sometimes used out West.

"Have a seat," Jon told me, his voice oddly flat.

Glancing from one serious face to the other, I was suddenly seven years old and coming to the principal's office for having put gum in Skippy O'Brien's hair. What was going on?

"I hope you weren't waiting long," I said. "Literally, I just got in."

Neither man replied, and a nervous flutter began to stir in the pit of my stomach. Buzz's two young directors were the epitome of metrosexual cool, the owners of the hottest up-and-coming advertising agency in Philadelphia. In the few weeks I had been working here, I had found their agency to be far more intense and high pressure than I had ever experienced, but at least a bit of ongoing levity usually lightened the mood. These two at the helm were often the most upbeat and witty of the bunch.

The mood of this room, however, was anything but light.

"We have a problem," Ric said as I sat in the passion red sculpted Lorenzo chair that was the focal point of his otherwise neutral-toned office. At my previous agency, Biddle & Sons, we hadn't had things like focal points. There, business was conducted and projects were executed amid piles of papers, mountains of discarded media equipment, and the cardboard-cutout detritus of decades of promotional campaigns.

"What's up, guys?" I asked, crossing my legs and trying to look comfortable in the oddly contoured chair. The first time I had ever met these two, they looked so much alike I assumed they were twins. With their precision haircuts and rectangular tortoiseshell glasses, they were almost identical despite the fact that Ric was older by several years.

The two men looked at each other, and for a moment I feared the worst, that the agency was about to declare bankruptcy or something. *Please, no, don't let it be that.* I hadn't even made the first mortgage payment on my new condo yet. If that's what was happening, mine would be one of the shortest, brightest, and ultimately saddest professional meteors ever to arc into oblivion across the Philadelphia sky. *Please, don't be that.*

"There's no easy way to say this, Sienna, so I'll just come right out with it. I'm sorry, but you're suspended. From work. Until further notice."

A bark of laughter escaped from my lips, so unexpected were his words. Suspended? Maybe I really *was* in the principal's office! What on earth was he talking about?

"I don't understand," I said. Was this some kind of joke?

"It has come to our attention that you are under investigation by the attorney general's office. We're not at liberty to say much more than that. Unfortunately, their investigation has had an impact on us and on our biz. Until we're able to learn more about what's going on, we're afraid we can't have you working here. I'm sure you can understand the difficult position we're in."

I exhaled slowly, wondering if that airplane had somehow brought me not to Philly but to the Twilight Zone instead.

"The attorney general? Of the United States?"

"Yes."

"What do you mean? What is this about?"

"We don't have a lot of details," Ric said. "In fact, we were hoping you could tell us what's going on, and maybe use this opportunity to explain things from your perspective."

"My perspective?" I said slowly, looking from Jon to Ric and back again. "I don't have a perspective. I don't even know what you're talking about. If there's some kind of investigation going on, then surely the government has me confused with someone else."

"No, trust me. They don't."

This was ridiculous. How could I be under investigation? And for what?

"Could it be that I have some unpaid parking tickets or something? Maybe I made a goof on my tax return? I assure you both, if the government has an issue with me that's in any way my fault, I will clear it up immediately, even if I have to go to the attorney general himself. This is absurd."

Both men simply sat there, their mouths tightly pursed as they studied me.

My mind was racing, but I truly couldn't think of a single reason why Uncle Sam would have any interest in me whatsoever. My life outside of work, what there was of it, was extremely quiet. Except for my family, a few close friends, and the man I was dating, the only people I interacted with on a regular basis were the clients who trusted me with their advertising needs and the coworkers in this office whom I had barely yet had the chance to get to know.

"You guys need to back up a little bit," I said, wishing one of them would say something, anything, to explain what was happening. "This doesn't make any sense."

Ric pulled the glasses from his face and carefully wiped them using the tail of his nonchalantly untucked Armani shirt. I had never seen the man wear a tie or jacket, but I had a feeling he spent more on clothes per month than my previous boss had per year.

"We can't go into specifics here," Ric told me. "Suffice it to say that we have learned that you are under investigation by the AG's office and are suspected of illegal activities of a significant magnitude. I can't tell you anything more than that. All I can say is that now that we know, we have no choice but to distance ourselves and our company from you before even more harm is done."

"We discussed our options," Jon added, watching his brother as he finished wiping his glasses and put them back on his face, "specifically of letting you go completely. But if it turns out you're innocent, that wouldn't be a wise move. So, after a lot of convo back and forth, we agreed to suspend you without pay until the sitch is resolved one way or the other. For now, we need you to get your things from your office, and the guard will escort you out to your car."

"We should add," Ric said, "that if you are exonerated by the government, you'll be fully reinstated and the salary you missed will be paid in full."

"What about Empower? I can't leave them hanging."

They had several ideas about how to handle that, none of them in any way acceptable considering that these were *my* clients, brought to this agency by me. I was so sure this government mess could be straightened out quickly that I begged them to let me contact the people in Boston to tell them I'd run into a "personal emergency" and ask for a small extension on next week's deadline. Ric agreed to go the extension route, but only if he could make the phone call himself.

"Fine, as long as you do it right now, while I can hear what you say," I replied.

Our negotiation reached, I gave him my contact's name and number and then sat back and listened as he made the call. The man was smooth, I would give him that. Within minutes it sounded as though he had the directors of Empower in the palm of his hand.

If I weren't careful, he just might end up romancing them right out from under me—which, I realized now, might have been his intention all along, his and his brother's. Maybe that had been their plan, to bring me here with the lure of big money, insinuate themselves with my biggest client, and then toss me out with some trumped-up charges that would likely disappear as soon as I did.

Was that what was really going on?

If so, then I had to wonder how it was that I found myself sitting across from these two schemers, they of the artfully absent consonants, who used words like "convo" and "sitch" as they cut me off at the knees. Talk about a hundred-and-eighty-degree turn! Had it really been just a month ago that they had finally wooed me over to their agency with an offer too good to refuse? The night I accepted, the three of us had toasted each other over tapas at Amada, smug at the knowledge that with their resources and my connections we would soon own the advertising in this town. Now it seemed as if I didn't even own the pencils that were in a cup on the desk in my office.

How could I have misjudged things so completely? I had always been a competitive person, driven to succeed in business and in life. Though I had celebrated numerous small victories while at Biddle & Sons, it was my biggest achievement that had caught the eye of the boys at Buzz, a wildly successful advertising campaign for Empower Sportswear for Women, based on a slogan and a marketing angle that had been mine from the start.

By jumping ship and coming over to Buzz, I wondered if I had I let ambition cloud my better judgment and dollar signs obscure the truth. How ironic that my prize-winning slogan for Empower just happened to be "In It to Win It." By wanting to win in business at any cost, I may have ended up destroying everything I had been working for all along.

"Extension granted," Ric said, hanging up the phone and interrupting my thoughts. "But if things aren't cleared up by this time next week, I'm reassigning the account."

His tone was final, as if I had now been dismissed. But I wasn't about to just get up and walk out of there. I fought the good fight for another ten or fifteen minutes, begging for more information even as the two of them insisted that a suspension was their only option and that they couldn't tell me anything more than they already had. They remained aloof but firm the entire time, except when I questioned their motives, at which point they both seemed genuinely offended. Either they were two very good actors or this suspension wasn't about trying to steal my clients after all.

In the end there wasn't a thing I could do, especially once they asked Shiloh to summon the security guard. He must have been hovering just outside, because a moment later he appeared in the office doorway, arms folded across his beefy chest, waiting to walk me out. Though I hadn't done anything wrong, and I knew this was just some terrible mix-up that would soon be straightened out, I couldn't help but feel embarrassed as I glanced over at him, my cheeks burning with heat.

I stood and stiffly walked to the door, pausing there to look first at Ric and then at Jon, my eyes boring into each man in turn.

"I'm not going to waste any more breath on defending myself against charges that you won't even explain, but I will be speaking to my lawyer about this, and I can assure you that when this absurd mess is straightened out, you'll owe me more than mere back pay. You'll also owe me a massive apology and a full explanation of how you think it's acceptable to treat an employee—any employee—like this."

Turning back around, I marched toward my office, my shoes clicking rhythmically against the distressed faux-pine floor. If not for my new condo—not to mention my new car—I wouldn't have merely threatened them with a lawyer but would have, in fact, quit this job entirely. I dearly loved playing with the big boys, and my time at Buzz had already become a daily roller-coaster ride of career high points, but when push came to shove, they were shoving me out the door, and I didn't know if that was something I would ever be able to get past or not.

At least Ric and Jon had had the decency to give much of the staff the afternoon off. The few people I passed as I marched down the hall with the guard in my wake made a point of not looking my way, not even for a moment. In a sense, their discreet avoidance was almost more embarrassing than if they had simply turned and stared, as I knew they all wanted to. To make matters worse, when I got to my office I saw that someone had put an empty cardboard box on top of my desk. Were they trying to insult me or be kind? Neither, I decided as I sat down and began opening drawers. They were simply being efficient. Everything at Buzz was all about efficient.

As the security guard watched silently from the doorway, I packed up all the personal items from my office. The whole process took only a few minutes, which wasn't surprising considering that I hadn't been there long enough to collect many things of a personal nature. That single, small cardboard box, once packed, was almost an embarrassment, really, as I couldn't help but compare it to the cases and cases of stuff I had carted out when leaving my ten-year stint at Biddle & Sons.

At least I had come into this job with my own laptop, so I wouldn't be computerless while this mess was being straightened out. It was still in its case on the chair, and once I was ready to go, the guard carried the box and two potted plants while I handled my briefcase and laptop.

We were silent when the elevator doors closed on the two of us and we rode down to the first floor alone. Once we stepped outside into the cool October air and began walking toward the lot half a block away, I wanted to say something, to tell this man that I hoped he knew this was all a big mistake, and that not only had I not done anything wrong, but I didn't even know what I was accused of doing. But I held my tongue. Why bother? Obviously, with these people I was guilty until proven innocent.

My mockingly shiny new Sebring practically glowed from its slot in the parking lot. We put the plants and cases in the front passenger seat, and then I popped the trunk and told him to set the box inside, next to the suitcase that was already there. I couldn't believe that just a short while before I had been wheeling that suitcase out of the airport, the return of the conquering hero. Now, as the guard simply turned and walked away, back toward the cold steel-and-glass skyscraper I had begun to think of as my new professional home, I couldn't help but feel like a military general who had been stripped of his stripes and left to slink from the parade grounds in shame.

Looking at the building, I let my eyes rove upward as I counted ten floors. The blue-and puffy-clouded afternoon sky reflected from the modern structure, making it impossible to see inside at this time of day.

But I didn't need to see to know that there were at least two pairs of eyes looking down at me, probably more. I resisted the urge to wave—or to make any other hand gestures that came to mind—and instead simply got in my beautiful new car. Even as I gripped the smooth leather wheel, it was as if I could feel the grip on my identity slipping away.

Who was I, Sienna Collins, if not the rising young star, creative genius, and mastermind behind one of the most successful sportswear advertising campaigns since Nike's "Just Do It"? I had never had to ask myself that before, so consumed had I been with my stellar career in the ten years since graduating from college. Now it looked as if I might have to face that very question. The problem was, I already knew the answer.

If I wasn't that person—that star, that genius, that mastermind—I wasn't really anyone at all.

TWO

My first stop was the office of my lawyer and best friend, Liz, the very same place where I had sat just last month and gone over the offer from Buzz with a fine-tooth comb, followed soon after by the condo closing. Though Liz's office was half an hour away, I didn't call ahead, probably because I knew that if she wasn't there or couldn't see me I would go into full freak-out mode. Instead, I simply drove as fast as I could, leaving uptown behind as I headed to Bryn Mawr. Fortunately, Liz was in and she agreed to see me, even though she was obviously swamped with work.

Her cluttered office was quite a contrast from the stark, trendy decor of Buzz, but as I settled into the overstuffed chair that she cleared by moving a stack of files, I couldn't help but think how much more at home I felt here than I had there.

As calmly as possible, I told her everything that had just happened. She listened intently, typing notes into the computer as I went. When it was her turn to speak, however, I was disappointed to realize that she didn't seem to care whether I was guilty of having done something wrong or not. She was all about the responsibility of my employer and the legalities of the suspension. After hearing her talk about that stuff for a good ten minutes, I simply held up both hands and asked her to change gears a little bit.

"I think the first order of business is to find out why I'm being investigated. Right now I care far less about my job than I do about whatever government mix-up is putting that job in jeopardy." I leaned forward to look at her intently. "You know me, Liz. You know I am an ethical and moral person. Whatever I'm being investigated for, if I could just find out what that is, I know I could get this whole thing cleared up."

Though she probably felt as clueless as I did about how to proceed with such an odd situation, she agreed to make some phone calls on my behalf to see what she could find out. But even as she said it, I saw her eyes traveling across the mountain of papers on her desk, and I knew she was wondering exactly when she would have the time to pursue such a bizarre matter. I asked what I could do to help, and she said at this point her best advice was that I go home, sit down, and create a detailed list of my financial assets— savings, CDs, IRAs, investments, etc.—to figure out just how long I could manage without a salary.

"I don't have to sit down to figure that out. I can tell you straight away. I'm overextended. I cashed in everything for the down payment on the condo."

"Everything?" she asked, her perfect eyebrows arching upward. "Sienna, you should know better than to do something like that!"

"I know, but my new salary was going to be so much higher that I didn't think it would be a problem."

"What about the massive sign-on bonus they gave you? How long can you live on that?"

"Not too long."

She raised one eyebrow.

"Most of it is now shiny and blue and parked at a meter just up the street."

Liz groaned. Then, placing her hands on the desk in front of her, she leaned forward and gave me the *look*, that same look she used to give me in college when it was time to start a new semester, and I would have to admit that I had spent my textbook money over the summer on things like clothes or activities or art supplies.

Needless to say, finances had never been my strong suit.

Lately, with so much starting to come in, that hadn't seemed to matter. But now that she was talking about security and investments and living within my means and going without a salary, anxiety began to curl up inside of me like a fist. I didn't know how to be poor. Correction: I knew how, I just didn't want to remember. I mean, I had never lived in poverty, but when I was a kid we were definitely on the lesser side of modest, our family of four living on my father's smaller-than-average pastor's salary despite the fact that he served a beautiful church in one of the wealthiest counties in Pennsylvania.

When I was in my mid-twenties, once all of the trials were over, I had ended up with several huge settlements. After paying off my many outstanding medical and legal bills and reimbursing my parents for their numerous expenses incurred during that difficult time, I wasn't sure what to do with the rest. Eager to live a normal life for a change, I had decided to stash it all in savings for the time being and act as if it didn't even exist.

After that I went out and landed my first real job, starting as an entry-level copywriter at Biddle & Sons. It hadn't been easy to cover the cost of living in the city on such a meager salary, but somehow I had managed. As I slowly climbed through the ranks at the agency, the settlement money remained in the bank untouched, though I had come close to tapping into it on more than one occasion. When things got really tight, I would consider looking for a position with a larger, better paying agency, but then we would land a big account, Mr. Biddle would surprise me with a bonus, and I would decide to stay. Some people would have hated the erratic, undependable nature of that income, but I actually found it kind of exciting.

Then a few years ago I began dating a man named Troy Griffin. A financial advisor and wealthy in his own right, Troy had learned about my settlement money and convinced me to invest in real estate. The housing market in Philly was hot at that time, so I took his advice and soon found that I liked the power of buying and selling. Troy did too. As it turned out, he was a lot like me—and surprisingly unlike any financial expert that I had ever known—in that he seemed to love the excitement of it all, the rush of walking out of a closing with a new set of keys in hand, the thrill of spotting a fixer-upper on some weed-choked corner lot with a faded "For Sale" sign posted out front. Two early house-flipping successes in a row only fueled our fires. During the months we dated, he and I were investing separately but simultaneously, and it reached near-obsession levels for both of us. We would spend hours in discussion and research, trying to predict the different places in the city where property values were rock bottom but sure to increase and bring a handy return on our investments.

Then came the crash. Except for those few early successes, almost everything else I got myself into ended up taking a sharp nosedive. As housing prices plummeted, I realized that such an aggressive financial strategy had been not just unwise but disastrous; it was all I could do to stay afloat. And though I had teetered on the edge of bankruptcy several times since then, I had always managed to avoid it, just barely squeaking by. Last spring, I had finally unloaded my last unwanted real estate holding and promised myself that I would never get into debt like that again. And I really meant it too. Had I not been offered the incredibly lucrative job at Buzz, I wouldn't even have looked at the fabulous new condos with the private balconies that had just gone up near the river. Not even when I found out they had fireplaces, built-in bookcases, and heated floors. Really, I promise.

"What about your bed-and-breakfast out in Lancaster County?" Liz asked me now. "Did you sell that off too?"

"No, you're right. There's still that. It keeps plugging along, earning a little profit every month. But the money's not enough to live on, and I really wouldn't ever consider selling, not unless it came down to a choice between that and living on the street in a barrel."

"A barrel?"

I smiled. "You know, like in the old cartoons? The little bum with his five o'clock shadow, so broke he doesn't even have any clothes, which means he goes around naked, wearing only a barrel held up with shoulder straps."

Liz didn't smile in return. Obviously, she hadn't learned the valuable lesson that when life handed you lemons, sometimes the best you could do was make obscure cartoon references, especially when somebody used those lemons to squeeze juice in your eye.

"Don't be politically incorrect, Sienna. People don't say 'bums' anymore."

"Don't lecture me on matters that are irrelevant, Liz. Come on, I'm trying to figure out why I'm on the verge of being fired. You know how hard I have worked to get where I am. Whether this situation renders me 'homeless' or 'house impaired' or whatever they call being a bum these days is beside the point. What am I going to do?"

Despite the sharp tone of my voice, a look of sympathy flashed across Liz's features. She didn't reply but simply nodded and looked down, turning her attention back to the notes and figures she had scribbled on the yellow legal pad in front of her.

That made me feel bad. Liz was a good friend, and I shouldn't be taking my fears out on her when she was only trying to help.

I leaned forward and placed a hand on her wrist, apologizing for my outburst.

"Look, I know I can be exasperating," I said softly. "I'm too impulsive, too undisciplined, too financially irresponsible. I appreciate that you can look past all that and still be my friend. I'm just lashing out at you right now because I'm frustrated and you're here."

"I know. Thanks," she replied, giving me a reassuring smile, one that said don't worry about it, I understand, and together we will figure everything out.

Just before I pulled my hand away, I noticed her eyes pause at my wrist. Trying not to feel self-conscious, I sat back and tugged on my sleeve, knowing that even the people who knew me best, who had been with me through everything and had seen my whole arm and knew what it looked like, could still forget sometimes and be taken by surprise, if only for an instant.

She cleared her throat and got back down to business.

"As long as the bed-and-breakfast isn't operating at a loss, I think you're right to hang on to it. Not to mention that I know you want to keep it in the family if at all possible."

"That's correct."

From that whole period of time Troy and I were dating, only one good investment remained: Harmony Grove Bed & Breakfast. Two years ago, when my grandfather died and left his property in Lancaster County to the various members of our family, Troy had convinced me to buy out my brother's share and join up with my father to turn our combined parcels into a small bed-and-breakfast in the heart of Amish country. Troy said he knew a man we could hire as manager of the place once it was up and running.

But first, to keep costs down, my dad and I had supervised most of the renovation ourselves, making the drive out as often as we could and even using up vacation time as we converted the place from an old Amish-built house to an elegant yet cozy bed-and-breakfast. Troy had helped us out a lot too, though the investment had lasted far longer than our relationship. He and I had broken up halfway through the renovation.

But at least his idea had ultimately paid off. That little five-bedroom bed-and-breakfast ran so smoothly in the competent hands of the on-site manager Troy had recommended that I barely gave it a thought more than once a month, when my tidy little handwritten profit check arrived. Last year, after my mother was diagnosed with multiple sclerosis, I had bought out my father's share of the place as a favor to him. Though that had extended my finances even further, so long as the profit checks kept rolling in, I knew it was still an investment worth keeping.

Now, as I sat in my old friend's office and thought about losing everything—my inn, my car, my condo—I realized that my current boyfriend, whose advice was far more conservative than Troy's had ever been, had been correct. Someone who had struggled with as much debt as I had, with only one good asset and a new job that had barely even started yet, had no business buying a condominium, much less one right on the river with a clear view of the Ben Franklin Bridge, even if it was going to keep my feet toasty warm on cold mornings.

Heath wasn't the only one who had warned me not to overextend myself. My parents had echoed his words, as had Liz, but I had been blinded by the heady figures Ric and Jon kept throwing at me, not to mention eager for the chance to meet and even exceed their expectations. How was I to know that something would come flying in out of left field like this and throw such a giant monkey wrench into my well-laid, albeit naive, plans?

"I suppose your next move is to put out some feelers about selling the condo. See if you can come up with other potential sources of cash, if it comes to that. In the meantime, I'll try to move heaven and earth on your behalf, putting out some inquiries with my government contacts and maybe threatening the Buzz boys with a lawsuit."

"You'll keep me posted?"

"I'll call you as soon as I make even a fraction of headway."

"All right. Thank you, Liz. I'll get out of your hair."

I stood to go, even though I would be leaving with no more answers than I'd had coming in. At least she would start the ball rolling. I could take comfort in that.

"No offense, but can I give you a little advice?" she asked as she walked me out.

"Sure. Advice that starts out with the words 'No offense, but...' is my favorite kind."

"Don't be sarcastic. No offense, Sienna, but I hope this situation makes you think long and hard about your tendency toward faulty decision making. If you hadn't—"

"I know, I know," I interrupted. "If I hadn't overextended myself, if I hadn't been so impulsive and self-indulgent—"

"I was going to say, if you hadn't let your own common sense be so swayed by a handsome man, you might not be facing such a precarious financial state now."

"You're talking about Troy Griffin."

She nodded.

"Don't worry, Liz. I am so done, and not just with Troy, but with all of the Troy Griffins of this world."

"I'm glad to hear it."

I opened her office door and stepped out into the empty reception area, turning to face her.

"Funny you say that, though," I added. "Would you believe that Troy actually called me out of the blue the other night? First time I've spoken to him in over a year."

Her eyes widened.

"What did he want?"

I explained that Troy had frequent business dealings in Lancaster County, and that he was one of my B and B's most regular customers. Late Monday night he had called to say that he was out there, staying in his usual room downstairs, when he had run across some old papers of my grandfather's and wanted to know what he should do with them. After some initial awkwardness, the call had ended up being fun, a simple reconnect with an old flame and an opportunity to brag a bit about my new job. It also helped that the timing had been good. When my cell phone first rang I had been bored to death, propped up in bed in my hotel room in Boston too wired to sleep but unable to find anything interesting on TV.

"Well, I just hope that was a one-shot deal. He didn't sound like he was trying to start things up again, did he?"

"Oh, gosh, no. Not at all," I assured her. "And just to make sure, I managed to throw Heath's name into the conversation quite a few times."

"Good. That's what I like to hear. Now Heath, *he's* a keeper, the perfect guy for you."

"You really think so?"

"Oh yeah. What's not to love? He's smart, handsome, successful..."

"So was Troy."

She squinted at me and began counting off with her fingers.

"And unlike Troy, Heath is dependable, solid, respected in the community..."

"Sounds like a job applicant, not potential husband material."

Suddenly, she reached up one hand and gently gripped my chin, looking into my eyes and speaking to me the way one would speak to a small child.

"He's what you *need*, Sienna. The very opposite of Troy."

I studied her face for a moment, thinking how beautiful she was, how elegant looking even now, at the end of a busy workday with her lipstick worn off and her clothes slightly rumpled. She and I were the same height with similar builds, but there the similarities ended. In college the guys liked to call us "Beauty and Cutie" when we were together. She was the Beauty of the pair, with her dark brown skin and long, elegant neck and classic features. I, of course, was the Cutie, with big eyes in a youthful face that I supposed didn't look too bad when I was all made up—but looked about twelve years old when I wasn't. Together, she and I formed quite a contrast, though after the incident senior year that would change my body and my life, I secretly thought a more accurate name for us would have been "Beauty and the Beast."

Right now, Beauty was still holding my chin, no doubt trying to make sure I really heard what she was saying. I got it, but I didn't appreciate being treated like a child by my lawyer, even if she was one of my best friends.

"You know, Liz, if you ever get tired of this job, I think you would make a very good kindergarten teacher."

She laughed, letting go.

"Sorry, point taken. Now get out of here, girlfriend. I have a client in a big mess, and if I don't get on it, pretty soon she'll be wearing nothing but a barrel."

THREE

Walking toward my car along the tree-lined street, I had to admit that already I felt better, more in control. Nothing about my situation had changed, but at least now I had an ally, one who would help me come up with a plan of attack.

Reaching my car and slipping inside, I tried to decide what to do next. I thought about going to see Heath, who was an emergency room doctor at Bryn Mawr Hospital just a few blocks away. I had no doubt that he would be a solid and comforting presence at this very difficult time. I knew he would believe me and support me, and maybe even offer to lend me some money if it came down to that, not that I would accept such an offer. Surely, he would be nothing but kind. Still, I was reluctant to go and see him. Just the thought of telling him what had happened made my cheeks flush with heat.

If only he hadn't objected so strongly when I accepted the new job and immediately put myself back into debt. I knew he wasn't the kind of guy to rub that in my face now, but he and I would both know the truth. He had told me so, financially speaking, but I had ignored his warning.

Starting up the car and admiring the gentle hum of its very new, very well-oiled engine, I decided to skip Heath for now and continue on to the one other place I could always find comfort and kindness and support: my parents' house.

Harold and Ida Collins still lived in the same parsonage in Radnor I had grown up in, a small converted carriage house that at one point had been connected with the massive estate next door. Their three-bedroom home was comfortable but small and dated, with wood-paneled walls, vinyl countertops, and kitchen appliances at least thirty years old. As a child I had loved living there, loved coming home down the curved driveway that first swept past the estate house and its beautifully manicured lawns before ending at the little carriage house that sat hidden in the trees beyond.

Once I reached middle school, however, I began to not love it quite so much. The more aware I grew of the modesty of our means, the more embarrassed I began to feel about everything: our tiny home, our second-hand clothes, our inability to afford the summer camps and tennis lessons and shopping trips the other girls in my class seemed to take as their right.

By the time I started high school, I no longer invited anyone over, preferring to socialize at their houses instead. Whenever I had to get a ride home from a friend, I would tell them to pull over and drop me off out front. If they wanted to assume that I was walking up the driveway to the huge stone mansion clearly visible from the road, that was their mistake, albeit one I wasn't quick to clarify. It wasn't until I went away to college and grew up a bit and began to appreciate my parents all over again for the wonderful people they were that I realized what an enormous brat I had been.

Now that I was possibly on the verge of pennilessness and maybe even bankruptcy, I couldn't help but think how grateful I was that the size of my parents' hearts far exceeded the biggest mansions in the world. They weren't in a position to help me out financially, but simply knowing I could plop down at their kitchen table and share my woes, without condemnation, to two pairs of loving, accepting, and sympathetic eyes was priceless.

Once I arrived, though, as soon as my father opened the door to greet me, I saw that his eyes were more tired and frightened and hurting than anything else. That's when I remembered what day it was. In my mother's ongoing battle with MS, she had gone for her quarterly treatment today, an infusion of a drug also used in chemotherapy.

After Dad's welcoming hug at the door, he whispered that she wasn't nauseated yet—he hoped that wouldn't happen at all this time—but that the body aches and fatigue had knocked her for a loop. She was lying on the couch, and when she opened her eyes and saw me, she broke into a broad smile and thanked me for coming, saying how much it meant to her that I would drive all this way just to see how she was doing after her treatment.

Though my heart was full of shame, I didn't correct her assumption. I wasn't trying to make myself look good; I just couldn't bear to make her feel bad. Instead, I acted as though that had been my intention all along, and I told my dad to sit down and rest while I made us all some tea. Shoulders visibly sagging, he plopped into the chair closest to the couch, leaned his head back, closed his eyes, and blindly reached out to take my mother's hand. In a near-simultaneous motion, her fingers simply moved to entwine with his and held on. She closed her eyes as well. Observing them, I felt that old familiar twinge of tenderness and security, the legacy of all children whose parents remained deeply and steadfastly in love.

My eyes filling with tears, I turned away and went to the kitchen to make some tea. I felt like a selfish, shallow idiot, and I knew God was using this situation to remind me that there were things in life far more important and more dire than government investigations, job suspensions, and money concerns.

Over the next hour, I devoted my energies to caring for both of my parents, cooking supper as I waited to hear back from Liz. Using ingredients I was able to dig up in the kitchen, I made a big pot of vegetable soup, and as it simmered on the old stove I threw together a batch of corn bread to go with it.

My situation was never far from my mind the whole time, though, and I kept discreetly peeking at my cell phone to see if I had missed anything. Liz didn't call, so I decided I would give her until 5:30 before trying her. She had told me to be patient, but patience wasn't exactly one of my virtues.

The phone finally rang at 5:17 p.m. My heart surged with hope, but then it sank just as quickly when I saw that the name on the screen wasn't Liz but Troy Griffin.

Again?

Holding the phone in my hand, I didn't answer it. Instead, I let it go to voice mail, thinking of how Liz had asked if Troy was trying to start things up again. Good grief, I hoped not. Our conversation the other night had been fine, but it had been about closure, not some new opening. When the phone beeped to tell me I had a message, I pressed the buttons and listened.

Hey, Si, it's Troy. I'm sorry to bother you again, but this is urgent. Really urgent. Can you call me back as soon as you get this? It's...it's important, okay?

And that was it, just a few short sentences, punctuated by the huffs and puffs of a man on the move, as though he were running and out of breath. Against my better judgment, I decided to return his call, though before it was over I planned on telling him to not contact me again.

I gave the simmering soup a stir, peeked at the corn bread in the oven, and then stepped out the back door for some privacy. Sighing, I called him back.

"Sienna!" he answered. "Thanks for returning my call."

"No problem," I replied, using the clipped tones of one who had other, more important things to do. "You said it was urgent."

"It is. Listen, have you ever heard of something called a Fishing Tree?"

I blinked, wondering if the man had lost his mind. This was his big emergency? Some sort of word game? I pictured him running on a treadmill, bored and killing time by calling me.

"You gotta be kidding. What are you doing, Troy, working a crossword puzzle? Watching a game show?"

"No, of course not. This is important. Just tell me, do you know what that is? Where it is? A Fishing Tree?"

"I'm sorry, but I do not have time for this." On Monday night when things were good and all was still right with the world, I hadn't minded hearing from Troy. But today, when I had been so vividly reminded of the impact our relationship had had on my finances and my life, I could barely tolerate the sound of his voice. "Troy, I have to go."

"No, wait! Please! It's...it's about your grandfather. About those papers of his."

I hesitated, trying to realign my thinking.

"What do you mean? What's going on?"

"It's hard to explain. In the papers, he says something about a Fishing Tree. Wait—hold on. Just a second."

As I listened to the sound of him fumbling with the phone, I made my way to the wrought iron bench next to the weeping willow and sat, wondering what this was all about.

"Sorry, Sienna. I'm afraid I'm not feeling so well. Like, dizzy. Real dizzy."

"You're not driving, are you?"

"No, no, I'm outside. In Harmony Grove. Been out here for hours, trying to figure out which one of the bazillion trees in here is the one your grandfather would have called the Fishing Tree."

I closed my eyes and began pinching the bridge of my nose. I knew he had called me from the bed-and-breakfast the other night, but I hadn't realized he was still there. And I sure couldn't fathom what this city boy, who had zero interest in the outdoors, was doing in the lush, wooded grove that had been designed and created by my grandfather. Most important, if this was about Troy trying to get in touch with his inner outdoorsman or something, what was so urgent about that?

"You probably have heatstroke, Troy. That can happen, even when it's not all that hot. If you ever actually went outdoors, you would know that."

"Ha-ha. Yeah, I know this might sound a little out of character, but I was reading through your grandfather's papers about this thing he kept calling the Fishing Tree and I just got really curious about it. Oh boy, hold on. I think I'm gonna be sick."

Pulling the phone from my ear, I tried not to listen.

"Sienna? Are you there?" his voice said loudly after a moment, so I put the phone back to my ear.

"I'm here. But I'm thinking that if this really is important we should talk later, when I don't have to listen to you losing your lunch."

"I didn't throw up, I just had to sit down. Maybe I'll be okay now."

Through the phone, I could hear the crunch and snap of autumn leaves as he settled himself on the ground. Was he serious? This was his big emergency? Wandering through the grove and hunting for a certain tree?

My irritation at this man bloomed into full-blown anger. I had no one to blame for my financial mess but myself, but at the very least I didn't feel like sitting here listening to this city boy play country rube when I had such bigger things going on in my life. Surely, this was the very picture of self-centeredness, that if something was important *to him*, then it was important, period.

I said as much now.

"Whoa, Nelly. Hold on, calm down. You sound angry. What'd I do?"

Was he kidding me?

"Troy, I don't have time for this! Today was an absolute disaster for me. You...you have no idea." Though I probably shouldn't have shared with him the details of that disaster, I couldn't help myself from driving the point home in a rant. "A few hours ago I was suspended from my job, my brand-new job at one of the top advertising agencies in Philadelphia. The suspension is without pay, and right now I'm facing the distinct possibility that if something doesn't change very soon I could end up having to declare bankruptcy."

"Suspended? You mean like a leave of absence?"

"Yes, an involuntary one. They even had the security guard escort me from the building."

"Why? What did you do?"

Somehow, the way he asked that question only served to make me even more furious.

"I didn't *do* anything, Troy, I was just summoned to the boss's office like a kid getting called in to the principal. I was told I was being suspended, without pay, until further notice. Apparently, I'm under investigation by the U.S. attorney general's office for reasons unknown, at least to me."

That seemed to stop him cold. Then, after a long moment of silence, he spoke.

"Say that again, Sienna? The U.S. attorney general's office is investigating you but you don't know why?"

"That's correct. Liz is looking into it, but so far she hasn't gotten back to me."

"Wow. I sure didn't see this coming. I wonder how they found out."

Maybe it was his words or something in his voice, but suddenly the hair on the back of my neck began to stand on end.

"Found out what, Troy? Does this have something to do with you?"

He didn't answer at first. Instead, I heard only more crunching and shuffling, as though he was getting back up, and then the rhythmic crunch-crunch of footsteps through fallen autumn leaves.

"Maybe you're right, Si. Maybe this isn't the best time to talk. Why don't I give you a call later?"

Suddenly, this had become the most important phone call of the day.

"Don't you dare hang up. You know something. Tell me what it is."

"I have no idea what you're—"

"Tell me, Troy! Now!"

This time he really did throw up, only I had no forewarning.

As disgusting as that was, I was willing to wait it out if it meant I might get some answers when he was done. After several long moments he came back to the phone.

"I'm so sorry about that. I don't know what's the mat...what's the...what's wrong..." he said, and I realized his speech was growing slurred. Had he been drinking? Was that what was going on? He'd been tossing back beers and wandering in the woods while looking for some stupid tree?

"Are you drunk, Troy?"

"Of course not."

"Then what's wrong with your voice? Why are you talking like that?"

"I dunno. I really, really don't feel good."

Suddenly, I was afraid he might be having a stroke or something, but then I realized the more likely explanation was that if he'd been out there a while, maybe he'd become dehydrated. Not being used to outdoor activities, he probably hadn't thought to bring along bottled water.

"Have you had any liquids lately? You could be dehydrated."

"I had a diet soda with lunch, but I've been out here ever since, looking for this tree. It's like trying to find a needle in a haystack," he said, though it came out sounding more like "neilinahaysta."

I told him enough with the tree, that he was to head straight back to the house, drink a big glass of water, and lie down. I didn't add that the sooner he did that, the sooner we could continue the important part of this conversation, and I could find out whether there was a connection between him and what had happened to me today.

"Where am I?" he murmured.

"You're in the grove."

"I know that, but what part? Which way is the house?"

Growing more concerned, I told Troy I was going to put him on hold and call Floyd to go outside, find him, and help him in.

"Floyd's out of town. Won't be back till tonight. Been gone since Monday."

My B and B's manager had been out of town for two days? Maybe that's why Troy was still there, to hold down the fort until Floyd returned, something I knew they had done in the past. Though I doubted Troy knew how to serve a delicious country breakfast to the inn's guests, at least he was handsome and charming, and as long as ladies were present, I didn't think they would have any complaints.

On the other end of the line, I could hear what sounded like metal clanking against metal, and I asked Troy what he was doing now.

"Trying to get back to the B and B like you tol' me to. It's just this latch, it's so complicated..." Another clank and then, "There, got it...no, wait. This isn't right. Where am I?"

"I don't know, Troy. What latch?"

"Jus' a latch on a gate. But it's okay. I think if I retrace my steps, like this..." More crunching as he walked. "No, tha's not right either. I jus' don't understand. Where *am* I?"

"I don't know, Troy. I'm trying to help you figure that out. It sounds as though you're all turned around. Are there any signs nearby? Any benches? Markers? Are you near the creek? Tell me exactly what you see."

"I see trees, Sienna. Lots of trees. I'm in a grove. What do you think I see?"

Sarcasm was good. At least it meant he wasn't out of his head. Just lost and confused and no doubt in dire need of liquids.

The stupid thing was that this shouldn't be a big deal. It wasn't as though he was lost in a national park or something. Then again, I guess to someone not used to the wild outdoors at all, the various trees and paths could begin to look alike.

What I really wanted to do was to call my cousin Jonah, whose farm was on the other side of the grove. But Jonah was Amish, and the nearest phone for him was in a booth up by the main road, shared by more of our cousins who lived on a farm across the street from that. The shared phone had voice mail, but in my experience it wasn't checked very often. If I left a message now, chances were good that they wouldn't hear it for several days.

The only other person I could think to call was my Uncle Emory, who lived on the other side of the grove. But Emory was mentally disabled, and though he knew the grove like the back of his hand, I didn't think I should put on him the responsibility of delivering Troy to safety.

"I think I see it now, what I did wrong before. I just have to—"

He stopped.

"Have to what?"

No response.

"Troy? You just have to what?"

"Shhh," he finally whispered. "Do you hear that? What is it?" I strained to listen but couldn't pick up anything. "Weird. I've never heard a sound like that before. Is it a machine? An animal?"

"I don't know, Troy. I'm not hearing anything."

"It's like a hum, a low hum," he said softly. "Like, I can almost feel it more than hear it. Sort of a rumble, you know? Almost like an earthquake, a tiny little earthquake."

I didn't know what to make of that. Was he having hallucinations? Should I hang up with him and call 911? While I tried to decide what to do, the phone remained silent.

"Are you still there?" I asked.

"Yeah."

"Still hearing it?"

"No. It stopped. I don't know what it was, but it stopped."

I stood, wishing I could drive there myself. But even without traffic it would take a minimum of forty minutes, and I was afraid he might not have that much time to spare if he really was hallucinating.

"Listen, Troy, I think you should call nine-one-one. You need some help." I didn't add that once we hung up I would call them too on his behalf, just to be safe.

"Wait a sec. I don' think that's necessary, I...oh...Oh!"

I cringed, afraid he was going to throw up again. Instead, he let out a little whoop.

"I see it! Way over there! I can see the roof of the B and B. Okay, I'm good. It's just a straight shot from here."

His voice still sounded slurred, but at least the end was in sight. I didn't know much about dehydration, but I had a feeling if he wasn't too far gone all he needed to do was drink some liquids and rest. If that wasn't enough, well, then we could call 911 after all.

"I'm sorry I bothered you with all of this, Sienna. Such a big fuss over a stupid tree. Anyway, I gotta go. I'll be all right. We can talk later."

"Troy, wait. *Don't* hang up."

The crunch of his footsteps changed, and I realized that as he walked it was sounding less like leaves and more like gravel, which meant he really was on the right track. The grove sat in a long, flat oval, and it was encircled around the perimeter by a gravel path. If he was on gravel now and could see the inn in the distance, then I had a general idea of where he was and I knew he wouldn't get lost again.

"Now that you have found your way, get back to what you were saying before. What did you mean, you didn't see this coming? Do you know anything about my being investigated?"

He didn't answer at first, but I knew he was there because I could hear his footsteps and his breathing.

"Troy? Talk to me. What do you know?"

He exhaled slowly.

"Look, I'll put it this way," he said finally. "Jus' don't blame me if the feds are on to things here, okay? Tha's Floyd's fault, not mine."

"Things?" I demanded. "What things?"

"Tha's all I'm saying. I didn't mess up. Floyd did. Look, I gotta go."

And then, without another word, he hung up.

For the next ten minutes, I tried calling him back, but he wasn't answering. I left several urgent messages in his voice mail, each one angrier than the one before. Finally, I switched tactics and tried calling the bed-and-breakfast directly, even though Troy had said Floyd wasn't there. That call also went to voice mail, and after I heard my own recorded self politely asking callers to leave a message and we would get back to them, I practically yelled into the phone, "Floyd, this is Sienna Collins. Call me on my cell phone. *Now.*"

I heard the back door opening as I disconnected the call, and I looked up to see my father standing in the doorway, concern etched across his features.

"Honey? Is everything okay?"

I tried to recover from the moment, squaring my shoulders and smoothing my hair. Should I tell him? I wanted to. But did he really need to take on my burdens when he was burdened enough already?

Trying to make my voice sound light, I simply said that I was having some issues at work, and that I was sorry I had to be out here fussing at people on the phone rather than visiting with him and Mom.

"Listen, she and I both know how busy you are, especially with the new job. It was an incredibly sweet gesture for you to come out here tonight, but please don't feel that you have to stay. You got some cooking done, and for that I am grateful. Almost burned the corn bread, but I got it out in time."

The corn bread! With Troy's call I had forgotten all about it.

"Anyway," he continued, "please don't think you have to stick around just because you feel like you should. It's the thought that counts."

If his words had come from anyone else, I might have seen them as suspect, thinking I wasn't wanted or something. But I knew him too well, and I was confident my father's selfless sentiments were genuine.

And though being with my parents really was where I belonged right now, I also knew I wouldn't be any good to either of them until everything was sraightened out. Bottom line, I needed to drive out to Lancaster County and confront Troy face-to-face.

FOUR

Fifteen minutes later I was on the road and talking to Liz, who said that so far she hadn't been able to come up with anything. I told her about my bizarre conversation with Troy, but she became so worked up at the thought that this situation might somehow involve him that I didn't have the nerve to admit that at that moment I was on my way to see him.

Better she learn that after the fact, once I had confronted him and forced him to give me more information. Liz promised to keep looking into things on her end, and after we hung up I couldn't help but feel as if the weight of the world was resting on my shoulders.

Seeing my poor mother and what she was going through had helped to put the whole mess in perspective, but there was no denying that it was indeed a mess, one very confusing, ugly mess, and right now the only hope I had of cleaning it up was walking down a gravel path at Harmony Grove, babbling about earthquakes and likely suffering from dehydration. Depending on traffic, the trip to the inn could take as little as forty minutes or as much as an hour and a half. Regardless, it was the only course of action I had for now. I headed west and continued to dial Troy's cell phone number every ten minutes or so along the way. Between calls, I gobbled down the large chunk of corn bread my father had pushed on me as I was leaving.

Of course, given the day I was having, traffic ended up being exceptionally heavy. By the time I turned from the main road onto the street that

led to my final destination, it was after 7:00 p.m. Even in my current distracted, angry, and frightened state of mind, the beauty of the scenery took
my breath away, as it always had.

Passing one patchwork farm after another, barely visible now in the fading light, I couldn't help but think how different my life would have turned
out if my grandfather hadn't broken away from the Amish faith back in the
forties and gone down a different path. If my father had been raised Amish,
would he have stayed in the fold? If so, if he had raised me to be Amish too,
would I now be living on a farm of my own somewhere, wearing a *kapp*
and picking vegetables with my five children and cooking meals on a pro-
pane-powered stove? Would the man who took me in his arms after a long
day have a beard with no mustache and wear broadfall trousers I had sewed
for him with my own hands?

Slowing as I reached the entrance to Harmony Grove Bed and Breakfast, I put on my blinker and turned into the driveway. Flanked on the right
by thick woods and on the left by an open pasture, the long driveway made
for a spectacular sight when there was light enough to see.

Uncle Emory's driveway ran parallel to mine but on the other side of the
pasture. And though my house was twice the size of his, he had something
I didn't: a covered bridge, very near the road, through which ran the beginning of his driveway over a lazy, trickling stream. Though technically not
on my property, that bridge was part of the allure of the B and B, and it was
clearly visible from the front windows of the bedrooms upstairs. The left
windows looked out over the grove, which was placed at an angle between
Emory's land and mine, and the back windows looked out on parts of the
grove as well, plus the graceful, tree-lined yard, and the small swimming
pool behind the inn that I'd had put in during the renovation.

Reaching the end of the driveway now where it widened into a small
parking lot, I saw two cars there. If memory served, the Honda was Floyd's.
I supposed the BMW was Troy's, though it could also have belonged to a
guest. I wondered if Floyd had just arrived home or if he'd been here all
along and Troy had lied to me earlier when he said Floyd was out of town.
Coming to a stop in the farthest slot, I got out of my car and placed my hand
on the hood of the Honda.

It felt slightly warm, which meant it may have recently been driven. Perhaps Floyd really had been gone.

Leaving all of my things in the car, I headed up the walk to my inn, startled to see that the exterior was completely bare of landscaping: no flowers in the flower beds, no hanging plants along the back porch, no blossoms beside the walkway that led to the pool. I peered into the distance, trying to see if anything was planted in the two giant clay pots that flanked the gate to the pool area, but it was too dark to tell right now.

Shaking my head, I paused at the bottom of the back steps, remembering what my father had told me. Last spring, when my mother was feeling better than usual, he had brought her out here for a mini vacation. I had been so excited for them and eager to hear how their trip went, but after they were back home my dad told me that I might want to know that as beautiful as I had managed to make this place on the inside, the outside was still incredibly bland and sparse, with no flowers—not even a single hanging plant. He knew I'd had trouble with this same issue the previous summer and that I would want to get a jump on things this time. I had e-mailed Floyd about the matter, and he had responded that he would take care of it. After that, I had never thought of it again until now. As I reached the back door and pulled it open, I realized that despite Floyd's assurances, nothing had ever been done in the matter. That made me nervous, because it led me to wonder what other tasks Floyd was supposed to have handled but hadn't.

At least the interior is nice and clean, I thought as I moved into the large sitting room inside the back door. I glanced at the elegant furnishings and fixtures, wishing I could simply enjoy wandering around the entire inn, inside and out, and letting my eyes linger on all the fabulous little touches that we had included in the renovation. It had been a while since I was last here. But that would have to wait for another time. Right now I needed to speak to Troy and most definitely to Floyd as well.

Despite the little bell that had jangled over the door when I came in, no one seemed to realize I was here.

"Troy? Floyd?"

I called out both men's names several times, and when they didn't reply I checked the kitchen and the office, both of which were empty, and then I went to the far end of the hall and knocked on the door to the room I knew Troy stayed in when he was here. He didn't answer, but I pushed it open anyway to see if maybe he was lying on the bed. I could tell that he was indeed staying in this room, as his suitcase was near the window and what looked like a wallet and keys were on the dresser. The bed was made but not neatly, as if he had simply gotten out of it and smoothed the covers. His window was open, and white lace curtains fluttered gently in the evening breeze.

I closed the door and returned to the main sitting area, coming back around to the door of the room where Floyd lived. I knocked on it, but he didn't answer, and so again I opened it up anyway and peeked inside. Floyd's bed was neatly made, with a navy duffel bag sitting on top. But he was nowhere in sight, and through the open door to his darkened bathroom I could see that no one was in there, either.

I decided they must be outside. Taking one more quick look in the kitchen just to be sure, I saw that at least one of them had recently been in there making themselves a sandwich. On the counter was an open jar of mayonnaise with a knife sticking out of it, and beside that a bag of bread and a plate with half of one sandwich made. As I had done with the car, I put my hand on the mayonnaise jar. It was cold.

It was growing so dark outside that I flipped on the exterior lights before going back out. I didn't see or hear anyone, but I called out their names again several times, each time progressively louder. When no one answered, I stood there in the silence for a moment, trying to see if I could hear anything.

Unlike Troy, I had always appreciated the outdoors and enjoyed getting back to nature, but that didn't mean it didn't take some adjusting for me too. Ears used to city noise always had trouble getting a handle on such complete country silence.

With only the chirp of crickets as accompaniment, I called out the men's names yet again and decided they must be further out back or maybe over in the grove. Perhaps Troy hadn't made it to the house after all, and Floyd was out looking for him.

Gripped by a disturbing sense of urgency, I called Troy's cell phone one last time, but he still didn't answer. Taking a deep breath, I then decided to try Floyd's phone. If he also didn't answer, I would call the police. Hoping it wouldn't come to that, I punched in Floyd's number and waited for it to ring at the other end of the line.

Much to my surprise, however, not only could I hear it ringing through the phone, but I could also hear an actual phone ringing somewhere not too far away.

"Floyd?"

He didn't answer, so I followed the sound, moving toward the solid fencing that surrounded the pool area. Could he be inside there? If so, why? It was too late in the year to go swimming, that was for sure. And he obviously wasn't planting flowers. His phone went to voice mail, so I disconnected the call and then redialed it again.

"Following the sound, I reached the gate and pulled it open.

That's when I saw Troy.

He was lying on his back beside the pool, dripping wet, with a huge, gaping wound that had been ripped through his trousers and clean into his thigh. Blood stained his pants around the wound and his eyes were open, frozen in a horrifying death stare.

Troy was dead. Looking at him, there was no question that he was dead. Yet still, instinctively, I ran to him—or I tried to, anyway. My foot caught on something on the ground beside the gate, something soft but solid that caused me to trip. I fell forward, landing on my knees and on both hands. Screaming more from the surprise than the pain, I turned to see what had caused me to fall.

It was Floyd, lying on the ground, facedown, a handgun clutched in his lifeless right hand. On the cement near his other hand was his cell phone, still ringing from my call. After one more ring it stopped, no doubt having gone into voice mail again. As I sat trembling—from pain, from fear—rocking back and forth, I couldn't help thinking, absurdly, that it didn't matter if I left a message or not.

He wasn't going to be answering it now.

FIVE

The 911 dispatch officer was excellent, his actions immediate, his voice deep and extremely calming as we stayed on the line together while I waited for the sound of approaching sirens. I hadn't heard anything yet, but he assured me emergency responders were on their way.

I couldn't begin to guess at what had happened here, but as I sat on the ground where I had fallen and looked around me and waited for help to arrive, I forced myself to take in everything and try to figure out what I was seeing. The first thing I noticed were footprints, faint marks on the cement that led from the pool to the gate. I was trying to describe them to the dispatch guy when I realized the prints were disappearing before my eyes.

"Water!" I said finally. "They're from pool water, and as they dry they're disappearing." I thought about that and then added, "Someone with wet feet walked from Troy's body across the patio and out the gate."

I thought I should take a few photos with my cell phone while the prints were still there, so I put the call on speaker phone, switched it over to camera mode, and snapped a few shots as best I could. The lighting wasn't great, so I didn't know if the images would be viewable or not, but I knew it was worth a try. In a few more minutes the prints would be gone completely.

I had just switched my phone off of speaker and put it back to my ear when I thought I heard a sound nearby. Whipping my head around, I realized, much to my astonishment, that the sound was a moan—and that it was coming from Floyd.

He was alive!

I was only a few feet away from him and could easily have checked his pulse, but suddenly I was frozen to the spot, my eyes glued to the gun in his hand. To my knowledge, Floyd wasn't a violent man, but for all I knew that gash in Troy's leg had been made by a bullet—and Floyd had been the one to pull the trigger.

Quickly and silently, I managed to get up and move backward until I was able to crouch down behind a canvas lawn chair. Perhaps in the semi-darkness he wouldn't notice me. At least I hoped he wouldn't. Positioned as he was on the cement between me and the gate, Floyd's body blocked my only exit from inside the fence.

Why hadn't I kicked the gun out of his hand when I'd had the chance? More important, why had I left both of my own guns in the car instead of bringing at least one of them with me?

Listening to him now, I decided that though he was still alive, he was completely incoherent. Still mumbling, his legs began twitching, though his hands remained still. I whispered all of this to the dispatch guy, adding that between moans Floyd's breathing sounded strange, heavy but with long, frightening pauses where he didn't seem to be breathing at all. Watching closely from my perch behind the chair, I noticed that his right hand had begun to move. Holding my breath, I waited to see if he might rise up now on his knees, gather his wits about him, and shoot me at point-blank range. Instead, his hand simply opened and shifted a little, unknowingly releasing his grip on the gun.

Without thinking, as fast as I could I jumped out of hiding, ran forward, and kicked that gun off to the side and out of reach. It skittered across the patio, coming to a stop at the base of a wrought iron table. Without a gun in his hand, this barely conscious Floyd wasn't nearly as much of a threat. And though I knew how to handle a gun myself and probably should have grabbed it for safety's sake rather than kicked it away, I had merely been moving on instinct.

I thought about retrieving it now, but something told me that leaving it where it was under the table would be the smarter move. Maybe I was being paranoid, but if that was the weapon that killed Troy, and if I was already being investigated for some sort of wrongdoing, then the last thing I needed was a murder weapon with my fingerprints all over it.

Catching my breath, I finally knelt down beside Floyd, wishing that Heath were with me now. As an ER doctor, he would have been in his element and known exactly what had happened to Troy and how to help Floyd. As it was, all I could do was report Floyd's condition to the dispatch officer at the other end of the line, who assured me again that help was on the way and that I should just sit tight and make sure I was in no danger myself.

Moments later, Floyd's moans and murmurs began to sound more like words. Leaning forward, I tried to hear what he was saying, but it took a few tries before I thought I understood.

"That creature, what was it?"

Gingerly, I reached out a hand, put it on his shoulder, and gave him a gentle shake.

"Floyd? It's Sienna. Sienna Collins. Can you hear me?"

I wasn't sure if he could or not. His eyes didn't open, and he just kept saying something about a creature. Then he added something new to the mix, blurting out more clearly, "What was that sound? What was it?"

In my mind, I could hear Troy from earlier, on the phone with me: *I've never heard a sound like that before. Is it a machine? An animal?*

"What was the sound, Floyd? Did it sound kind of like a machine? Was it a hum?"

He didn't answer so I shook him again.

"Floyd! It's me. Sienna. What did it sound like?"

That time, he opened his eyes, though obviously with great effort.

"Sienna?"

"Yes. I'm here. An ambulance is on its way."

"Am I dead?" he asked, again closing his eyes.

"No, you're still alive. Are you hurt?"

Mumbling, and then, "I don't know."

"You don't know if you're hurt?"

"I don't remember."

I spoke into the phone, explaining what was happening and asking what could possibly be taking so long.

"It feels longer than it is," the dispatch guy replied. "You should be hearing sirens any second now."

Frustrated and afraid, I turned my attention back to the man who still lay on the ground in front of me. Unlike Troy, whose hair and clothing were soaking wet, Floyd's body was completely dry. I also didn't see any signs of blood, though of course he was lying facedown, so he could have had an injury in the front.

"What happened here, Floyd? Did you shoot Troy?"

"No. Troy's dead."

"I know, but how? What killed him?"

Floyd simply moaned, so I tried a different approach.

"Floyd? Can you tell me about the sound you heard? What was it like?" Thinking of my call with Troy, I added, "Did it sound like a hum?"

"Lower," Floyd rasped. "More like rumbling."

I swallowed hard, remembering Troy's words: *I can almost feel it more than hear it. Sort of a rumble, you know?*

He opened and eyes and stirred a bit more, as if trying to look around. But the effort was too much for him, and after a moment he seemed to pass out again, his face landing flat against the cement.

"Floyd," I said, shaking his shoulder and trying to wake him up. "Come on, man. Hang in there."

Again, his breathing sounded off, and for a moment I feared he had stopped completely. But then out of the blue he sucked in a great gasp of air and spoke.

"The creature...breathed fire...just like a dragon."

"Fire?"

"But it wasn't a dragon. I don't know...what it was. It was big...and black and shot out a burst of fire."

I stared at the pale, puffy lids of his closed eyes, trying to make sense of his words. They were slurred and slow to come out, but his tone was adamant.

"Floyd, why were you out here? How did Troy end up in the pool?"

"I heard a scream. I was in the kitchen and a woman screamed, so I grabbed the gun and...came out."

I waited for him to go on, but he did not.

"A woman? What woman? Where is she?" I demanded, wondering if those had been her prints leading from Troy's body. "Who was it, Floyd? Who screamed?"

"Nina. It was Nina."

I sat back on my heels, worried now for yet another person. Nina lived across the street in the little cluster of houses that ran along the main road. A friend of our family for many years, she was also the part-time aide and caretaker for Uncle Emory.

"Where is she now? I don't see her. Are you sure she was here?"

"The creature musta got her. Carried her off."

Heart pounding, I stood and turned in a slow circle, peering into the darkness along the fence, looking both for Nina and for whatever creature it was that Floyd kept talking about. Were we in danger? Should I retrieve his gun from under the table and stand guard? There didn't seem to be anyone or anything else inside the fencing with us, so at the very least should I close the gate so that nothing could get in? Except for the metal gate, the fencing itself was stucco with tile embellishments, solid and thick, though only about four and a half feet high. Closing the door wouldn't keep everything out, but it might help, depending on what might be trying to get in.

Before the dispatch guy could tell me what he thought I should do, I finally heard sirens in the distance. The noise quickly grew louder until it could have been a hundred different sirens, all speeding toward us. I simply stood there waiting next to Floyd, and as soon as I could tell that personnel were out of their vehicles and within earshot, I began yelling.

"Here! Here! We're over here!"

Soon I was surrounded by what felt like a dozen people, most of them in uniform, all of them looking as if they knew exactly what to do. As yet more responders arrived, the crowd grew: paramedics to work over Floyd, uniformed officers to guard the scene, armed gunmen fanning out across the lawn and probably into the grove beyond. With all of the activity, I could only hope they would find Nina before it was too late for her, as it was for Troy.

Much of what happened next felt like a blur of uniforms and bodies and movement, punctuated by the crackle of radios and walkie-talkies. A man in uniform led me to the nearest chair, the very same one I had hidden behind just a short while before, so that I could sit down. For some reason, he seemed to think that if I didn't sit soon, I might fall down. He may have been right. As more and more activity went on all around me, I realized my entire body was trembling and that I was gripping the armrest so tightly that my knuckles practically glowed white in the near darkness.

I sat there and tried to gather my wits about me, fully aware that this situation would have been traumatic enough on its own, but I had a personal history that made it about a million times worse. Closing my eyes, all I could do was try to block memories of the one other time in my life when I had been surrounded by these same types of sounds and sights, the milling about of busy, uniformed law enforcement officers who had responded to a cry for help and tried to make right what should never have gone wrong in the first place.

Finally, a different officer came over to me, an attractive African American woman who introduced herself as Georgia Olsen. She asked me if I was okay, if she could get me anything, if I had been hurt in any way. How could I tell her that even just the concerned but professional tone of her voice brought back memories from that one night so long ago, brought them crashing over me like waves beating furiously against a pier?

Had it really been ten years? Right now it felt more like ten days, or maybe even ten minutes.

Georgia could probably see that I was losing my grip on my emotions because she helped me up, took me by the elbow, and led me out of the pool area, along the walkway, and up the steps into the main room of the bed-and breakfast. Somehow, I ended up on the couch with a glass of water in my hand, a blanket on my lap, and an EMT at my elbow preparing to take my pulse. I couldn't find it within myself to stop him and tell him he should go for the other wrist. Instead I just sat there like an observer of my own body and watched as he pulled up my left sleeve to reveal the scarred and mangled skin that it had been hiding. A true medical professional, he didn't wince or even react to the sight but instead simply switched to the other arm and continued with what he was doing. Georgia, on the other hand, allowed her gaze to linger a little too long before politely looking away.

The EMT finished checking my vitals and began asking me strange questions, such as did I know what date it was and who was the president of the United States. For a moment, a small part of me wanted to answer in ways that were totally bizarre, like "1923" and "Tony the Tiger," just to see how he would react. But I resisted the urge, afraid he might misinterpret the joke. At least I was thinking humorous thoughts, which had to be a good indication that I still had my wits about me.

After checking me over, he said I looked okay but asked if I wanted to go to the hospital anyway. I told him that I did not, that there was no need, that I wasn't hurt. Even the pain from my earlier spill on the sidewalk was gone.

I thanked him and then watched absently as he placed his equipment back in its case, picked it up, and headed outside. Once he was gone, something inside of me wanted simply to slip away, to take a long rest or merely lapse into blessed unconsciousness. But then Georgia was sitting on the coffee table in front of me, one strong hand on my arm, giving me a gentle shake.

"Sienna? I know he said you're fine, but we can still take you to the hospital if you want. What do you think?"

Telling myself to snap out of it, I shook my head and assured her I really was fine.

"Is there someone we could call to come be here with you? A family member? Friend?"

That was a good question. I gazed into her concerned brown eyes, my mind lingering in some sort of haze, one where the world wasn't evil and people didn't try to hurt you and they understood that when you said no, you meant no.

Finally, I shook my head, telling her I had plenty of family in the area but that I didn't need anyone to come here and babysit me, that I was just fine on my own, thank you very much.

"All right. Well, you stay here for now, and I'll come back and check on you in a bit."

"Okay. Thanks."

As she walked away, I leaned my head back and closed my eyes and did the only thing I could think of to do: I prayed. It wasn't the warm, confident, solid prayer of my youth, but a mere whisper from one who hadn't truly cried out to God in a long time and wasn't even really sure these days if he was listening.

Keep me safe, keep me from harm, keep me in your loving arms.

Ten years ago those were the words my counselor had suggested, three simple sentences I should be able to remember and utter even in the midst of crisis, even when the part of me that had been so wounded wanted to give up and simply go away.

I don't know if it was the prayer or the glass of water or the earlier, calming ministrations of the EMT and Officer Georgia, but slowly I began to feel myself returning to the moment. Taking several long, slow, deep breaths, I tried an old anxiety-fighting visualization tool, one I hadn't had to use in a long time. Just as I did years ago, I closed my eyes and tried to imagine all of my problems, all of my cares, all of my anxieties washing away in the sea, carried off like shards of driftwood on the tide.

SIX

By the time Officer Georgia came back to check on me, I was feeling more like myself and somewhat recovered from the shock of all that had happened. Still, the fact that I had lost control so badly was embarrassing. As I tried hard to show that I was now present and focused and could be helpful to all that was going on, I just kept wishing that these people knew me, that they understood what I was really like, strong and brave and not some frightened, trembling nut case who had to be led around like a child and coddled back to sanity. Most days I was a victor, not a victim.

I guess Officer Georgia eventually got the point because she stopped looking at me as if she thought I really could use a babysitter and instead had me run through, step-by-step, everything that had happened since the moment I arrived. When we were finished, she told me the detective in charge of the case would be here soon, and he would be going through things with me again later, probably in much more detail.

After that she went back outside to attend to things there. I did the same, though I tried to stay out of everyone's way. Mostly I hovered around listening and watching, trying to ascertain what was going on. Apparently, Floyd had continued mumbling and talking the whole time they stabilized him, placed him on a stretcher, and rolled him toward the ambulance.

I couldn't imagine what had happened to him to make him sound so crazy. According to one exchange I overheard between the paramedics, he wasn't wounded anywhere that they could see. His blood pressure was very high and his airways were dilated, but so far they had no idea what had happened to him to get him in this state. They were going to run a tox screen at the hospital for drugs, which I felt sure would come out positive. However they had gotten there, I had no doubt that drugs were definitely in Floyd's system.

Knowing the detective would be here soon, I tried to decide how much I would have to tell him beyond the fact that I owned the inn and I had been the one to stumble across both bodies. I wasn't sure if I should volunteer the information about my suspension and government investigation or not. On the one hand, if he found out about all of that some other way, my omission might make me seem as though I had been hiding something. On the other hand, I had no idea if that was even related to this, despite my strange phone call with Troy earlier.

Obviously, I had to call Liz, tell her what had happened, and ask her what to do. Slipping into the bathroom, I pulled out my cell phone and made the call with my heart in my throat, praying she would be more sympathetic (about what I had been through) than angry (that I had come out to see Troy). She didn't answer her home phone, office, or cell, and in a way I was relieved. I knew if she understood the situation here fully, she would insist on being present during my interrogation—something I thought would make me look far more guilty, not less. Leaving a simple message on her cell to call me when she had a chance, I decided to wing the detective's questions on my own. I would answer honestly, try not to fill the silences or volunteer excess information, and above all keep my mouth shut otherwise as much as humanly possible. Nothing was wrong with presenting a modified version of the truth, I told myself as I put my phone away and returned to the main room.

Hearing a commotion outside, I went to the door and looked out, wondering if Floyd's "creature" had been caught. Instead, I realized, the excitement was about Nina. They had found her, alive but unconscious, lying on the driveway that ran through the covered bridge next door. I wanted to know if she had been mauled, as Troy had. I heard someone say that though she had no visible wounds anywhere, her vitals were dangerously bad.

Because she was soaking wet, the police thought she had been the one to pull Troy from the pool. That reminded me of the footprints I had photographed earlier. I quickly reviewed them and, with Georgia's help, texted them to the detective who would be handling this case.

I then wandered to the pool area and peeked over the fencing, taking in the sight of Troy's body all over again. With several technicians hovering over him, he looked like a butterfly being pinned down in a collection.

Everyone was waiting for the medical examiner to arrive, but the general consensus was that the wound in his leg didn't look like a gunshot at all but instead a long, deep cut. Poor Troy! We may have had our issues, but he hadn't deserved to suffer like this. I thought of his family—his parents, his sisters, his extended relatives—all who would soon learn of his fate. Blinking back fresh tears at the thought of their pain, I said a prayer for them and turned away.

From the pool I went to the driveway, which was lined with emergency vehicles of all sorts, even two fire trucks. Out at the road, stationary red and blue rotating lights revealed even more vehicles, clusters of onlookers, and a cop directing the slow-moving traffic. It was too dark to see Nina's parents' house from here, but I wondered if they had received the news yet. Probably so, if not directly from the police then from nosy neighbors who were no doubt watching the scene closely, taking it all in, and spreading gossip like wildfire. Nina was about my age, but she lived in an apartment over her parents' garage, a move she made a few years ago after her only child was killed in a car accident.

I was about to head back inside when I noticed someone new coming onto the scene, a man who looked to be in his mid-thirties, with curly hair and strong features. Obviously muscular in an hours-at-the-gym-everyday kind of way, he wasn't my type, but I found something very compelling about him all the same. Georgia greeted him in the driveway, and as they spoke, it struck me that there was an intensity to his bearing, like a tiger about to pounce, that gave him an aura of danger and excitement. As Georgia brought him over and introduced us, I saw intensity sparkling in his eyes as well.

His name was Mike, and he was polite and very businesslike, saying he would need to interview me in a little while, but there were other things he had to do first. He didn't seem happy to find me outside, close to the fringes of the activity, and he asked me to please go into the house and stay there so that I wouldn't inadvertently contaminate the scene.

Cops and technicians were inside as well, though, so finally I just got myself out of the way completely by sitting down in a rocking chair near the fireplace.

Waiting for the detective to come in and start questioning me, I tried to calm my nerves by allowing my eyes to wander around the room, which we had decorated in a manner intended to delight the senses and soothe the soul. Truly, the renovation had been a labor of love, from the classic moldings around the ceiling to the understated window treatments throughout the house to the tastefully displayed gift shop area near the front window of this main room. Looking toward those gifts now, I thought how nice it would be to wrap myself up in one of the folded quilts that were part of the display. The quilts we sold were made by my Amish cousins, and just looking at their handiwork now made me smile.

My cousin Jonah and his wife, Liesl, in particular, were two of my favorite people in the world. They lived nearby, and though we always enjoyed being together when I visited Lancaster County, we hadn't been able to find a way to stay in touch otherwise. They didn't text or use e-mail, and I didn't write letters. They didn't travel outside of the area very often, and I didn't come out this way much anymore. About our only common ground would have been telephone conversations, but because they didn't have a phone in their house but instead took calls from a phone booth outside, that wasn't exactly easy, either.

At least they were the kind of people I could go without seeing for months at a time and then pick right up with again almost exactly where we had left off the time before. My grandfather may have left the Amish faith of his youth and chosen a different path, but I had nothing but respect for the Amish people I knew. They always brought with them such a calming influence.

When I heard two of the cops clumping down from upstairs and talking about guests, I realized it hadn't even occurred to me that other people might be here, that the three rental rooms upstairs could contain dead or unconscious or babbling bodies as well.

Leaning forward, I listened intently to their conversation and was relieved to hear that all three rooms were empty. Still, I had to wonder why that was. The inn was almost always booked solid, so if there were no guests here tonight, there must be some reason for that. Had guests been here earlier? If so, had they witnessed what happened?

Might they have been victims somehow themselves?

Concerned, I moved to the check-in desk near the gift shop area and took a look at Floyd's guestbook, which showed that all three rooms had indeed been reserved for the night, though whether the guests had actually showed or not, I wasn't sure. A phone number was jotted beside each name, so I decided to give them a call to see if I could get more information.

That was my plan, except that none of the numbers worked. All three calls resulted in recordings that announced the numbers were out of service. How odd. There was nothing else I could do for now, but I decided that later I would go to the office to see if I could find more complete and/or accurate records to try again.

Tomorrow I would also have to deal with canceling any upcoming reservations, at least for the rest of the week and weekend. I hated to do that, especially now when I needed every penny I could get, but with Floyd in the hospital and a death in the pool, I really had no choice.

When the detective was finally ready to speak with me, we sat near the fireplace in a pair of matching rockers. As I took a deep breath and tried to calm my nerves, he pulled out a small notebook from his pocket and opened it up, pen poised at the ready. He told me he wanted me to walk him through the events of the evening again, which I did, step-by-step. When I was finished telling him all I had seen and heard, he had me clarify my connection with the inn and my relationship with Nina, Floyd, and Troy. Troy was the hardest to explain, especially given that I still felt it prudent to omit certain facts. I avoided the government investigation issue by focusing primarily on our personal history, explaining to the detective where Troy and I had met (at the Frida Kahlo exhibit during a benefit at the art museum), how long we had dated (about ten months), and when we had broken up (almost exactly two years ago, during the period of time when we were involved with the renovation of this inn).

Reading through his notes, the detective returned to more current events.

"You said he called you this afternoon?"

"Yes. I can even tell you what time," I said as I pushed the buttons on my phone to reveal the list of my most recent calls. According to that list, Troy's call had come in at exactly 5:17 p.m., and we had spoken for about fifteen minutes. I showed the detective where I had tried calling back a number of times over the next hour and a half, but that he hadn't answered.

"You say he sounded strange on the phone?"

"First he said he was feeling sick and dizzy. Sometimes his words were slurred, and he seemed confused." I went on to tell him about the sound Troy said that he heard, which was similar to what Floyd had described, a deep rumble. "The other night when Troy and I talked he sounded fine, but today he definitely wasn't himself."

"Do the two of you speak often?"

I shook my head, saying we hadn't spoken at all for months, but we had talked twice this week, the first time being on Monday night, when I was in Boston on business.

"I was surprised to hear from him, but I didn't mind. It was kind of nice to catch up, actually. Mostly, he was calling to tell me he had found some papers of my grandfather's, and he was wondering what he should do with them."

A uniformed officer came into the room, interrupting us to talk with Mike about some technical issues outside. As they spoke, I thought more about my talk with Troy on Monday, realizing that he hadn't been calling that night just to ask what he should do with the papers. He had been reading through those papers and had some specific questions that had arisen from them.

Closing my eyes, I tried to remember our conversation, or at least the parts of it that were relevant here.

We had spent a few minutes catching up on each other's lives, and then he explained the reason he was calling, saying he was out at the B and B and had run into some old documents of my grandfather's.

"I was just going to put them back where I found them," he had said, "but in several different places I noticed that they refer to diamonds. Remember looking for diamonds during the renovation?"

"Do I? We practically tore the whole house apart!"

The story of the diamonds was a complicated one, but essentially it involved Grandpa Abe's first wife, Daphne, whom he had met and married over in Germany right as World War II was coming to a close. Daphne had become pregnant while still a newlywed and had ended up dying in childbirth. The baby survived, a son my grandfather had named Emory. A few years later, Abe and little Emory had returned to the states, where Abe remarried and had one more child, another son, my father Harold.

Two years ago, when my grandfather passed away, we learned that his will included "certain assets" that he was leaving to Emory, assets that had once belonged to Daphne. The will didn't specify what those assets were, and no one knew what he had meant, not even the lawyer.

We were about to dismiss the matter outright when my grandmother piped up with a theory, that the assets in question were actually diamonds. She knew for a fact that Abe's first wife had inherited a cache of diamonds from her parents. What happened to those diamonds after Daphne died my grandmother didn't know, but she had a feeling Abe had held onto them for his son, brought them back to the states, and had hidden them away for safekeeping until his death.

It was an exciting thought, and even though technically the diamonds belonged solely to Emory, we all wanted to find them for him. During the renovation, Troy and my father and I had looked high and low, even dismantling parts of the house in our search, but we had come up empty, and eventually we decided that either the diamonds were hidden so well they would never be found, or Abe hadn't brought them with him to the States in the first place.

We had the lawyer pursue the matter as well, hoping he might find diamonds listed on an official customs declaration form or something. But nothing ever came of it—no proof, no first-person sightings, and no idea where those diamonds ever ended up. Poor Emory received everything he had coming from his father's will except for those "certain assets." It was anyone's guess as to what my grandfather's true intentions had been.

I had forgotten about the matter until Troy called me on Monday night to talk about it. As we reminisced about our search for the diamonds during the renovation, I suddenly got my hopes up, wondering if these newly discovered documents held clues as to their location. But when I asked Troy, he said they provided no new no hiding places or anything like that, just more vague references that would lead to nowhere.

"But I thought you'd like to know about them just the same," he had added. "So those diamonds never turned up, huh?"

"Nope. We never found a thing," I said, shaking my head sadly. "Whatever my grandfather was talking about, I guess we'll never know."

Sitting here now, with Troy dead outside, I opened my eyes, a new and disturbing thought beginning to permeate my brain. What if he had been lying on Monday night when he called me? What if those documents he found *had* provided new clues about the diamonds, clues he then tried to follow? That would mean he hadn't stuck around here for a few days so Floyd could go out of town. More likely, he had gotten rid of Floyd so he could go on a treasure hunt by himself.

If that were true, it would explain what he had been doing out in the grove today. Troy was no outdoorsman, but he would endure almost anything that might lead to a hidden fortune in diamonds. In fact, on Monday night he had even said as much himself.

If this were true, then the bigger question that remained was whether or not his search had anything to do with the fact that he was now dead.

SEVEN

When Mike finished his conversation and returned his attention back to me, I decided to share with him what I was thinking. Had Liz been there, she might have told me to be quiet. On the other hand, if there was a treasure-hunting element to this case, that would actually be a good thing for me personally, as it would help take away any focus that might point toward my government investigation/work suspension problem.

I launched into a full explanation about the will and the diamonds and the papers Troy had found. Just as I finished, we were interrupted again, this time by the news that the medical examiner had arrived. Mike excused himself, saying he would be back and for me to stay inside and out of the way.

I agreed, though after he was gone, I moved through the house all the way to the screened porch, which was close to the pool area. From there I would be able to hear and see what was going on outside while technically remaining inside, as directed.

Stepping onto the wooden slat flooring of the porch, I realized that the night air was getting chilly. Pulling my dress jacket more tightly around me, I moved to a wicker chair near the back, turned it toward the pool area, and sat there in the darkness.

Though I could barely see over the pool fencing, I could easily hear the conversation between Mike and the ME. She confirmed right away that the wound on Troy's thigh had definitely not been caused by a gunshot. Instead, she said he had been stabbed by something jagged.

"I'm thinking of a woodworking tool, like a circular saw, maybe? Or a gardening trowel, a hoe. Something with a sharp edge, but jagged. Not like a knife."

"The other victim said there was some kind of creature here," Mike said. "Does it look like it could have been done by an animal?"

I leaned forward, listening intently for her reply.

"Yes and no. Some sort of big sharp claw could have done this. The nature of the cut mark would be consistent with that. The problem is, claw marks usually show up as several parallel lines, not just one, especially with the big cats. So I don't think it was a mountain lion or a cougar or bobcat. I suppose it could have been a bear, if that bear happened to have one prominent claw." She went on to say that whatever animal had done this, if indeed an animal had done this, at the lab she would be able to look more closely at the wound and check it for evidence. "A gash this deep can hold plenty of debris."

"So was that cut the cause of death? Did he bleed out?"

"I don't know yet. The froth in his lungs and the nasal hemorrhaging both point to drowning. The skin on his feet tells us the body wasn't in the water too long. I'd say half an hour at most. The skin on his hands...I'm not sure what's going on there. It's blistered and red, see?"

They were both quiet for a moment, and then he murmured something I couldn't quite make out. Judging from her reply, there was something under Troy's fingernails—a residue of something white that had managed to remain despite his having floated in the pool.

"If you look here," the woman said, "you can see he also bit his tongue, which tells me he may have had a seizure."

Mike asked about other signs of a struggle, other cuts and bruises. She replied that she could see no visible signs of forced drowning, such as bruises around the neck, shoulders, or head. Nothing like that at all.

"There *is* massive bruising around this gash in his thigh," she added. "We'll check the rest of his body at the lab for other cuts and contusions, but I don't see anything else that jumps out at me right now."

I couldn't understand Mike's next remarks, but it sounded as though he was saying that regardless of how Troy died, whether from bleeding to death or drowning or a seizure, there was no question that he had been bleeding heavily from his leg, and that by following the trail of blood they might be able to trace his steps backward to see where he was when he first got hurt. Mike barked out orders then, and several cops sprang into action, moving toward the driveway, probably to retrieve some sort of equipment that would help them find Troy's trail of blood in the dark.

"Looks to me like someone attempted mouth-to-mouth after pulling him out of the pool," the medical examiner said. "But I'd wager he was dead and floating at least a little while before that futile attempt at resuscitation."

Someone else spoke then, the policeman who had apparently been the one to find Nina unconscious out on Emory's driveway. He felt that she was the one who pulled out Troy and tried mouth-to-mouth, given that when they found her there were a few flecks of dried blood on her lips and her clothes were soaking wet. In response, the ME said that sounded likely, especially if she had no cuts of her own inside her mouth or anywhere else.

Listening and watching all that was going on out there, I saw some technicians using what looked like a portable black light, shining it toward the ground around the pool area and then moving outward, over the back corner of the stucco wall, then across the yard toward the grove. If Troy's wound really had been caused by an animal, I hoped the men would be careful. Lancaster County was made up primarily of farmland, but there were enough wooded areas, especially right around here, that an animal could hide in and maybe even strike again.

Floyd had said the creature he saw was black, which made me think perhaps it had been a bear. Certainly, Pennsylvania had lots of bears. I myself had seen bear scat many times when hiking in the Poconos—but that locale was several hours from here. Lancaster County was too densely populated for bears to proliferate, though I supposed it wouldn't be unheard of for a bear to pass through once in a great while.

Suddenly, Mike emerged from the pool area and spotted me there on the porch, startling me from my thoughts.

"Sienna?" he asked, moving closer to the screen that separated us.

"Yes," I replied, pulse surging, afraid he was about to fuss at me for eavesdropping. Instead, he simply asked if I might have a property survey or something else handy that they could look at, something that would show how far the woods and grove extended, and where it sat in relation to nearby homes and farms. I said I would see what I could find, but a quick search in the office produced nothing.

Instead, I grabbed a pen and some paper, thinking that at the very least I could draw out a simple sketch for them. I carried the pen and paper into the kitchen, sat at the table, sketched out the property's front and back, and then added the row of houses across the street. Moving in a circle clockwise, I added Uncle Emory's house next door and then Jonah and Liesl's farm after that, around the corner from Emory's place, with their property line abutting his and mine. Finally, I added the homestead directly behind mine, an old defunct chicken farm. Moving the rest of the way around to the left, I scribbled in thick woods that covered several acres and ended at the road.

Once all of that was done I added in all the outbuildings I could remember, including my shed and Emory's barn. I didn't try to do that for Jonah and Liesl's farm, though, because as with most Amish farms, it had too many outbuildings to count, much less draw correctly.

The only area I was fuzzy on was the road that led to the chicken farm. I knew several isolated homes were along in there, but I wasn't sure where to place them in my drawing, so I guessed. Finally, I drew in the centerpiece of everything here: Harmony Grove itself. Scribbling a wide, flat oval of trees to represent its boundaries, I finished with a wiggly line down the middle for the creek and a little bridge over the creek at the very center.

Mike came inside just as I was finishing up, took a look at my sketch, and asked if there was a copy machine here where he could make some duplicates. I offered to do that for him, and by the time I returned from the office to the kitchen with twenty copies in hand as requested, he had been joined by two other cops, whom he introduced as Rip and Charlie.

The four of us sat at the table, and I went over the map in detail, explaining how all of the land had originally been owned by my great-grandfather, who had divided it up among his children. Because his son Abe had decided to become a welder, not a farmer, he had been given the wooded, non-farmable portion of land, a large tract that was rocky and hilly with a creek running through the center.

"Of course, what wouldn't have been suitable for farming was perfect for creating a grove," I added. "In the end, my grandfather's greatest legacy came from the one piece of land no one else in the family even wanted."

EIGHT

Georgia came inside to tell Mike that they had managed to find the place where Troy's bleeding had started, about five hundred feet back from the pool. She added that the ground there was grassy and dry with no good shoe or footprints, though it did look as if a struggle of some kind had taken place there, with some ruts and torn grass and the like.

Mike asked the question I felt sure we were all thinking. "Any signs that struggle was with an animal?"

"Yeah, we can't rule that out. A couple of gouges in the dirt could be claws, but we're not sure what kind. We need better lights out there, and we need to widen the search. If it was an animal, maybe we can find a print somewhere else on softer ground."

"How about signs that it wasn't an animal? Any grease or oil or something that would indicate a machine of some kind?"

"Nope. Nothing of the sort. Mostly just blood on grass."

"Which way did the victim go once the blood flow started? Straight to the pool?"

"Yeah, but not exactly in a straight line. It looks as though he was weaving around some, though whether from confusion or because he was being pursued, we can't know. The splatters were closer together at the end than at the beginning, which indicates he was slowing down as he became more impaired."

Everyone was quiet for a moment, considering this new information.

"I hate to be gross, but did you find the place where Troy threw up when he was on the phone with me?" I asked, knowing that that evidence might help them piece together the logistical parts of this puzzle.

"Not yet, but we've got an eye out for that. A change in the weather is coming our way, so we're working things as fast as we can."

"Yeah, I heard rain," Charlie added, "though it's not supposed to get here till Friday."

Next to me, Mike sucked in a deep breath, held it for a moment, and then exhaled.

"Okay," he said wearily, "I hate to do this because we know what will happen, but we have to put the word out." Handing her the remaining duplicates of the sketch, he told Georgia to delegate the contacting of the people in all of the homes I had drawn.

"What do we tell them, exactly?" she asked.

"Just let them know that there might be some sort of wild animal loose in the area and for them to be careful and to try to stay inside if possible until we have more information. While you're there, also find out the times that each of them was home today and if they have seen anything unusual or relevant."

Georgia studied the sketch for a moment, looking confused, so finally Rip jumped in to explain it to her.

"This whole area here, it's kind of like a clock. A big square clock." Pointing toward me, he added, "She's at twelve o'clock, you got her uncle at two o'clock, the Amish folks at three o'clock, the chicken farm at six o'clock, and then mostly just woods after that, all the way back up to twelve."

"I see," Georgia replied, nodding.

Once she seemed to have a handle on things, she, Rip, and Charlie headed out, leaving me alone in the kitchen with Mike.

"Excuse me while I prepare dispatch for the onslaught," he said to me, pulling out his phone and making a call.

I was trying to stay quiet and out of the way as much as possible, but when he hung up I couldn't help asking what he had meant by that. He rolled his eyes.

"You have no idea. As soon as word gets out, we'll start getting calls on sightings of bears, mountain lions, panthers, you name it. It never fails. People watching for something often see what they want to see. A neighbor's cat in the shadows becomes a cougar. A stray dog becomes a wolf. It's human nature, and thoroughly predictable, but because we can't know which leads are credible and which aren't, we have to follow up on all of them, unfortunately."

"Then you should probably know that it might get even weirder than that," I said, wondering how to explain.

Mike looked at me, tilting his head in curiosity.

"As in?" he asked.

"As in, you may not be aware of this, but rumors have persisted for years that Harmony Grove is haunted, that it's full of ghosts and eerie lights and even werewolves. That's ridiculous, of course, but with all that happened here at the B and B tonight, I wouldn't be surprised if those rumors start up again, big time."

Mike nodded, considering.

"So, basically, along with the calls we're already bracing for, we're also going to get reports of Bigfoot, Yeti, Sasquatch, vampires—"

"Space aliens, werewolves, specters, you name it."

"Lovely."

"I'm sorry. I wish it wasn't this way. But having seen Troy's wound up close, I'm almost ready to believe in werewolves myself."

"Hate to say it," he replied, "but I know exactly what you mean."

Our eyes held for a moment, and then he cleared his throat, breaking our gaze.

"Speaking of Troy," Mike said gruffly, reaching into his pocket and pulling out his notebook, "is there anything else you need to tell me about him? We were interrupted just as we were finishing up our interview."

"Only that the more I think about him being out in the grove today, the more sense it makes that he was there looking for diamonds. You have to understand that to get Troy Griffin outside and into nature would just about take something that extreme, believe it or not."

"In other words, you're confident he wasn't simply out for a stroll?"

"Absolutely confident. I mean, I suppose he could have been cutting through the grove to visit one of the neighbors." Mike raised an eyebrow in question, so I added that Troy was friends with almost everyone around here, that he had come to know them during the renovation. "But I think he was out there hunting for buried treasure. Troy simply didn't do nature. He never went outside, not even around here where it's so beautiful."

Mike flipped through several pages in his notebook before speaking.

"An older couple who lives across the street said they noticed Troy out in the grove a whole lot, off and on, for the past two days. Said he was carrying something around with him the whole time, a stick or a pole or a tool or something. Neither one can see distance all that well, but they figured he was just doing yard work."

I laughed.

"Yeah, right. Troy wouldn't know a hoe from a hole in the ground. If they saw him out in the grove, there had to be some very good reason he was there. Something in my grandfather's documents must have made him think he had a clue about where the diamonds were hidden. Judging by our last phone call, that would be on or in or under or around the Fishing Tree, whatever that is."

"You have no idea."

"No, especially without getting a look at those documents."

"Well, we've searched Troy's room and his car and found nothing like that in either. If they're still around here somewhere, they're hidden really well."

Mike quickly skimmed through his notebook one last time before shutting it and saying we were done for now except for one more thing.

"You said that during your call it sounded like Troy was fooling with a latch of some kind? A metal latch?"

"Right. That's when he was first sounding confused and weird. He got it open but then he realized he was all turned around and it didn't matter. After that he retraced his steps."

"Where do you think he was at that point? Could you show me on your sketch where any gates or latches would be?"

"Sure," I said, grabbing the pencil and moving back to the table.

Sitting there beside the detective, ignoring the vaguely pleasant scent of his aftershave, I leaned over the drawing and put a mark on the gate to the pool area, and then on the gate to a small defunct garden that used to be out back but was now just a fenced-in rectangle of weeds.

"The chicken farm probably has some gates," I added, pointing to that part of the sketch. "Troy could easily have wandered over there by mistake, so you might check with the guy who lives there. He's a little odd, but nice enough. His name is Burl Newton."

"I know Burl," Mike said, though he didn't elaborate.

"It's wooded back there where our property lines meet. I can see Troy getting confused. I doubt the same thing could have happened over at Jonah and Liesl's farm. I mean, I'm sure they have a number of gates, but theirs would all be out in the open, not hidden in the trees."

"How about next door at your uncle's house?"

I couldn't think of any gates that might be at Uncle Emory's, as his entire property consisted of a small one-story house, the barn behind it, an old springhouse beyond that, and the long driveway out front that passed through the covered bridge near the road.

"No latches there at all that I can think of," I said. "Which just leaves the grove. There are four gates in there, at each of the entrances: north, south, east, and west."

Mike's brow wrinkled. "The grove is fenced in?"

"No. All four gates are purely ornamental. That's probably why I didn't think of them when Troy and I were talking. Maybe in all of his confusion he was trying to open one of those gates without realizing that all he really needed to do was walk around it."

The more I thought about it, the more I decided that made the most sense. I drew in all four gates on the map, and when Mike took it back from me I could tell he seemed to think this was the most likely scenario as well.

He thanked me for my help and stood, asking if by any chance I was an artist.

"For a fast doodle, this is pretty good," he added, "not to mention accurate, judging by what I know of this area."

"Thanks. I do like to fool with art in my spare time, but it's just a hobby."

After Mike went out, I stood in the open doorway and listened as he asked for more lights in the grove and began assembling teams to move in there.

I heard him ask his people who among them were competent as hunters, and then he delegated to them the job of searching the grove for animal prints, scat, and any other signs they would know to look for.

It sounded as though he was eager to get out into the grove as well. And while I didn't relish the thought of being mauled by a wild animal, I realized that if I went along with him and the technician he was going to take with him, I could probably be a big help. As children, my brother Scott and I practically lived in the grove, and I still knew it better than almost anyone.

Summoning my nerve, I called Mike over and offered my services. At first he seemed hesitant, but when I stressed that the grove was very unique and difficult to navigate in daylight, much less in the dark, he finally relented. He agreed that it might be a good idea to have me go out with him and his technician, but just to be safe he would add two extra men, armed officers who would flank the three of us and watch for animals as we went. I said I just needed to grab a windbreaker from my car and then I would join them where the teams were assembling on the far side of the pool area.

When I got to the car, I thought about grabbing one of my guns from there as well, but then I decided against it. I didn't want to create any unnecessary suspicion that could end up leading these people in directions I didn't want them to go. Also, not everyone who owned a gun really knew how to use it, and though I was well trained myself, I didn't want them to be worried that I might accidentally shoot somebody's foot off.

Pulling the windbreaker on over my dress jacket, I joined what was to be our little five-person group: Charlie, Rip, Mike, the technician, and me.

"Let's keep our eyes and ears open," Mike said, looking at each of us in turn.

In response I noticed that the two gunmen instinctively patted their firearms, and for a moment I regretted my decision not to arm myself too. Instead, I would have to trust in the protection of others, something that had been difficult for me to do ever since that night ten years ago, when I learned that the only person I could ever really count on to save me was myself.

The technician handed me a flashlight, a heavy, powerful one that shone a long bright beam out in front of me. Everyone else in our little group had one as well, and once they had all turned them on and made a final equipment check, it seemed we were ready to go.

Excitement crackled in the air. At Mike's command, we headed out toward the grove together, walking side by side, five parallel beams of light slicing through the darkness like claws ripping through skin.

NINE

As we walked together toward the grove, I tried to give a brief explanation about it, one that would help Mike and the others understand its unique design. Trying to focus on the illuminated ground in front of me rather than thoughts of any creatures that could be lurking in the shadows beyond, I told them how my grandfather had gone off to Europe in World War II, during which he met and fell in love with a German woman named Daphne. The story of how their relationship came to be was fascinating but far too complicated to go into now. It also wasn't relevant to our search, so instead, I rattled off information I knew would resonate with these men in uniform, where my grandfather was inducted and trained and assigned.

"Having been raised in an Amish home, he was a conscientious objector, so he was sent to Virginia, to be trained at the Medical Replacement Training Center in Camp Pickett." I went on to explain that my grandfather's older brothers had remained stateside during the war, but that Abe had decided to go a different route with his CO status, entering the service as a noncombatant army medic. "He and Daphne were married near the end of the war. They stayed in Europe, and their only child, my uncle Emory, was born about a year later."

Up ahead I caught a glimpse of the main gate, so I cut to the chase and explained that Daphne's grandfather had been a renowned scholar, and many years before she was born he had joined with an arborist to create a very unique grove behind the family home, one based on the epic poem *The Metamorphoses.*

As soon as I said "poem" I could tell I was losing their attention, so I simply added that Daphne died giving birth to Emory, and when my grandfather moved back to the states a few years later, he decided to re-create that grove here as memorial to his late wife. I didn't add that Daphne and her entire family had deeply loved the grove, nor that she had in fact been named from one of the main characters in the poem.

"So what makes a grove a grove?" Rip asked.

"I think it's the same thing as an orchard," Charlie said.

"No, I think a grove means it's just one certain type of tree, not a variety," Mike ventured.

"Technically," I said, "a grove is simply a grouping of trees where the ground is kept clear of undergrowth. The trees don't have to be fruit bearing, nor do they all have to be the same kind." Hoping my correction hadn't sounded rude, I added, "I mean, I'm sure Harmony Grove has plenty of underbrush now, but when my grandfather was alive it didn't. He tended it constantly, keeping it immaculate."

Up ahead, our beams of light illuminated the main gate and reflected off the brass plate on the left door. Other, smaller reflections from closer to the ground shone back toward us as well, so before anyone might think that those were animal eyes looking at us, I quickly explained that they were markers.

"Markers?"

"Yes, you know, like little signs about the different trees? My grandfather knew how to do metal work, so he made them for all over the grove."

"Oh, I know what you mean by markers," Charlie said. "Where they'll have the common name for a tree at the top and then the scientific name under that? Like, Pine Tree and then *pineaniculus treealiopulas?*"

Everyone chuckled.

"Kind of like that," I said, smiling, "except most of these markers don't identify the types of trees but instead have poem excerpts *about* the trees. You'll see when we get further inside. Some of the markers never made much sense to me, but at least they're interesting. The whole grove, really, is fascinating—it's full of unusual plantings, with a beautiful bridge over the creek and lots of ornamental touches."

Mike asked if any of the markers in here said anything about a Fishing Tree, which was the thing Troy had called to ask me about earlier today.

"I've been thinking about that. I do remember one that says something about dolphins, and maybe another that has to do with fish, but I'm not sure where either of those is. With at least a hundred markers in here, it could take some time to find them—and even if you did, there's no way to know if one of those is what my grandfather meant by the term Fishing Tree or not."

What I didn't mention were the more bizarre markers in here, including one that referred to "walking skeletons," another to something called "Blood Street," and even one about werewolves, which was no doubt how those particular rumors were started.

We reached the gate and stopped there, all of us shining our lights up on the beautiful wrought iron arch, the words "Harmony Grove" spelled out in the curve of that arch. On the left door, etched in a brass plate, were these words:

Through me what was, what is, and what will be are revealed.
Through me strings sound in harmony, to song.

"Is that from the Bible?" Rip asked.

"No, it's from Ovid's *The Metamorphoses*," I replied.

"Meta who?"

"*Metamorphoses*. It's an ancient epic poem, kind of like *The Iliad*? *The Odyssey*?"

"I read *The Odyssey* in tenth grade," Charlie volunteered. "Didn't understand a word of it."

We all smiled.

"*The Metamorphoses* is a little easier to understand, I think. Basically, it's a love story about Phoebus and Daphne. He loves her desperately, but she's not interested in him at all."

"Can you blame her? Who could love somebody with a name like Phoebus?"

Charlie joked, and again, everyone chuckled.

"This ironwork is gorgeous," Mike said, using his flashlight to inspect the gate. On the left, below the brass inscription, was an arrow pointing an upward angle and extending beyond the inner frame of the door. That arrow, like the rest of the door, was made from wrought iron, but its tip was covered in shiny brass. The right door featured a similar arrow, also pointing inward and upward, but its tip was a dull metal. When pulled closed, the two arrows crossed at the center. "Did your grandfather make this?"

I nodded. For years I had been told that my artistic talents had been passed down to me from my grandfather, though my dad always insisted that those talents had skipped a generation along the way. Now as I looked at this incredibly beautiful gate and the grove that lay beyond, I felt a deep sense of pride. Abe Collins had been a strange and remote man in his lifetime, but there was no question he had also possessed an enormous amount of talent.

While the technician went to work on the gate's latch, checking it for Troy's fingerprints, and Mike studied the ground around both gates, looking for footprints or other evidence, Rip and Charlie seemed more interested in reading the nearby markers than watching for beasts in the shadows. Rip read the first one out loud, an excerpt from the poem, which provided an explanation for the design of the gate:

> He landed on the shady peak of Parnassus and took
> two arrows with opposite effects from his full quiver:
> One kindles love, the other dispels it.
> The one that kindles is golden with a sharp glistening point.
> The one that dispels is blunt with lead beneath its shaft.

"Who's the he?" Charlie asked.

"He who?" Rip replied.

"He, there. With the arrows. Who's he?"

Wishing the two men would cut their who's-on-first banter and focus on keeping us safe, I jumped in to explain that the poem referred to a Cupidlike creature who started all the trouble by shooting Phoebus with an arrow that kindled love in him but then shot Daphne with one that dispels love. Thanks to those arrows, poor Phoebus was destined to unrequited love forever.

"Unrequited love forever?" Charlie cried. "Sounds like you, Rip!"

Their guffaws earned a sharp reprimand from Mike, who reminded them of their purpose for being out here. Thus chastised, they manned their posts, flanking us with their backs to the group and their flashlights shining out into the night on each side.

As Mike and the tech worked and Rip and Charlie stood guard, I remained silent, trying not to be in the way.

"Is this gate usually closed or open?" Mike asked me, still studying the dry, dusty ground around it.

"Open. Actually, the only gate of the four that usually stays closed is the one we call the German Gate. If Troy got turned around and was fooling with a latch trying to get it open so that he could get back to the inn, that probably would have been the one that confused him."

According to the technician, this gate was offering nothing in the form of solid evidence, and he was ready to move on.

"Okay then, Sienna," Mike said. "Why don't you lead us to the German Gate."

It was clear across on the other side of the grove, so rather than follow the meandering path that encircled it, I suggested we cut straight through instead. We headed out, once again playing our beams in front of us, watching and listening for any unusual sounds or movements.

After a few minutes Rip and Charlie's chatter started up again, this time wondering how an Amish man, who probably hadn't been educated beyond the eighth grade, had ended up building a grove full of literary references.

"The literary references came from Daphne's grove back in Germany," I reminded them. Though I said nothing more, I wanted to jump to my grandfather's defense and insist that the Amish often found many ways to continue learning long after they were finished with school. But though my grandfather had been a well-read and obviously gifted man, the reason for the grove's literary ties had nothing to do with either.

As I thought about it, I remembered what my dad always said, that while this grove may have begun as a mere copy of another one across the sea, at some point it had taken on a life of its own, growing and expanding far beyond its original, more modest re-creation.

We pressed onward, growing silent as the grove thickened around us. In daylight, the canopy of treetops overhead was simply awe inspiring, but here in the dark, where they blocked the light of the moon and stars and a mist hovered over the ground, it simply felt otherworldly.

I wasn't the only one getting the creeps. I noticed that both Rip and Charlie had drawn their weapons and were holding them at the ready, just in case. Seeing the looks on their faces, I decided that if there really was a creature out here somewhere, I wouldn't want to be it right now. Just as quickly, I realized they needed to be careful. With other teams also working the grove, they could all end up shooting each other.

"Let's not be trigger-happy," Mike said, as if he could read my mind. "We have other people out here, remember."

"We know, boss."

Wondering if any of those teams were nearby, I began to direct the beam of my flashlight toward the trees that surrounded us rather than on the path in front of us. As I did, I noticed something odd.

"Wait," I said, pausing on the path. Playing my beam along the ground around some of the trees off to one side, I realized I was seeing holes, dozens of holes that had been dug in the ground. "This isn't right. Someone has been out here digging."

"Someone or some*thing*," Rip said, moving gingerly toward one of the holes to take a closer look.

The technician and Mike moved in as well, squatting to study them, and after a moment both agreed they could clearly see shovel marks. These holes had been made by a human, with a tool, and not by a creature. Mike stood up, looking at me.

"Seems like your treasure-hunting theory was correct, Sienna. Probably what the folks across the street saw your ex-boyfriend carrying around out here was a shovel."

While it was certainly comforting to know that these holes hadn't been dug by some beast, seeing them now certainly raised more questions than it answered. If Troy really had been out here in the grove searching for treasure, was it possible he had succeeded in his quest? Before he died, had Troy actually found our family's mythical diamonds?

As the technician took some photographs and our gunmen stood guard, I noticed that Mike was shining his light all around the area, looking for markers and then reading them. I joined him at one, a metal plate next to a tall, old oak.

"What are you thinking?" I asked.

"That there must have been a method to his madness. The grove is huge. Troy couldn't have just gone digging at random. I'm thinking that there must be something right around here that indicates a Fishing Tree."

I helped as well, skimming the text on each plate I could find.

"What do you think of this one?" Mike asked, pointing.

It read:

> *They set sails to the wind,*
> *though as yet the seamen had poor knowledge of their use,*
> *and the ships' keels that once were trees*
> *standing amongst high mountains*
> *now leaped through uncharted waves.*

"This is the closest one yet, given that it talks about ships and water," he said.

"True, but it doesn't mention fish. Somewhere out here, there are at least two markers I can think of that are way more specific about fishing than this."

We weren't far from the middle of the grove, and it struck me that perhaps the Fishing Tree was the name of the grove's centerpiece, the delicate bay laurel that sat just on the other side of the bridge and was flanked by a circle of beautiful wrought iron benches. We kids had always called that one the Kissing Tree, but perhaps that was just our name for it and my grandfather called it something else. Certainly, it was the most significant tree in the grove, the one around which all of the others had been planted. If my grandfather had referred repeatedly to any one tree in his papers, it more than likely would have been that one.

I explained my thinking to Mike, so once he and the technician had finished examining the area for evidence, he used his radio to call in a follow-up team and our little group pressed onward.

"What do sailboats have to do with the story?" Rip asked as we went.

"Yeah, and where were they going in that ship?" Charlie added.

I explained that before the main point of the story—the part with Cupid's arrows and the whole unrequited love thing—Ovid gives a long, fictional tale about the forming of the earth.

"There's even a great flood. I think the quote on the marker comes from that part. The flood destroys all of humankind, and the ones who are left have to start over and repopulate the earth."

"Sounds like the Bible to me," Mike said.

"Similar elements," I replied, "but this story is definitely not biblical. Instead of our one real God, the world Ovid describes is created by many mythical gods. In fact, it's the gods that keep messing up things for the humans, from what I recall."

"So when does the Cupid guy start doing his bit?"

"About two thirds of the way in. After that, the whole rest of the poem tells what happened to poor Phoebus and Daphne."

We came to the bridge, which was so narrow that we had to cross in single file. As I started over, I thought back to the many times Scott and our Amish cousins and I had played here. We had elaborate pretend games about an ogre who lived underneath. Striding quickly across the wooden planks now, I could only hope there weren't any real ogres hiding under there, just waiting to come out and grab me around the ankles.

TEN

Once our little group was on the other side of the bridge, we found ourselves facing the centerpiece of the grove, the bay laurel tree. As we stood there taking it in, I was surprised to realize that while most of the grove seemed neglected and untended, someone had been taking care of this area recently. Here, there were no fallen limbs or intrusive weeds or even any autumn leaves. In fact, I realized, looking down at the ground, the clearing had recently been raked, the ridges created by a rake's tines still visible in the dust. Before I could point this out, the technician picked up on it as well. Telling us not to move in any closer lest we contaminate any evidence, he very carefully and thoroughly began examining and photographing the scene.

While we waited, Mike and I read the markers etched into plaques mounted on the benches circling the tree. Nearby, Charlie and Rip stood guard.

"So what happens to Phoebus and Daphne?" Rip asked, which made me smile, knowing that he was genuinely interested in the poem's story.

"In a nutshell? He pursues her, she runs from him, and when he's about to catch her she begs the heavens for help and is turned into a tree. A bay laurel."

I added that the markers on these benches, when read in sequence, provided the climax of the poem, starting with the final chase through the wilderness, followed by her plea for help, and then that bizarre transformation of human into tree:

Her strength was gone, she grew pale,
overcome by the effort of her rapid flight,
and seeing Peneus's waters near cried out
"Help me, father! If your streams have divine powers
change me, destroy this beauty that pleases too well!"

Her prayer was scarcely done when
a heavy numbness seized her limbs,
thin bark closed over her breast,
her hair turned into leaves,
her arms into branches,
her feet so swift a moment ago stuck fast in slow-growing roots,
her face was lost in the canopy.

Only her shining beauty was left.

I read the next one out loud, its words familiar simply because as children it had always made us giggle:

Even like this Phoebus loved her
and, placing his hand against the trunk,
he felt her heart still quivering under the new bark.
He clasped the branches as if they were parts of human arms,
and kissed the wood.

"That's why we always called this one the Kissing Tree."

"Is that this Ovid guy's version of a happy ending?" Charlie asked, frowning.

"The poem's a tragedy. Unrequited love, remember? It doesn't have a happy ending." I read the next plate in the series:

But even the wood shrank from his kisses,
and he said "Since you cannot be my bride, you must be my tree!
Laurel, with you my hair will be wreathed,
with you my lyre, with you my quiver.
Just as my head with its uncropped hair is always young,
so you also will wear the beauty of undying leaves."

"Okay, that's pretty sad," Rip said. "Since you cannot be my bride, you must be my tree? I mean, personally, I'd like to find my soul mate, but I'd rather have no one at all than fall in love with a tree."

We all laughed.

"Is that where it ends?" Charlie asked.

"Almost. There's one more," I said. "I'd read it to you, but it's on the marker over where they're working."

I hadn't thought that either Mike or the tech were even listening to us, but they must have been because the tech paused in what he was doing to read it for us.

"It says, 'The laurel bowed her newly made branches and seemed to shake her leafy crown, like a head giving consent.'"

"At least it ends on an upbeat note," Mike commented. "Sort of."

"Yeah," Charlie replied, "'cept that's a bay laurel and this is zone seven. Not gonna be a happy ending for *this* tree."

I wasn't sure what he meant, but Rip understood and soon the two men were discussing trees and gardening and climate zones. Apparently, Charlie was of the opinion that bay laurels could never survive a Pennsylvania winter and in this region should always be planted in giant pots, ones that could be moved inside when temperatures began to plummet. Rip disagreed, insisting that if you nursed one along carefully enough and protected it until its roots had been well established in the ground, that it could be done. His was the winning point, because I was pretty sure that this was the very same bay laurel tree that had always been here.

Both men finally quieted down, focusing again on their guardsman duties. I waited quietly nearby, shining my flashlight out into the grove, looking for more holes in the ground. I felt hopeful that we would find something, but despite my searching and the efforts of both Mike and the technician, they couldn't find any special evidence in this area either, nothing except that which we had originally observed, the tended and raked ground.

We continued on toward the German Gate. As we walked I began picking the brains of the two gardeners, wondering if perhaps the Fishing Tree had received its name not from the quote on its nearby metal marker, but instead for some horticultural reason. The two men tossed around ideas for a while, but they couldn't come up with anything.

"No 'catfish rose' or 'trout vine' or anything like that?" I pressed.

Charlie replied that fish heads and fish powder were sometimes used as fertilizer, but otherwise he couldn't think of any plant or tree that had "fish" in its name. Rip said something about it was ringing a bell, and he offered to look at his gardening books at home and let us know.

"I think you're both barking up the wrong tree," Charlie quipped, making us smile.

Our smiles faded as we neared our destination: the German Gate.

As children we had always avoided this area, not liking the violent and dark poetry on the markers here or even the trees themselves. Unlike the rest of the grove, which featured a wide variety of tree types, the ones on the other side of the German Gate were all the same kind, beech trees I think, and they had been planted in straight, tight rows, like soldiers standing at attention.

Unlike the rest of the grove, which mimicked its German original, this section had been entirely of my grandfather's design. If the grove was shaped as a sort of long oval, this section was a bulge on the outside of that oval. The gate was closed, blocking the entrance to the bulge, though of course all one needed to do to get into it was walk around the gate. Its lettering faced inward, into the grove, the words *"Jedem das Seine"* spelled out in a stark, art deco style amid the wrought iron, crisscross pattern of the massive doors.

Taking it all in, as an adult I could appreciate the symmetry of the creation, but I still didn't like it. Standing there, playing our lights along the closed gate and the rows of trees beyond, it struck me that I should get more information about why my grandfather had decided to add this extra part to the grove. Maybe my father would know, or my grandmother. I should ask, as well, where the quotes on the markers among the beech trees had come from. Though the quotes in the rest of the grove had been pulled from *The Metamorphoses*, the ones in the bulge beyond the German Gate were from some other source, and now I wanted to know what that source was.

Even on this side of the gate, though, where the quotes were still from

Ovid, the choices were strangely disturbing. Looking down, I read the one nearest to where we stood:

> *Immediately every kind of wickedness erupted*
> *into this age of baser natures:*
> *truth, shame, and honour vanished;*
> *in their place were fraud, deceit, and trickery,*
> *violence and pernicious desires.*

Next to that was my least favorite of all, because it was surely one of the ones that had started rumors in the past:

> *He himself ran in terror, and reaching the silent fields*
> *howled aloud, frustrated of speech.*
> *Foaming at the mouth, and greedy as ever for killing,*
> *he turned against the sheep, still delighting in blood.*
> *His clothes became bristling hair, his arms became legs.*
> *He was a wolf, but kept some vestige of his former shape.*
> *There were the same grey hairs, the same violent face,*
> *the same glittering eyes, the same savage image.*

"These markers are freaky," Charlie said, reading another one out loud. "'Her sons' dreadful bodies drenched Earth with streams of blood'? What's up with that?"

"Yeah, how about this one?" Rip replied from the other side of the path. "'These progeny were savage, violent, and eager for slaughter, so that you might know they were born from blood.' Good grief."

"Guys, come on," Mike scolded. "Stay on task here."

Both men snapped back to attention, but as they focused on their duties as watchmen, they asked me to read them some more.

"Here's the one closest to the gate: 'War came, waving clashing arms with bloodstained hands.'"

Rip shook his head.

"I gotta say, this Ovid fellow was one dark guy."

He wasn't the only one, I thought. Watching the technician pull out his tools and go to work checking for fingerprints on the gate latch, all I knew for sure was that my simple, Amish-raised grandfather had grown up to become one very odd, very complicated fellow. No wonder people thought this place was haunted.

"What do the words in the gate mean?" Mike asked, shining his light on them. "*Jedem das Seine*? Is that German?"

"Yes. I don't speak German myself, but Jonah says it means 'To each his own' or something like that. Why those particular words on this particular gate, I have no idea."

Mike kept looking at it and squinting.

"I've seen this before," he said slowly. "Somewhere else, in a photograph or something. Not necessarily with trees around it, but this gate…I've seen a picture of a gate that looks just like this one."

I could tell he was trying hard to remember where, so I didn't speak. Instead, I simply waited in the darkness beside him, hoping that by figuring that out, he might shed some light on why it had been put here and if that could relate in any way to the family diamonds or to Troy's death. All five of us were silent, the night deathly quiet around us. Even the crickets didn't chirp here. The only sound was the wind rustling the branches above. Finally, Mike shook his head and said he couldn't remember but it might come to him later.

Suddenly, I spotted movement from the corner of my eye, beyond the rows of beech trees on the other side of the gate. Rip saw it too, and before I had even gasped, his gun was up, pointed and cocked, and he had taken cover behind a nearby tree.

Seeing what was happening, Mike and Charlie drew their guns as well, Mike moving toward me in one fluid motion and pulling me with him behind another tree. It wasn't wide enough for both of us, so rather than leaving him exposed, I silently moved on to the next tree and crouched down, watching to see what would happen. By that point, we had all managed to take cover except for the technician, who had simply hit the dirt at the base of the gate and lay still.

Seeing the man trapped there, exposed and without cover, Mike whispered sharply for all of us to turn off our flashlights. The figure was beyond the reach of our beams anyway, so we did as he said. Once my eyes adjusted to the new darkness, I was relieved to see that the technician, dressed all in black, nearly disappeared from view.

No one fired. No one even spoke. Instead we all simply waited and watched, frozen, peering through the night at what had emerged from the shadows and seemed to hover there in the distance at the crest of the hill. Clad in a long, white flowing gown, the slim, diaphanous figure moved silently beyond the trees through the mist. Holding my breath, I tried to understand what I was seeing. I just hoped, more than anything, that it was an actual person and not what it really looked like.

A ghost.

ELEVEN

After a moment the figure in the distance moved downward into the hollow, disappearing from view. Waiting to see if it would emerge, I began to wonder if by thinking it was a ghost that I was doing the exact thing Mike said people tended to do, see what the eyes were expecting to see rather than what really was.

Human or not, there was no doubt that someone or something was out there.

"I'm going in," Rip whispered, and he began to move quietly in that direction, around the side of the closed gate and into the beech trees, zig-zagging from tree to tree for cover.

If I'd had one of my guns with me, I would have gone too—not because I'm foolhardy or especially brave, but simply because the thought of being proactive was far less frightening to me than staying put and waiting to see what would happen next. Charlie whispered he was going in as well, but before he got very far a light suddenly appeared in the distance, in almost the same exact spot where the figure had first emerged. Moving along eerily in the silence, the light reached the crest of the hill and paused for a long moment, but rather than following along down into the hollow, it seemed to change course and come toward us instead. Hovering just a few feet off the ground, the yellowish glow dimmed and brightened as it floated closer.

The light finally came to a stop about fifteen feet beyond the gate. We waited, guns drawn and ready, my heart pounding furiously in my chest.

"Who goes there!" Rip suddenly demanded from his hiding place up ahead. The beam of his flashlight burst to life from among the beech trees, illuminating the path where the light was hovering.

We all flipped ours back on as well and pointed them toward the same spot, beams meeting in the center like spokes to an axle. What our illumination revealed wasn't some otherworldly creature. It was simply a man, holding a lantern.

"I am Jonah Coblentz," the man called. "Is everything all right?"

"Jonah!" I cried, relief flooding my veins. "It's me! Sienna! Your cousin Sienna!"

Even as the men were already lowering their weapons, I called out to them that it was okay and not to shoot. Making my way toward Jonah—around the gate, through the trees, and back onto the path as quickly as possible—all I could think of was how grateful I was that these officers of the law had had the presence of mind not to shoot too soon.

"Sienna!" Jonah exclaimed as I reached him. "What are you doing out here?"

"At the moment I'm thanking the Lord you didn't get shot!"

I threw my arms around him and held on tight. He tried to hug me in return, but with a lantern in one hand and a rifle in the other, it was a little awkward.

Releasing our embrace, I stepped back and looked at his familiar face. Though I hadn't seen my cousin for almost a year, not since a visit last Christmas, in the lamplight he looked exactly the same, and I told him so.

"Except maybe the beard is another inch longer," I added. Like all Amish men, he had stopped shaving everything but his upper lip the day he got married. That had been eight or nine years ago, and every time I saw him he looked more and more like his father.

In the midst of our little reunion, Mike came around the gate and joined us, asking Jonah if someone else had been with him.

"*Jah*, that is my wife, Liesl."

Pointing my flashlight toward the place where the white figure had disappeared, I saw that it was back again, much closer now and peeking out from behind a tree. It really *was* Liesl, and though she waved at me enthusiastically, she neither spoke nor came any closer.

"What's wrong with her? Is she okay?"

Jonah chuckled.

"*Jah*, she is fine, just embarrassed. We were already in bed when the police came knocking, and we were so concerned about the animals that we rushed right out to check on everything without stopping to think."

Looking again at my cousin's wife, I suddenly realized what he was saying. Though her nightgown was extremely modest, her hair was down. Her long, lovely, never-been-cut hair was loose on her shoulders and hanging free. To her mind, she might as well have been out here stark naked. The only time Amish women ever let their hair down was in the privacy of the bedroom with their husbands.

That also explained why I hadn't recognized what I was seeing earlier. Had she been wearing the apron and cape she wore in the daytime, no doubt I would have spotted that telltale Amish silhouette, remembered that beyond the beech trees lay their farm, and figured out that it was her. Instead, a figure in a white gown had no context, and my mind had gone to "ghost."

As Mike and Jonah briefly conversed, I thought about running over and giving Liesl a hug, but I wasn't sure if that would only embarrass her further. To be safe, I simply waved in return and stayed where I was. After Mike crossed back to the other side of the gate to help the technician, Jonah and I chatted, me explaining what I was doing with the police, him telling me how sorry he was to hear about Troy, not to mention Floyd and Nina.

"I am relieved to say that the animals are all fine," he told me. "There were no signs of any wild beasts at all. Now we are on our way to Emory's. Liesl wants to check on him and make sure he is okay."

"I should have thought to check on him myself," I admitted, "or at the very least called my father about all of this by now."

When Grandpa Abe died, the responsibility of his mentally disabled son had fallen to my father. Unsure about what to do, my dad had had his older brother Emory tested for competency, and we all had been relieved to hear that he could live alone as long as he had daily part-time help. Nina, a home health worker who lived across the street and had been a longtime family friend, had easily filled the bill. Just to make sure things were working out with the new arrangement, my father had begun coming out to see Emory more often. Things had floated along smoothly ever since—or at least until my mother had become so sick. Now my father had almost no time or energy to spare for his brother. I didn't even want to think about what might happen if poor Nina ended up not pulling through.

"You haven't told your family yet?" Jonah asked, his eyebrows disappearing under the rim of his hat.

"My mother isn't doing very well," I explained. "She had one of her treatments again this morning."

"Ah. Then your father has enough on his hands already," Jonah replied. "Do not worry, Sienna. Liesl and I and will take care of Emory. Even if Nina didn't come today at all, I am sure that is not a problem for him. He makes out okay. My bigger concern is how he reacted when the police came knocking on his door tonight. He is terrified of men in uniform, you know."

I put a hand to my mouth, now feeling even worse.

"Oh, dear. I didn't know."

"It is okay. Liesl and I have a key to his medication box. There are pills we are allowed to give him if he gets too upset. Do not give it another thought; we will take care of it."

"Thank you, Jonah. We'll talk tomorrow, okay?"

I could tell that Mike and his men had finished with the gate and were waiting for me, so I gave Jonah a hug and thanked him again for being such a huge help. He insisted that no thanks were necessary. Emory was family, and this was just what families do.

"You two be careful out here," I said as we parted. In reply, Jonah held up his rifle and said he had things covered.

As I made my way back through the trees, I thought about that. An Amish man with a gun? Perhaps later I would ask him about it. It was my understanding that the Amish were never willing to bear arms, not for any reason. I realized there was so much about my own family heritage I didn't know or understand. Once my grandfather left the faith, he also left all that part of himself behind.

Mike explained that it didn't look as if Troy had been at the German Gate after all, so we pressed onward, checking first the Corn Gate and then the Peace Gate. In the end we had to conclude that whatever latch he had opened during our phone conversation, it wasn't any of the four in the grove.

Feeling overwhelmingly disappointed as we crossed back to the B and B, I realized that our entire jaunt had served only one good purpose evidence-wise—that of finding the holes that had recently been dug. I was feeling hopeless and every bit as confused as before when Mike's radio crackled to life and we heard at least one interesting bit of news: One of the cops who was an avid hunter had found some very unusual animal scat among some trees not far from the pool area. The scat had been overlooked by everyone before because of its appearance. I wasn't interested in hearing the details, but it sounded as though it included a piece of fruit so large and nearly undigested that an untrained eye might not realize it had passed through an animal at all.

"Do you recognize what kind of creature it came from?" Mike said into the radio.

"Negative. It's not like anything I've ever seen before. I can tell you what it *didn't* come from." He then went on to list every animal, large and small, that we had been considering thus far. When he was finished, Mike asked the man what he thought their next animal-tracking move should be.

"Once it's daylight, we can check for prints in the mud alongside the stream in the grove," the man's voice said. "The ground should be softer and wetter there, so if there really has been a wild animal around, that'll be our best chance for finding any tracks." He added that it was also probably time to call in the game commission.

Radio chatter continued all the way back to the B and B, with the officers who had made the rounds knocking on doors finally reporting in. I was only half listening, but I smiled when I heard one of them say that the Amish couple around the corner seemed more interested in the safety of their livestock than themselves. I knew they were talking about Jonah and Liesl, who took excellent care of all of their animals.

From another report, we learned that Burl Newton, the former chicken farmer who lived directly behind me, hadn't been home when they knocked on his door. But police had continued moving down Burl's road, notifying other neighbors, and when they came across a backyard party in progress several houses down, they ran into Burl there and were able to talk to him.

"Said he walked over from his place around six o'clock, and that he didn't hear or see anything unusual along the way."

From another report, I was glad to learn that one couple who lived across the street from the B and B confirmed my arrival around 7:15 p.m. They also said that Floyd's car had been gone for a few days, but that it had shown up tonight a little before 6:30 p.m.

According to the various reports, not one single person they spoke to in the area had heard or seen anything strange all day or night prior to the peal of sirens arriving around 7:30 p.m.

Mike thanked his people for their reports, and then we continued the rest of the way to the B and B in silence. By the time we reached the pool area, I was relieved to see that Troy's body had finally been removed from the scene.

Though we had no real answers yet, things seemed to be winding down for the night, and I was starting to wonder what I was going to do about sleeping arrangements. My bed-and-breakfast apparently had plenty of empty rooms, but with its manager in the hospital, no other guests around, and a potential murderer and/or creature running loose outside, I wasn't too keen on staying here all alone. I was too tired to drive back to my parents' home in Radnor, much less all the way to my own place in Philly. That basically left only a few options, none of them that desirable: Impose on family, either by staying next door at Emory's or with Jonah and Liesl, or lock up my empty bed-and-breakfast and pay to stay at a local hotel. As it turned out, neither was necessary.

TWELVE

Apparently, the crazy calls about animal sightings had already started to come in, and just in case folks might take it upon themselves to go creature hunting and possibly destroying evidence, not to mention shooting each other by mistake, Mike decided to post several of his men on the grounds for the night. Just knowing they would be out there made all the difference as far as I was concerned.

"We need you to remain in the area, if possible," Mike told me, "at least for the next few days. If not, be sure to notify me before leaving."

"Will do," I said. Then, after a long pause and some internal debate, I added, "Just so you know, I have firearms and a license to carry. I plan to be holstered from here on out."

He wanted to see my permit, so together we walked to my car. On the way I asked if he was feeling as pessimistic as I was, if he thought we would ever be able to make sense of all the strange things that seemed to have happened here today.

"I think the bulk of this case lies in the medical evidence," he replied. "We should know a lot more about what happened to Troy after the forensics are all done."

"How about Floyd and Nina? Do you think they were poisoned somehow?"

At the car, I handed my permit to Mike, and as he studied it I decided to get my suitcase and things from the car to bring them inside. When I opened the trunk and spotted the cardboard box from my office sitting in there, I was reminded of the sum total of the disasters that had taken place today.

"Poison. Sure, that's one possibility. It's also possible that Floyd and Nina had been partying, and that maybe they partied just a little too hard."

"What do you mean? Drugs? You think Floyd and Nina are in the state they're in because they were taking *drugs*? That's ridiculous!"

Mike shrugged. "They could have been inside getting high, heard a disturbance out by the pool, gone out there to see what it was, and tried to help Troy by pulling him from the water and doing mouth-to-mouth and all of that. Floyd could have passed out, and when Nina tried to get home, she made it as far as the bridge and then passed out as well."

"What about the things that Floyd said? The fire-breathing creature he was talking about?"

"Floyd was totally out of his head."

I nodded. "Okay, but drugs? Come on. I doubt that either Floyd or Nina were in the habit of taking drugs." I went on to defend them both, though even as I explained what a wonderful manager Floyd was—so wonderful that he handled everything here without my help at all and had been turning a profit for me practically since day one—I remembered Troy's words on the phone, and I knew there was a chance that Floyd wasn't nearly as great as I was saying he was. But I wasn't ready to share that with the police just yet. Instead, I focused on Nina, explaining how she had known our family for years and that my grandfather had trusted her implicitly.

Refusing Mike's help I pulled my suitcase from the trunk and slammed it shut for emphasis.

Mike studied my face for a moment and then spoke. "Then maybe you can tell me why Nina had six little white pills in a baggie in her jeans pocket."

"White pills?"

"Ativan. Easy to come by, easy to abuse."

"Did you talk to her doctor? It could have been prescribed for her."

Mike shrugged. "We're looking into that. Her parents said that as far as they know she was given Xanax back when her daughter died, but they had never heard of her ever getting Ativan. We'll see. Even if she did obtain it legally, it takes more than the prescribed dose to knock somebody out like that. As I said before, the tox screen should tell us more. Often it all comes down to the medical."

"Emory has pills to calm his nerves," I said, remembering what Jonah had told me. "Maybe they belonged to him and she just had them on her because she'd been over there taking care of him."

Mike handed me back my permit.

"So you're thirty-three, huh?" he asked out of the blue, and I realized he had done the math from reading my birth date.

"I know, I know. People always think I'm younger than I am," I said, returning the permit to the glove compartment. "When I was in my teens and early twenties, I hated it, but these days I'm starting to see its value."

"Yeah, you don't look a day over twenty, maybe twenty-five at the most. On the other hand, even thirty-three is young to be the owner of a beautiful place like this."

I thanked him for both compliments, explaining that I had done a fair amount of real estate investing in the past, but Harmony Grove Bed & Breakfast was mine mostly thanks to my grandfather's will.

Mike asked me to go on, so as he took my suitcase and briefcase and I retrieved the two potted plants, I explained that the will had divided my grandfather's holdings six ways, leaving various assets to his ex-wife, his two sons, his two grandchildren, and one charity.

"His ex-wife?" Mike asked as we headed toward the house. "I thought she died."

"His *first* wife died, remember? I'm talking now about his second wife, my Grandma Maureen. They were married for less than ten years, I think. She divorced him back when my father was still a child."

"Must have been a pretty amicable divorce if he named her in the will."

"Actually, they rarely had any contact at all anymore. We were surprised at first when we found out he'd given her the grove, but the more we thought about it, the more it made sense. His obsession with that grove was a large part of what had come between them and ultimately ended their marriage, so I guess he figured it was the least he could do. As Grandma Maureen says, when you marry a widower, it's hard enough to compete with memories of his late wife—but nearly impossible when he dedicates the bulk of his land to a living memorial of her."

"I can see her point."

"Anyway, Emory got about five acres, which included the smaller back house, the barn, the springhouse, and the covered bridge out front. Like I told you earlier, he was also supposed to get the assets left to him by his mother, Daphne,' whatever those were, but he never did."

We reached the door and stepped inside. I told Mike just to set my bags at the foot of the stairs as I continued.

"My dad got three acres, which included the main house and the shed. That was it for the buildings on the property, but my brother and I got the land that was left, two six-acre parcels that sat on each side of our father's three."

I set the plants on the mantel.

"I was doing a lot of investing back then, so when my dad and Scott and I were trying to decide what to do with our parcels, I tried talking them into combining all three and turning this place into a bed-and-breakfast. Scott wasn't interested, but he really wanted to see the whole property stay together and in the family, so he sold us his share cheap. That, combined with my land plus my father's land, was enough to make this place happen. My dad got my mother to agree by painting a picture of their retirement, saying that when that day came when he would no longer serve at the church, the two of them could move out here to the B and B and take over its management. Of course, that was before she was diagnosed with MS."

"How about the grove itself?"

"My grandmother retained ownership of the grove, but she was happy to let us use its name for our bed-and-breakfast."

"And the pool? Was it here already?"

Changing my mind about the plants, I moved one of them to the wide sill of the back window.

"No, we had the pool put in ourselves. Before we started the renovation, we thought the house might need to be gutted, but once we got down to it, it was in better shape than we'd expected. So we used the surplus in our budget toward a pool, something we felt would give this place a competitive edge over most of the other B and Bs in the area."

Mike pulled the notebook from his pocket and began flipping pages. I had thought we were mostly just having a conversation, but when he did that, I realized that the detective was still in full detecting mode.

"So this place is co-owned by you and your parents? You said earlier you were the sole owner."

"We were co-owners at first. But then later, after it was up and running, my mother's condition grew worse, and she had to quit her job as a church secretary." I explained that we knew my parents would need every penny they could get, so even though I was already pretty strapped by that point, I wanted to do what I could. With some creative financing and my grandmother's help, I had been able to buy them out. "Ever since then, it's been all mine."

Seemingly satisfied, Mike closed the notebook and slid it back into his pocket.

"Like I said, impressive."

Our eyes met and held. After a beat, I looked away, moving toward the door to retrieve the rest of my things from the car.

"So if that's what happened to all of the land, what went to the charity?" he asked as we stepped outside and headed down the walk.

"The what?"

"You said your grandfather's will divided things six ways, the sixth being a charity. What did the charity get?"

"Oh, they didn't get any land, they got money, what was left of Grandpa Abe's savings. It wasn't a fortune, but they were very appreciative.

"What was the charity?"

"The Holocaust Memorial Museum in DC."

We reached the car, and I opened the trunk again to get out my FAA-approved gun box. Mike was silent as I unlocked and opened the steel container to check on my babies: a Kahr MK40 autoloader and a Ruger SP-101 double action revolver. They both seemed fine, but as I closed up the box it struck me that Mike hadn't said a word the whole time.

"What's wrong?"

"I'm just surprised," he said. "The Holocaust Museum? Why there?"

"Daphne was Jewish. I'm sorry, didn't I mention that before?"

"No. You didn't," he said, his voice so emphatic that it startled me.

"Yes, her whole family was killed during the Holocaust—parents, siblings, aunts, uncles, cousins, everybody. She was the only surviving member. Then she ended up dying while giving birth to Emory."

"So Emory's Jewish," Mike said. "I did not realize that."

"Well, half Jewish, anyway, I guess you could say." I corrected, closing the trunk and handing him the metal box before getting some extra ammo from the glove compartment. "I guess you could say he's half Jewish, half Amish. How's that for a combination?"

"This is unbelievable."

I wasn't sure what difference it made, and for a moment I was afraid that the detective was anti-Semitic. Bristling, I was about to call him on it when he saw my face and quickly explained.

"Maybe we weren't properly introduced before," he told me, dark eyes meeting mine. "My full name is Mikha'el Weissbaum, born and raised in Elkins Park, Pennsylvania, son of Morty and Rivka Weissbaum."

I got the point. Mike was Jewish too!

We both laughed over our misunderstanding, but when he saw me grab three extra boxes of .40 S&W ammo on top of what was already in the gun box, our moment of levity evaporated with the seriousness of his face. And I hadn't even told him about the 125-grain jacketed hollow points in my briefcase.

"I hope you know how to handle those guns. I don't want you shooting any of my men."

"Don't worry. I'm fully trained, and I go to the firing range two or three times a month to keep up my skills."

Mike replied that whether I was proficient with it or not, I should never let a gun give me a false sense of security, adding that I still always needed to be aware of my surroundings, lock doors, and follow all of the other safety measures that required not much more than presence of mind and common sense.

"You might even want to learn some self-defense techniques," he said as we walked back toward the door. "I actually teach a class in Krav Maga if you're interested."

"Actually, I've taken classes on self-defense before," I told him, explaining that my favorite was RBSD, which was reality based self-defense. "I also box, and I have a mean uppercut."

With my free hand I demonstrated my best move, accidentally exposing my bad arm. He looked at my scar, but unlike most people who saw it and then glanced self-consciously away, he allowed his eyes to linger, a question forming there.

For some reason, the disfigurement I was usually careful to hide and rarely talked about outside of my inner circle didn't seem like such a big deal. I didn't even mind explaining it to him. There was no need to go into detail. I just told him that when I was in college I had been the victim of a violent crime, and my scars had come from that.

"Hence the guns, and the self-defense, and the boxing, no doubt."

I smiled. "All on the recommendation of the counselor who helped me work through the trauma," I replied. "Well, I take that back. She wasn't too keen on the guns. But the boxing and the self-defense were both her idea."

He didn't ask the nature of the incident, though it struck me that as a cop it might not be difficult for him to look me up on some database and read all about it for himself. Somewhere out there were surely reams and reams of police reports, evidence logs, trial transcripts, and more. Smoothing my sleeve back down I told him that the single biggest lesson I had learned in college was that I'd better protect myself because no one else ever would. We reached the door, and I paused, adding, "I just wish I could have protected Troy too."

"Protected Troy? You weren't even here."

"No, but if I had come sooner, maybe I could have gotten here in time to save him."

I stepped inside, put the ammo down on the table, and took the gun box from Mike. He remained in the doorway, pulling out his car keys, ready to go.

"Maybe," he said, looking at me intently with those deep, dark eyes. "Then again, maybe you would have arrived in time to be killed right along with him."

THIRTEEN

I didn't realize how exhausted I was until I closed and locked the front door. Wearily, I carried my things up the stairs, through the small upstairs sitting/reading area, and down the hall to the end. This back room was my favorite, the one I stayed in whenever I came here. It was smaller than the other two, but I liked the way it was tucked in at the end of the hall, and it gave the best view from the house of the grove.

As I set my things down and unzipped my suitcase, I thought about how fortunate I was that I still had all the stuff I had packed for my trip to Boston, otherwise I wouldn't have had toiletries or spare clothes or other things with me now. I sat on the edge of the bed, took a deep breath, and let it out slowly, willing myself to relax. I needed to call my parents and tell them what had been going on here tonight, but it was late, and they would be sound asleep after an incredibly trying day. The news was going to be very upsetting to both of them, I felt sure, and would likely keep them up the rest of the night if I called now. I decided to wait until morning.

Next, I thought about calling Heath, who was also surely asleep by now. If he spotted this mess on the news first, I knew he was going to be upset and hurt that I hadn't called and told him myself or asked for his help.

So why hadn't I contacted him yet? Heath was my boyfriend, after all. We had been dating for almost ten months, and intentions on both sides were serious. I loved him, and I had no doubt that he loved me.

So why? At first there was the pride issue, of course; the embarrassment of my suspension at work and my newly precarious financial situation. But beyond that, after I had arrived here and the dominoes began toppling, when I had finally been able to make a call, why had I only dialed Liz and not Heath as well?

I had no doubt he would have come immediately just to support me, to hold my hand, to keep me feeling safe. I should have wanted him here, if for no other reason than the fact that Heath possessed a deep calmness, one born from the time he spent in Bible study, meditation, and prayer. Heath had grown up in a more conservative church than I had, which led to different stands on some theological matters, but at least he and I were in total agreement on what my dad called the "big rock issues" of our faith. On smaller, less important matters, where wise debate could be heard from both sides, we sometimes landed on opposite ends of the spectrum.

The most notable area that had been a bone of contention for us practically since our very first date was the issue of self-defense, pacifism, and nonviolence. I was raised to believe in the concept of just war and the moral obligations of a democratic society, and after what happened to me in college, my willingness to bear arms became much more personal. Heath, on the other hand, had been strongly influenced by Mennonite grandparents, and though he wasn't a Mennonite himself, their pacifist ideals had resonated with him.

Neither Heath nor I were the type of people who enjoyed unnecessary conflict, so after several strong arguments on this particular topic, we finally agreed to disagree. Ordinarily, that would have been the end of it. But even with our truce, the matter hadn't been solved but merely shelved. Someday, if we took this relationship all the way to the altar, this issue would have to be figured out. To most people that might have seemed silly, but to me it was deadly serious. Having been a victim of violence once, I couldn't imagine being married to a pacifist. My bottom line in every discussion had always been that I spoke from experience, which in my opinion trumped theory every time.

Thinking about Heath now, I decided that one reason I hadn't contacted him was because of his feelings about nonresistance. Heath knew I had a gun but he hated it, and he absolutely never wanted to be around it or be forced to watch me handling it. Given that, is it any wonder that I actually felt safer without him around? Being here alone, I had the freedom to exercise whatever self-protective options I needed to. Were he here, I might be tempted to defer to his preferences, and that could be a fatal mistake.

Aside from that, I really would have wanted him here. With his calm demeanor and logical thought processes, he was ideal to bounce things off of, whether trivial or significant. He was also incredibly smart, and I had a feeling his medical knowledge would come in quite handy just now. After all, that's what Mike kept saying: It all comes down to the medical.

Tapping the button for my contacts list, I even went so far as to get Heath's number up on the screen. I just wanted to hear his voice, to hear him tell me everything would be okay even if we both knew it wouldn't.

I almost pressed the dial button, but in the end I decided not to call. We could talk in the morning. There was no reason to wake him up just so his night could be as complicated and restless as mine.

I was about to put the phone away when I realized I had one voice mail message waiting, one that had come while I was out in the grove and probably hadn't heard it ringing. It was Liz, calling to say there were no new developments but that she would keep me posted if anything came up. Listening to her message, I could tell she hadn't learned anything about what was going on here. No doubt she assumed I was back in Philadelphia, safely tucked up in my own bed, and not in Lancaster County, embroiled in what may very well be a murder investigation. Tomorrow, of course, I'd have to bring her up to speed first thing, right after I spoke to my parents and to Heath.

Putting the phone in my pocket, I turned my attentions to the metal gun box on the bed beside me. Before I went to sleep, I wanted to thoroughly check and load both weapons. I did that now, and when I was finished I focused on my various holster options. Though I usually carried my auto-loader in a gun purse and left my revolver in the car as a backup, while I was here I planned to use my fanny pack holster instead so that I would be armed at all times. And I planned on sleeping with both guns in easy reach.

My body was so exhausted that I knew I should climb in bed and try to get some rest. Unfortunately, my brain wasn't tired at all. It was firing on all cylinders, and I could tell sleep would be a long time in coming. A night owl by nature, it wasn't unusual for me to be up this late even on a normal night. If I stayed up another half hour or so, just long enough to settle my mind and leave it more open to the possibility of sleep, I didn't think that would hurt anything.

I decided to go down to the office and do a little poking around, maybe look for my grandfather's documents and figure out what had happened to tonight's guests. Patting the MK40 in my holster and reassuring myself that it was there, I headed downstairs. I may not know Floyd's office systems or his specific business practices or even the names of our most frequent guests, but I thought if I could orient myself to some of that now, at least it might make me feel a little bit more in control.

I had to say this for Floyd, the office was incredibly neat. There were no sticky notes on the computer, piles on the desk, or scraps of trash around the trash can. Unlike my desks at home and at work, which usually looked as though a tornado had blown through, this place was positively pristine. I had tried to do a little better at Buzz, feeling oddly out of place in a company that practically made neatness a job requirement, but it simply wasn't in my nature. Even in a fancy tenth floor windowed office full of streamlined furniture and sleek storage devices, I couldn't seem to hold my act together, at least not perfectly, and certainly not like this.

I began by looking in drawers and cabinets, trying not to be jealous of the color-coded folders as I did so. I had my eye out for anything related to my grandfather, but all I could find were documents and forms and other supplies related to the running of the inn.

When I hired Floyd two years ago, his only sticking point was that he be allowed to run the bed-and-breakfast his way, which I quickly realized was another word for the precomputer stone age way. He wouldn't take the job, he had told me, if it meant he had to learn computer systems and software programs. I was reluctant to agree, but in considering his request I asked him to show me the systems he would be using, and they seemed so simple and accessible that in the end I met his demand. Just in case he changed his mind down the road a bit, I had supplied him with an inexpensive PC, and it was still sitting on the center of the desk where I had put it the day I brought it here. Booting it up now, I was curious to see if the man had, indeed, learned to automate, even just a little bit. I had had to teach him how to use a basic spreadsheet, if only so that my financial statements could come to me via e-mail, something that was necessary for my digital lifestyle. Otherwise, I had no idea if he used the computer for anything else or not.

Sitting in his chair, I clicked around a bit, not surprised to see that Floyd had hardly been using it at all. Of course, he had gone in once a month to do the spreadsheets for my sake, but otherwise the hard drive was nearly as empty now as it had been when I set it up. It didn't take long to figure out that Floyd kept no guest information on the computer at all. But I needed to find the correct phone numbers for the people I had tried calling earlier, so I crossed to the file cabinets and did things the old-fashioned way, digging through a bunch of receipts before finding the guest registration forms.

Setting them on the desk, I retrieved the registration ledger and brought it back to the office, using the names written there to search for their corresponding file cards. My hope was that Floyd had accidentally transposed something in the ledger, and I could get the correct numbers this way. Floyd's files were so neat that I quickly found cards for all three guests. But when I compared them with the ledger, I saw that the phone numbers had been written out exactly the same on both.

That meant I would probably have to go online and hunt down phone numbers for these people that way. I wasn't in the mood to go through all of that right now, but I planned on looking into it in the morning. For now, I simply started looking up the names of all the people who had reservations coming in the next seven days, pulling their guest information cards, and setting them in a neat pile on the desk. Tomorrow I would go through the pile one by one, calling each one of them to say that we had had a problem at the inn and would need to cancel their reservation. I would also offer to help them find some other place to stay, though that might not be such an easy task this time of year. Early October in Lancaster County was prime fall foliage season. I would do the best I could and hope that most of them wouldn't take me up on my offer of help.

Suddenly I realized what a blessing Floyd had been. He had handled things so fully that I had been able to collect my checks and not give the B and B another thought. That wasn't the best way to run a business, I knew, but with my crazy schedule in the city, there weren't enough hours in the day as it was. I could only hope that Troy had been lying or wrong or confused when he made it sound as though Floyd was up to something that had led to my investigation by the attorney general. If that were true, and even if I were able to clear my own name from the matter, I would still be facing the huge problem of finding someone to replace Floyd.

Closing down the computer, I decided that the old cliché was true: You don't know what you've got till it's gone. With Floyd gone, at least temporarily, I was the de facto manager here, a job I sure didn't want for long.

As I tucked Floyd's chair under his desk, turned off the light, and closed the office door, it occurred to me that perhaps the only way I was going to find out what Troy had meant about Floyd getting me in trouble with the government was from Floyd himself. I hoped he would have a speedy recovery because I had plenty of questions that couldn't wait.

Before I went toward the stairs and up to bed, I turned the other way and went down the hall and through the dining room to Troy's room. I would have liked to go inside and search every nook and cranny for the mysterious papers of my grandfather, but I had been told to keep out for the time being, and the strip of yellow police tape stretched across the doorway emphasized that point. It probably wouldn't have done any good anyway, I decided, because the police had already searched the room thoroughly earlier. Even more important, the officers had taken away Troy's suitcase and his belongings, so already they had reduced the number of potential places I could have searched.

Instead, I just stood there in the doorway for a moment, one hand resting on the reassuring bulge of my gun, and thought about the fact that Troy was dead. He was really, actually dead. Why did that seem so surreal?

I wish I could have comforted myself in the knowledge that he had gone quickly, but as almost two hours passed between his call with me and my finding his dead body by the pool, that left a two-hour time span during which he very likely had suffered, first from whatever had cut him, and then from whatever had drowned him.

The best-case scenario in this rotten situation was that everything that had happened was all an accident, or more accurately a series of accidents. At least if there had been no malice involved, things could settle down sooner, and life could get back to normal.

Well, not exactly normal. Not for Troy or for the people in his life. Floyd and even Nina might be okay in the end, but all that was left for Troy was for his body to be buried and mourned. Just thinking about that now, I was surprised to find myself overwhelmed with sudden grief.

I thought about my relationship with him way back when, about the good times, the laughter, the excitement. Troy was nothing if not exciting—not to mention handsome and adventurous, with vivid green eyes that crackled with intensity. He gave off such an air of competence that it was no wonder I had allowed myself to trust him too much. If I could forgive him for all the bad that had come near the end, for all the fallout from what our relationship had cost me, literally cost me, I might find more peace about his death.

FOURTEEN

Once I climbed into bed it didn't take long for me to fall asleep, despite the clicking of the heater as it kicked in, a clock down the hall that sounded a faint bong every hour on the hour, and the occasional crackle of the police radios of the men standing guard outside.

I'm sure I would have stayed asleep till morning if only there hadn't been one exceptionally loud radio crackle when one of the policemen was passing under my window below. That noisy squawk popped me straight out of a dream, the kind that leaves your heart pounding and your body shaking. I opened my eyes and looked up at the ceiling, trying to figure out what had awakened me, where I was, and if I should be scared. But then just a second later another squawk and some chatter followed, and I realized that's all it was, the comforting sound of the lawmen outside.

Turning my head toward the clock, the pounding and shaking subsiding, I saw that it was 4:42 a.m. Lovely. I hadn't even turned out my light until nearly 3:00. Even if I slept until nine or ten in the morning, I knew that still wasn't going to be enough, especially not now.

Flipping over on my other side and trying to get comfortable again, I closed my eyes and waited for sleep to return. My body was sore from the earlier fall, and in that strange way that the mind and body have of working together, I realized I had been dreaming that a shark had hold of my wrist and kept biting and wouldn't let go. At some point during the dream, my mind had changed the shark into a sea turtle, and by the time I was awakened, the turtle was a scuba diver, twisting my wrist and fighting me as he tried to stab my thigh with his knife.

It was a silly dream, yes, but thinking about it now, my pulse began to quicken. The water. The struggle. The pain.

Lying there in the bed, I could feel sweat beginning to bead along my forehead. My hands grew clammy, my breathing shallow. Helpless to stop it, I felt the old, familiar anxiety rise up inside of me, gripping my lungs and squeezing out all room for air. Sitting up, trying to ignore the frenzied roiling of my stomach, I rubbed my wrist and arm and told the bad feelings to go away.

It had been a while, but now those feelings were back, the last vestiges of emotional holdover not born of tonight's events but certainly stirred up by them.

Water. My dreams always came back to water.

Recognizing the panic that now threatened to overwhelm me, I closed my eyes, trying to remember the most important thing my counselor had taught me ten years ago: *Move through the discomfort, not around it, so you can move on.* She had shown me how to let yucky feelings happen without avoidance, without denial, and without any substances to numb the pain. Just let them happen, let myself feel them, and then let them go, handing them over to God.

If only that weren't so hard to do! How much simpler it would have been to mask the pain with the anesthesia of alcohol or drugs or whatever—or my personal anesthetic of choice, activity—rather than allow myself to *feel*. The busier I stayed, the more I ran, the more I achieved, the longer those uncomfortable feelings were held at bay. But now that the old memories had risen up and were combining with a new trauma, I knew I was walking into the danger zone. A new job and a major new campaign contributed to the problem. If I weren't careful, I might find myself filling my outer world so completely that not only did it smother the inner pain but everything else inside of me as well.

I touched the floor with the tips of my toes and tried deep breathing. In. Hold. Out. In. Hold. Out.

Move through the discomfort, not around it, so you can move on.

Rising, I stepped to the window and pulled the white lace curtain aside. Looking out at the night sky, I couldn't believe how many stars were visible to the naked eye. Hundreds. Thousands. Far, far more than I could ever see from my windows in the city.

"'Praise him, all you shining stars,'" I whispered out loud, not even sure which psalm I was echoing. I tried another, desperate for comfort. "'He made the moon and stars to govern the night. His love endures forever.'" That wasn't quite right, but close enough. Either way, it didn't help.

If you can't pray in your own words, pray in Scriptures.

Move through the discomfort, not around it, so you can move on.

Breathe in. Hold it. Breathe out. In. Hold. Out.

Give it over to God. He's big enough to handle it for you. He made the moon and the stars.

The night sky.

The night.

That night.

Spring break, senior year in college, one whole week in a Virginia coastal town.

Seven days of sun and sand and relaxing with three of my best friends.

Six nights of having our tiny little hotel room all to myself, blessedly quiet for studying while my friends were out painting the town.

They knew I didn't like the bar scene, that I preferred a good book to an evening of drinking and dancing. I was the overachiever even then, driven to succeed, the one who always chose work over play. All week they had tried to get me to come along, and each night I had declined, saying I wasn't interested and I needed to study. Knowing I was a Christian— a pastor's kid, no less—didn't stop them from pressuring me.

Then came that last night. Maybe I went to shut them up. Maybe I went because I was bored, tired of the quiet, and ready for a break. Most of all, maybe I went because, as I watched them get ready, giggling about the outfits they would wear and the nail polish they would use and the cute boys they hoped would show up again tonight, I suddenly felt about fifty years old. Life couldn't always be about quiet and studying and getting ahead.

True, I didn't drink and I couldn't stand the smell of smoke and I wasn't crazy about having to yell over the din of music. But even if I were more ambitious and disciplined than most, that didn't mean I had to work 24/7. Soon I would face graduation and a career and the beginning of a mature, responsible, adult life. On this last night of spring break of my senior year in college, it was time for me to act not fifty or forty or even thirty but twenty-three. My age. It was time to act my age.

And so I went.

We ended up choosing a well-known restaurant/bar, a local landmark built on a pier jutting out over the water. The food was wonderful, the waiters young and friendly, the prices affordable. My friends and I had a great time at dinner, laughing and joking and flirting with every halfway decent guy that looked our way, just for kicks. We felt alive and beautiful, tanned and relaxed from our week in the sun.

After dinner, we moved from one side of the place to the other, from the noisy restaurant to the noisier bar, which was twice as big and ten times as full. The music was pumping, if way too loud, and soon all four of us were out on the dance floor, enjoying the moment, having a good time. The place was crowded, yes, not to mention hot, but there was something very freeing about being in the crush of all those bodies, in the dark, moving to the beat of the music.

A guy who had been making eyes at me in the restaurant all evening soon squeezed his way into the tight space next to me. He was cuter up close than he had been from across the room, with sun-bleached hair and tanned skin and teeth so white they practically glowed in the dark. Yelling to be heard over the music, he said his name was Damien and that he couldn't believe his rotten luck, that a beautiful girl like me was starting my vacation on the very night he was ending his. Yelling back and forth, I realized that because he hadn't seen me out partying all week, he assumed I had just come into town.

I told him no, that I had been here all week, spending my days on the beach and my nights with a good book.

"Lucky book!" he teased, laughing.

With all his compliments, Damien smelled of beer, and I could tell by

the look in his eyes that the bottle in his hand wasn't his first of the evening. But he was cute and he made me feel like the prettiest girl not just in
the room but in all of Virginia, and on that night I was trying very hard to
act my age.

We ended up dancing together for more than an hour, at one point the
dance floor so full that even when we wanted to take a break and sit down,
we couldn't get through the crowd to do so. I had started my evening with
soda, and when we finally managed to squeeze our way off the floor and grab
a table along the side, Damien offered to get me another. Back from the bar,
he handed me an open cup of what I thought was cola. It smelled like cola.
It tasted like cola. But soon the room started spinning, and Damien's face,
which had been looming close all night, began to go in and out of focus.

Later, much later, lab tests would show that the drink he brought me had
indeed been cola. But somewhere between the bar and our table it had been
modified with some Rohypnols, more commonly known as roofies. This
stranger had roofied me.

At the time, all I knew was that if I didn't lie down soon, I just might fall
on the floor. Ignoring the cigarette butts and the sticky goo on the table's
surface, I simply folded my arms and laid them on the table, and then I put
my head down. Damien's arm was around me in an instant, and I was so
relieved that he understood how badly I needed a little support and some
fresh air. Practically carrying me from the bar, Damien moved more quickly
than I would have thought possible, given the crowd, until we were outside.

The thing was, he kept going. Not only did he keep going but suddenly
we weren't alone. Others were coming with us too. Other guys, some of
them very big and very drunk, all of them moving in step in a way that to
my drugged brain almost felt choreographed.

Somewhere in the back of my mind, a voice was telling me to run. I felt
weak and confused, but finally I obeyed, breaking away and heading back
down the pier toward the open-air restaurant. A number of people saw me;
in fact, most of the diners that sat along the outside row of tables had a very
clear view of a girl who was stumbling and running toward them. Some
stared. One woman gaped, first in surprise and then disdain.

But not one person did a thing.

Later, one woman told police that she and her husband *wanted* to stop those boys from what they were doing, but they were afraid. Another said sure, she saw those boys heading out of there with that girl; she had thought about telling the manager or trying to stop them, but then she "saw that girl's face and how absolutely plastered she was and figured she was getting just about what she deserved." In the end, no one tried to help me at all.

When Damien and his friends caught up with me, they laughed and grabbed me and pulled me away, and soon the restaurant's patrons were back to their meals, their chatter fading into the background behind us.

I must have passed out completely after that, because the next thing I knew, I was in a different place and time: not inside but out, not sitting on a chair in a bar but lying on my back on a gnarled old wooden pier, no longer surrounded by my friends but instead by a circle of Damien's friends, drunken young men on every side, who seemed to be forming a human privacy wall around us. About the only constant between the before and after was Damien's face. It was still looming too close, but now it was over me, looking down at me.

I screamed, a scream so loud and bloodcurdling that I couldn't believe it had come out of my own mouth. He was struggling with my pants, which he couldn't quite get undone or torn off, especially once I started fighting back. All I could do was scream louder and louder in the hopes that I would be saved, in the hopes that someone would hear me and rescue me.

But Damien had a plan for drowning out my screams. Later there would be testimony that said, essentially, he and his buddies had been trying to accomplish this very scenario several times during the week, but that something had gone wrong each time. In this their last try, they had covered every contingency. If the girl woke up too soon, and if she started hollering, they would simply holler louder, and hoot and laugh and cover the sound of their victim's screams with the simple noise of a rowdy group of drinking buddies on a Friday night at the beach.

Though I clawed and scratched and fought as hard as I could, I was no match for the muscular Damien. I even heard myself growing hoarse, but it didn't matter. When I could no longer scream, Damien's buddies were louder still, chanting amid the yelling, hopping up and down on the old wooden dock, stomping in a rhythm to match their chant.

Had they attempted to pull this off anywhere else that night, it would have ended differently. But because they chose to rape me on an older part of the pier that wasn't used anymore, way out on the section that was dark and chained off and closed to the public, there were other factors at play.

Of course, I didn't know that then. All I knew was that one moment I was pinned to the ground and fighting for my life, and the next moment that ground had dropped out from under me and I was falling.

Later, just to explain the complexities of that collapsing pier would take two days of testimony during the trial. But beyond the experts and their charts and the buck-passing city officials lay the truth: In the end, I was saved because of a lazy code inspector, rotting wood, and a crumbling underwater foundation.

My salvation wasn't without a price. As the floor disappeared from under me, and screams erupted all around me, I felt the whoosh of flight and then the slam of water against my back as I struck the surface. Plunging into the depths, my arm was speared by a cluster of razor-sharp steel rods mounted in cement on the seafloor, pointing skyward just under the surface.

Bodies rained down all around me, many of them speared as well, the shower of rotted planks and other detritus hitting the water with splintering, thundering crashes.

I don't know how I got loose. I don't know how I got away from the shrieking, tumbling boys who in their panic were only managing to push each other under the water. I don't know how I ended up half a block away, floating free in the Atlantic Ocean with my toes just touching the sand, the blood-red waves gently pushing me toward the shore, my arm a mangled pulp.

Somehow I made it all the way to the beach. Cradling my shredded and broken and bleeding appendage against me, I felt almost no pain. That would come later. All I knew then was that I had to get to safety, I had to get help, I had to get to a doctor before it was too late. Cursing the sand that kept shifting under my feet and slowing me down, I finally reached more solid ground, the sidewalk and then the street where a patrol cop on a bicycle just happened to be passing by. Already, someone had reported screams and crashing sounds from the closed part of the pier. First responders were already on their way. But when that man saw me, saw my torn clothes, saw my bleeding arm, he immediately called for help.

Everything after that had been handled very well: police, ambulance, hospital, doctors, lawyers, counselors. Every step of the way, through every part of my ordeal, it seemed as if God was sending me the very people that could help me best, starting with a team of brilliant doctors at the nearest hospital who managed to reattach my arm and hand.

Eventually, I was released and sent back home, my care transferred to the hospital there. Of course, throughout everything, my family rallied around me like never before. My school deferred my classes for as long as I needed. My mother found me one of the very best Christian counselors in the country, who just happened to have an opening at her office in Bryn Mawr for three afternoons a week.

More surgeries followed, more pain than I could ever have imagined, but with the healing on the outside came healing on the inside as well. Even my three friends, who struggled mightily with their own guilt about that night, finally came around and understood that I blamed them no more than I blamed myself.

Everyone expected me to hate my attacker, to feel vindicated when we learned he had not survived his injuries and had died from internal bleeding. How could I explain that, dead or alive, Damien hadn't been the only villain that night?

For starters, his buddies were more than complicit. At least most of them got their just desserts: All were hurt when the pier fell apart, several quite badly. Down the line, those who survived were charged and tried and convicted almost to a man.

Beyond that, though, were the others, those who didn't facilitate or encourage what was happening but who saw it when it could have been stopped and chose to look the other way. *How*, I would rail in my darkest moments, *how could someone stand by and do nothing even as a girl is being dragged from a bar, nearly unconscious, by a group of drunken, rowdy guys?* Even if others in the bar hadn't realized what was happening, what about the people in the restaurant? I knew they had seen us.

Those were the ones who never had to pay, who weren't charged with any crime, whose only punishment for looking the other way once all was said and done was to endure a lifelong sense of shame that surely clung to them like the stench of bar smoke. They were all to blame for what happened to me, for what could have happened. If not for the collapse of the pier, I would have been raped, perhaps by the entire gang.

Seven operations later, though I had worked through the crisis, emotionally speaking, there were still many scars that lingered, both inside and out. My mangled arm was a constant reminder of the one night I decided to loosen up, abandon my standards, and act my age. The night that changed my life forever.

Now, standing at the window of my little room at the inn and looking up at a thousand stars, I remembered one session with my counselor, how angry she had become when I had referred to this hideous arm as my mark of shame. She kept insisting that it was not a mark of shame but one of survival.

Once I got into self-defense, shooting, and boxing, and I was strong and knowledgeable and better understood how to defend myself in *any* situation, I finally began to believe it. Eventually I decided to take it a step even further, telling myself that my scar wasn't a mark of shame or of survival but in fact a secret mark of power. I wanted to get to the point where I could wear these scars under my sleeve as strongly and surely as Clark Kent wore an "S" hidden on his chest. I told myself that this was my best proof that in the end I wasn't a victim but victorious.

Someday, surely, if I told myself that enough times I would finally come to believe it. Taking a deep breath, I took in as much air as I could, held it for a long moment, and then slowly blew it out.

Better.

I felt better.

As always, my counselor was right. I could move through the discomfort to the other side. I could trust God to be here with me as I did, to carry this burden for me.

But that didn't mean this beast called up from the depths was going to stay back down. For the past ten years I had done everything humanly possible to keep myself from feeling powerless. And then along came today, in which crisis after crisis managed to strip away any illusion of power and control that I had ever had. In a single day, my whole world had begun to crumble, not like the instant plunge of the pier, but more like the shifting of sands under my feet as I tried to get to shore.

I reached up and smoothed the curtains, the trembling gone, certain that I would do whatever it took to protect myself, protect my inn, clear my name, and find the answers to all the questions that had suddenly appeared.

I wouldn't do it just for me but also for Troy. Yes, he had had his issues, and yes, in many ways I wished he and I had never met. But he had still been a friend to me. He didn't deserve to die this way. Most of all, if foul play was involved, he surely didn't deserve to go to his grave at the hands of someone else before his time.

I knew what it felt like to be someone's victim. That might have happened to me in the past, but not anymore. Not for me. Not for Troy.

Not on my watch.

FIFTEEN

When I woke, it took a moment to get my bearings. Where was I? Watching sunbeams dance across the mahogany armoire in the corner, for a blessed moment I realized I was in my favorite room at Harmony Grove Bed & Breakfast and all was right with the world. Then memories came rushing back: the scene at Buzz, the visit with Liz, the call from Troy, the bodies at the pool, the endless questions. I was at Harmony Grove Bed & Breakfast all right, but all was definitely not right with the world. Not with this world, anyway.

I could have done with a few more hours of sleep—the clock on the bedside table said 8:02 a.m.—but there was much to do and I was awake, so I swung my legs over the side of the bed and sat up. Thinking of my middle of the night panic attack, I felt much better now and in a way almost relieved that it had happened. I was glad to know I had been able to push through it. Today I felt stronger and more determined than ever to get this entire situation straightened out.

My stomach rumbled, and I realized that except for that piece of corn bread my father had insisted I take for last night's drive out here, I hadn't eaten since breakfast the morning before—not even a bag of pretzels on the plane. I dug out a protein bar from my suitcase and ate it quickly, hoping I could get something more substantial later.

But before I dressed for the day, I needed to call my father and Heath to let them both know what was going on. I also had to give Liz the whole truth, which wasn't going to be easy. I wasn't eager for any of these calls, but they needed to be made. As it turned out, no one answered, so I left messages for all that didn't include details but just a simple request to call me back as soon as they could.

My cell phone rang as I finished getting dressed. It was Heath.

For some reason, the sound of his voice brought tears to my eyes. If he were here with me now, I would simply lean into his arms and hold on for a while. He must have been able to hear some of that longing in my voice, because before I could even tell him what was going on, he asked me what was wrong and if my trip to Boston hadn't gone as well as I had expected.

"No, things in Boston went beautifully."

"What is it, then? You don't sound like yourself."

Trying not to cry, I began by making the bed as I spoke.

"You're right. Things aren't good, Heath. In fact, I'm in the midst of a major crisis. Several, actually. I would have called and told you about everything last night, but I was tied up with the police until well after midnight."

"Police? Sienna, what's going on?"

Tucking in the sheets, I explained everything that had happened from the moment I arrived at Buzz to the moment I went to bed. He listened intently, his outrage growing as I spoke. Unlike Troy, whose reaction to the news that I had been suspended was "What did you do?" Heath's immediate response was, "Are you kidding? What could those idiots be thinking?"

That vote of confidence was sorely needed and caused fresh tears to spring into my eyes. Smoothing the bedspread, I continued my tale, though when I got to the part where I left my parents' house to come to Lancaster County, I was afraid Heath might not be so generous. But again he surprised me, saying simply that he hoped that weasel Troy 'fessed up once I was able to confront him face-to-face.

"Well, no. That's where things took a major turn for the worse."

Propping the pillows against the headboard, I took him step-by-step through my entire horrific night. When I was done, I held my breath, waiting for his response.

"I'm on my way."

"Heath, no. Wait. You can't just come out here. That's not fair to you."

"I certainly can and I will. Do you want me to run over to your place and get anything for you first? Some clothes or whatever?"

"No, but thank you. I'm fine. You can come this weekend if I'm still here, but don't take time off work for this."

Even as I tried to convince him not to come, I wasn't sure if my motivation was purely selfless (I knew how hard it was to get time off from the hospital, and I hated him having to do that for my sake) or not (that small part of me that wanted to be free to defend myself however I saw fit). Perhaps it was an equal mix of both. We debated back and forth for a few minutes, and in the end I convinced him to finish out the workweek and come tomorrow night. As we talked, I made my way to the office downstairs, turned on the computer, and sat down at the desk.

"If you want to help, there is something you could do from there," I told him. "You're good with money and with math. Would you be willing to look at the books from the B and B to see if you spot anything fishy?"

"Of course," he answered, sounding almost disappointed that I hadn't asked for more than that.

"I hate to sound callous and self-centered, but what happens if Floyd doesn't get better, Heath?" I asked as I waited for the machine to boot up. "He's the inn's sole employee. What about the day-to-day mechanics of running this place? I don't know how to do that, not to mention I don't have the time or desire. I'll have to cancel pending reservations and eventually hire someone else." The more concerns I voiced, the more new ones that popped into my mind. "And that's not even thinking about the PR ramifications of all of this. Can the B and B recover from the taint of death? What am I going to do? And what about my job? I've only been there a few weeks. They don't know me or my character. After all I've done to get this far, if I end up losing my position at Buzz I'll lose my home, my car—"

"Shhh, Sienna. Shhh. Calm down. Take one step at a time. Things might be much better today. The police could have made all sorts of progress last night."

"That's true."

The computer was ready, so I went online, attached the B and B's financial records to an e-mail, and sent it off to Heath for his perusal.

"First things first," he continued. "Do you know if Floyd kept good insurance on the inn, just in case? There could be ramifications."

"I hadn't even thought of that. I actually have no idea. I'll look around as soon as we hang up."

Heath waited until the file came through but then he had to go, so I promised I would keep him up to date with things via text, and he said he'd call on his very next break. "I love you," he added before hanging up.

Slightly overwhelmed by a wave of emotion and needing an immediate distraction, I went to the files and began looking for some perfectly labeled, color-coded folder for insurance. There wasn't one, at least not that I could find, so I returned to the computer and tried to take a look there. Though I doubted it, perhaps Floyd had ordered the policy online.

I was feeling antsy, wishing Mike would get here and tell me if they indeed had made any progress last night, as Heath had said. With one eye on the window and the long driveway out front, I continued to click around on Floyd's computer. Unable to locate any files on his hard drive regarding insurance, I went into his web browser, hoping to find some activity that involved insurance companies there.

Scanning the brief history, I wasn't surprised to see that the cache had never been emptied. The man used his computer so little that, even after two years, there wasn't much there. Movie times. Weather. TV schedules. Mapquest. Google Earth. Baby names. Phone lookups.

Wait a minute, baby names? I looked closer at the history to see that the site had been accessed often. Did Floyd have a baby, or maybe a pregnant girlfriend? Scanning the dates, I could see that he had been looking at baby names about once a month for two years. How strange, especially given that he had no children of his own, at least not as far as I knew. Clicking on the site itself, the link brought me to the results of his most recent name search: Nadeem, Vortimer, Anselmo. Those were unusual names, for sure, and I clicked on each one in turn to learn that the first was Arabic, the next Arthurian, whatever that was, and the third was Spanish.

Had Floyd been helping people of various ethnicities name their babies?

Was he writing a novel and trying to come up with character names? Maybe he just liked learning about name origins the same way some people studied etymology. All I could hope was that Floyd wasn't doing nefarious deeds, such as baby selling or illegal adoption, and using this site to name real stolen babies. Surely that wasn't it.

Though I didn't plan on sharing this odd finding with Mike just yet, I would certainly tell Liz about it and see if it raised red flags for her or if she could come up with a reasonable explanation.

Running through the browser history one last time, I noticed the addresses for some sites that had been visited early on, when the computer was new. I had made those searches myself, and they were for several different online hotel and bed-and-breakfast customer review sites. I had written up and posted the listings, but I had never thought to go back and see how our ensuing customers had rated us.

Going to each of those sites now, I located the listings for Harmony Grove Bed & Breakfast, but I didn't see any reviews of the place at all. I tried even more sites, but no matter where I looked, I couldn't find one single opinion or customer review for my inn, not even on Trip Advisor, which seemed to have every other bed-and-breakfast in the world picked apart by virtually everyone who had ever stayed there.

In a sense, this lack of feedback was even stranger than Floyd's monthly obsession with baby names. Everybody had an opinion these days. Even the nightly news solicited opinions. We lived in a world where people weighed in on everything, everywhere—especially online in matters of travel.

So why wasn't anyone reviewing Harmony Grove Bed & Breakfast?

Feeling strangely unsettled, I kept looking but couldn't find a single review. Beyond that, I realized that the inn offered no online booking capability, and it had never even been listed anywhere other than those first few original postings I had done. Even if Floyd wasn't computer savvy, his job as manager included getting the word out about the inn. Instead of providing me with answers, my research had created new questions. Who were the inn's guests? Where were they coming from? And why didn't they review the place once they had been here?

Again, I feared that these were answers I could only get from Floyd himself. Glancing at the clock, I wondered if he was still out of his head or if he might now be awake and coherent and able to explain things to me. I tried calling the hospital where I assumed he had been taken, but they didn't show him as currently registered, and I didn't feel like calling other hospitals in the region to track him down. Hanging up the phone, I sat back in the chair, closed my eyes, and thought back to when I had first hired Floyd.

Our interview had been recommended and facilitated by Troy, who had met Floyd Underhill through his work with one of the big hotels in downtown Philly. In their dealings since then, Troy said, he had come to respect everything about the way Floyd did business. Originally from Camden, Floyd might seem a bit rough around the edges sometimes, but he had been working in Philly's hospitality industry for years and knew how to run a place like this better than anyone.

During our interview Floyd seemed nice enough, but he wasn't exactly the wonder boy Troy had described. More than anything he seemed tired to me, and I had a feeling he wanted this job primarily so that he could leave the city and its frenetic pace and settle down out here in the country in a cushy job he could perform without much effort. Still, when it came down to numbers, Floyd talked a good game, explaining that he had so many contacts in the industry that he could begin filling the inn immediately, showing a profit by the end of the first quarter. I wasn't sure how atypical those claims were until I interviewed two other highly qualified candidates and listened to each of them go on and on about building a customer base and generating word of mouth, etc., saying that they couldn't promise a full house for the first year, possibly two. Needless to say, I hired Floyd.

Until yesterday, that had seemed to be one of the smartest decisions of my life.

As an advertising specialist, I had always planned to throw my full energies into promoting this place once we were open, spreading the news via marketing, public relations, advertising, and other avenues. But as it turned out, Floyd was as good as his word and had begun raking in the dough almost right away. Every time I called from the city to see how things were going, he told me the B and B was booked solid, the customers were delighted, the gifts were selling like hotcakes, and all was well. Much to my relief, this place was so full, so fast that I never had to spend any time or money on promotions for it. After having focused on the renovation for so long, my work at Biddle & Sons was beginning to suffer, so as soon as I was sure Harmony Grove Bed & Breakfast was in good hands and would continue to thrive without any help from me, I put it on the back burner and focused on my job in the city.

The first year this place was open, I had come back and stayed several times just to check on things, see how Floyd was doing, and visit with family in the area. My last such visit had been in December for a lovely, relaxing post-Christmas vacation. Now here it was the following October, and I couldn't believe that since that holiday visit ten months ago I hadn't returned even once.

Obviously, my absence had been a huge mistake. Why had I trusted Floyd so implicitly? Why hadn't I smelled a rat? My parents couldn't understand how a brand-new bed-and-breakfast in an area filled with many others just as nice or even nicer could generate such an instant and thriving customer base. I should have questioned that as well.

Back then I figured it was about location, location, location. This was a fantastic place for an inn, right in the heart of Amish country, on beautiful grounds with a pool, next to a grove and a covered bridge, and surrounded by Amish farms. I had told my parents that Floyd knew what he was doing and that he was probably having the guests funneled here through a specific travel agent or Realtor. Again, I should have asked for more specifics from Floyd himself.

In light of what Troy had said on the phone yesterday, I saw now that other things about this place didn't quite add up, either. When my parents had paid a surprise visit here last spring, the bed-and-breakfast had been devoid of other guests and generally untended. The breakfast Floyd prepared for them—breakfast being a key element to any B and B's success—had been skimpy and bland and left a lot to be desired.

Where were last night's guests, for that matter, and why didn't any of their phone numbers work?

These questions and more were rolling around in my head when my cell phone rang.

It was Liz.

Before I launched into an explanation of what had happened since last we spoke, I let her update me on what she had managed to accomplish thus far on her end. The news wasn't great, but it wasn't surprising either—not yet, anyway. She said the attorney general's office confirmed that I was a "person of interest" in an ongoing investigation, but they were not willing to divulge further details at this time.

"I made it very clear that if they want to talk to you, they have to go through me," she said. "So if anything happens at all, do not say a word to anyone. Just tell them, 'Speak to my lawyer.' That's your mantra, Sienna: *Speak to my lawyer.* Okay?"

Knowing she was going to kill me when she learned of the hours I had spent in the company of the police last night, I mumbled an assent and listened as she continued.

"I also spoke to the Bobbsey Twins at Buzz, and they are standing firm on their 'wait and see' position. Until this matter is resolved, it definitely looks as though you're not going to have an income. Right now, there isn't anything else I can do to force the issue. At least they're aware that I have an eye on them and that I'm watching out for your interests."

"I wish I could afford to walk away from Buzz completely."

She was quiet for a moment, probably deciding whether to chide me yet again about the car and condo or not.

"I understand how you feel," she said finally. "But what's done is done. Let's just let things play out for now. We don't really have much choice otherwise. At least I get the feeling that something big is going to happen soon."

"Maybe it already has," I replied. Taking a deep breath, I launched into my tale, probably giving it far too quickly but afraid that if I even paused for a moment she might start yelling at me. When I was finished, the line was silent as Liz processed all she had learned. When she spoke, the gentleness in her voice surprised me.

"Oh, hon, I'm so sorry. Are you okay? Any anxiety attacks?"

Leave it to Liz to be sweet just when she had the right to be mean. I told her about the one in the middle of the night, of how I had handled it, of the way I was feeling this morning. She seemed more concerned for my emotional well-being than anything else, and I was so touched that, again, my eyes filled with tears. It wasn't even 10:00 a.m. and already this was turning out to be a very weepy day.

As we talked, Liz helped me feel better about things, reassuring me that I had handled the police's questions correctly. She would have liked to have been here last night, she said, but given that they hadn't charged me with a crime—and didn't seem to suspect me of anything at all—she said it had been okay to answer their questions without her. She also reinforced my decision not to divulge the facts about my suspension or the government's investigation.

By the time we hung up, I felt relieved and energized, eager to find some answers to the puzzles surrounding me. I decided to start with the small stack of reservation cards, call my upcoming guests to cancel their reservations, and while I had them on the phone ask how they heard of Harmony Grove Bed & Breakfast in the first place. Perhaps they could fill in some of the blanks Floyd wasn't here to fill in for them. My plan was to start calling the phone numbers listed on the cards.

Except that none of those numbers worked.

Some people were scheduled to stay more than one night, so for the four rooms over the next five days there were nine different people with reservations.

And not one of them had a working phone number?

I went online to search for names, numbers, and addresses. Not only could I not find any of these numbers, I couldn't find these addresses, either. Trying to pull up records using just name, city, and state, my search was fruitless for card after card. Feeling very uneasy, I typed in the last one, a couple listed as "Mr. and Mrs. Anselmo Rodriguez."

Anselmo?

That was one of the baby names. I again went into the browser history, looking at prior baby name searches and finding several other matches there. Last month's baby name search had given the names Mackenzie, Paige, Sara, and Zoe. One of the reservation cards was for "Sara Mackenzie"; another was for "Zoe Paige."

As fast as my fingers could fly across the keyboard, I scanned all of the history in more detail, realizing that the phone numbers on the reservation cards had come from failed reverse phone lookups. The addresses that had been searched out via Mapquest and Google Earth matched the address on some of these cards. In every case, they were addresses that didn't quite exist: empty lots or incorrect house numbers. In most cases these were merely a few digits beyond the highest-numbered houses on the streets, so that where an address on a card might be written as "542 Oak Street," the satellite image on the screen would show that the last two houses on Oak were numbers 539 and 540.

Sitting back in my chair, heart in my throat, I realized that Floyd hadn't been naming babies at all.

He had been creating fictitious guests.

SIXTEEN

To me, the obvious question now was whether there had been no guests at all (with these names merely for show) or if there had been guests, but they had stayed here under falsified records (because they wanted to hide their identities). I had no idea which of the two it was.

What about credit card records? Names had to be correct for those. Was that what this was about? Identity theft, stolen credit cards? Could that be the subject of the government's investigation?

Tearing the file drawers apart in search of credit card receipts, I could find none. The office had a small safe mounted inside a lower cabinet, so I went to that now, thinking about the combination. When we first installed it, my father had set the numbers himself, using my mother's birth date. I was afraid Floyd might have changed that in the past two years, but once I was able to stop my fingers from shaking long enough to rotate the dial correctly, I found that it still worked. The lock clicked free, and when I swung open the door I could see that the contents included a few hundred dollars in cash and the small, handheld credit card imprinting machine I had received when setting up our merchant account.

Pulling out the machine, I studied it closely. It looked brand new, as if it had never been used. I thought about the paper imprinting slips that had come with the machine. From what I could recall, there had been several boxes of those. Going to the cabinet of office supplies, I looked around and finally found slips on the top shelf—several boxes' worth—each one still taped shut and coated with dust.

Trying a different approach, I went back to the computer and opened up the spreadsheet, scanning the in-and-out flow of the money that came through Harmony Grove Bed & Breakfast. From what I could see, nearly every transaction had been in cash. I got these statements every month. Why had I never noticed that before?

Closing my eyes and pinching the bridge of my nose, I tried to think. Who in this day and age used cash for anything? Even fast-food drive-throughs took credit and debit cards. Yet here, quilts were selling for more than a thousand dollars, paid in cash. Stays at the B and B totaling hundreds of dollars a pop, paid in cash. Opening my eyes, I continued to study the data in front of me. I realized that not only had our customers paid us with cash, but much of the outgo from this place had been handled in cash as well. The largest expenditures were to the Amish families who provided the items for the gift shop: Five thousand dollars for quilts and other cloth goods just last month. Two thousand dollars for wooden toys the month before that.

Studying the spreadsheet, it looked as though our quarterly tax payments had been paid by check, as had the utilities and other miscellaneous bills. But it was as if almost everything else had been paid for with cash, from the office supplies to the groceries to the housekeeping services and more. It simply didn't add up. I knew Floyd was a technophobe and liked to do things the old-fashioned way, but this was ridiculous. What about our tax returns? Did he have receipts to match all of these expenditures?

The first year, I had gone through the tax return Floyd had prepared before he sent it in. It had looked great, so this year, when I was busy with other things, I hadn't even bothered checking it. Wondering if the government's investigation had to do with the IRS, I dug through more drawers until I found two big, fat expanding folders labeled "Taxes," one for each year. Twisting open their metal clasps, I looked inside at the many slips of paper there. At least there were tons of receipts included—Office Outlet, Jonah and Liesl Coblentz, SuperBrand Foods, and more—clipped together by month. Each one I pulled out to check showed the form of payment listed as cash. I would have to go through these receipts carefully later, perhaps with the help of an accountant, but from what I could see things seemed to be in order.

Putting the folders aside for now, I once again tried to think the situation through.

Floyd was a cash-based guy. I could at least understand that somewhat. But how could all of these customers also be cash based? *No one* was cash based these days. Even when I had cash on me, I still used my credit and debit cards whenever possible, just to earn the free points the cards gave me. I wasn't unique in that, not at all.

So why all the cash? Could Floyd have insisted on it from our customers, telling them we didn't take credit cards? That didn't seem likely, and it certainly wasn't true. What was I missing here? What dots was I not connecting?

The guests had fake names and nonexistent phone numbers and addresses.

These same guests always paid in cash.

Judging by the lack of Internet activity, it was almost as if no one had ever stayed here at all—at least no one with an opinion who had posted a review.

The place was scruffy and untended outside.

When my parents came in the spring, they had been the inn's only guests, their morning meal less than impressive.

My room upstairs had dust on the lampshades and a cobweb in the corner, despite the fact that Liesl had been paid for cleaning just last week, according to the financial records.

Taking all of the above into account, I began to realize that of the two options I had considered regarding the fake names, the most likely possibility was that there were no guests at all. If that was the case, then where was all the money coming from? How could there be so much cash flowing in and out if not from paying guests at the inn and from sales in our gift shop? We sold a ton of quilts and wooden toys here. If there were no guests, then who was buying all of that stuff?

Sick to my stomach, I realized that Harmony Grove Bed & Breakfast could be involved in something highly illegal, though I couldn't begin to fathom what. No wonder the U.S. attorney general's office was investigating me. No wonder Troy said that such an investigation would have been Floyd's fault. Certainly, something very fishy was going on.

At this point, what I needed to do was to verify the amount of traffic this place was actually getting on a regular basis. The neighbors across the street certainly seemed to keep tabs. I could ask them directly about the traffic flow and the inn's comings and goings. I could also look into the room-cleaning situation as well. Though Floyd did the daily cleaning, Liesl was the inn's more thorough once-a-week housekeeper. When she came each time, was she washing sheets from the beds and scrubbing out the bathrooms? Surely a cleaner would be able to tell if a room had actually been used, even after the tidiest of guests.

I called Liesl first, leaving a message on her family's voice mail. I knew she probably wouldn't get that message any time soon, so if I didn't hear back from her shortly I would pay a visit in person instead. First, though, I would call up a neighbor or two.

Using the computer to look up the numbers of the people across the street, I started with Mrs. Finster, an older woman who lived alone in the smaller gray house on the corner. The least verbose of them all, my hope was that our call could be short and sweet. When she answered, I was momentarily tongue-tied, but then I blurted out that I was following up on some reservation issues in Floyd's absence and hoped she could help me out. What I learned from our ensuing conversation was very disturbing.

According to her, almost no one ever came and went from Harmony Grove Bed & Breakfast other than Floyd himself. About once a month a "dashing young man with dark hair and a fancy car" would come and stay a few nights. Occasionally there was another car or two, though not often and not for long.

"Did you ever wonder why a bed-and-breakfast seemed to have no guests?" I asked, knowing that the dashing young man had been Troy.

"Frankly, dear, I didn't even realize the place was still open for business. To be honest, I was glad things were so quiet. When it first opened and looked so beautiful, I was afraid that traffic on this street would increase terribly. When it turned out that almost no one ever came at all, more than anything I was just relieved."

I thanked her for the information and ended our call when movement out of the front window caught my eye and I saw several cars turn into the driveway. Most were police cars, and for a moment I was terrified they had come here to arrest me. But when I opened the back door and stepped outside, I realized they were simply here to follow up with last night's investigation.

Mike's greeting was pleasant enough but all business, and from the deliberate, energetic nature of his body language, I had a feeling there had been some sort of break in the case. I was hoping he would tell me what they had found, but all he did was inform me that his people had some things to do both inside and out and he hoped they would be finished here soon so the crime scene could be released.

"Do you know yet what happened last night?" I asked.

"We've made some progress," he replied, reaching for the radio on his belt. "I'll explain in a bit. Right now I have to get out back with the rest of the team."

With that he walked away toward the pool, talking into the radio as he went. Unsure of what to do, I kept out of the way and watched and listened as cops and technicians went into Floyd's and Troy's rooms and into the kitchen and began searching them even more thoroughly than they had last night. Hovering in the background, I tried to figure out what was going on. It sounded to me that they were searching for drugs, drug-related paraphernalia, and poison.

So poison really had been involved. Suddenly, I was quite glad I had eaten my own protein bar this morning for breakfast, and that I hadn't had a thing from the kitchen, not even a glass of juice.

"Sienna?" Georgia called from Troy's bedroom. "Could you come here a minute, please?"

I hurried into the busy room, finding Georgia and a technician standing at the small door in the back corner, one that wasn't even visible from the main doorway thanks to the massive dresser that nearly hid it from view.

"What's in here?" Georgia asked me, pointing toward the door. "We checked it out yesterday, but I just wanted to make sure we weren't missing anything."

"Missing anything?"

"Yeah. It's such an odd little room down there. Is there more to it than this?"

The door she was referring to was the key selling point to this room, the main reason why it cost more to stay in here than in any of the three rooms upstairs, even though they were bigger and had better views.

"It's a private wine cellar," I explained, adding that we had created it during the renovation, under Troy's guidance, and that one bottle of wine of the customer's choice was always included for free with every three-day rental of this room. "The old basement under the house had two entrances, one here and one off of the kitchen. The basement isn't huge, but since we weren't really using it for anything, we decided to wall off this back corner and create the illusion of an old European wine cellar. I even faux painted the walls. As you've seen, there's nothing down there except the big wine rack full of bottles and a little bit of room to stand and study them and make your choice."

Georgia told the technician to go on down, and then she squinted at me and asked if I had a liquor license.

"Of course. Why, is that surprising?"

She shrugged.

"I dunno. I guess it's just not that common for a bed-and-breakfast to deal in alcohol. 'Cept maybe for the ones that serve mimosas with Sunday brunch or something.

My cheeks flushing with heat, I didn't admit that as a Protestant I had always felt somewhat conflicted about serving alcohol. Instead, I simply explained that it had been Troy's idea. He had said customers would jump at the chance to have access to an entire wine cellar all by themselves. He predicted that the complimentary bottle of wine that came with the room would frequently be followed by the purchase of more bottles as well. He had been right. From what I could recall, Floyd had reported that the average guest in this room seemed to purchase two or three bottles *per night* in addition to the free one. Given the vast markup on alcohol, the proceeds had been impressive indeed, at least on paper.

Of course, at the moment I wasn't sure what was true and what wasn't, nor even if this room had ever had any guests in it other than Troy. But I didn't bring that up now. Instead, I explained the thinking behind his plan, that most folks who liked wine fancied themselves as connoisseurs and enjoyed playing sommelier. To encourage sales, I had covered the walls down there with pretty, artfully-framed signs that described various vintages and their salient characteristics. I had also placed the most expensive bottles right at eye level, with the complimentary ones at the bottom of the rack.

"So you're a wine connoisseur too?" Georgia asked as we listened to the clink of wine bottles from the technician below.

I shook my head.

"No, I don't drink. I got the information from the liquor salesman who helped us choose the stock."

I didn't add that the whole thing had been a major bone of contention between my parents and me, the only real argument we'd had throughout the entire renovation process. As a pastor, my father didn't want anything to do with the sales or promotion of liquor. Looking back now, I understood his position completely, and I felt a surge of guilt as I remembered how dazzled I had been by Troy's financial projections, and how strongly I had argued to my father that this one simple little wine cellar could be one of the biggest cash cows of the entire business.

I couldn't recall the details of our argument now, but it had been quite heated, I remembered that. In the end, my dad had given me an ultimatum, saying that if the bed-and-breakfast was going to sell or serve wine that he wanted no part in it. I had acquiesced begrudgingly, frustrated that the little cellar had already been built and prepared and only needed the wine bottles to be ready to roll.

For me, obviously, I had allowed the dollar signs to outweigh my principles.

A few months later, after I bought out my parents' share and the inn became fully mine, I had suppressed those principles even further, faxed over the original purchase order Troy and I had worked out with the liquor salesman, and told Floyd to stock the cellar as directed and up the price of the room accordingly.

Now the technician was emerging from the stairwell with a bottle of wine in each hand, and it struck me that the poison they were seeking might have been hidden in one of those bottles. Nearly a hundred bottles of wine were down there, some of them extremely expensive. Was it possible they would have to open and test each one? I sure hoped not.

Given the current precarious state of my finances, my job situation, and my inn, that wine collection was one of the few tangible assets I owned outright.

On the other hand, perhaps God was simply allowing me now to reap what I had sown.

Maybe Troy had paid that price as well.

SEVENTEEN

As it turned out, the police weren't planning to open the wine at all—at least not yet. For the time being, the tech just wanted to get a better look at some of the bottles by the window in order to check the seals and study their clarity. I listened as he and Georgia discussed getting some lighting down there, and I had just come back from retrieving an extension cord for them when I ran into Mike.

"There you are, Sienna. Got a sec?"

"Absolutely."

"I have a question for you about the property." Pulling from his pocket the sketch I had drawn last night, he said he needed to know about all of my outbuildings. "Your picture shows a large shed out back and an outdoor storage closet here, next to the pool. Is there any other outdoor storage at all?"

"No, that's it."

"How about inside the house? Where do you keep pesticides, tools, things like that?"

I explained that the tools were kept in the basement and that the bug sprays and ant bait were on a rack just inside the basement door, at the landing. "At least that's where they used to be, though I suppose Floyd could have moved them at some point."

"Okay, thanks," Mike replied, folding the paper and sliding it back into his pocket. "That's all I need for now."

He turned to go, but I reached out and put a hand on his wrist.

"Look, I know you're busy, but can you bring me up to speed at all? At least tell me how Floyd and Nina are doing?"

Mike glanced at his watch and said he had a few minutes, but we should get out of everyone's way. There was activity all around us, so I suggested we move out to the side porch.

"Nina's not doing too well. She's still unconscious," he told me as we walked across the dining room.

"How about Floyd?"

"He's much better. Awake and talking."

Mike pushed open the door and we stepped out into the cool morning air of the screened-in porch.

"What does he say about last night? Has he been able to explain what happened?"

Mike rolled his eyes and said that Floyd had an explanation, yes, but because of his present condition it wasn't fully reliable. "According to Floyd, he was in the kitchen making himself a sandwich when he heard a woman outside screaming."

"Nina?"

"Yep. He says he heard the scream and grabbed his gun. He found Nina at the pool, where she had just pulled Troy's body out the water. She was trying to do CPR on him, but Floyd had to convince her it was no use because Troy was already quite dead."

Picturing Troy's open eyes, I knew exactly what he meant.

"Floyd says he and Nina were arguing about it when they heard a strange noise coming from the other side of the fence. They turned to look, and that's when a big black creature rose up out of the brush and emitted a burst of fire. Floyd doesn't remember anything after that."

"He still says it was big and black?" I asked. "Yeah, with hollow eyes."

Trying to picture it, I couldn't help but shudder.

"Don't get too worked up just yet, Sienna. Floyd tested positive for drugs. I've seen people on hallucinogens who thought their vacuum cleaner was a giraffe, so I'm not putting much stock in his story. Floyd may *think* that's what he saw, but the information isn't very reliable, given that he was quite high at the time."

"Which drug? Was it Ativan, like you suspected?"

"The info isn't that specific yet. So far, tests show some sort of tranquilizer, so it could be. It'll be a few days before we know for sure."

"What does Floyd say? Does his doctor have him on tranquilizers? Nerve medication? Something like that?"

"No, Floyd swears he's never taken anything stronger than aspirin his whole life."

"So he was drugged by someone else," I said, knowing all too well how easily that could happen.

"Possibly."

"How about Nina? Same drug?"

"Nina did test positive for the same drug, plus one other."

I looked at Mike, waiting. He hesitated a moment, as if he had already divulged more than he should have. Then he spoke.

"She also had some sort of toxin in her system, the same toxin found in the victim."

"Toxin? Do you mean poison? Nina and Troy were definitely poisoned?"

Mike nodded. "Nina had such a small amount we're thinking she probably was contaminated when she gave Troy mouth-to-mouth, or possibly from the water in the pool as she pulled him out. In any event, it doesn't look like she was exposed to enough of the toxin herself for it to be fatal. But between that and the tranquilizer, she's still unconscious and may be for a while yet."

I turned and looked out at the sweeping lawn, the autumn leaves, the pastoral scene that surrounded us. Poisoned. Amid this paradise, people had been poisoned.

"So that's Troy's official cause of death," I said, just wanting to understand clearly. "He was poisoned."

"Technically, no, but causally, yes."

"In English, please?" I asked, turning back toward him.

Mike explained that Troy's official cause of death was drowning, but that he had been poisoned first by a central nervous system toxin that caused convulsions, which then caused the drowning.

"Though why he was in the pool when the convulsions began is anyone's guess," he added.

As I pictured the scene Mike was describing, I suddenly felt faint and had to sit down. I reached for the nearest chair and lowered myself into it, causing the wicker to squawk and crunch as I did. I exhaled slowly.

"How did it happen? Where? Who did this to him?"

Mike sat on the chair across from me and tried to explain what they knew thus far.

"The ME says it wasn't cumulative, like someone putting arsenic in his coffee every day. That would point more toward intention, premeditation. This was likely a single acute exposure."

"Exposure, how? Through food?" I asked, thinking of the technicians in the kitchen.

"Probably not. The ME doesn't think the poison was ingested, but at this point it's still a possibility. We're rounding up all open containers on the premises to have them analyzed, just in case."

Not wanting to end up like Troy—or Floyd or Nina—myself, I was glad to see all of the food go.

"The ME says that overexposure to certain pesticides can cause convulsions," Mike continued. "She thinks Troy was contaminated through direct contact with the skin. He must have received a sudden, lethal exposure to some toxin yesterday afternoon, probably through his hands. The skin there is blistered front and back, plus there are slight trace elements of a chemical powder under his fingernails. Of course, any other residue on his hands would have been washed away in the pool. It's probably too diluted to show up, but we're testing the water anyway."

"I don't understand. How did this happen? Was it an accident?"

"That's one theory. Judging by the physical evidence and what we've been able to figure out about Troy's day yesterday, it could have had something to do with the tools he was using for his treasure hunt in the grove. Depending on how and where those tools were stored, there's a good chance he accidentally did it to himself. Maybe he was rooting around in the shed for a shovel and accidentally stuck his hands in a container of concentrated pesticide. Or maybe the shovel itself had inadvertently become coated with a toxic substance while in storage, and then as Troy used it and his palms began to sweat, the moisture helped speed that toxin into his bloodstream. However it happened, our hope is that by taking a thorough look in and around all of the structures on the property, we'll find the shovel and other digging tools he was using, along with whatever pesticide or hazardous chemical was involved. A team is also searching the grove for pesticide concentrates right now. If we can find the substance that killed him, we might be able piece this puzzle together and rule it an accident."

Feeling overwhelmed, I stood and walked to the screen, looking out toward the grove. It was just so big. If Troy had been poisoned by something already out there, trying to find that poison would be like searching for a needle in a haystack.

"What about the cut on his leg?" I asked, my eyes still scanning the beautiful trees in the distance.

"The ME says the structure of the wound is looking more like an animal than an implement. By running the cut mark through the database, she ruled out the most obvious culprits: a chain saw or garden trowel or other known tools. She believes it was done by a single claw. There was also an enormous amount of bruising to the hips, thighs, and abdomen, so whatever got him got him good and hard."

"Man," I whispered, glad I was still facing away from Mike as tears suddenly filled my eyes.

"The cut was to the bone," he continued, oblivious to the effect his words were having on me, "and fortunately debris was lodged in the tissue. They're running tests now, growing cultures. We should get more info soon."

"Wow," I whispered. Poor Troy. Poisoned, attacked, drowned. What a way to go. Wiping away my tears in frustration, I turned back from the window and returned to my chair. "Troy said he was dizzy and feeling ill the whole time we talked yesterday. He must have been contaminated before he even called. At that point the poison was already working its way into his system."

Mike pulled out his notebook and flipped to a page where he had obviously worked out a timeline.

"ME says exposure to the toxin likely occurred between 4:00 and 5:00 p.m. Troy called you at 5:17, so that would be correct. By the time he called you he'd been poisoned and probably didn't even know it."

"After he hung up on me, how long was it before he died? Did the medical examiner give an exact time of death?"

"Exact, no, but she gave us a range, and by combining that with other factors we've been able to narrow it down to him dying somewhere between 6:10 and 6:30 p.m."

"So he hung up with me at 5:30 and was attacked and had gone into convulsions and drowned within the hour."

"Yes."

I didn't know why all of this information was hitting me so hard, but I felt tears welling up again. Perhaps as the sequence of events became more tangible, the fact that Troy really was dead was beginning to sink in. Whether his death was intentional or accidental almost didn't seem to matter as I thought about how much he must have suffered.

"Thanks for telling me all of this," I said softly, knowing Mike had things to do. I hoped he would get back to them before I began to cry in earnest. When he didn't rise to leave, I assured him that I was okay and that he could go back to work.

Still he hesitated, and when I looked at him through my tears I could see there was more he wanted to say.

"Listen, Sienna, this whole accidental poisoning angle isn't the only theory we're working. There are other possibilities."

"What do you mean?"

"Now that we've had a chance to do some background research, we've uncovered some things that complicate matters."

I waited for him to go on, suddenly afraid from the look on his face that he had found out about my government investigation. From there, he might even have assumed that I had played a part in Troy's death somehow. Was I about to be arrested?

"It's starting to look like Troy Griffin had a gambling problem, not to mention some shady associates."

Relief flooded my veins, and I had to force myself to remain expressionless. That wasn't what I had expected him to say, not at all.

"Gambling problem? What kind of gambling?"

"*Every* kind. Cards, dice, horses, sports, you name it. Your ex-boyfriend was a real high roller. He went to Atlantic City all the time. In the past few months, he was there at least twice a week, sometimes every night."

I should have been surprised by this news, but as I thought about it I realized I wasn't. Back when we were dating, Troy loved playing poker with his buddies or taking clients to casinos.

He had even talked me into going to Atlantic City with him once. I had no interest in gambling, but a client had given Troy two front row tickets to a concert by one of my favorite bands, so I had agreed to go. We had ended up having a great time, making the easy one-hour drive from Philadelphia, enjoying the concert, and sharing a free dinner in a restaurant afterward. Before heading back home, Troy had insisted on playing a little roulette in the casino, saying it was a matter of etiquette because the reason we'd been given the free concert and dinner was so that we would spend some money at the tables.

We only stayed about an hour, which, with a few good wins, was just long enough for him to lose several hundred dollars. Except for that, our evening had been great fun.

"He used to gamble when we were dating," I said to Mike now, "but I didn't think he was addicted. Not then, anyway. Not to my knowledge."

The more I thought about it, though, the more I realized that our real estate ventures had been like gambling to him. The further we went with it, the more he enjoyed it. The bigger the risks we took, the more excited he had grown. No wonder he had urged me on so. He was feeding the need that burned inside himself at my expense.

"As it turns out, Troy is—well, *was*—very much in debt," Mike said. "When there's a death, heavy debt is always a red flag, either for homicide or suicide."

My eyes widened.

"You think Troy committed suicide? That he poisoned himself on purpose?"

"No. I'm thinking homicide, given the players involved."

I leaned forward, placing my elbows on my knees.

"You think Troy was killed over a debt he couldn't pay?"

"Possibly."

I took in a deep breath of air, trying to match what Mike was saying with what we already knew.

"If Troy was in debt to some sleazy loan shark or something..." I began, my voice trailing off as I thought for a moment, "at least that would help explain the treasure hunt. Troy found those old documents on Monday. Maybe he had tapped every other source, and finding those diamonds was his last hope for settling up his accounts."

"Which in itself was another kind of gamble, I guess, given his chances of actually finding them."

"Though maybe he did," I said. "Maybe he found the diamonds, and he was killed not because he couldn't pay the debt but because when he paid it, the debtor learned about the diamonds and wanted all of them for himself."

"Troy owed a lot of money to a lot of nasty people. Ones who have killed for far less."

I thought about that, my mind going back to our one evening in Atlantic City. That night it had seemed as though Troy had known a lot of people, including some very stereotypical mobster-types: The well-dressed Italian with the steely gaze and a moll on each arm; the pair of Russian toughs in Valentino suits who never took off their sunglasses, not even when we were introduced; the Asian businessman with a nasty scar across his throat and an obsequious entourage around him. Troy knew them all, and on the way home when I had teased him that they looked like the United Nations of mobsters, he had simply laughed.

A few minutes ago, when Mike told me about Troy's nasty associates, I had been picturing some greasy little bookie or a wisecracking loan shark in ill-fitting clothes. But now my mind was suddenly full of images far more sinister.

"Mike, are you saying that you think Troy's death was a mob hit of some kind?" I asked, not wanting to hear the answer. "The man who was killed in my pool yesterday, the man I once dated, was in the Mafia?"

Mike held up one hand, palm outward.

"We don't know that he was one of them, just that most of his clients have ties to organized crime."

I tried to understand the implications, wondering how this could possibly be true.

"You think Troy's death was a mob hit," I repeated, my stomach tightening from deep inside.

"Mob hits are usually a lot simpler than this. A gunshot or a stabbing, But not poison. At least not that I've heard of. So, again, we'll have to wait and see. I'm just saying it's a possibility."

The radio crackled at Mike's hip, and he excused himself to answer it.

"Weissbaum."

"Where are you, sir?" a woman asked, probably Georgia.

"Out on the side porch. Am I needed in there?"

"Nope, stay put. I'll come to you. Big news."

Mike stood and turned toward the door, but I stayed where I was, feeling a bit faint. On the phone yesterday, Troy had said that my investigation by the government was likely Floyd's fault. Did Floyd have ties to the Mafia too? Could he have done something with my inn that had caught the government's attention? If so, that could very well be why I was under investigation, because somehow Harmony Grove Bed & Breakfast was connected with the mob.

Georgia emerged from the house, her eyes sparkling. At the moment, I didn't want to hear her "big news."

I had enough big news of my own.

EIGHTEEN

"We just found out that a black bear was caught and killed in Holt-wood a couple of hours ago," Georgia said, waving her radio toward us triumphantly.

"A big one?" Mike asked.

"'Bout two hundred and fifty pounds."

"That's big enough."

"A homeowner let his dog out and spotted the bear digging in the trash can. He had to shoot the bear to save the dog."

I stood and moved toward them, asking where Holtwood was.

"It's a little town about ten miles west of here, near the Susquehanna River," Mike replied.

They were both excited, certain that the bear was the big black creature Floyd had spoken of and what had cut Troy with its claw last night. Incredible. Listening to them talk, it sounded as though bear sightings in this area were rare but not unheard of. Attacks, on the other hand, were a different matter.

"I can't remember the last bear attack on a human that I've heard of, not anywhere around here," Georgia said, shaking her head in wonder. "That's a real shame."

"Let's work with the game commission to run a few tests on the bear to see if we can establish a stronger link with the vic. Have them do a tox screen, look for a tissue match, and see if it has a prominent claw."

"Yes, sir."

"Call the ME too. See if she can think of any other tests that could tell us if the gash on Troy Griffin's leg really was made by that bear. I want to be completely sure before we relax our guard."

"Will do."

Georgia went back into the house, and Mike turned to me triumphantly, saying that perhaps one question had been answered.

"Sounds like Floyd didn't imagine his black creature after all," I agreed.

"Yeah, but I'd feel even better if this one could breathe fire."

Mike excused himself, saying we could talk later, and then he went outside through the porch's screen door.

After it had fallen shut behind him, I stood there for a moment trying to process what I had just learned. It would take a while to wrap my head around the Mafia connection, but I had a feeling that finally I was on the right track. Whatever Floyd had done to get me investigated by the government, it very likely involved organized crime.

I needed to tell Liz, but I didn't feel like having a conversation that involved right now, so I sent her a quick text instead: *Just learned that Troy had been involved with the Mafia! Relevant?*

She replied almost instantly: *Could be! Will explore further. I'll be in touch.*

I was putting the phone away in my pocket when it rang. Pulling it back out, I looked at the screen expecting to see Liz's number, but instead it was my father. This was another conversation I was not eager to have, but I knew it was inevitable. I answered, trying to keep my voice sounding light.

My father's voice, on the other hand, sounded every bit as tired and worried today as it had yesterday. I hated having to burden him at all, but I knew he would find out what was going on out here eventually, and that it was best I tell him myself now. Of course, I left out most of the details, including my job suspension and the government investigation. Instead, I focused on the series of events he would most likely be reading about in the newspaper.

"Remember that phone call I got yesterday when I was at your house?" I asked.

"The one where you sounded kind of angry? The problem at work?"

"Um…it wasn't about work. I just said that so you wouldn't be worried. It was Troy. Troy Griffin." He was quiet for a moment, so I continued. "He was calling from the bed-and-breakfast. He was lost out in the grove and saying some pretty strange things. Then he hung up on me. He wouldn't answer when I tried him back, so when I left your house, I drove out to Lancaster County to talk to him face-to-face."

"Oh, Sienna, I know Troy was important to you at one time, but I sincerely hope you're not thinking about starting things up again with him. You're not, are you? He doesn't begin to compare with Heath. In your heart of hearts you have to know that."

I walked toward the screen door, opened it, and stepped outside. I needed some fresh air, even more than I was getting on the porch.

"Of course I know that, Daddy, but that's irrelevant now anyway. Troy is dead. When I arrived here last night, I-I was the one who found his body. He had drowned in the pool. Here at the B and B."

My dad gasped. After a moment of being speechless, he found his voice and started asking questions, wanting to make sure I was okay and trying to figure out what had happened. Like Heath, he wanted to come right away to help handle things and make sure I was all right, but I wouldn't let him. We went around a little bit on that one, but in the end I got him to agree that right now his place was with his wife, not out here with his daughter. Once he had voiced all of his concerns and sympathies, and I had given him back every reassurance that I could, I moved on to the next part of what I had to say.

"The thing is, Daddy, the circumstances around Troy's death were very odd. The police are trying to figure it all out." I told him about the horrible gash on Troy's leg and the bear that had been caught ten miles away just this morning. Then I explained Mike's theory about the poison and the convulsions and the drowning, saying that Troy had probably handled some sort of pesticide that had done him in. In response, my dad was appropriately horrified, but I was glad his mind never seemed to go toward the idea of foul play. With his only daughter out here, and him with his hands full back there, the last thing he needed to know was that a murderer might be on the loose, especially one sent by the mob.

Then I told him about Floyd and Nina, saying that they had been found near Troy, both unconscious. I had already explained that Troy had likely been poisoned by a pesticide, so while I didn't say the same about Floyd and Nina, my father seemed to draw the conclusion that all three had shared the same fate, but that poor Troy was the only one who ended up losing his life from it.

"I hate to burden you with any of this at all," I said, "but I had to tell you because of Emory. With Nina in the hospital, I wasn't sure what we should do." I went on to explain that Jonah and Liesl had looked in on Emory last night, but I couldn't expect them to fill Nina's shoes for very long.

Without missing a beat, my father said that he would contact a local home health agency and set something up. As he spoke, I could already hear him flipping through his trusty Rolodex.

"You remember. They sent some workers out when your grandpa broke his hip. What was the name of that one we liked so much? Heidi? Helga?"

"Hilda, I think."

"Hilda! That's it. I'll ask for her. She was good with Emory, and from what I recall he seemed comfortable enough with her."

I felt so bad that my father had to fool with any of this right now, but it had to be done, and as Emory's guardian, he had to be the one to do it. He found the company's contact information and said he would call as soon as we hung up. Before we did, he asked about insurance on the inn, saying that I needed to call my insurance broker right away, if I hadn't already. I was too embarrassed to tell him that I had left all of those matters to Floyd, and not only did I not know who my insurance broker was, I wasn't even sure if I *had* an insurance broker. I managed to evade the issue, but as we ended the call, I couldn't help feeling just a little bit like a liar.

Slipping the phone in my pocket, I realized I was standing very near the gate to the pool area. I wasn't sure what things would look like in there in broad daylight, but I wanted to see. Would there be a chalk outline where Troy's body had lain? Any law enforcement officers still in there, working the scene? Hesitating for just a moment, I finally forced myself to step forward and take a peek through the bars of the gate.

As soon as I did, I regretted it. I could see no chalk outline or any technicians, but what I could see was blood, dried blood, that had come from Troy's leg and spilled on the cement patio and dried to a horrific rusty brown. Turning away immediately, I decided to find Mike.

With one hand resting lightly on the bulge of the gun at my waist, I followed the sound of voices around the fencing and crossed the yard to the far side of the shed. As I went, I thought again about Floyd and his possible involvement with the Mafia, and it struck me that there might be another explanation for the baby naming business on his computer in the office. What if the guests who stayed in the inn were mobsters? If so, then perhaps the reason the records were falsified was to allow them to be here incognito. That wasn't a comforting thought—mobsters sleeping in my beds, eating in my kitchen, swimming in my pool—but at least it might answer one question in a way that made sense.

When I reached the shed, I found it humming with activity. It was also a big mess, and it looked as if the cops in protective gear had been carrying everything from inside the shed to the yard and spreading it out on the grass. Hanging back and listening to their conversation, I let my eyes rove over bicycles, tennis rackets, a croquet set, some clay pots, and old hose. Most of the recreational items had been purchased by my parents and me from yard sales we had visited during the renovation. I had forgotten about most of it, but now that things were lying all over the grass as if we were about to have a yard sale of our own, I felt sad. These items were for our guests. As I wasn't even sure if we ever had any actual guests, I had a feeling that these things had remained untouched since the day we had put them here.

At least there was one good find among the junk: my punching bag, one also bought at a yard sale but put here specifically for me. I had mounted a hook in the shed roof's overhang and had pulled out this punching bag and hung it up every time I came out to work on the renovation.

Oh, what I wouldn't give for a good workout with that punching bag now! I decided I would come out here later and do just that, once I was sure all was well and I would be safe.

Rip emerged from the shed, walked over to Mike, and began rattling off a list of all the chemical substances they had found inside, things such as paint, paint thinner, and antifreeze.

"That's about it, boss. No pesticides at all, and no yard tools except a big snow shovel."

Mike had acknowledged my presence with a nod when I had first come walking up, but now he turned and spoke directly to me, asking where we kept our lawn tools.

"I know you said tools were in the basement, but all they found there were screwdrivers and pliers. What we need are the shovels and hoes and things like that."

"As far as I know, we use a lawn service. They bring their own tools."

"Yeah, but everybody has the basic stuff."

Seeing the blank look on my face, he persisted.

"You can't tell me this place wouldn't have a rake. Maybe some clippers? Especially here, with all these trees. What about the grove? Surely you have some gardening tools for the grove."

I reminded him that the grove belonged to my grandmother. "But you're right. There used to be some tools for that in the barn over at Emory's. That's where my grandfather kept them, and they probably stayed there after he died. Now that I think about it, during the renovation we needed some wire cutters. We sent Troy over there to get some from my grandfather's old toolbox. He couldn't find any, so he came back with garden clippers instead."

"Great. Thanks."

Speaking to the others, Mike told them he wanted them to take a good look at the barn next door. They worked out the logistics, and it sounded as though some would drive over and some would walk so that they could check the progress of the teams in the grove along the way. Mike said he wanted to speak to the homeowner before they started their search, so he told the ones who would be driving to wait to come over after he called and gave them the go-ahead.

"Technically, we don't need permission to search there, but we need to be careful on this one. I'd like him to be clearly informed. Trust me, the DA is not going to want any search and seizure problems down the line, not given the history."

I wondered what history he was talking about, but before I had a chance to ask, Mike turned to me and asked if I would come along to show them the best way to get there from here and to be there when he talked to my uncle. I was relieved to be included, and we all set off together, moving briskly across the lawn.

We made good time as we headed through the main gates of the grove and up the path toward the bridge at the center. We talked as we went, and I couldn't help but think how much safer it felt in here today than it had last night. Now that the sun was out—not to mention that the bear had been caught—the grove wasn't nearly so terrifying. Instead, it was its beautiful, familiar old self, the slice of paradise I knew and loved.

We made it to the bridge and onto the other side, pausing to speak with several teams of technicians we encountered along the way. Though everyone seemed to be working hard, it didn't sound as though any breakthroughs had been made. As we neared the far side of the grove, Mike asked me to explain to everyone about my uncle's mental condition.

"Oh, yeah," Rip said. "There's something wrong with this guy, right?"

"Yes, he has a mental disability," I replied. "He's impaired but high functioning."

"How is he able to live alone?" someone asked.

In response, I explained about the evaluation my dad had had done after my grandfather died, and how Nina had subsequently been hired to check in on Emory every day and make sure his basic household needs were being met.

"He's a sweet man, very gentle," I told them, wondering how to explain. "He just doesn't always come across that way because he doesn't understand things like social niceties and body language. But he has a great memory; his brain sort of locks in on facts. He loves birds and insects, squirrels and chipmunks." A chipmunk scampered by just as I said that, darting up the nearest tree. "When I was in college, I told Emory that a bird had built a nest in a hanging plant outside my dorm and had laid some eggs in it. He started asking me questions about what color the feathers were, how big the eggs were, what color the eggs were, and on and on. Finally, I took a picture of the nest and its eggs and mailed it to him. Within a month, the eggs had hatched, the babies had grown and learned to fly, and the nest had been abandoned. But Emory has continued to ask me about those birds every time I've seen him since."

As we continued our passage through the grove, I thought about my great-grandfather, who had originally owned two hundred and fifty acres. When he died and his land was divided among his sons, my grandfather's portion had included thirty-five acres of land and two houses. Abe had still been over in Europe at the time, raising his motherless son with the help of a German nanny, but when he received word that his father had died and of his inheritance, he had come home, his little boy in tow, and moved into the main house. He had hired a woman named Maureen to be Emory's caretaker, putting her up in the smaller house for propriety's sake. Despite their separate residences, Abe and Maureen had fallen in love. Once they were married, she moved into the big house, and they put the little house on the market as a rental. By that point Abe had installed electricity in both homes, much to the heartbreak of his Amish mother and siblings, who had long held out hope that he would one day return to the fold and be baptized into the faith.

Maureen gave birth to my father a few years later, and their family of four lived there in the big house together—at least until Maureen filed for a divorce and moved out, taking my father with her. Eventually she settled in nearby Chester County, though as he was growing up my dad had spent summers back here in Lancaster County with his father and half brother.

About fifteen years ago, Grandpa Abe had tripped on the basement stairs of the main house and broken his hip. After two surgeries and several months of rehab, he had decided that he had no business living in that big, two-story house, and that he would do better to move himself and Emory over here to the little house and rent out the main one instead. They had done exactly that, Grandpa Abe and Emory living here together without further incident until my grandfather's death two years ago.

Now Emory lives here all alone, I thought as we finally emerged from the far side of the grove and into Emory's yard. Straight ahead and a little to the left was Emory's home, a modest, one-story structure that had originally been built many years ago for an elderly family member. Once that person died, it was my understanding that over the years the house had been used by other family members as well. With just two bedrooms, it wasn't big enough for a whole Amish clan, but it had done in a pinch for more than a few newlyweds.

"You guys wait over here," Mike was saying, interrupting my thoughts. He pointed toward an old picnic table under a nearby shade tree. "Sienna and I will go the rest of the way alone. We don't want to spook the guy. We just want to get permission to search."

Thus, while the rest of our group relaxed in the shade, Mike and I continued on to the house. When we reached the door, Mike stood back and let me knock. After a moment the door swung open, and I was face-to-face with Uncle Emory.

NINETEEN

My uncle looked the same as he had the last time I'd seen him, short and round with tufts of gray hair on his balding head and the sweet, vacant eyes of one who viewed the world with a mix of wonder and confusion.

"Hi, Uncle Emory. Long time no see. How are you?"

"Do you still have any common house finches?" he replied, opening the door wider so that we could step inside. As we did, I told him that no, I hadn't seen any for a long time. I didn't try to hug him. Emory didn't like physical affection of any kind.

"This is my friend Mike," I added, gesturing toward the detective who came in behind me.

"I had shoofly pie," Emory said to both of us, not bothering to acknowledge Mike with a greeting or even a nod. "Nina couldn't come today, but Liesl did. She's a better cook than Nina."

I laughed, glancing at Mike.

"Well, don't tell Nina that or you'll hurt her feelings," I said.

"Okay."

I heard a woman's voice calling from the kitchen, and I realized that someone else was here. Moving further into the room, I was thrilled to see my cousin Liesl just emerging from the kitchen doorway, wiping her hands on a towel.

Dressed in the modest garb of the Amish, her hair tucked tightly under her *kapp*, Liesl looked far more appropriate today than she had last night. We greeted each other with a warm hug, but as we pulled apart the expression in her eyes warned me not to bring it up right now, not in mixed company, not even if I was dying to tease her. Which I was.

"Can I have more pie?" Emory asked, moving to the table without waiting for a reply. As he sat down and carefully took a paper napkin from the holder and tucked it into his collar, Liesl introduced herself to Mike and whispered to both of us that Emory had had a difficult night but that he was doing much better today.

She went to the kitchen to cut him another slice of pie, calling out to ask if we would like some as well.

"I don't think there is enough for everyone," Emory said quickly, shaking his head. Though I felt sure there was plenty for all, I understood that he wanted to keep it for himself, so I said no thanks and that we hadn't even had lunch yet, so we shouldn't be eating pie anyway.

I glanced at Mike, who was looking around the room, taking it all in. Seeing things through his eyes, I realized that this old place looked tired, in need of new carpet and drapes, its handmade furniture still solid but scratched and worn. Had Emory received the assets left to him by his mother as he was supposed to, we could have afforded to fix this place up for him.

Though I truly hadn't been fishing for a meal, Liesl returned with not just a plate of pie for Emory but also two plates of hot chicken salad on lettuce for Mike and me. I tried to refuse, but my growling stomach was giving me away. Mike seemed equally famished, and so we both gratefully accepted Liesl's offering, especially after she returned with a plate for herself as well and joined us at the table.

After a silent shared grace, we all dug in, that first bite so delicious that I had to take a moment just to savor it.

"What's the crunchy part on top?" Mike asked enthusiastically.

"Crushed potato chips," Liesl said, smiling. "Makes a nice touch, *jah?*"

We chatted as we ate, and then turned to the task at hand. Getting Emory's attention, I told him I had brought along my friend today because he needed to ask him something.

"Okay, but he still can't have pie."

"That's all right. I enjoyed the salad instead," Mike said easily. "Emory, I wanted to know if my people could take a look in your barn as part of our investigation. Is that okay with you?"

"Sure, go ahead. But be careful. There's a Dark-eyed Junco by the door."

"A Dark-eyed Junco?"

Emory put down his fork, tilted his chin upward, and began making a high-pitched, rapid tweeting sound with his lips.

"Is that a bird, Emory? A Dark-eyed Junco is a bird?"

"Yes, a common North American songbird. The nest has three eggs in it. I looked at it but I didn't touch it." In a higher, more singsongy voice, he added, "'Never, ever touch baby birds or their nest because then the mother might not come back.'" I smiled, recognizing the patient, instructive tones of Grandma Maureen that he was quoting. Emory was almost as good at mimicking voices as he was at making bird calls.

"Okay, then," Mike said. "Since you don't mind, we're going to head on out to the barn. But I promise I'll tell all of the policemen to watch out for the birds and their nest."

As if Mike had flicked a switch, suddenly Emory put down his fork and began rocking back and forth and humming. I knew it was the word "policemen" that had done it. Emory hadn't realized what Mike was saying before, but he certainly got it now. Liesl saw what was happening and immediately placed a comforting hand on her cousin's shoulder.

"Remember, Emory? Jonah talked to you about this last night. Policemen won't hurt you. They are our friends. They can help us if there is a problem."

"They'll take me away."

"Not if you haven't done anything wrong."

Emory didn't reply. Instead he simply continued the rocking and the humming.

"I'll be out there with them," I told him. "Will that make you feel better?"

He didn't answer but simply began to hum louder.

"He was like this last night," Liesl said softly, looking from Mike to me.

"It just got worse and worse. In the end, we had to give him some of his pills just so he would go to sleep."

"What kind of pills?" Mike asked, sitting up straight.

"Um, I think they are called Ativan? He doesn't need them very often, but we can give some to him if he gets worked up."

"Can I see the bottle?" Mike asked.

Liesl looked at me, eyebrows raised, and I nodded that it would be okay. Turning my attentions to Emory as Liesl led Mike from the room, I tried to think how my grandfather would have handled this moment.

"Hey, Emory, do you still have that movie called *The Amazing Ibis?*" He didn't reply, so I simply got up from the table and moved over to the TV area in the next room. Making a big show of looking through old VHS tapes, I could see from the corner of my eye that I had his attention, at least somewhat. When we were younger, this was his favorite show, one he watched over and over.

"Well, look at that. Here it is. Do you mind if I put it on right now?"

He didn't answer, but I turned on the TV and the VCR and popped in the tape anyway, adding that I could probably cut him one more sliver of pie to eat while he watched the show.

Calmed somewhat, Emory carried his fork and plate to the easy chair that sat directly in front of the TV. Soon the old documentary was playing on the television, and Emory's rocking slowed to a stop as he was swept into the action. I took his plate and carried it and our dirty dishes into the kitchen. When I returned with the promised extra slice, I gave Emory's plate back to him and then stood there next to his chair and watched the show for a few minutes as he ate. Mike and Liesl returned, and then he and I were able to make our exit.

As Liesl walked us to the door, I told her that my father was arranging for a caretaker and I would keep her posted on that.

"I'll come find you later so we can talk," I added.

"Please do," she urged me, her voice and eyes emphatic. She gave me another hug and then softly closed the door behind us. Moving down the front step and onto the walk, I took a deep breath and let it out slowly, thankful that the crisis had been averted, at least for now.

"Well, what did you see? Were his pills the same dosage that Nina had in her pocket?" I asked as Mike and I reached the end of the walkway and started along the worn path along the edge of the lawn.

"Yeah, but the script was filled two months ago. Except for the few that had been recorded on his medicine log, there were only six other pills missing and unaccounted for."

"Meaning..."

"Meaning that the six pills in Nina's pocket no doubt came from here, but that she hadn't taken any of them yet. Whatever she and Floyd were intoxicated with, it probably wasn't Ativan after all, at least not Emory's Ativan."

We headed toward the group waiting under the tree, both of us lost in thought. Up ahead they saw us coming, and when Mike gave them a thumbs-up signal, they all rose and began making their way toward the barn ahead of us.

Feeling uncomfortable, I apologized for Emory's behavior, adding that I had no idea why the mention of policemen had made him act that way.

"Cops were here the night his father died," I mused. "Maybe Emory associates the uniforms with people coming and taking his dad away."

"It probably goes further back than that," Mike replied, pausing to step around a cluster of rose bushes that protruded into the walkway and needed pruning. "He probably associates uniforms with being arrested."

"Like on TV, you mean?"

Mike didn't reply, so I glanced at him and was startled by the sideways look he was giving me.

"Wait. You mean Emory himself? He was arrested? When? Why? How do you know?"

"I read through his records this morning." Mike paused near my grandfather's old vegetable garden, his eyes scanning the weed-filled furrows. "You didn't know?"

I shook my head.

"I'm sorry. It was a long time ago, before you and I were even born. I shouldn't have mentioned it."

I pressed him for dates, and finally he told me that the first time Emory had trouble with the law he was just a child of about ten or eleven. The second time, he was older, a young adult of about twenty.

"I never heard this before."

"It's true."

Mike knelt and studied a half-rotted pumpkin that was nearly hidden in the tall grass.

"Was he charged with a crime?"

"I don't know details about the first time. He was a juvie then, and those records are sealed. The second time, from what I could see, he was charged, but your grandfather worked things out with everyone involved and the charges were eventually dropped."

"What was he accused of doing?"

Mike poked at the pumpkin with a stick.

"I'd rather not say. You might ask someone in your family about it. Maybe your father knows and could tell you. I shouldn't even have said this much. I just assumed you knew."

I stood there for a moment, trying to understand what he was saying. Poor Emory was so clueless in certain areas that I had to wonder if perhaps he had accidentally committed a crime, such as walking out of a store with a candy bar in his hand without paying for it. Whatever had happened, it had to have been an accident. Emory was about as innocent and guileless as they come.

"Does this look like scat to you?" Mike asked, holding back the weeds with his stick.

Trying not to be grossed out, I leaned over to take a closer look, wondering why he was doing this if the bear had already been caught. Reaching for another stick, I pushed more of the weeds out of the way and then I couldn't help but laugh, pointing toward its stem, which was still attached to the vine.

"Spend much time tracking wild animals, do you?" I teased.

"Okay, okay, so I'm a city boy at heart. I just spotted the orange of the pumpkin and thought maybe it was similar to what my guys found over near your pool."

Mike tossed his stick aside and stood.

"Why were you reading Emory's file anyway? Surely you don't think he had anything to do with Troy's death."

He shrugged, brushing the dirt from his hands.

"This property offers direct access to the grove. Nina was found in this driveway. That makes Emory a POI."

"POI?"

"A person of interest. Don't worry, Sienna. Your uncle has an alibi for the time span we're focusing on. He was at work all afternoon, and then he went over to his boss's house for dinner. He didn't get back here until almost eleven last night."

Mike gestured toward the barn, and we continued on our way. While I was glad Emory had an alibi for the time in question, I had to wonder how Mike knew all of that.

"Did you interview him?"

"Didn't have to. Emory's boss brought him home last night, and they arrived here at the same time as two of the patrolmen who were going around warning neighbors about a possible animal on the loose. They got the information on his whereabouts at that time."

"Ah." No wonder Emory had gotten so worked up last night. He had come home from dinner to find two cops at his house—cops who wanted to know where he had been and what he had been doing.

Mike excused himself to call the other part of the team and tell them to drive on over. When he hung up, I spoke, trying to sound casual. I wondered if he had looked up my name and found me on some government investigation list somewhere.

"So...were there other POIs? Find anything surprising?"

We reached the barn and paused, looking through its cavernous doorway at the activity inside. Soon even more officers and technicians would be here as well, hunting for tools, testing chemicals, trying to solve a puzzle with far too many pieces.

"You might say that I came up with more than I bargained for on a couple of hits," Mike replied evenly.

Then he headed into the barn with the others and got down to work.

TWENTY

Hovering along the fringes of the action, I had just managed to locate the Dark-eyed Junco nest in a low bush beside the barn when I heard what sounded like gunshots in the distance. I immediately took cover behind the bush and drew my weapon. Watching, waiting, my heart pounding, I suddenly realized that no one else seemed alarmed or had even reacted at all.

Lowering the gun, I listened intently, wondering if I was imagining things. Then I heard the sound again, just as Mike came walking past.

"It's a nail gun, Collins," he said dryly, "not a shotgun. You can holster your weapon."

He continued on past, leaving me there behind the bush with my cheeks burning. Between this incident and the earlier animal scat he thought he'd found, I guessed we were even.

As the distant "bang" happened yet again, I realized that what I had been hearing was, indeed, the sound of nails being shot, not bullets. Slipping my gun back into its fanny pack holster, I was just glad that I hadn't done something really ridiculous, such as yelling "Hit the dirt!" to all of these cops.

Feeling like an idiot, I slunk away in search of the noise's source, which sounded as though it was coming from the springhouse, a picturesque little structure that sat on the far side of Emory's house. Built in the early nineteen hundreds, the springhouse had straddled a cold water creek and was designed to provide refrigeration of sorts thanks to the shallow, rectangular depressions in the floor where perishable foods could be placed. The running spring water would keep those food items cold without the chance of them washing away down the creek. I couldn't imagine having to store perishables this way, but without any other source of refrigeration, I supposed it was better than nothing.

The staccato sounds of the nail gun were definitely coming from there now. Moving closer to see what was going on, I finally spotted a man perched on top of the roof. It looked as if he was repairing some of the roof tiles, holding them down with one hand while securing them in place with the nail gun he held in the other. Uncertain as to why anyone would be trying to repair this old building that no longer served any purpose, I came even closer. That's when I saw my cousin Jonah standing nearby, his hands on his hips, looking upward as he chatted with the man on the roof.

"Jonah?"

"Sienna! Hey! You remember Burl Newton, don't you?"

Shielding my eyes from the sun, I squinted up at the wiry, tanned guy on the roof, who was giving me a wave.

"Of course I do. Hi, Burl. How have you been?"

"Can't complain. Jus' had a little free time, so I thought I'd come over and fix this roof like I been promising Emory I would."

"Don't believe him," Jonah said, grinning. "I think he is doing this now so he can get a closer look at everything going on here with all of the policemen."

"What *is* going on here?" Burl asked. "I thought they was next door, over at your place."

"Yes, I would like to know too," Jonah said. "I was just coming to check on Liesl when I saw all of this activity."

Without going into detail, I told them of Mike's pesticide theory, bringing both men up to speed on the general progress of the investigation and ending with the news of the bear that had been caught this morning in Holtwood.

"*Ach*, I am so glad. Liesl said the children could not go outside until the matter is solved. The girls are doing fine, helping their *grossmammi* in the kitchen, but the last time I went in there the boys had shaped the piecrust dough into little cows and were lining them up around the table for milking time."

I laughed, thinking boys would be boys whether Amish or not. I warned Jonah that the police wouldn't be sure about the bear until the lab tests had come back, but that it didn't sound as though that would take too long.

"So what's wrong with the springhouse?" I asked, changing the subject and again shielding my eyes to look up at Burl.

"Bunch of squirrels gnawed a hole clean through some roof tiles. Ain't all that big of a hole, but it's letting rain into the beams, rotting the wood. If it don't get repaired, eventually this one little hole could cause the whole roof to come down. Not that it would matter, really, but you know Emory."

Yes, I knew Emory, and I remembered now that Burl did too. An odd and reclusive man, he was nevertheless Emory's oldest friend. They were the same age and had grown up living on back-to-back properties, easily able to visit and play together as small children without ever having to venture out onto any road. Of course, at some point Emory ceased to mature, intellectually speaking, while Burl had continued to grow up, so their friendship had by necessity transitioned into something else. Though I had never really warmed up to Burl myself, I knew he kept an eye on his old childhood buddy, and I was touched to see him here now, fixing a useless old building just because it mattered to my uncle.

This particular springhouse hadn't been functioning for years, not since this branch of the creek had dried up and left it without any water. Still, the unused structure had remained, giving a lovely, picturesque touch to the old-timey feel of the property. It was just a shame that it was hidden away like this where more people couldn't see it.

When we were doing the renovation next door, my mother and I had really wanted the springhouse to be part of it. Our feeling was that if we could have the structure moved from back here out of sight to a far more prominent spot in front of the inn, its rustic beauty would enhance the whole feel of Harmony Grove Bed & Breakfast. Between that and the inn itself and the covered bridge, the entire scene would have made a beautiful vista, something straight out of a storybook.

We had offered to buy the structure from Emory, with the secret hope that he would tell us just to take it, no payment required. Much to our surprise, however, he had turned us down flat, saying that the spring-house was not for sale and would never be for sale, and that it needed to stay exactly where it was forever and ever. At the time we had been surprised most of all by the vehemence of his response. Later on, however, I figured out what the issue was. With its open-air structure and wide rafters, the springhouse provided a perfect habitat for all sorts of birds and small animals.

Even now, as Burl was making such a racket up on the roof, a myriad of birds twittered from nearby trees, probably waiting for us to go away so they could return to their nests.

"Hey, listen, I was sorry to learn of your father's death last year," I said to Burl. "If I had heard about it in time, I would have tried to come out for the funeral."

"Why?"

I was so startled by the question that I couldn't think of an answer. My comment had been meant as a social nicety, not an actual statement of intent. Obviously sensing the awkwardness of the moment, Jonah interjected that even though I hadn't known the man very well myself, I had probably wanted to pay respects on behalf of the Collins branch of the family.

"Yeah, well, don't worry about that. Ain't like the man's been missed— not by Collinses or anybody else, for that matter."

That was true, though I was surprised to hear Burl admit as much about his own father. As a child I had been terrified of Mr. Newton, a surly, grizzled old recluse who once threatened my brother and me with a pitchfork when we ran into his yard to retrieve an errant baseball.

Suddenly, activity over at the barn seemed to increase. From where I stood, I could see several technicians darting in and out, talking on their radios, barking out orders. I wanted to know what they had found, so I excused myself from the two men and retraced my steps around to the front of the barn where I could watch and listen more closely.

From what I could tell, the commotion was over some chemicals that had been found in a storage closet. They had apparently discovered all of my grandfather's old welding and metalworking solutions, along with the various fertilizer supplements and pesticides he had used in his care of the grove. Of particular interest to the police was a certain pesticide in the form of a white powder. I heard one of them say that the warning label even listed "convulsions" in a list of side effects from overexposure.

Another vehicle arrived, a big, dark van with no back windows, and I moved out of the way even further as a group of people in Hazmat suits got out and went into the barn. The whole thing felt like overkill, but they must have known what they were doing.

A little while later, they began to emerge from the barn carrying large, sealed bags, inside of which they seemed to have placed full containers of the various chemicals they had found, especially the main pesticide in question. More bags followed, and judging by their shapes and sizes, I could tell that those were full of gardening tools, including several shovels.

I wasn't sure what all this meant. I told myself that it would be good news if the police could prove that Troy's poisoning had been an accident. Then, perhaps, all other lines of investigation—into organized crime, into Emory, even into me, at least at the local level—could be closed down.

On the other hand, I had to wonder what Mike's interest in Emory was in the first place. If Mike knew Emory had an alibi for yesterday afternoon and evening, why had he gone into the old police records this morning? What had Emory's old arrests been about anyway?

I couldn't ask my father without worrying him to death, and I didn't want to put any of the older Coblentz relatives in the uncomfortable position of having to tell me family gossip about one of my own elders. Wondering who I might ask, I heard the nail gun going off again, and it struck me that perhaps Burl could fill me in.

I walked back over to the springhouse. Burl was still up on the roof, only now he was sitting fully atop it, straddling the crest as if it were a horse he was riding. Jonah was gone; I assumed he had headed over to the house to see his wife.

I had hoped that when Burl saw me he would come down to the ground so we could talk more easily, but instead he just waved and kept going on with what he was doing. I decided to plunge ahead anyway. After glancing toward the house to make sure there weren't any open windows through which I might be overheard from inside, I spoke.

"So, Burl, you've known Uncle Emory your whole life, right?"

"Pretty much. Since we was about three or four, anyway."

"Did you know that when he was younger he was arrested by the police?"

"Yeah, of course."

"Can you tell me about it? What happened back then?"

"You mean the first time or the second time?"

My pulse surged. "Both. Can you tell me about both?"

"What's to tell?" he asked, shooting off three quick nails in a row. "First time, it ended up getting him institutionalized. That was a shame. I really missed him. He didn't come out of that mental home for years."

Burl set down his nail gun and picked up a different tool, some sort of drill that was too loud to talk over. As I waited for a break in the noise, I tried to figure out which way to go with my questions. I knew Emory had been in an institution when he was younger, but I had never known the circumstances that had put him there.

"The second time he was arrested, he was older," Burl said when he finally released the trigger on the drill. "Things were handled a little different that time. But my family didn't press charges, so the police eventually let it go."

"*Your* family? What kind of charges were they? What happened?"

Burl didn't answer, so I put a hand over my eyes and looked up at him until he replied.

"Look, I really hate to say. It's all water under the bridge. I don't hold nothing against Emory for it."

He began drilling again, and I could tell by his very body language that he didn't want to discuss the situation. But I wasn't going to give up that easily, not until I knew the truth. The next time the drill stopped, I jumped right in with my next question.

"What were his crimes, Burl? What had Emory done that was bad enough to get him arrested?"

Without answering, Burl began to put his things away. I wasn't sure if he was finished with the job or simply wanting to escape my questions. Finally, as he swung a leg over the crest of the roof and inched his way down the slope to the top of the ladder, he spoke.

"He killed some animals. First time was a rabbit, out in the woods. That didn't have nothing to do with us. Second time it did, though. Second time was a dog. My dog."

"Emory killed some animals? Killed your *dog*? I can't believe that," I said, walking to the base of the ladder and holding up a hand to take the drill from him.

"It's true," he replied, handing it down to me. "First time he was practically caught red-handed. Even admitted it. Second time, he was older, maybe a little wiser. Denied it like crazy, but everybody knew. The injuries were exactly the same."

"Injuries?" I asked, squinting. "What kind of injuries? Since when does a little boy killing a rabbit in the woods constitute a crime anyway, especially back in the fifties? Boys go rabbit hunting all the time."

Burl started down the ladder, not answering until he got to the bottom.

"He wasn't hunting, Sienna. Just killin' for pleasure, I guess."

I frowned, unable to comprehend what this man was saying.

"Emory Collins. Killed some animals."

"Yep."

"I don't believe it."

Burl reached the bottom of the ladder and stepped onto the ground, turning to face me.

"Believe it. It wasn't too hard to figure out who done it. And like I said, first time around he even admitted it."

Stunned, I stood there beside the springhouse, silent, as Burl took his tools from me, carried them over to his open toolbox, and set them down inside.

"Emory *loves* animals, Burl. There's no way he would ever hurt one. Not him. Ever. Never, ever."

Burl moved the ladder inside the open springhouse, setting it up directly underneath the spot where he had been working on the roof.

"Look," he said, glancing at me over his shoulder, "if it helps, Mister

Abe did everything he could to make things right. He was so heartbroken about it. Even paid my daddy a lot of money for a new dog and for our pain and suffering."

"What about the dog's pain and suffering?" I asked, though why I was sounding angry at this man I had no idea. He had been the victim here, not the perpetrator.

I had never really liked Burl, but I realized now that he must be a good man to have forgiven his old friend of something like this. I wondered if somewhere along the way he might have been influenced by the Amish, who were emphatic on the topic of forgiveness. That would be about the only way I could think of to explain Burl's ability to get over such a major transgression.

"It takes a big man to forgive something like this," I added.

"Aw, my daddy didn't care about that ol' dog. He was jus' happy to get some money."

"I was talking about *you*, Burl."

He glanced at me, eyes wide, and then he blushed and looked away.

"When it happened with the dog," he said gruffly, "your grandpa said that it musta been like in that famous book by, uh, Steinbrenner, I think, about the two brothers and the mouse?"

I thought about that as he walked around the side of the building and retrieved a heavier piece of equipment, one with a handle and wheels. He lifted and rolled it to the doorway of the springhouse, and then he tried to get it inside and down the steps. I jumped in to help, and though he insisted on doing it alone, I insisted even harder on helping. Together, we got it over the threshold and down the steps, where the air was perceptively cooler inside.

"Steinbeck?" I said, coming up with the name at last. "*Of Mice and Men?*" Looking around at the mossy stone chamber, I realized Burl had already brought several other pieces of equipment in here too and had propped them against the side wall, ready for use.

"Yeah, that's it. Mister Abe tol' us how the retarded fellow in that story would just be loving on a mouse and would love it too hard and would end up killing it by accident."

So that was what my grandfather had done, explained this aberration in

166 MINDY STARNS CLARK

his son by giving it a literary reference? I had news for him. I had read that book, and the deaths caused by the man in the story had happened because he didn't know his own strength, not because of anything that involved killing for pleasure. Not at all. To my understanding, that was the territory of serial killers, not simple but lovable literary characters. Watching Burl roll his machine to the base of the ladder and set it there, I took a deep breath and blew it out slowly, everything shifting and realigning within my brain.

No wonder the police thought Emory was a person of interest.

TWENTY-ONE

Burl wasn't finished with his work, but he was clearly finished talking with me. He flipped on the machine, which I had a feeling was an air compressor, and then he grabbed some tools and headed up the ladder to go at his repairs from the inside.

The sound of the machine reverberated within the old stone building so loudly that it hurt my ears. Stepping out of the building and onto the grass, I looked toward my uncle's house just fifteen feet or so away and wondered if I could ever face him again. Had I ever known who he really was at all?

It happened a long, long time ago, I told myself, but that didn't help. All I could think was that any person—whether mentally disabled or not—who could kill an animal for no reason was one very sick, deranged monster. If Emory had done that to his only friend's dog years ago, would he have hesitated to do the same to a person now?

Emory was so protective of the grove, I had to wonder. Could he have caught Troy in there digging around and messing it up and then attacked him out of anger? Surely, that was the question Mike had been asking himself as well, regardless of Emory's alibi. I had never really seen Emory angry before, but I had certainly seen him agitated. Was he really capable of something like this?

Suddenly the familiar panic surged up again, and as my heart pounded and my hands began to sweat, I knew I had to do something fast if I didn't want to end up completely incapacitated. Pressing my hand against the solid

barrel of my gun for reassurance, I tried deep breathing, tried telling myself
all of my little sayings, tried my three-sentence prayer.

Keep me safe, keep me from harm, keep me in your loving arms.
Keep me safe, keep me from harm, keep me in your loving arms.
Nothing helped.

Feeling almost dizzy from anxiety, I moved toward the driveway. Right
now, more than anything, I needed to put some distance between myself
and my uncle. Not sure where else to go but wanting to be safe, I walked
over to rejoin the police. As I went I realized that most of the cops were no
longer in the barn but were out in the grove instead. Mike was standing with
several others in the shade of a nearby tree, but when he saw me he broke
away and came walking over.

"There you are," he said. "I was looking for you earlier. Wanted to let you
know..." His voice trailed off as he stepped closer and got a good look at my
face. "Sienna? Are you okay? You look sick. I mean, you *look* fine, but you
look as though you feel sick."

Acknowledge the anxiety to someone else, I could hear my counselor
say. *Admitting it freely robs it of its power.*

"I'm having a panic attack," I whispered, my heart now pounding so
loudly that I felt sure he could hear it too.

He bent his knees slightly so that we were eye to eye, looked at me
intently, and asked if something had happened. "Something new, I mean?
Just now?"

I shook my head, so ashamed of my trembling hands, of the sweat that
was making my clothes cling to my body.

"I was talking to Burl. He told me about Emory. About his arrests. The
news just...it got to me." I wanted to tell Mike it wasn't a big deal in itself,
that it was simply tapping into my own personal trauma from ten years ago.
But my throat had grown so tight that it was hard to get words out. "I'll be
all right. I promise. It's just my own...baggage. Things here keep stirring
up feelings from the other...From the past."

"Gotcha," Mike replied softly. Then he did the strangest thing. He
simply stood up straight, placed one hand on each side of my shoulders,

and pulled me toward him, just slightly, tilting his head forward so that his temple pressed firmly against mine.

"Put your hands on my elbows, close your eyes, and just breathe," he whispered, holding both of us perfectly still. Somehow, I found our strange stance instantly comforting and protective, as if we were in water and had formed a three-point hold to buffet ourselves against the waves. We stood there like that for some time, his hands strong and firm on my shoulders, the skin of his cheek blazing against mine.

"I once had a dear friend who suffered from an anxiety disorder," he said softly without moving. "She taught me how to help."

Closing my eyes, I wondered if I could teach this stance to Heath. Then I wondered if it was wrong of me to wonder whether Heath, with his feelings about nonresistance and his aversion to guns, could ever make me feel as safe as Mike was making me feel right now.

"This does help," I whispered. "Very much."

I knew we couldn't stay like that forever, especially with others around. Finally, I told him I was okay and he could let go. He did as I asked, though he seemed reluctant to move away from me completely.

"You need to do something physical, to exert yourself," he said, trying to gauge by looking into my eyes whether I really was okay or not.

"I saw my old punching bag behind the shed. But that's too much trouble. I'd have to put all of the junk away first."

"Maybe you could jog the track around the grove a couple of times."

"I'd love to, but it's not safe," I replied, shaking my head. "Not yet, anyway. Not for sure."

Gesturing toward the grove, he assured me that with this many people around, he doubted that either murderers or wild animals or anything else could do anyone much harm today.

"Between my department and the game commission and the USDA, we have about eight different teams in there looking for evidence. Must be forty or fifty people, at least. You'll be safe. Just stick to the path so you don't land in a hole and twist an ankle."

"Have they found more holes out there?" I asked, noting that though my heart was still pounding furiously in my chest, my breathing was already a little more steady and sure.

"In three different areas of the grove, yes. For one man, Troy did a lot of digging in just two days' time."

"He must have been desperate to find those diamonds," I replied.

Running a hand through my hair and gathering it up off of my neck to cool down, I felt grateful that this man had been here in this moment to help me through. The panic was beginning to subside.

"I do feel better. But you're right, a quick run really would help right now."

"Then go for it. Stick to the outside path, and I'll let everyone know we have a jogger coming through."

Before I could object, he whipped out his radio and started talking into it. I could feel the hot burn of my cheeks as I listened, waiting to hear what he would say and hoping he wouldn't totally embarrass me.

"Heads up, people, this is Weissbaum. I've asked Miss Collins to take a jog around the outer path of the grove a few times, just to give the whole place a once-over to see if she notices anything else amiss. Don't interrupt her and don't get in her way. Clear?"

After a moment came the replies:

"Clear."

"Got it."

"Understood."

And so on.

Tucking his radio back onto his belt, Mike grinned at me mischievously and said that should suffice. "I'll be here when you make it all the way back around, if you need me."

Studying the angled plains of his cheeks, the strong features, the intense eyes, I couldn't help but wonder how this handsome man could be so kind despite working in a field where he dealt with criminals and violence and evil as a matter of course day after day.

"Thank you," I said softly before turning to go. "Oh, wait. What were you going to tell me?"

"What?"

"A few minutes ago. You said you had been looking for me to let me know something."

"Oh yeah. To let you know that the investigation has been expanded and that these other government agencies are joining in on it. Right now your driveway is probably as full of cars as it was last night. I just didn't want you to worry if you went back over and saw that."

"Okay. Thanks."

I didn't ask if there was some specific reason for this new development or if it was all part of his investigation. But as I reached the path and moved from a walking pace into a slow jog, the rhythm of my feet hitting the ground began pounding out the words over and over: *government agency, government agency, government agency.*

Did the investigation that had gotten me suspended involve any of the officials out here now? Was it possible that some of the people who had parked in my driveway weren't even really here to learn more about Troy's death but about me or my B and B instead?

Feeling powerless and afraid I might once again be overwhelmed with panic, I forced my mind away from these unanswerable questions and instead decided to focus on my run, on the task that Mike had fictitiously laid out for me. I decided to actually look things over now, nodding at each cluster of people I passed, allowing my eyes to scan the grove around me for anything that might feel like a red flag. Focusing on something outside of myself seemed to help almost immediately.

Just the sight of these beautiful trees, of the flashes of red and yellow and orange among the green, of the sun-dappled shade flickering on the path ahead of me, was so calming and peaceful that I already felt a hundred times better. I wasn't thrilled to be running in blue jeans with a heavy gun strapped to my waist, but I could deal with it. This wasn't about physical fitness anyway but about mental fitness. At least I wasn't jogging in slacks and heels.

I had come into the grove just past the German Gate, turning right to run forward toward the main road as I went around the wide oval, the grove on my left. I knew that the full loop of the path equaled exactly one mile, which meant that an easy jog should take about ten or twelve minutes to get all the way around once. Hopefully, just once would do. There were so many more important things I should be accomplishing than merely running from a panic attack.

After jogging slowly for just a few minutes, I reached the first big curve, which turned me so that I was running parallel to the main road. I slowed to a walk as I neared the midpoint for this side, the entrance to the grove we always called the Peace Gate. Reaching the gate now, I paused to look up at it and enjoy its optical illusion, the curving wrought iron that at first glance always seemed to form a simple, abstract design but upon further study revealed within that design the outline of doves—some in flight, some nesting, one perched on a wrought iron limb. The inscription for this gate read:

> *This was the Golden Age that, without coercion, without laws,*
> *spontaneously nurtured the good and the true...Without the use of*
> *armies, people passed their lives in gentle peace and security.*

The markers in this section were similarly utopian and benign, much as they were at the opposite end of the grove, in the area around that we called the Corn Gate. Filled with images of peace and prosperity and good will, for the most part they were simply boring. As kids, we much preferred the more dramatic verses in the center of the grove that dealt with the ill-fated romance of the poem.

"Is there a problem, Miss Collins?" a voice called, and I looked up to see a cluster of technicians working nearby, eyeing me with concern, as if I had found something questionable in my survey of the grove.

"No. No problem at all. I was just admiring the beautiful gate."

"This whole grove is beautiful," one of the women in the group said as they got back to work. "Once this case gets solved, it really ought to be opened up to the public, you know?"

"That's true," I said, giving them a wave as I started moving again. As I ran I wondered why my grandfather had chosen to keep the grove private and within the family rather than donate it in his will to be used as a public park.

Maybe because diamonds really are hidden in here. Maybe he couldn't

risk taking this place public because someone else might find them before
we did.

Trying to keep my mind clear and refusing to think about that now, I continued jogging along the path and around the curve that positioned me so that I was running away from the main road, with the B and B off to my right. In a few minutes I would reach the grove's main entrance, the gate with the two arrows and the words "Harmony Grove."

For some reason, that was the gate that always made me miss my grandfather the most—probably because of the many times I had seen him standing there in its opening, surveying the grove in front of him, and observing us children as we ran and laughed and wove in and among the trees.

Though we had visited here a lot when I was a child, always spending plenty of time when we came, I hadn't loved the man who was my father's father, mostly because I hadn't known him well enough. Abe Collins had been an incredibly silent person, and when he spoke at all it was always about mundane matters, never of thoughts or memories or revelations or matters of the heart. Lack of communication had been a big issue during his marriage to Grandma Maureen. Though he hadn't been much of a husband to her, he had been a good father to his two sons and had deeply loved them both to the day he died. Grandpa Abe had been so reclusive in his lifetime that we had expected his funeral to be a quiet affair, with only a few family members and neighbors in attendance. Instead, we had been deeply touched by the entire Coblentz clan, who had come out in force, filling the parking lot with their buggies and the pews with their peaceful stillness. At the front of the room had been no casket, open or closed, but instead a single, framed photo of my grandfather, who had asked that his body be cremated instead. Thanks to a very thorough eulogy given by his pastor, by the end of that service I knew more about Grandpa Abe than I had ever learned during his lifetime.

Passing the main gate now, I pictured him and thought of all the surprising facts I had learned about him the day of his funeral.

Born to Amish parents, the youngest son of seven children, Abe Coblentz had shown a flair for art at a very young age. Afraid his special talents might create pride in the young man, his parents had attempted to channel his artistic abilities in a practical and useful direction by arranging for an apprenticeship with a blacksmith once Abe's official schooling was complete. A quick study and a hard worker, Abe had soon proven himself invaluable on the job.

He was sixteen and still working for the blacksmith when the Japanese bombed Pearl Harbor. One by one, each of his older brothers had been called into the service and subsequently approved for conscientious objector status, though their road during the war years had not been easy. Tormented by soldiers, demeaned by officials, and treated almost like prisoners of war throughout every stateside work assignment they had been given, Abe's brothers had written home weekly, asking for prayer for the strength to endure. In the fall of 1942, the government lowered the age of the draft from twenty-one to eighteen, so by the following February Abe's invitation from Uncle Sam had arrived as well.

Soon he, too, was approved for CO status, but unlike his brothers, Abe had shocked his entire family by requesting to serve in the war as a noncombatant. Once all the red tape had been cut, Abe found himself in training as an army medic, after which he was sent to Europe and into the very heart of the action.

Not much was known about Abe's war years, except that they had changed him in many ways. Rumors back home were wild and varied—that he was a coward, that he was a hero, that the men in his battalion hated him, that they loved and respected him—though no one knew which rumors were true and which were not. About all that was known for sure was that, as a member of a unit of the American Fourth Armored Division of the Third Army, Abe had been among those liberating several Nazi concentration camps, including Ohrdruf and Buchenwald.

Abe had not been baptized into the Amish faith before going off to war, but his entire family had held out hope that once he returned he would confess and repent of his sins of supporting the war effort, join the church, and find himself an Amish bride. Instead, word was received in the summer of 1945 that Abe had married a survivor of Buchenwald, a Jewish woman named Daphne, and that he intended to stay there in Europe after his tour of duty was complete. Months later, the family learned that Abe and Daphne were expecting a baby, due to be born just a few weeks after their first anniversary.

That spring, however, Daphne had gone into early labor, her body still weak from the ravages of Buchenwald, and though the child survived the difficult birth, Daphne did not. At that point, as a young, widowed. noncombatant soldier with an infant son, the assumption was that Abe would return home, to his Amish roots and loving family. Instead, he had shocked them all yet again by hiring a nanny for the infant and remaining in Europe.

Abe and his motherless child lived there until he got word that his father had passed away back home. At the desperate, pleading request of his mother, and with the promise of a portion of the family land and homes that he had inherited, Abe had finally returned to the states with his young son. There, Abe had delivered one last, shocking blow to his family: Immediately following his honorable discharge from the U.S. Army, he had filed a court order to legally change his last name from Coblentz to Collins. When asked why, he had replied that it was an attempt to erase the shame of association with a religious sect that endorsed nonresistance. The conscientious objector had done an about-face at some point during the war, deciding that there could be no excuse, no honorable reason at all, *not* to fight, at least not when the enemy was as dark and evil as the Third Reich had been.

After that, the battle lines had been drawn, so to speak. And though they would never stop praying for him and never stop loving him, the various members of the Coblentz family had left Abe alone to live in *and* of the world as he was so determined to do.

Rounding the third curve of the grove path, the one that would bring me to the Corn Gate, I slowed again to a walk and thought about the enigmatic man and how his decision to break away from the Amish faith had resonated through the subsequent generations. Because something inside of him changed, something that no one else had ever truly understood, I was the creative director of an advertising agency in Philadelphia rather than a young Amish wife and mother in Lancaster County. Did I owe him thanks for that? At times a part of me longed for an Amish life, for its peace and simplicity and spiritual purity. Another part of me knew that theirs was a road I would never have chosen to walk down. After the funeral, I realized that thanks to my late grandfather, that was a choice I had never been forced to make.

TWENTY-TWO

Reaching the Corn Gate, I stopped and read its inscription, mounted on a brass plate amid the cornstalk pattern of the wrought iron:

Spring was eternal, and gentle breezes caressed with warm
air the flowers that grew without being seeded. Then the untilled
earth gave of its produce and, without needing renewal,
the fields whitened with heavy ears of corn.

Thinking of my grandfather now, picturing his labors over every element of this entire, magnificent grove, I was suddenly consumed with a wrenching sense of guilt. In his will, he had requested that our immediate family gather in the grove in one final, memorial act to bury his ashes there. Though the funeral service had been held several days after his death, there had been no rush on the private memorial and ash-burial. The grove had been sorely neglected in my grandfather's last few years of life, and we all wanted to see it get fixed up a bit first before we held our little ceremony there. My grandmother hired a team of arborists and landscapers to do the job, but once they were finished we never could seem to find a date that worked for everyone.

Soon after we had finally chosen a date, my mother had been diagnosed with MS. Consumed with her care, we had postponed the gathering indefinitely, but even after she started the quarterly chemo treatments, we had never rescheduled the memorial service in the grove. Though we would mention it now and again, none of us had made of point of insisting that we follow through on my grandfather's final wish.

Shame on us. Shame on all of us. Abe Collins may have been an odd and unknowable man, but he deserved better than to have his final remains sitting in a plastic bag in a dusty cardboard box in the back of my father's closet.

Continuing onward, I decided that honoring this wish would be one positive result of this awful situation. When everything surrounding Troy's death had been solved, I was going to move heaven and earth to rally the family and make sure my grandfather got the send-off he deserved. He had blessed us with this magnificent grove. It was the least we could do in return.

As I rounded the final curve, the one that would lead me to the German Gate where I had started, I decided that this leisurely jog around the grove had been just what the doctor ordered. In one sense, it had calmed me down and helped push away the panic. In another sense, it had whetted my appetite for more activity. What I now wanted, more than anything, was to hang up that punching bag on the hook at the shed and go a few rounds with all of my might.

A sharp pain suddenly stabbed at my shin, and I let out a yelp before I even looked down to see what had happened. Expecting to spy some sort of creature or beast rising up from the earth to devour me, I was shocked to realize that I had been the victim of a man-eating blackberry bush.

I stopped, pulling up my snagged pants leg to get a closer look at the tiny dots of blood on my skin. I felt like an idiot for squealing, even more so when about six people suddenly materialized from somewhere up ahead, including Georgia, ready to take on whatever danger I had encountered. I apologized, assuring them that I had simply been scratched by a blackberry bush and that I really shouldn't have reacted like that.

"Those look like Marc Jacobs jeans you got on, girl," Georgia said. "I woulda screamed too."

We all laughed, and then everyone returned to their work.

I was about to finish out my jog when something dawned on me. I hesitated, thinking.

The blackberry bush. I remembered the blackberry bushes, because we used to come out here as kids and pick enough berries for my mother to bake a pie. They grew beside a marker that referred to "blackberries cling-ing to tough brambles." But that wasn't important.

What was important was that somewhere in this very same region was the marker about the dolphins.

I wasn't sure how or why I remembered. I just knew that the dolphin marker was near the blackberry marker and that both of them had been among my favorites in the whole grove. If the one about the dolphin signi-fied the Fishing Tree, I may have found the location Troy had sought in his search for the diamonds.

Walking around to the other side of the blackberry bushes, careful to give their thorny limbs a wide berth, I scanned the closest marker and then kept going in an ever-widening circle. Three markers away, I finally found it:

There are dolphins in the trees, disturbing the upper branches and stirring the oaks as they brush against them.

The marker sat in front of a big oak tree, and I could remember as a child staring up at the broad limbs, wondering if they had ever really held dolphins.

Was this the Fishing Tree?

If so, had Troy found it too?

There were no holes in the ground that I could see, though as I stepped back to take a wider look, something about an uneven patch of dirt caught my eye. Bending over and peering closely, I thought what I was seeing looked like a shallow hole that had recently been dug but then filled back in.

Grabbing a stick from the ground, I poked at the dirt, trying to see if it really was loose. Almost as if I had popped the top off of a lid, a clump of brown dirt flipped away, revealing something altogether different under-neath.

Inside the hole was a mixture of a little dirt with a whole lot of white powder.

Within half an hour this part of the grove had been cordoned off, with the key investigators from the various branches of law enforcement among the few who were allowed to venture inside. I tried to watch and listen for a while, but everything seemed to take so long, and it felt as though I had been watching and waiting around for things all day.

Right now, I needed to *do*.

I turned and walked away, weaving through the cluster of technicians who were chattering about this latest find.

I heard them spouting all sorts of theories about the white powder, the most logical being that it had been put there for the treatment of moles. Why else would someone dig a hole in the ground and fill it up with a toxic substance that way? Soon we would know more about what the substance was, at least, and I heard someone say that a special expert was being brought in to consult.

As though there weren't enough experts around here already?

Tired of the lot of them and eager for a workout, I was thrilled to see when I got to the shed behind the B and B that someone had picked up the mess that had been made earlier by the cops. Not only that, I realized, but the punching bag had been hung from the hook, as if someone had known that's what I wanted.

Mike. It had to be. He must have radioed one of his people to come over here and get it set up for me.

Feeling flattered (at his attention), nervous (that his interest in me was more than professional), and guilty (that I might just be interested in him too), I decided to take out all of my emotions on the bag itself.

After safely putting aside my gun and rolling up the bottoms of my pant legs, I started right in, first by bending my knees and balancing on the balls of my feet. Tucking in my elbows, I raised my hands to cheekbone level, tightened my abs, and began hopping lightly from foot to foot, shifting my weight back and forth as I rotated around the bag.

Careful not to lock my elbows, I waited another moment and then suddenly stepped forward on my left foot and shot out a quick jab into the bag, followed by an uppercut with my right. Gaining a little more confidence with each thrust, I followed with five more jab/uppercut combos in a row, exploding my fist out each time as I did, rotating my shoulders, driving the punch for the jab and then quickly snapping back with my left and whipping upward with my right, using the force of my hip to drive the uppercut. Again, bam, *pow*. And again, bam, *pow*.

Soon, sweat was trickling down my back and I was lost in the focus and energy of the workout. This bag was old and limp, and my hands had no protection at all, but I didn't care. At the moment, I felt brave and powerful, my scars pulsating for all the world like Superman's blazing red "S."

I had just switched to a right cross when something suddenly moved into my peripheral vision. Spotting a blur of black from the corner of my eye, I reacted without thinking, suddenly twisting to deliver the hardest right cross I knew how to give, thrusting the force of my hip and shoulder into the punch that swung directly at whatever had loomed into view. The punch connected and sent my victim sprawling.

Pulling back, I kept both hands up in a defense position, looking down to see that I had taken out not a beast or a creature but a man.

And older man.

An older, Amish man.

Horrified, I apologized profusely. He was rubbing his cheek where I had connected just below his eye, and already the skin was bright red and rising into a swollen lump. My hand was killing me, so I could only imagine how his cheek was feeling.

Assisting him into a sitting position, I apologized again and again, collecting his hat from where it had landed in the grass and dusting off the black felt before handing it back to him. The man was silent the whole time I tried to explain, probably still reeling from the shock of coming around a corner only to be decked by a raving lunatic who had mistaken him for a wild beast.

When he was ready to get to his feet, I insisted on helping him up and steadying him until I was sure he was okay. When he finally spoke, it was to explain that he had come here at the request of the police and had been looking for Detective Mike Wiessbaum.

"Someone said he was out this way, so when I heard the noise I thought maybe I would find him here."

I explained that Mike was in the grove and that I would deliver him there myself, though not until we had put some ice on the lump that had already doubled in size and was turning into a fairly significant shiner. Picking up my fanny pack holster and quietly strapping it on, I could only hope he didn't realize it held a gun.

Walking together to the B and B, I introduced myself and explained that I was the owner and the granddaughter of the man who had once lived here, Abe Collins.

"*Jah*, I knew Abe well," the man said, removing his hat as we stepped inside and holding it in his hands.

He remained in the main room while I went on into the kitchen. Digging through the cabinets until I found some plastic bags, I triple-bagged some ice from the freezer and rolled the whole thing up in some paper towels.

"Here you go," I said, coming out and handing it to him, wincing as I watched him touch it to his face. "You might want to get a look in the mirror," I added, pointing to the one that was mounted on the wall over the fireplace. "I just can't say enough how sorry I am."

He did as I suggested, looking up at his own image with wide eyes as he placed the ice bag more fully against his cheek, just above the line of his beard.

"I see you favoring your hand. You might make one of these for yourself as well."

"Good idea."

Once I had done that, the two of us headed out to the grove together, both icing our injuries and chatting as we went. I learned that his name was Jeremy and that he worked over at Lantz Farms in Quarryville.

"I've always loved that place," I said, adding that as kids we would gladly tag along whenever an adult needed to go there. As a child, I had been fascinated with their vast collection of Amish-built swing sets and playhouses, but as I grew older I spent more time in the floral shop instead, admiring the magnificent creations in the refrigerated flower cases.

As Jeremy and I walked, we passed several clusters of officers and other personnel, and though we received some strange looks with our injuries and ice bags, no one asked what had happened. When we came near the group in the grove, I apologized one last time to Jeremy, promising it wouldn't ever happen again as long as he didn't pop out of nowhere and startle me so, especially when I was already so jumpy. He said not to worry, and that he knew now to keep a wide berth from the feminine young lady with the very manly right cross.

Unable to keep from grinning at the compliment, I managed to catch Mike's eye from where we stood at the perimeter of the scene, and he broke away from what he was doing to come toward us now. Taking in the sight of Jeremy's eye, my knuckles, and both of our ice packs, he simply shook his head and said, "I don't even wanna know."

As my new friend was now safely delivered into the arms of the law, I stepped out of the way as Mike led Jeremy forward and began introducing him to some of the others as "the expert I was telling you about, Jeremy Lantz."

Jeremy *Lantz*? I knew that was a common surname around here, but I had a feeling he didn't just "work at" Lantz Farms but instead was the owner. How very Amish of him to have been so modest. I was just glad I had said only good things about the place.

Catching snippets of the conversation that was happening around the dolphin marker, I realized that Jeremy Lantz of Lantz Farms had been called in as an expert on pesticides. Careful not to touch anything, he knelt beside the powder-filled hole, took a good look, and began to speak." Seeing how the others listened and made notes as the man talked, I felt an odd satisfaction at how they so naturally and immediately deferred to his knowledge. Because formal schooling for the Amish ended after the eighth grade, I knew that some people thought they were backward and unintelligent. But Jeremy Lantz was living proof that they were nothing of the sort, and that for most Amish their learning began far sooner than grade school—and continued on for the rest of their lives.

Standing there, watching and listening, I assumed Jeremy would explain the method behind this powder-filled hole. Instead, he seemed as puzzled by this sight as everyone else.

Thinking about it myself, a very disturbing question suddenly popped into my mind. What if my grandfather had dug that hole and filled it with a toxic substance not to treat moles or termites or any other garden pest, but instead to serve as a deterrent to whoever might come looking for his hidden cache of diamonds?

Technically, not to mention posthumously, that would make Grandpa Abe a murderer.

TWENTY-THREE

My pocket buzzed several times while I was standing there trying to listen, so finally I broke away to see who was trying to get in touch with me. I wanted to dump my half-melted ice pack first, but with no trash can around I ended up pouring its contents onto the ground and tucking the leftover plastic bag in my pocket.

When I looked at the screen I saw that I had two texts, one from Liz and one from my father. I checked his first, relieved to learn that he had lined up a temporary replacement for Nina through the same agency that had cared for Abe when he broke his hip years ago.

Next, I switched over to Liz's message, which said: *Great tip! I have been able to confirm investigation is almost definitely mob related. Nothing beyond that for right now, but I have some feelers out and will keep you posted.*

I tried not to think about the darker side of the confirmation. On the one hand, any news was better than being completely in the dark. On the other hand, now that I knew "almost definitely" that I had been linked in some way with organized crime, I had entered a whole new playing field. Somehow, a big black beast breathing flashes of fire was a preferable danger to some nameless, faceless monster with a gun and a directive to kill. Whether Troy's death had been a Mafia hit or not, I wouldn't sleep soundly until this investigation was completely over, all truths had come to light, and my name had been cleared. Even then, I could only hope I wouldn't end up on someone's bad side. I had seen enough gangster movies to know how that would turn out.

Trying to get those images out of my mind, I texted back a simple thanks to Liz.

"Do your thumbs ever get tired?"

I looked up to see my cousin Liesl coming toward me, grinning.

"Not as tired as my voice would get if I had to do all of this through phone calls instead," I replied, also smiling, as I pressed "Send."

Liesl stepped closer, surveying the busy scene.

"So what is going on now? I was just heading home to help with supper, and I saw all the commotion." She gave a small wave to Jeremy, who was deep in conversation but nodded politely in return.

"A few new developments," I said, offering to walk her the rest of the way home and bring her up to speed on the way. I didn't add that I was worried about her. I would feel much more comfortable with my MK40 and escorting her than I would at watching her walk away by herself, unarmed and alone. To my experience, the Amish often weren't as tuned in to personal safety as others were, though whether that was because of their "God's will be done" mentality, or the fact that they were such a non-litigious group, or something else entirely, I wasn't sure.

Breaking away from the crowd in the grove, Liesl and I cut across the path along the edges of the beech trees behind the German Gate, up the rise of land beyond that, and then down into the shallow gully that delineated her property line. As we walked, I explained about the pesticide in the barn and the powder in the hole. I didn't bring up anything about Emory's arrest record—no reason to spook her too, especially given how much time she had been spending with his care—but I did bring up the diamond angle, wondering if perhaps their side of the family knew anything about that. She didn't think so but promised to ask some of the older relatives if they had ever heard of Abe having had some diamonds.

We reached the top of the next rise at the edge of their pasture, and as always the site of the vista in front of me took my breath away: the patchwork fields, the gleaming white structure of the rambling old farmhouse, the cows grazing beyond the fence. While we continued to walk toward the house, I told Liesl I had a few questions I wondered if she could answer. She nodded, glancing at me curiously.

"It's about the B and B. First of all, what can you tell me about the amount of traffic that goes in and out of there? I'm sure you don't watch that closely, but it would be helpful if you could make a guess how often it seems full or empty. Also, have you ever noticed anything special or unusual about the people who stay there?"

"I am sorry, Sienna, but I have never seen anyone stay there other than Floyd," she replied. "Oh, and Troy. He would come every once in a while. But otherwise, no. No guests at all."

An entire bed-and-breakfast, tucked away in Lancaster County and making a profit, and only one customer once in a while? If not from guests, then where was all of the money coming from?

"How about the cleaning you do over there?" I pressed. "Can you tell if the rooms have been stayed in or not?"

"I do not do any cleaning there. Or least not much, anyway. Floyd calls me when he needs me, but he has not needed me all that often."

"When was the last time you cleaned?"

"Two or three months ago, I think. He asked me to come and give the whole place a good once-over. Mostly, that meant dusting and vacuuming and mopping. You know, it wasn't like the toilets were filthy or the bathtubs needed scrubbing or anything. I cleaned them, of course, but mostly I just dealt with a few cobwebs and some dust, especially upstairs."

Though I had half expected to hear what she was now telling me, her words still punched me in the solar plexus, leaving me winded and unsteady.

"What about the sales in our gift shop?" I asked weakly, afraid now to hear the answer. "Have you sold a lot of quilts and toys and things through there?"

Now she was the one to look concerned.

"No, not at all. You and Troy placed that one big order in the beginning, of course, but there have been no orders since."

I ran a hand through my hair, suddenly exhausted and weighed down by the endless series of questions that continued to hammer me, the kinds of questions that had no easy or obvious answers.

"Didn't all that seem strange to you, Liesl? A bed-and-breakfast with no guests? A gift shop that doesn't stock gifts?"

She shrugged. "I was disappointed about the gift shop sales, and I did wonder how you could afford to keep the place open without any guests, but I did not think it was any of my business."

She and I walked along in silence until I said, "I made a big mistake here, Liesl. I was busy with my job in Philadelphia and didn't pay attention to this place. I trusted Floyd—and Troy—and now I'm in a mess."

"I am sorry, Sienna. I know how hard you worked on the place and how hopeful you were about it as a business," she said, no doubt assuming that my "mess" was merely financial.

If only I had been that lucky! Even bankruptcy would have been preferable to what I had now: an inn with no guests but plenty of income, ties to organized crime, and the government breathing down my neck. I wanted to defend myself somehow, to say that beyond negligence and general naïveté, I hadn't done anything wrong. Liesl didn't seem to have passed any sort of judgment on me, but I wanted her to know that if things took a turn for the worse and I ended up being charged by the attorney general for some nefarious deed, that I wasn't a criminal. My only crime was one of neglect.

But in the end I didn't say anything else about it. Instead, I simply asked her to keep me in prayer and then changed the subject, inquiring about the kids. The rest of the way to the house, I learned all about Daniel's troubles with penmanship—or, as she said, "penning"—in school, Jenny losing her first baby tooth, little Annie's first words, and more. It always amazed me that though Liesl and I were about the same age, she had married at nineteen, had begun having children soon after, and hadn't stopped yet. Currently, she and Jonah had five kids ranging in age from one to nine. I couldn't imagine a more horrifying prospect, but parenthood suited her very well.

"And you and Jonah? The two of you are happy?"

She looked at me strangely before answering that yes, they were fine, and why did I ask?

"I guess because I have enough trouble making a relationship work with just two of us. I can't fathom trying to do it with half a basketball team."

Liesl laughed melodically, saying it wasn't always easy with little ones underfoot, but they managed to do okay.

She and Jonah had always seemed to be happily married, and I wanted to ask her about that now in order to learn what their secret was. But we lived in such different worlds that I had a feeling that, even if she could articulate it, whatever it was could never translate to my relationship with Heath—or with anyone else, for that matter.

"Someday I hope to have a marriage like that. Like yours. Like my parents'," I said instead.

"*Jah,* I wish that for you too. But it will take the right person, especially because you are so much like me."

I smiled, knowing exactly what she meant. Our worlds couldn't be more different, but our personalities were very much the same.

"I see it like this," she added, eyes twinkling, lowering her voice. "Jonah is the string to my kite."

"The what?"

"You know me, Sienna. I am the type of person who is full of ideas and plans and enthusiasm, flitting around back and forth, all too often in a frenzy."

This Amish gal with her steady, peaceful life didn't know from frenzy, but I held my tongue, supposing it was all relative.

"I may be a kite," she continued, "but that is okay because my husband is a string. With him, I can still fly. But this way I can fly without completely flying away."

I was speechless for a moment, amazed that with that simple analogy I understood what she was saying.

We reached the clothesline, and Liesl paused, lifting up her hands to feel along the seams of the first few items hanging there. As with most of the Amish homes in this area, their clothesline was mounted at an upward angle so that she could easily stand at one end to hang the clothes, but as she fed the line through the pulley, they would be swept much higher off of the ground at the other end, away from the dust and dirt that was kicked up by the animals and farm implements.

"From what I hear, you have been seeing someone. A doctor, I believe?"

I smiled at the thought of the old familiar Amish grapevine.

"Yes. His name is Heath Davis. We met in January and have been dating since."

"And you met how?"

I explained that Heath had been working in the emergency room one night when my dad had had to bring in my mom. A rash had broken out all over her body, and they were afraid it was a side effect of her chemo drug.

Dad had called me in the city that night and told me I should come too, that it was important. Fearing the worst, I flew straight from the office, where I had been working late, to the hospital in Bryn Mawr. It wasn't until I arrived there that I learned my mother was absolutely fine, and that the rash had come from a reaction to the generic laundry detergent my father had recently bought and started using. The "important" reason I had been summoned was that they wanted me to meet her nice young doctor, a handsome and intelligent man who just happened to be a Christian *and* single *and* "exactly the guy" for me. Mortified, I was screaming at them on the inside even as I forced a polite smile and shook the good doctor's hand and accepted his invitation to go upstairs to the cafeteria for some coffee. By the end of that single encounter, I had stopped plotting ways to get even with my parents and had begun hoping Heath would call to ask me out on a real date. Which he did before I even got back home that night. We had been seeing each other exclusively ever since.

Liesl finished her inspection of the drying clothes, saying that they needed another hour or two yet, and we continued on past a lush vegetable garden toward the house.

"I hear that rain may be coming our way. Cooler air too," I said, hoping to move the subject away from my love life.

"So will you marry this doctor, do you think?" she asked, not to be deterred.

I hesitated, not sure how to reply. Heath had broached the topic of marriage several times, but each time I told him we hadn't yet been dating long enough to have that sort of discussion yet. The truth was, I wasn't sure if the timing had anything to do with my reluctance to discuss it or not. Heath could be the string to my kite, I had no doubt about that, but in our case I didn't necessarily see that as a blessing.

Sometimes, what I most wanted wasn't a string at all but another kite, flying wildly alongside mine, the two of us soaring together as high as we both could go.

TWENTY-FOUR

"I don't know if Heath and I will end up getting married or not. Ask me again in a year. Right now it's too soon to tell."

Liesl studied my face, and I knew what she wanted to say. I wasn't getting any younger, my biological clock was ticking, I would never know any blessing greater than that of a loving husband and children. I felt sure she was right on all three counts, but I would rather stay single forever than decide too quickly and regret it for the rest of my life.

"Well, I hope we have the chance to meet him soon," she said finally.

"He'll be here this weekend," I replied. "So now that I think about it, you might want to make sure the coast is clear before you...well, you know..."

She paused, one hand on the doorknob.

"Before I what?"

I shrugged.

"Before you go running around the woods in a nightgown with your hair down."

She squealed, swatting me with her hand as both of us laughed.

As we opened the door of her home and stepped inside, we were greeted by Liesl's mother-in-law, my cousin Lucy, not to mention the most incredibly delicious smell that had reached my senses in a long time.

"Lucy! Am I smelling what I think I'm smelling?" I gasped, thinking of the delectable casserole she always served with pitchers of homemade chicken gravy.

"*Jah*. As soon as they said Sienna was in town, I went outside to pick some celery for the filsa. I will send Jonah over with it later." The older woman enveloped me in a hug, smelling like sage and other spices, her embrace a welcome comfort to my weary soul. "How are you, sweetheart? I am so sorry for all the trouble you are having over at Harmony Grove."

I didn't want to talk about it, so I thanked her for her concern and immediately asked about her health, knowing that cousin Lucy could go a good hour on her gallstones alone. Launching into the tale of her latest myriad of problems and treatments, she turned back toward the counter where she had been kneading some dough. As she did, Liesl gave me a wink before interrupting to ask about the children.

"Annie is napping, and Jenny and Nellie are downstairs scrubbing the baseboards."

"I am so sorry you have had to keep them inside all day," Liesl said as she removed her shoes near the door and tied on her apron. "Where is Jonah?"

"He went to pick up the boys from school. Until they know for sure about the wild animal, he does not want them walking home alone."

"Good idea," Liesl replied, though I had to wonder if the kids would be any safer in a horse-drawn buggy than on foot, should a wild beast actually materialize.

"Let me tell the little ones hello and then I will chop the carrots," Liesl said.

I was about to go with her when Lucy replied, "No rush. Sienna and I will catch up here while you do. She has not even heard about my sciatica yet."

Biting her lip to keep from laughing at my self-made situation, Liesl gave me a look and then disappeared down the basement stairs alone. Stuck in the kitchen for the time being, I offered to help, and soon Lucy had me at the sink as she tried to describe the levels of pain that shot down her legs at various points during the day.

I usually couldn't stand the tedium of washing dishes by hand, but today the warm water felt good on my sore knuckles. Taking my time, running a dishcloth around the inside of a mixing bowl, I wondered what Heath was going to say when he learned that I had been working out with the punching bag just one day after I had fallen and landed on my hands and knees. Neither he nor my surgeon approved of my exercise of choice, but I persisted regardless, convinced that my mental health was even more important than my physical health, and boxing was one of the most mentally healthful things I knew how to do. At least I had hired a trainer to come up with some accommodations that might prevent injury, not to mention to teach me the best ways to compensate for a weak left jab that wasn't likely ever to get any stronger than it already was.

With Lucy at the stove and me at the sink, strains of childish laughter occasionally filtering up the stairs, for a while it almost felt as if time was standing still. As Lucy went on about her ailments, I half tuned her out, thinking instead about my own situation, of how ironic it was that all of the chaos of last night and today had been happening out here in Lancaster County, one of the most bucolic and pastoral places in the world. I was always on guard for danger when I was in Philly, but never here. Here, I had always felt safe. Until now. I could only hope once this mess was behind me that I could learn to feel safe at Harmony Grove again.

"Towels for drying are in there," Lucy instructed me suddenly, pointing toward a cabinet door. I supposed that was her polite way of saying that I was moving a little *too* slowly. As she returned to the biscuits she was cutting from the dough and the tale she was telling, I rinsed and dried the bowl, set it on the counter, and moved on to the other items that were waiting to be washed.

Moving into the rhythm of washing, rinsing, and drying, I thought how quiet it was here, even with Lucy's nonstop monologue. Being around my Amish relatives always served to remind me how noisy my world had become back home, how stressful and busy I kept every moment of every day. I could appreciate the quiet now, but as a younger woman, as much as I loved my Coblentz relatives, I usually kept my visits here short, often finding the quiet tones and the slow pace almost excruciating. Any brain that was used to constant stimulation in the foreground and background would have had a hard time sitting at a kitchen table and shelling a pile of beans with nothing but soft, occasional conversation to help pass the time, not even music from a radio.

During the renovation, when I was spending more time with the relatives than I had in years, I had even done an experiment, privately taking note of how I was feeling and when. Over and over, the way it went was that at five minutes, I would finally stop listening for a radio or TV in the background. At fifteen minutes, even if the company was interesting and the conversation stimulating, I would find myself glancing at my phone wondering if e-mails had come in, discreetly checking for texts. At twenty-five minutes, I would wonder to myself how these people could possibly live like this. Weren't they bored out of their minds?

It usually took about an hour before my muscles would finally start to relax. By the two-hour mark, I would find a stillness I forgot I could even experience. To their credit, this kind of silence was intentional. As isolated as the Amish often seemed, it always surprised me how very aware they were of the impact noise could have on a life and the damage confusion and chaos could wreak on a soul.

Ultimately, beyond that hard-won stillness came the true goal: a oneness with God. Was it any wonder I always felt spiritually renewed when I spent time in Amish country? By turning down the noise of my life, I was able to hear those still, small whispers of a loving God, whispers that filled my heart and never failed to refresh my soul.

TWENTY-FIVE

The current stillness was interrupted, just as I was finishing the last dish, when two little bodies burst out at the top of the stairs calling my name. Liesl appeared behind them, explaining that she hadn't even told the girls I was here until they finished with the job they had been sent down to do. The noise of our greeting must have awakened the smallest one, because soon we heard a little cry bleating from the crib in the next room.

"Quit your *Brutzin*," Liesl called out to the baby as she went to get her up from her nap.

I let Jenny and Nellie lead me across the wide, open room to the couch in the sitting area. They were both talking at once, and though I was flattered that they seemed to remember me, they had obviously forgotten that I didn't speak Pennsylvania Dutch. As that was all they spoke, and they wouldn't learn English until they got to grade school, we had to communicate through hand gestures and facial expressions instead.

"Jenny is telling you about the new animals that her father has purchased for the farm," Lucy said as she checked the biscuits in the oven. "Says she named the big one Peanut."

"*Er isst aus meiner hand heraus*," Jenny added, and when I looked to Lucy she interpreted.

"He eats right out of her hands."

I was about to ask Lucy if these new animals were horses or cows—or maybe even goats—when the front door opened and Jonah and his two sons came inside. Now the whole family was here.

For the next few minutes, as Lucy manned the kitchen and Jonah worked to replace an empty propane tank in a floor lamp at her request, the children clustered around me on the couch and chatted softly with each other in Pennsylvania Dutch. Stephen, the oldest one at nine, was also the shyest of the bunch, but I noticed that even he stayed nearby, settling in a chair and listening to his siblings and finally interpreting some of their words into English for me. I asked him how school was going so far this year, and he was listing his favorite subjects when Jonah interrupted to say that as soon as he was finished with the lamp they would be heading outside to do chores.

"You must stay close to me, remember," Jonah added sternly, "and your little brother will need to remain inside this time."

Seeing the flash of disappointment on the younger boy's face, I suddenly felt guilty, as if their imprisonment was all my fault. I could only hope that the matter would be resolved soon.

Liesl finally emerged from the next room carrying a tiny bundle of adorableness, apologizing that it had taken so long but that the baby's hair had come loose in the crib and had needed to be combed out and rebraided.

Little Annie, still hung over from sleep, nestled on her mother's hip, clutching a soft pink blanket and blinking with wide blue eyes as she took in the scene. I hadn't seen her for almost a year, and I couldn't believe how much she had grown. I gave her a broad smile, and much to my delight, when Leisl stepped closer, Annie suddenly held out both arms and leaned her body down toward mine, despite the fact that she was far too young to remember me. Leisl said something to her in Pennsylvania Dutch and then bent down to transfer her.

Annie came to me easily, settling on my lap and leaning her head back against my shoulder as if she felt right at home. Despite all the confusion and torment of the past twenty-four hours, I allowed myself that moment simply to breathe in the smell of the little angel in my lap, listen to the cadence of the family chatting about their day, and watch the good-natured interplay over at the stove between Jonah and his mother as he snatched one of the biscuits she had just taken out of the oven.

As Annie grew more awake, she sat up straighter and engaged with the other kids. Eventually, she slipped from my lap onto the floor completely and toddled away, leaving her little blanket behind as she ran, laughing, to her father. Running my fingertips over the fabric's fuzzy softness, I wondered if I would ever have reason to own a blanket like this one, if I would ever have a little angel of my own. Suddenly, I was overwhelmed with sadness.

Even if Heath wasn't perfect in every way—even if he was cautious when I wanted him to be daring, deliberate when I yearned for spontaneity, and mature when I wished for his sillier side to come out and play—he was an incredibly good man, dedicated and loving and gentle and honest and everything else a woman could dream of in a husband. I had seen him with his nieces and nephews and knew he would be an excellent father, that he could give me children and companionship and devotion and security for the rest of our lives.

If only I could learn to love him the way he loved me.

The children moved away to sit at the kitchen table and enjoy an afternoon snack of homemade biscuits and honey. Lucy invited me to join them, but before I did I carefully folded the little blanket, unable to resist pressing it to my face and breathing in its precious baby smell. As I set it on the empty cushion beside me and then stood, I realized that Liesl had caught me. She was watching from across the room, and tears suddenly sprang into her eyes.

Terribly embarrassed, I was about to make some excuse and beat a hasty retreat when the door burst open and one of Jonah's workers came inside.

He blurted out something in Pennsylvania Dutch and in response Jonah passed his daughter over to his mother, grabbed his hat, and headed outside. Liesl spoke to her mother-in-law and started for the door as well. Some of the children tried to follow, but Liesl set them straight on that notion with a single look. Quickly, I told Lucy I would talk to her later, and then I followed Liesl, asking what was going on as I caught up with her and we strode quickly across the lawn, retracing the path we had taken not too long before. Jonah and his worker were walking even faster and were far ahead of us now.

"It is something about the new animals in the back cages," Liesl said. "The emus."

Emus? That must be the animals the children had been talking about.

"I don't know what's wrong," Liesl added. "But the police are all there, and they said they needed to speak with us right away."

TWENTY-SIX

"Since when did you have emus?" I asked as we continued to race across the field.

"Just since the spring," Liesl replied. "It is a new business venture for us."

She didn't elaborate, so I stayed quiet the rest of the way. As we neared the back of their property, not far from the grove, I saw that on the far side of an old outbuilding they had installed several huge wire pens, each one of them at least six feet high and twenty or thirty feet long. Sure enough, inside the pens I could see emus, tall, brown birds with beady eyes and spindly legs. Several technicians were also in there gathering soil samples.

I stood back from Liesl and Jonah as Mike explained to them what was going on. According to him, several important tests had now come back from the lab, tests that provided information to the authorities that they hadn't had before. Not only did the bear that had been caught and killed in Holtwood that morning have no detectible ties whatsoever with Troy or his injuries, but fecal flotation tests for debris found in the gash in Troy's leg had come back positive for "avian coccidiosis," which meant that his wound had been caused either by a bird or by some implement that had been contaminated by birds.

Birds?

In a way it was almost laughable, given Floyd's "big black creature" and the rumors of werewolves and all our fears of a wild, raging beast hiding somewhere out there in the woods, preparing to strike again. Instead, we were left scratching our heads and feeling kind of silly, trying to figure out how a bird or something bird related could possibly have inflicted such a massive wound. As I heard Charlie telling Rip, "It's like we were all waiting for Bigfoot to show up and in walked Tweety instead."

To make matters even more confounding, there were bird-related elements to all three of the properties that had direct access to the grove: Burl with his former chicken farm, Jonah with his emus, and Emory with his Dark-eyed Juncos and numerous other songbirds. Now samples were being collected at all three locations, samples that would be tested for coccidiosis. Of the three locations, the one that came out positive for the parasite found in the wound would be the one they would zero in on.

Working from the other end of things as well, now that evidence of avian coccidiosis had been detected inside Troy's cut, a second, far more specific test was being done, one that would identify the exact species of coccidiosis involved, whether galliform (chicken), ratite (emu), or passeriform (perching birds). My understanding was that these two sets of tests—the one that would determine which location had coccidiosis and the one that would determine which type of avian species the coccidiosis found in Troy had come from—could each take several days to complete. It would be a race to see which results would come in first, but either one should give enough information to narrow the scope of the investigation significantly.

In the meantime other evidence was still being sought, and almost everyone at the scene seemed to be theorizing about how to interpret this new information. When I heard that Troy's injury was bird related, my first thought was of a falcon or an eagle or some other fierce bird of prey. But the more I thought about it, the more I realized that even the fiercest of raptors couldn't injure a man to the extent that Troy had been injured. On the other hand, when given our current choice between chickens, emus, and songbirds, the word "fierce" didn't exactly come to mind either. I knew emus could kick, but I doubted they could inflict the kind of injury Troy had suffered.

Eventually, when I began to feel that I was more in the way than anything else, I told Jonah and Liesl that I was going to head back to the B and B, but for them to have someone call my cell if they needed me.

"Not to worry, cousin. God is with us," Liesl whispered, giving me a quick hug, her words far more confident than the expression on her face.

Walking toward the grove and through it to the other side, I spotted clusters of officials along the way. Many of their conversations sounded fascinating, and as I passed group after group, I listened to the different theories that were being proposed. One police officer told of a type of bird in Australia that could actually kill a man, an ostrich-sized creature called a cassowary that lived in the wild and ate small animals as a matter of course. Another talked about falcons' beaks, which he said were uniquely configured to cut through the spinal cords of their victims. I heard stories of angry seagulls killing house pets and aggressive geese putting people in the hospital. But when someone suggested that a hoard of angry woodpeckers could have descended upon Troy en masse and done that kind of damage as long as they were working together, I felt things had taken a turn for the ridiculous.

By the time I reached the B and B, I had learned that other, even more important scientific evidence had already come back as well. The white powder in the hole in the grove matched one of the containers that had been found in Emory's barn: a pesticide known as chlordane. Testing Troy's blood for that specific substance had confirmed that chlordane was indeed the toxin that had been instrumental in his death.

Sitting on a bench in the yard behind the pool area, surrounded by activity, I used my phone to go online and look up chlordane. I learned that it had been used widely in the United States from 1948 to 1983, but at that point had been banned by the EPA for all uses except termite control. That had lasted until 1988, when the EPA had banned chlordane altogether.

Apparently, the substance was a known carcinogen, but I wasn't interested in reading about the effects of long-term exposure. Instead, I googled "poisoned by chlordane," my search revealing that an acute exposure could cause, among other things, "blurred vision, confusion, staggering, convulsions, central nervous system depression, and death." Poor, poor Troy.

While digesting that information, I began to wonder if simply possessing a toxic substance that had been outlawed for more than twenty years would constitute some sort of crime in and of itself. If so, that would mean that Emory could be in big trouble because, technically, it had been found on his property. While I was still having trouble processing the news I had learned earlier about my uncle, this was a separate matter entirely, one that could cause problems for him despite the fact that he had nothing to do with it.

Wanting to know more, I scanned the people around me until I spotted Mike, but I could tell he was too busy to be interrupted. Instead, I noticed Georgia standing nearby and asked if we could talk. Moving away from the others, I expressed my concerns to her, saying that clearly the pesticide had been sitting in that barn for years, and that it had been put there long before that building and its contents had ever even come into Emory's hands.

"I mean, Emory shouldn't have to pay the price for the fact that his father didn't clean out an old storage closet before he died, should he? Please tell me he's not going to be arrested for this."

Taking me by the elbow, Georgia led me further away from the others and spoke just above a whisper.

"Honey, we wouldn't be out to hang something on your uncle that clearly wasn't his doing. Gosh, who doesn't have old cans of bug spray lying around? No, the bigger question isn't why the outlawed substance was in the barn in the first place, but how it got from there to those weird holes in the grove."

I blinked, wondering if I had heard her correctly.

"Holes? Plural?"

Glancing around and lowering her voice even further, Georgia confirmed that they had now located two more holes within a fifteen-foot radius of the one I had discovered, holes that had also been filled with chlordane and topped with dirt. Stranger still was that the Hazmat guys had discovered some unusual objects hidden within the white powder in all three holes.

"What kind of objects?" I asked, wondering if they had located the diamonds or even just a container that could have held diamonds at some point.

Georgia said that one hole had a bunch of old nails and screws mixed in, another had a rusty old jar lid, and the third held the bottom half of a broken trowel.

"That's weird," I said.

"I know."

I thought about Grandpa Abe and my earlier fear that he had created those pockets of pesticide as protection for the diamonds. I shared my theory with Georgia now, but before I had even finished she was shaking her head back and forth.

"No, babe, you don't have to worry about that. Grandpa didn't have anything to do with this. These holes were dug recently. The Hazmat guys said probably within the last few days, but certainly since the last time it rained. They said it was fortunate we found them when we did, because rain would have dissolved the powder and caused some serious problems. Even as old as it is, that stuff is still real toxic, and it would have made one heck of a poison mud stew."

Looking out toward the grove, I tried to picture what she was saying. Like a minefield, it was almost as if those pockets of powder had been put there as traps, waiting to catch someone when they least expected it. Rain would have eventually washed the powder away, but in the meantime would only have served to exacerbate the problem.

Georgia and I were interrupted when a call came through that she was needed at Burl Newton's place right away. Wanting to see what was happening, I offered to show her the nearest path, a shortcut that would lead from where we were standing in my backyard through the thick brush to the Newtons' chicken farm. We walked quickly, moving single file where the brush was thick, and emerged directly behind the Newtons' house. From there, we turned left and cut across the scruffy backyard toward the cluster of officers who seemed to have gathered around one of the old henhouses.

Charlie was there, and when he spotted us walking toward him, he grinned, saying that it looked as though we had finally hit pay dirt.

Apparently, one of the technicians who had been gathering fecal samples to test for coccidiosis had stumbled across an old trunk hidden underneath some raised nesting boxes. Inside of the truck was an entire collection of cockfighting paraphernalia. Whether that equipment had played a part in Troy's injury or not, even possessing that stuff was against the law. By the time we arrived, Burl Newton was already in handcuffs and being led toward a police car, though he wasn't going quietly.

204 MINDY STARNS CLARK

"If I'da known that stuff was hid inside there, why would I have given you permission to open up that trunk in the first place?" he was demanding. "I'm tellin' you, that stuff belonged to my daddy, not me! I've never even seen it before!"

The man sounded desperate, and though the thought of cockfighting turned my stomach, I couldn't help but feel sorry for him at the moment. If he was telling the truth, then his situation now was similar to Emory's, with both men in the position of having to pay the price for old things left behind by their fathers, illegal things that until now had gone unnoticed by the sons or the law.

Burl had always come across to me as a shifty and secretive man, one who tended to made me feel uncomfortable for no real reason. But after our conversation earlier today and learning about his kindnesses toward Emory both now and in the past, I was more inclined to give him the benefit of the doubt in this situation. As I watched him being forced into the back of the police car and driven away, I offered up a little prayer on his behalf, asking that above all else God would help each person involved with this investigation find the truth behind every question, every confusing element, and every lie.

As Georgia stepped in to handle the paperwork involved with this new find, I watched and listened as a technician rattled off a quick description of some of the items inside: clippers and tools, syringes and medicine, scales, chains and leashes, knives, electrical tape, and more.

"Wait a minute, what do we have here?" the tech said, carefully pulling from the trunk with his gloved hand a curved, jagged blade about three inches long. It was shaped like a scythe, and I couldn't help but think that it looked like a miniature version of the tool that the grim reaper was always pictured carrying in his hands.

One of the officials in the crowd explained that in cockfighting, blades like that were actually taped to the gamecocks' ankles, pointing back and upwards, like spurs on a pair of cowboy boots.

"When roosters fight, they kick, and those blades do a lot of damage," he said.

"Yeah, they don't call it a blood sport for nothing," another added, looking around at each of us in turn. When his eyes met mine, he seemed startled, his head jerking slightly back, his eyes widening for an instant and then darting suspiciously away. Immediately, he whispered something to the man next to him, and then they both looked straight at me, their expressions a mixture of what looked like incredulity and anger.

I didn't know what this was about, but given that they were both some sort of government officials, I had the sudden, sickening feeling that I had just come face-to-face with two of the people who had been investigating me.

TWENTY-SEVEN

Almost immediately after spotting me, the two men turned away and strode quickly toward a cluster of cars parked near the house. Wanting to know who they were and what was going on, I thought about going after them and demanding an explanation. But then I hesitated, thinking that the longer this investigation of theirs remained hush-hush and in the background, the longer I was still free to move around and remain privy to all that was going on. Thanks to my lawyer's inquiries, the AG's office knew that I knew they were investigating me, and yet nothing official had happened yet, no interrogation or notification or anything. For some reason they had thus far chosen to remain silent. Because of that, I realized confronting them now could very well make matters worse for me, not better.

Instead, I turned my attention to Rip and Charlie, who were conversing about the case nearby.

"I'm thinking the blade in the trunk there is gonna test positive for that cock-a-doodle-osis stuff," Charlie said. "Even better if it has Burl's fingerprints on it and the vic's blood as well. 'Cause then it would be case closed, and we'd have Burl Newton not just for possession of cockfighting paraphernalia but also for the murder of Troy Griffin."

"Wouldn't be a sure thing, Charlie. Don't forget, Griffin died of drowning possibly caused by the poison, not from the cut in his leg," Rip said, giving me a wink and a smile when he realized I was there and listening in on their conversation. "Whoever cut him and whoever poisoned him could be two different people."

"Cut, poison, same difference, sort of," Charlie replied. "At least some good physical evidence could link Burl to the scene of the crime. Then it would all be downhill from there."

We all watched as one of the technicians backed up a van from the gravel driveway and toward us across the grass between the chicken coops.

I asked both men if Burl had an alibi for yesterday afternoon and evening.

"Well, yeah, sort of," Charlie replied, explaining that Burl had walked to a neighbor's house around 5:00 for a barbecue and had stayed until police showed up last night around 11:00, when they were notifying everyone along the street about a possible wild animal on the loose.

"Were those times verified by the neighbor?" I asked.

"From what I understand, there were about six or seven guys there, and they'd already gone through a couple cases of beer by the time our men arrived. Every one of those guys gave a time they had come, verified by the homeowner and each other, but I wouldn't exactly count their information as a hundred percent reliable. Most of 'em were drunk as skunks."

Recalling the timetable Mike had constructed, I knew the cut in Troy's leg had happened at some point after he hung up on me at 5:30 and before he died, which was 6:10 at the earliest and 6:30 at the latest. If Burl was telling the truth, he couldn't have been around to inflict the wound, though of course the timing regarding the poison left a lot more leeway than that.

"Almost there," Georgia said loudly, directing the van as it inched closer to the heavy trunk.

I moved out of the way as I thought about Charlie's comments. Had Burl killed Troy? The two men knew each other, having met during the renovation. But that had made them barely more than acquaintances, certainly not friends—or enemies, for that matter. If Burl had killed Troy, then why? I decided to ask Charlie if he had a theory for a motive to go along with his belief in Burl as the murderer.

"Look around you. Poverty's a great motivator—especially if ol' Troy was out there diamond hunting, like you said. I bet he dug up those diamonds, and Burl saw the whole thing and just snapped. Wanted that ice for himself and killed to get it."

"Will you guys be searching Burl's house to look for diamonds?" I asked, wondering if his theory could possibly be correct.

"Not right away. Probably not till we get some evidence back from the lab that will justify a warrant."

Could Burl have killed from greed? Certainly, he was poor, much poorer than I had realized if his home and property were any indication. Every building, including the house, was sagging and peeling and so ramshackle that it looked as if the next strong wind would take the whole place down. That was odd, considering that Burl was a handyman and had the skills to fix things up. The only explanation for this state of disrepair was that he couldn't afford the materials he needed to get the job done.

Then again, maybe Burl was just lazy. Goodness knows, he was an incredibly slow worker, so maybe he just hadn't gotten around yet to all of the repairs that needed doing. During the renovation of the B and B, Burl had come over to ask us for work several times, but we were already using a top-notch team of Amish carpenters and didn't need him. Still he persisted, so just to be nice my father had finally hired him to do a single task, one that should have taken a day at most. Four days later, Burl finally finished. All my dad could say to me once Burl was paid and gone was thank goodness we had agreed on a rate that was by the job, not the hour. Now that I saw how very poor the man was, my mind was flipping back and forth between feeling bad for not using him more back then, even if he was slow, and being glad we hadn't, just in case he was a murderer.

"Well, whatever you say, my money's on the Amish farmer next door," Rip told us, obviously forgetting that the Amish farmer next door was my cousin.

"Careful, Rip," I said evenly. "That's my family you're talking about."

He didn't seem embarassed but instead held up both hands and said, "Sorry, but one of his emus has been having stomach problems, which according to the tech wouldn't be unusual if it was infected with that particular parasite."

"So you'd base a murder charge on a case of the runs?" Charlie teased.

"Not murder," Rip countered, "more like an accident, at least regarding the cut, if not the poison. This morning some of the boys found an animal print in a muddy spot along the creek in the grove, one that could be a match for the bigger emu. If it is, that would mean the animal had been loose out there last night and could have attacked the victim."

"And maybe breathe fire too," Charlie added, eyes rolling as the three of us watched the trunk get loaded into the van.

"Could an emu inflict that kind of damage?" I asked Rip, feeling anxious for my cousins. Jonah and Liesl couldn't be held responsible if Troy had unknowingly unlatched their emu cage and set one of the large birds free and then got hurt by it, could they?

Worse, officials didn't actually suspect Jonah of some sort of foul play, did they?

"Well, that's what they've been talking about over there for so long. According to some expert the game commission brought in, emus are pretty docile, but they will kick if they're cornered."

"And that kick could gouge a grown man's thigh to the bone?" I asked incredulously.

Rip shrugged.

"It isn't likely, they said. Some bruising, yeah, that's to be expected. But that cut has got them pretty perplexed."

He went on to explain that emus have three toes with the middle one prominent, the nails textured in a way that would be consistent with the marking of the wound. In fact, he said, the medical examiner herself was the strongest proponent for the emu-did-it theory. Listening to the two men now, I decided I wasn't going to form any opinion at all but instead would wait to see what might develop next. As Mike had said just last night, it would all come down to the medical. Right now, that involved a parasitic infection specific to birds, and as soon as the results were in we would be closer to many of the answers we sought. ·

For now, I wanted to get back over to Jonah and Liesl's to make sure they were okay. Rip and Charlie decided to come too, having grown bored once the van had driven away with the trunk safely inside. Georgia joined us as well, and together the four of us walked toward a different cut-through than she and I had taken before, one at the very opposite end of Burl's property. That path would allow us to bypass the grove completely and emerge at the back corner of my cousins' farm.

Moving along the tree line to the point where the cut-through began, we passed a widely spaced row of small, A-frame-shaped structures behind one of the Newtons' old chicken coops. Two technicians were working in and around the old rusty metal structures, no doubt collecting samples in their search for the source of the coccidiosis.

"What's all this? Dog houses?" Georgia asked.

"Gamecock houses," Charlie replied. "See the pegs in the ground in front of each one? The roosters get a leash hooked from their ankle to that peg, with just enough play to let them move around but not quite enough to reach the other roosters."

"Otherwise, they might kill each other," Rip added as we reached the entrance to the narrow path and started down it single file.

I shuddered, remembering the roosters who used to make so much noise back here. Unlike in movies and television, these roosters crowed at all hours of the day and night, regardless of the sunrise. We always knew they lived in those little "rooster huts," as we called them, but never in my wildest dreams had I suspected that they were gamecocks. Then again, as a child I doubt I would have even known what gamecocks were for.

"Do you guys know if Burl's father ever got in trouble with the law for cockfighting?" I asked, remembering Burl's denials as he had been led away in handcuffs, saying that the items in that trunk had belonged to his father and not to him.

"I dunno, but I'm sure Mike has checked that out by now," Rip said, reaching up to help with a low-hanging limb. "He likes tracking back people's histories good and thorough."

Not wanting to think about that, at least not in relation to myself, I asked Rip more about the emus as we continued onward. Soon we were getting a lesson in what he said the emu expert was calling "the cattle of the future." Apparently, emu meat was as tasty as steak but much lower in cholesterol, emu oil was used in the health and beauty industries, and emu hide could be turned into fine leather. For someone who wasn't afraid of hard work, emu farming could be a very profitable venture indeed.

By the time we got to the cages, I felt much more knowledgeable on the topic. Just one official was still hanging around and talking to Jonah, though from their conversation it didn't sound as though there had been any new developments beyond what Rip had already told us.

Spotting Liesl sitting on the ground not too far away, I left the others and headed straight there instead. As I drew closer, I could see the sadness and despair on her face. I didn't say a word but instead simply sat down next to her, putting an arm around her and pulling her close. She rested her head on my shoulder, and after a moment she began to cry.

Though I didn't join her in her tears at that moment, I knew exactly how she felt.

TWENTY-EIGHT

Liesl and I sat there together for a while as the sun moved below the horizon and streaks of orange slowly disappeared from the purple sky. As darkness descended and the moist evening air grew cooler, all around us began a twinkle of fireflies. There were just a few at first, then dozens, then what soon seemed like hundreds or even thousands. As far as the eye could see, tiny yellow-white lights sparkled, flickered, and glimmered like twinkle lights on Christmas Eve. Looking out at the tiny points of light that hovered amid the trees of the grove, I couldn't imagine that any place in the world could be more beautiful than this.

Liesl didn't even seem to notice. Instead, she sat up straight, wiped her eyes, and apologized for her tears.

"Why are you apologizing? This situation is totally cry-worthy."

"Because God is in control. His hand is over all of this, Sienna. If I really believe that, there is no need to cry, not even if my husband is accused of wrongdoing."

"Has Jonah been formally accused of anything?"

"Not yet, but I am afraid..." Her voice trailed off as she shook her head, biting her lip to keep back more tears.

"Did he have anything to do with Troy's death?"

"No," she whispered.

"Then we have to trust that the truth will out. If it doesn't—"

"Whether it does or doesn't, I must wish for *God's* will to be done, not mine. Not my husband's. God's. At all times, in all things. It is that simple."

Her words reverberated there between us. Sitting side by side in the encroaching darkness, thinking about the choices she had made and the life she lived, I began to wonder if Liesl's faith ever wavered at all. Despite everything, deep in the night, had she ever woken up and found herself questioning the life she had chosen?

Whenever I compared Liesl's world to mine, I knew I could never live out my faith in the ways that she did, or at least not to such extremes. For her, being Christlike was an ever-present effort, one that began when she woke up in the morning and continued all day long. From clothing to transportation to technology and more, she lived a life of surrender, simplicity, and selflessness.

I, too, strove to be Christlike as much as possible, but I knew I missed the mark more often than not. Part of me was deeply remorseful about that, deeply repentant. Another part of me, however, rebelled against the very thought of it, against all of the rules that had been drummed into my brain since childhood.

Don't drink, don't smoke, don't have premarital sex, don't gamble, don't curse, don't, don't, don't.

Good little girl that I was, I had fallen in line with every one of those "don'ts"—but in the end my good behavior had earned me nothing. The nondrinking, nonsmoking, nonpartying virgin had very nearly been gang-raped. After that, it seemed to me that all bets were off. Given what I'd been through, why shouldn't I now be able to live my life the way I wanted to? What was so bad about wanting more—more money, more success, more safety? Didn't I deserve that? Didn't God want that for me?

Or were those the very things God was now calling me to surrender?

Glancing at my cousin, my heart aching with the need for answers that wouldn't come, I knew that this wasn't a path I needed to go down now. Instead, I reached into my pocket and pulled out my phone and clicked on my favorite Bible app. If I couldn't find answers for myself, I could certainly locate some biblical encouragement for my cousin. I typed in a few search phrases—birds, God's will, justice—finally landing on Psalm 106:3, which seemed to fit the moment.

"Here you go, from the Psalms," I said, holding up the screen to read the verse out loud. "'Blessed are they who maintain justice, who constantly do what is right.' That's you and Jonah, constantly doing what is right. God has your back, cousin."

Tentatively, Liesl reached out and took the phone from my hand.

"You have a Bible in this thing? That is not King James, is it?"

I grinned, reaching out to tap a button.

"Now it is."

"Look at that!"

Reaching out again, I tapped another button, this time changing the version from King James to the Luther Bible, which was in German.

"*Ach!*" she cried, nearly dropping the phone from surprise. Gripping it more tightly, she read the words of the verse aloud. "'*Wohl denen, die das Gebot halten und tun immerdar recht!*' Sienna, this is astonishing! Unbelievable!" She handed it back to me, shaking her head in wonder, saying she had no idea that a cell phone could do that. "Perhaps those things are not *all* bad."

Not wanting to get into a technology debate, I tucked the phone away and changed the subject.

"So what's the story with the emus, Liesl? I didn't even know about any of this. You said you have had them since spring?"

"*Jah*, once Jonah had to stop training racehorses. He needed something else to supplement our income, so he did some research and decided that emu farming would be a wise choice." She went on to say that it had been a great adventure for the whole family—at least until now.

As Jonah was primarily a farmer, I had forgotten that he trained racehorses on the side. It had always seemed an odd choice to me for a Christian to make, but then again I thought the same thing about all of the Amish tobacco farms in the area, not to mention the Amish vineyards that grew grapes for local wineries.

"What happened with the racehorses?" I asked, wondering if he had been convicted about the matter somehow and had decided to give it up.

"*Ach,* a big mess. It is not important now. Troy got Jonah in trouble with a horse's owner and with the men who had arranged for the training. They all decided to take their business elsewhere."

I looked at Liesl, my eyes wide. *Troy* had something to do with it? Since when were Troy and Jonah involved in any way, connected by anything other than me and my relationships with each of them?

"What do you mean?" I hissed, desperately hoping she hadn't mentioned this particular fact to the police. In matters of the law, the Amish could be very naive. With a few honest words, my cousin could have incriminated himself in some way, ending up with major problems that a little less honesty and a simple chat with a lawyer could have prevented.

Liesl looked at me, obviously startled by the tone of my voice.

"What is wrong?"

"You said Troy got Jonah in trouble. How? What happened?"

She shrugged.

"Troy got information from Jonah that he used in a sneaky way, to make money."

"Can you elaborate?" I asked, my stomach beginning to tighten into a knot. "But quietly, please," I added, looking up to see that Rip and Charlie had left but that Georgia and the official remained, both of them talking to Jonah.

"Well," Liesl whispered, "last winter Troy started coming over whenever he was at the inn, chatting with Jonah and watching him train the horses. Jonah thought Troy was simply being friendly, if perhaps a bit overly curious. Then one day we found out that Troy had had other motives for his visits. He was taking the information Jonah was giving him about the horses—both the ones currently in training and some that Jonah had trained previously—and he was using that information to place big bets on their races."

My mind reeled as she continued.

"One of Troy's wins was especially lucrative, thanks to a huge bet he placed on an unknown young filly Jonah had trained named Sweet Becky. I do not remember how it all happened exactly, but one of the horse's owners grew suspicious of Troy and his big win with this horse that was a bit offset in the front legs and had no pedigree and no real experience. Prior to that race, the only people who were aware of Sweet Becky's potential were her owners and trainers and handlers. So the owner began asking around, and that is how he learned that Troy and Jonah knew each other. Jonah was the leak that led to Troy's win."

"Didn't Jonah know that he should have kept information like that confidential?"

She shrugged again.

"Jonah knew not to be a *Blabbermaul,* but he also did not think it was necessarily a secret. Usually, this situation does not come up, you know? The track is more than a hundred miles away from here. It is not like he has the opportunity to talk about the horses' prospects with anyone who would care or be interested in betting. It never crossed Jonah's mind that Troy would take advantage of their friendship like that."

Trying to keep my voice low, I asked if that was when the horse training had come to an end.

"*Jah.* Sweet Becky's owner was very angry. He said 'Loose lips sink ships' or some such crazy phrase. And that was that. Not only did this man tell Jonah that he would not use his services again, we believe he put the word out so no one else would use him either. It was very sad."

"Poor Jonah."

"*Jah,* but he had to admit it had been his own fault. He should not have talked about the horse to anyone, not even someone he thought was a friend."

I took a deep breath and let it out slowly, fully aware that if not for me, Troy and Jonah would never have met, and my cousin wouldn't have ended up losing part of his livelihood.

"What happened between Jonah and Troy after that? Did they have words?"

"They had a very strong argument, *jah.* But what could be done? Jonah said his piece and Troy tried to make excuses, and in the end my husband and I were reminded that we are to be a peculiar people, set apart, not tossing around information with someone from outside the community. Now and then the Lord reminds us of that with hard lessons." Looking toward the emu cages and the three people who seemed to be wrapping things up and preparing to leave, she added, "Perhaps now, with this new turn of events, there are simply more lessons we need to learn."

We both stood, but before we went to join the others, I asked Liesl if they had told the police anything about the Jonah-Troy gambling connection. Much to my dismay, she nodded, saying they had spoken at length with Detective Weissbaum and several others and had given them the entire story.

I couldn't imagine what police must be thinking now, or how they might be planning to proceed, but I wanted to speak with Mike as soon as possible so that I could plead Jonah's case and vouch for his outstanding character. Of course, at this point, depending on whether Mike had learned about my own government investigation problems, my vouching for Jonah might not mean a whole lot.

Liesl introduced me to the man who had been at the cages, and it turned out that he wasn't any sort of law enforcement agent as I had thought, but was rather an emu expert the game commission had called in as a consult. His car was parked at Jonah and Liesl's house, as was Georgia's patrol car, so for my own safety and at her suggestion, I decided to walk to the house with all of them and let her give me a lift home rather than cut back through the grove by myself.

With that settled, Georgia reported in via radio and then whipped out her big police flashlight to lead the way. Crossing the field, we three women were mostly silent as the two men continued to chat about emus, both of them referring to things like "vestigial claws" and "aspergillosis." I could tell that the man was impressed with Jonah's knowledge of the big birds and didn't seem the least suspicious that there had been any foul play here—or fowl play, as the case may be.

When we reached the driveway, I was glad to see that Mike was there waiting for us—or, rather, waiting for me, judging by the expression on his face. After telling Jonah and Liesl goodbye, I stood there awkwardly, certain that the handsome detective had finally learned the truth about me. Mike spoke to Georgia for a moment, and then she turned and gave me a little wave as she and the expert headed to their cars, which were parked side by side further up the drive. Obviously, he had told her that he would be taking me home—or perhaps straight to jail, for all I knew.

A few minutes later we were in his car and pulling out onto the road. I was going to wait for him to break our silence, but when he drove past the driveway for Harmony Grove Bed & Breakfast without turning in, I felt my stomach lurch.

"Where are you taking me?"

He took his time answering, pausing first to reach into the console between us and pull out a small container.

"Nowhere," he replied, popping the container open with his thumb and shaking out a toothpick. "We need to talk away from the others. I thought it would be best if we just took a little ride and chatted in the privacy of the vehicle."

Toothpick clenched between his teeth, he snapped the lid back on and returned the container to the console before he continued.

"I just got reamed out by my superiors for letting a civilian have such complete access to what is still technically a crime scene. I'm afraid from here on out you're not allowed to wander around outside on your property. These people don't want you in the yard or the pool area or the grove, nor do they want you anywhere near Burl's property or Jonah's emus. Is that understood?"

"Yes," I said, my heart pounding. No doubt, the two men who'd spotted me at the chicken farm earlier were the instigators of this new restriction. Did that mean they had told Mike that I was under investigation? "Sounds like that about covers everything."

"Not everything, Sienna," he replied, chewing furiously on the toothpick. "Not even close."

Putting on his blinker, Mike made a right turn onto the road that would lead to Strasburg.

"Here's the deal," he said. "What started out as a simple investigation of a possible homicide has mushroomed into something far bigger. I have spent much of this day trying to figure out why representatives of various government agencies have been finding it necessary to involve themselves with my case. See, the EPA, I can understand. They heard we have a toxic substance in the ground, and they're nervous. The game commission we brought in ourselves to help with the wild animal issue. Given the poison and the coccidiosis found in the vic's wound, I can see why we were next joined by BAHDS, and some VFOs and AHIs of the PADLS. Once we found the cockfighting equipment, the USDA was understandably on the scene. After talking to Jonah, it was no big surprise to see a woman from the PSHRC. On top of all of that, I even get why the FBI finally showed up. Given what we know now about Troy Griffin's manner of death, there are elements of this case that could apply on a federal level."

I swallowed hard, a bit lost in all of this alphabet soup as he continued.

"But here's what I don't get. Out there today I had to accommodate several other kinds of federal agents, and in the meantime I also have calls coming in back at the station from the PDOR, the PDOB, and even the DOT! What do any of those places have to do with anything?"

Mike was obviously getting worked up, but instead of answering his question, I asked him to provide some clarification regarding the acronyms, saying that it was pretty hard to follow what he was telling me when I didn't understand what all of those initials meant. In response, he listed them out, counting off on his fingers:

BAHDS was the Bureau of Animal Health and Diagnostic Services.

PADLS was the Pennsylvania Animal Diagnostic Laboratory System.

VFOs were Veterinary Medical Field Officers.

AHIs were Domestic Animal Health Inspectors.

USDA was the U.S. Department of Agriculture.

PSHRC was the Pennsylvania State Horse Racing Commission.

Those all made sense to me too. Unfortunately, it was the next batch of clarifications that turned my stomach:

PDOR was the Pennsylvania Department of Revenue.

PDOB was the Pennsylvania Department of Banking.

DOT was the U.S. Department of the Treasury.

"Is that clear enough for you?"

"You said there were other kinds of federal agents there as well?" I pressed. "What other kinds?"

"ATF guys, for one," he said and then added, "that's the Bureau of Alcohol, Tobacco, Firearms, and Explosives, though why they showed up is anybody's guess. The only firearm involved was Floyd's gun, but since when do ATF guys pop up for a routine summary offense? The weapon was never even discharged at the scene."

"Who else?"

He turned right again, and I had a feeling he was simply going to drive in one big rectangle until we ended up back where we had begun.

"Well, here's the kicker, Sienna. The whole reason you and I are having this conversation is because of two agents who pitched a fit to my boss a little while ago. They were yelling about you being over at Burl Newton's place, hanging out with the cops and listening in and watching them gather evidence. I have been told to put a stop to all of that or else."

"What kind of agents were they? What federal agency?" I closed my eyes, waiting for him to say they were from the U.S. attorney general's office.

"What agency?" he echoed, chomping furiously. "I'll tell you what agency. They were from the Secret Service."

TWENTY-NINE

 My eyes flew open.
"Secret Service?"

He nodded.

"The United States Secret Service?" I repeated.

"Yeah. Two Secret Service agents observed you at the scene and said that from here on out if we didn't *contain* you, they would *detain* you."

"Detain me how? Like jail?"

"They didn't specify, but I'm sure that's what they meant."

"On what grounds? Why would the Secret Service have an interest in me? Aren't they the ones who protect the president?"

"One and the same. I had the distinct feeling they had come here because of you. Would you like to tell me what on earth you might have done to attract their attention? Did you send a threatening letter to the White House? Maybe date a known assassin? Take a bomb-making class from a terrorist?"

I shook my head, desperate to know if we would ever get to the bottom of this crazy, mixed-up mess.

"No, no, and no. Obviously, they don't suspect me of anything substantial, or they would have already done something about it."

Mike didn't reply, though if he chewed any harder on that toothpick he was going to imbed the wood into his gums. He seemed to be waiting for me to volunteer some information that would shed a little more light on things, but at the moment I was practically speechless. Before I spoke at all, I simply had to get a better handle on what this news about the Secret Service meant.

"Give me a minute," I managed to mumble as I pulled out my phone, went online, and googled "duties of the Secret Service." After clicking on several links, I found the information I was looking for, a full list of the areas over which the agency had jurisdiction. I knew there had to be more than just the protection of the president and his family and other high-ranking U.S. officials. Sure enough, according to their website the Secret Service was also in charge of financial crimes, including counterfeiting, forgery, fraud, money laundering, and more.

Financial crimes. That would explain the involvement of the Departments of Revenue and Banking and the Treasury today. It could also indicate the one element that had been verified by my lawyer, that somehow all this had to do with organized crime.

When I added everything up, what did it leave me with? Which of the financial crimes from the Secret Service list was the most likely possibility?

I thought of my inn.

My beautiful inn, where almost every transaction was done in cash.

My beautiful, elegant inn, where all of that cash added up to a nice profit.

My beautiful, elegant, profitable inn, which had no guests and no sales from the gift shop and no explanation whatsoever for all of that cash.

Scanning the list of crimes again, I thought about counterfeit, which was a possibility. But the one I kept going back to, the one that seemed most likely, was money laundering. Couldn't money laundering involve lots of cash being funneled through a business?

"Bear with me," I said to Mike, and then I texted Liz about this new development and asked if I could level with the detective. She replied immediately, insisting that I not talk unless she was present.

But things are escalating. I think Floyd has been using HGB&B for money laundering for the mob! I typed in return.

"Who are you texting over there?" Mike asked, glancing at the phone in my hand.

"A friend. We're tossing around some ideas."

Before he could reply, the phone began to vibrate in my hand.

"Liz?" I said, answering it.

"Are you with the detective right now?" she asked, her voice sounding all business.

"Yes."

"Can he hear me?"

"I don't think so."

"Okay. Here's how it is. I'll talk, you listen."

"No problem."

"All right. We're walking a very thin line here, Sienna. I know you're not in a position to tell me why you think Floyd has been laundering mob money through your bed-and-breakfast, but I'll take your word for it. My bigger concern is that you don't breathe one word of this to the police until I can be there with you and they can conduct a formal interview. Not a word."

I had known she was going to say that, but I wasn't too happy about it. Mike had been nothing but decent and kind to me—not to mention quite forthcoming. And in return I was going to withhold important information that might help him unravel his case. It wasn't fair, and it didn't feel right.

Still, I wasn't stupid. I knew everything I said to him might eventually be held against me in a court of law. When it came down to it, the only course of action I could take right now was the one that would most likely keep me out of jail.

"Are we clear on this, Sienna?" Liz's voice demanded through the line.

"Yes, but when do you see that happening? Soon?"

"What, me coming out there? I have court in the morning, but I can come out there tomorrow afternoon."

"Okay."

"I know this is hard. Are you all right?"

"Yeah. Just...you know."

"I know. Hang in there, baby. I'll see you tomorrow."

"Sounds good."

I disconnected the call, trying to decide what to say to Mike. He was obviously waiting for me to share the fruits of my conversation, but I had received my orders from Liz, and they were to keep my lips zipped.

"Well?"

"Well...I'm afraid there's nothing I can tell you," I said, thinking that technically that wasn't a lie. According to Liz, there was nothing I could tell him—at least not until she was with me.

Mike was quiet for a long moment, chewing thoughtfully on his toothpick.

"But you have some ideas about what's going on."

Turning my head away from him and looking out the side window, I replied, "Maybe." Turning back, I added, "But I also have a good lawyer who doesn't want me sharing half-baked theories with the police without her being present."

The silence that suddenly rose up between us was nearly deafening.

"Whoa," he finally whispered. "Did *not* see that coming."

"I'm sorry, Mike," I said softly. I felt like dirt, especially when he glanced at me and I could see the flash of betrayal in his eyes. "It's not like I have anything concrete. Just a theory about why all of those different agents are involved."

"A theory you're not willing to share."

"Not yet. But soon. I will, I promise. Tomorrow, in fact."

"Unbelievable."

He made the final right turn that would bring us back to the B and B. Leaning my head against the headrest, I looked out at the passing darkness and felt a sad sense of loss. Mike had already begun to feel like a friend, and now I had ruined our friendship. That much was obvious, from the silence that filled the car to his body language, which was shouting loud and clear.

We were nearly back to the B and B when he finally spoke again, but this time his voice was remote and coldly professional.

"If that's how you want to play this, Sienna, fine. Just so we're clear, like I said earlier, you are not to be outside at the B and B at all, other than on your driveway. That's it—no lawn, no grove, no pool area, nothing. If you want to visit your cousins, get in your car and drive over there, but do not cut across by foot. And absolutely, positively do not go anywhere near the home or property of Burl Newton. Is that understood?"

"Yes."

"Stay out of things and watch your step. Otherwise, you might find yourself behind bars, courtesy of the Secret Service."

"I understand. Thanks for letting me know."

He turned into the long driveway, and I realized that all of the cars that had been there earlier were now gone. Still, it was clear that someone was inside the B and B because I could see movement through the open front windows. I asked him if that was one of his men, but he said no, more than likely it was Floyd.

"Floyd? He's out of the hospital?"

Mike glanced at me as he came to a stop.

"The hospital released him this morning."

"Where's he been all day?" I asked, realizing that must have been why the hospital hadn't had him listed as a patient when I called.

"Down at the station."

"Down at the station? Why?"

"The firearm violation," Mike said, putting the car into park and turning it off. "Our people worked it out, but it took a while."

"You mean the gun he had last night? How was that a violation?"

Mike spoke, but his voice still sounded flat and cold.

"Unlawful possession, thanks to his criminal record. Though as I said earlier, it looks like it'll be treated as a summary offense."

He opened his door to get out, but I remained frozen in my seat, wondering if he had just said what I thought he said.

"Floyd has a criminal record," I repeated.

"Yes."

"As in prison? The manager of my inn has been in prison?"

"Yes. You didn't know that?"

Suddenly angry, I reached for the car door and whipped it open.

"No, I didn't know that!" I cried, climbing out and slamming the door. Remaining on the opposite side of the car, still chewing the toothpick, Mike stood there and watched me rant. "Here we go again! First Troy with his gambling and Emory with his past. And now Floyd? Is there anyone else I need to know about? Maybe Nina's parents are really drug runners? Jonah and Liesl are into human trafficking? Burl Newton has a history of dressing up like a clown and terrorizing preschools?" He did not smile. "Does every person involved here have some big, dark, law-breaking secret?"

As soon as those words were out of my mouth, I knew they were a mistake. Mike remained silent for a long moment, making his point. When he spoke, it was in a voice as cold as ice.

"You tell me, Sienna."

I took a step back, smoothed my hair, and tried to collect myself. He was right. Though I had done nothing wrong, I was certainly keeping my own share of secrets.

"Tomorrow," I whispered, feeling suddenly deflated. "I promise I'll tell you everything I know tomorrow."

There was an intensity to his expression that was nearly frightening. I knew that not only had I made him angry on a professional level, but that I had hurt him deeply in some personal way as well.

Perhaps the damage could be mended after the fact, once Liz came and I could talk. Right now, I had bigger issues to deal with—namely, an employee who was likely using my inn to launder money and, oh, by the way, never thought to mention that he was an ex-convict.

"Before I go in there and confront Floyd, at least let me know the nature of his crime. Was it violent? The man who runs my business isn't a murderer or something, is he?"

Mike studied my face for a moment before shaking his head.

"No. Strictly white collar."

"How much time did he serve?"

"Three years."

"Where? Some cushy white collar 'confinement facility'?"

"No, Rahwey."

I swallowed hard, my eyes wide.

"Floyd Underhill spent three years at Rahwey State Penitentiary? That's *huge*, Mike. That's hard core."

"Yep, sure is."

"An ex-con, who was at Rahwey no less, has had free rein over this place for two years? I trusted this man with my business here, implicitly."

He shrugged, hands out and palms up.

"What can I say? Maybe you should have checked his references."

He was still hurt, I understood that, but now his attitude was making me angry again.

"Floyd's big reference was Troy. I didn't think I needed any others. Obviously, I'm not a very good judge of character."

"Funny, I was just thinking the same thing about myself."

Our eyes met and held, his sparked with challenge, mine with fury. Did he really want to dwell on *us* right now? Good grief. There were far more important things going on at the moment.

"You have a lot of nerve, Detective, acting all hurt and put out with me and everything. Get over it. You know very well that you would do exactly the same thing. There's not a cop alive who wouldn't keep his mouth shut if he were in my shoes right now."

His head jerked slightly back, and I could tell I had struck a nerve.

"Now, if you'll excuse me, I have an employee to talk to."

With that, I marched around the front of the car and up the walk toward the door, my head and heart pounding with rage. But before I could even get there, Mike grabbed my elbow, jerking me to a stop.

"Sienna, wait!"

"What?"

He didn't let go but instead held on with a firm hand, his body very close to mine, so close I could smell his aftershave, blended with the scents of sun and sweat and earth.

"You need to settle down first before you go in there. I understand why you're upset with Floyd, but bursting into the inn in a rage and confronting him like that isn't going to help anyone. He's an old guy. He had a rough night and an even rougher day."

I met Mike's eyes, which were black as night, mere inches from mine.

"You're afraid I'll take him down like I did Jeremy Lantz?"

His lips tilted ever so slightly at the corners but he resisted a full smile.

"Yeah, something like that. Just calm down first, that's all I'm saying."

His hand still gripped my arm, my scars pulsating under the heat of his fingers. Holding his gaze, I could see his eyes flicker with intensity, an intensity that felt both exciting and frightening at the same time.

"Sienna?" a voice said from not too far away, a man's voice.

Startled, Mike and I both turned quickly to see who had spoken. He was standing at the edge of the driveway, his face half hidden in shadow.

Heath.

THIRTY

"Heath! What are you doing here?" I blurted out as Mike and I moved apart. Realizing how odd I probably sounded, I tried again, making my voice much warmer this time. "I mean, I'm so glad you came. You just startled me. I-I wasn't expecting you until tomorrow."

My boyfriend stepped forward into the light, his eyes moving from me to Mike and back to me again. My cheeks were burning, though I hoped there wasn't enough light by the back door for him to see. Heath walked up to me, and I quickly moved to embrace him, my heart full of mortification, guilt, and embarrassment.

"What's going on here? Is everything all right?" he asked as our hug ended. He looked again at Mike, obviously not sure how to read the scene he had just come upon.

"Nothing. Yes. I mean, let me introduce you," I said. "Heath, this is Mike Weissbaum, the detective investigating Troy's case. Mike, this is Dr. Heath Davis." I hesitated and then added, "My boyfriend."

Much to my surprise, Heath slipped an arm around my shoulders and held me there, almost possessively, a move that for him was very uncharacteristic. He then offered his hand to Mike for a shake. Mike paused just a beat and then accepted it, the two men gripping so tightly as they shook each other's hands that I was afraid there might be a crushing of bones. After that, I was glad when Mike said he was, in fact, just on the point of leaving when Heath had arrived.

The handsome detective nodded at me and then walked away, whistling as he went down the walk toward his car. As I watched him go, my heart grew heavy with shame. Why had I been playing with fire like that? Right now, the last thing I needed in my life was more drama.

Trying to assuage my guilt—and maybe to keep Heath from looking into my eyes at that moment—once Mike had rounded the corner I gave Heath another hug. He held me tightly in return, though I wasn't sure if the fervency of his embrace was due to suspicions that had been awakened or simply from concern about my well-being.

"I know you said not to come until tomorrow, but I couldn't stand it anymore. I couldn't even think straight. A few hours ago, I almost prescribed acne meds to a guy with gout. That's when I decided I had to get out of there. All it took was a quick shift switch with one of my partners and now I'm covered through Monday."

"Why didn't you call?"

"I was afraid you would tell me not to come."

Heath pulled back from our embrace so that he could look into my eyes and study my face. Still feeling flushed from the surprise and embarrassment of his unexpected appearance, I had to force myself to look him in the eye.

"Sienna, are you sure you're okay?"

I nodded. "I'm fine, Heath. Absolutely fine, I promise."

With a flicker of light, I realized that something had changed inside the house. Looking at the windows, we could see that the kitchen light had been turned off and Floyd's bedroom light turned on. After a beat, the light for his bathroom turned on as well, and that was followed a moment later by the faint sound of running water.

"Sounds like Floyd's getting in the shower," I said. "Good timing. I have to have a serious talk with him, but it would probably be better if I filled you in on things first."

"Walk with me to my car to get my stuff. Tell me everything."

"First, you tell me what you thought about the books. Were you able to get a good look at the file I sent you?

"Yes."

"Then I have a feeling I already know what you're going to say."

"Oh?"

"That the books look perfect, everything ties out great, and there are no issues at all with one exception. It seems very odd that everything here is being done—"

"In cash," he said in unison with me. "Bingo. How did you know?"

Speaking softly but quickly, I tried to give him a recap of events, picking up from where he and I had left off this morning and taking him through my day up to what I had learned about the Secret Service. As he listened, I could see that he was wearing his "doctor" face, almost as if the events and discoveries here were symptoms he could collect, analyze, and then diagnose. In a sense, I realized, that was exactly what was needed: a diagnosis, one that would explain whatever sick, strange things had been going on at my inn in my absence and without my knowledge.

I was nearly finished with my recap by the time he had unloaded his suitcase and other items from the car and we returned back up the walk to the door. Not yet ready to confront Floyd, I listened at his bathroom window for a moment, just to make sure the shower was still running, and then we stepped inside the back door.

I had been so intent on bringing Heath up to speed that I completely forgot this was the first time he had ever been here. Stepping into the main room, I told him to put his things down at the foot of the stairs for now. As he did, I caught a glimpse of his face and was surprised and pleased by what I saw there. His eyes were wide as he looked around in wonder, taking it all in.

"Wow, Sienna, this is your humble little bed-and-breakfast? You have to be kidding me. Honey, this place is incredible!"

I beamed proudly, as if the B and B were my child and had just taken the blue ribbon at the gymnastics meet, the science fair, and the beauty pageant all in one. Looking around the room, I tried to see the place through Heath's eyes and had to admit that it really did pack quite a punch.

"Are you hungry?" Heath asked, holding up a brown bag he had carried in from the car, and as he did, I recognized its delicious, familiar scent.

"Please tell me that's what I think it is."

"Yep," he replied, eyes twinkling. "You know I can't live without my General Tso's chicken."

Heath was teasing. He wasn't crazy about Chinese food but he had gone there for takeout because he knew it was my favorite. Being this thoughtful was so like him. And how had I repaid him? By practically throwing myself into the arms of another man the first chance I got!

I suggested that we eat in the dining room, and we made our way there together, Heath's eyes taking in every design element and architectural touch along the way. After he put the bag down on the large mahogany table and I began to unload its contents, I felt a surge of gratitude so overwhelming that my eyes filled with tears.

Seeing those tears, Heath immediately took me in his arms and cradled me there for a long moment. No words were necessary between us. It was enough that he was here and that he cared.

He was just a little over six feet tall, but sometimes when I stood this close to him, he felt like a giant to me. Looking up at the smooth, chiseled plains of his handsome face, his piercing blue eyes, his neatly cut sandy brown hair, I felt again the surge of attraction that had hit me the first night we met and had done so every time I had been with him since. Even more good looking, though, was the man he was on the inside: kind, gentle, solid. My rock.

Maybe it was a good thing that he had come out here to Lancaster County earlier than expected. Whatever seemed to have been drawing me to Mike paled in comparison to the feelings I had for Heath, something I hadn't realized until just that moment.

"Thanks for coming," I whispered, meaning it.

"I couldn't not," he replied before taking my chin in his hand, tilting it just so, and giving me a kiss.

By the time we heard Floyd finally emerge from his room, Heath and I had served up our plates in the kitchen, heated them in the microwave, and were back at the dining table about to start eating.

"Hello? Is someone here?" Floyd's voice called, interrupting our grace.

"Amen," Heath said softly.

"In here. The dining room," I called.

Floyd's head popped out from around the corner.

"Sienna? It's you! I *thought* I heard somebody."

He came all the way into the room, dressed in casual clothes, his hair—or what there was of it—still damp from the shower. He walked directly over to Heath, holding out his hand for a shake and introducing himself as Floyd Underhill, manager of Harmony Grove Bed & Breakfast.

What a joke.

Floyd gave me a light hug, and though I expected to feel a surge of my earlier anger toward him, at the moment my overwhelming emotion was one of pity. No wonder Mike had told me to go easy on him. He looked exhausted, with dark circles under his eyes and an unhealthy pallor to his skin.

"We have a lot to talk about, Floyd," I said gravely.

"We sure do!" he replied. "Man, that smells good. Mind if I grab a plate for myself first?"

Heath and I looked at each other and then back at Floyd. I was thrown by his enthusiastic response and relieved when Heath rose from the table and replied for us both, escorting Floyd to the kitchen and describing the food choices that awaited there as they went.

I needed a moment alone to gather my wits about me. Judging by Floyd's upbeat and enthusiastic demeanor, he had no idea where our conversation was about to go. Obviously, he thought I was still clueless about his past history and his current exploits, and he was gearing up to blow a little smoke as usual. But I had news for him. Where there's smoke, there's fire.

And I was about to turn up the heat.

THIRTY-ONE

By the time Floyd returned to the room, I was feeling much more in control. Watching him as he settled across from me to eat and chat, I tried to picture him in prison orange, sitting in a dingy cafeteria among hardened criminals. Somehow, that wasn't so easy to do.

With his balding pate and pudgy features, Floyd looked to me the way he always had, like the neighbor who keeps to himself but gives a friendly wave when he goes out to get the paper, or the uncle who comes to the family gatherings but never talks about much more than the weather or the latest ball game. Floyd was forgettable, nondescript, unnoticeable.

Perhaps that was what made him such a good criminal.

"I found out this morning that you're the one who called nine-one-one last night, Sienna," Floyd was saying as he smoothed a paper napkin on his lap. "I'm sure glad you showed up when you did, or I might have died. Can't wait till they find out what happened to me."

"And to Nina," I reminded him. "And Troy."

"Well, yes, of course."

Heath entered with a glass of milk and set it down in front of Floyd, saying, "Here you go."

"Ah, thanks so much. Man, I'm beat. All I wanted all day was a shower, a decent meal, and a comfortable bed. Bet I'll sleep like a log tonight. Are you guys staying over? Guess you'll want the Oak Room, huh?"

He speared a piece of sweet and sour chicken with his fork and popped it in his mouth.

"Oak and Birch," I replied at the same moment that Heath said, "Separate rooms. Thanks."

Floyd nodded, still chewing, and I realized that this was how he was hoping to play it, just acting friendly and innocent until he could wolf down his meal and escape to his bedroom.

Good luck with that.

"We have to talk, Floyd," I said, noting his almost imperceptible reaction to my words. Except for a brief pause in his chewing, he didn't seem startled by my statement at all but instead simply nodded his head, maintaining his bland expression. "Let's start with your version of events from last night. I want to know everything."

Floyd swallowed, dabbed at his mouth with his napkin, and launched right in, telling us how Troy had shown up on Monday for an overnight stay but then had decided to extend that stay for a few days. On Tuesday morning, Troy had offered to cover things if Floyd wanted to take a little time off, which he did. After an overnight visit with family in Jersey, Floyd had just returned yesterday evening and was making himself a sandwich in the kitchen when he heard a woman scream. The scream had come from outside, so Floyd retrieved the gun from his bedroom and ran out to see what was going on. There, though the screaming had stopped, he followed the sounds of splashing, only to find Nina on her knees beside the pool, dripping wet and trying to do CPR on an obviously dead Troy.

Floyd had finally convinced her to give up when they heard a strange sound from not too far outside of the fence, a low, deep rumble followed by a rustling. They both turned to look, and everything after that was fuzzy.

"I'm awful tired of saying this and having people look at me like I'm crazy, but I know what I saw. It was some kind of creature, a big black thing that rose up from the bushes and shot out a burst of fire. I don't remember anything after that. They said I was talking crazy in the ambulance, but I don't remember any of that at all. I just remember seeing the flash, and then I woke up this morning in the hospital."

Having finished his tale, Floyd took another big scoop of chicken and popped it into his mouth.

"What do you remember about the creature, Floyd?" Heath asked. "Any chance it could have been an emu?"

Floyd laughed, nearly choking on his food.

"An emu? Like, one of those big, stupid birds?"

"Yes."

"No, man. No way. This thing wasn't a bird. It had arms, not wings. It had hands."

"Hands? Like human hands?"

"Kind of, I guess. When it stood up—"

"On two legs?"

Floyd hesitated, thinking.

"Yeah, on two legs. It just rose up on its hind legs, like a polar bear or a gorilla might, but real fast like. Then it shot fire at me. I don't remember anything else after that."

Heath and I looked at each other, and though we didn't say anything, I knew we were both thinking the same thing, that it really didn't seem that Floyd was lying. He may have been a criminal, but in this matter it sounded as though he was telling the truth—or at least what he perceived as the truth.

"After dinner I'd like to try something, if you're game," Heath said to Floyd. "Maybe I can help you remember more."

"What do you want to try?"

"It's called 'guided relaxation,'" Heath explained. "It involves closing your eyes and listening to my voice and letting my words help you to relax. Then we go through the whole sequence of events, step by step. Sometimes when your brain isn't stressed and working so hard to recall every detail, you're actually able to come up with more memories."

"Sounds like you want to hypnotize me or something."

"No, not at all," Heath replied. "This is completely interactive, no altered states necessary."

"Heath's a doctor," I added. "They use this method sometimes when there's been a trauma."

Floyd looked skeptical, but he agreed to do it if we thought it would help.

"I think it's worth a try," Heath said, nodding.

"Tell us about Nina," I said next. "What was she doing over here?"

Floyd shrugged, saying he didn't know. He took a bite, chewed, and swallowed, and then he added, "Maybe she and Troy were starting up again."

"Starting up again?"

"They dated for a while. Well, if you can even call it dating."

Heath and I looked at each other, eyes wide.

"What do you mean? When?"

"Last spring, for a couple of months I think. It was no big deal. She would come over whenever Troy was here, stay with him, and then go back home when he left."

No big deal? Troy and Nina? Sleeping together? In *my* inn? The very thought made me sick. I put down my fork, thinking that, even for Troy, this was a new low. Oblivious to my reaction, Floyd went on to explain that Troy had broken things off with Nina a few months ago, but that with her being here yesterday, maybe they had gotten back together again.

"For that matter, maybe that's why Troy wanted me to go out of town," Floyd added.

"Do the police know about their relationship?" I asked, wondering why Mike had never brought it up to me.

"Beats me."

Heath held out both hands to stop us both, a puzzled expression on his face.

"Wait a minute. I'm confused. Sienna, the way you talk about this Nina person, I've been picturing an older lady and not someone who would catch the eye of a mover and shaker like Troy, not even for a casual affair."

I apologized for giving Heath that impression, saying Nina and I were about the same age but that her life had gone down a different path than mine. I guess I did tend to think of her as older just because of all she had been through.

"I mean, she was married at eighteen, had a child by nineteen, and divorced her husband a year or two after that. Then a few years ago, her daughter was in a serious car accident. The girl survived, barely, but then later she died from ongoing complications. It was tragic."

"Oh, wow, how sad," Heath said.

"Anyway," I continued, "she wasn't exactly Troy's type, but I guess when in Rome, you know?"

Floyd laughed.

"You're kidding, right? Nina is everybody's type. Everybody with a pulse, that is."

Startled, I asked Floyd if he was implying that Nina made a habit of sleeping around.

"No, not at all," he said, shaking his head. "I'm just saying she's hot." Looking at Heath, he winked and added, "*Smokin'* hot, if you know what I mean."

Floyd's words were inappropriate, but in light of Nina's current plight, in the hospital in serious condition, I thought they were incredibly so. I was glad that Heath did not respond with a knowing leer or a wink of his own but instead simply turned his attention to the plate in front of him and ate some more of the Chinese food.

"Hey, listen, folks, this was delicious," Floyd said after finishing his last bite, crumpling up his napkin, and dropping it onto his empty plate. "Thanks so much for sharing with a hungry old man. Right now, I'm going to hit the sack. I'm bushed. Maybe you and I can try that relaxation thing tomorrow, okay, Doc?"

Floyd scooted his chair back from the table, but before he stood I told him he wasn't going anywhere, not yet.

"We're just getting started here," I said, a reckless anger suddenly rising up inside of me and filtering out through my words. "I have questions and I want answers."

"Can't it wait till morning?" Floyd said, avoiding my eyes as he grabbed his plate and stood up. "I'm just so exhaust—"

"Sit down!" I yelled, slamming my hands on the table.

The gesture was effective, and he sheepishly lowered himself back into his chair.

"For starters, why don't you tell me about your criminal record?" I said, focusing on the man sitting across from me, shoulders hunched, eyes downcast.

"What about it?"

"It wasn't exactly on your resume when I hired you."

"I know," Floyd said, barely audible.

"Why not?"

"Why do you think? 'Cause if you had known, you wouldn't have hired me. And I really wanted this job."

I laughed sarcastically.

"I'm sure you did."

"Look, I know it sounds bad, but you need to understand the whole story," Floyd said.

Then he proceeded to give us that story in detail, from growing up as a street punk in Camden to falling in with a bad crowd as a young man to getting caught and convicted and then "fully rehabilitated" in prison. He went on to speak glowingly of his life after that, when a kind parole officer helped him land a job at a hotel in Philly. There, Floyd had begun to learn the hospitality business and soon realized he had a gift for it, which, according to him, had turned his life around. All in all, the story was quite compelling.

But I knew it was just that. A story.

"What crime were you convicted of, Floyd?" Heath interrupted to ask, the first words he had said in a while.

"Yeah, Floyd, do tell. What could possibly have been bad enough to send you up the river for three years?"

Eyes darting away, he replied that he had "just passed a couple bad checks, is all."

"Right. A couple of bad checks got you three years at Rahwey," I scoffed.

"Okay, well, so it was more than a couple. I'm not proud of that fact, but it's not like I stabbed somebody. It was check kiting."

"Check kiting," I echoed. "Is that anything like money laundering? Or was that a skill you learned after you decided to move out here to Lancaster County and turn my bed-and-breakfast into a cash-washing machine?"

At first Floyd tried to look shocked. In a performance worthy of an Oscar, he was also by turns appalled, offended, and astounded. Between the faked customer records, the rooms that stayed clean, the gifts that never sold, and more, I had plenty of evidence to throw in his face to refute every protestation. But when it came down to it, I didn't need to say a word. Like a mother waiting out a toddler who is pitching a tantrum, I simply sat there, arms folded across my chest, as he ran through his whole string of denials. Finally, he slumped there at the table, defeated.

"You get your profit check every month," he growled, eyes downcast, "what do you care if things don't quite add up?"

Again I didn't reply, and after a moment he spoke again, this time looking right at me.

"Frankly, Sienna, I think it takes a lot of nerve to show up here like this and pretend you wanna be so hands-on all of a sudden. You haven't called or come by in almost a *year*. But now that the heat's on, you show up, all indignant-like, asking questions, making accusations. Give me a break."

He was right, of course. That was no way for anyone to run a business, and there was no denying I had taken the hands-off approach far too literally. But that was also no excuse for what he had done. I couldn't believe he had the nerve to try to turn this back on me. Seething with rage, I took a deep breath, now clearly able to picture Floyd in that orange prison jumpsuit.

"Whether Sienna involved herself with the day-to-day running of the inn or not," Heath interjected calmly before I could speak, "she still had every right to expect you to conduct honorable business practices on her behalf. Instead, you took advantage of the situation in the worst way."

"I trusted you!" I blurted out loudly. "Yes, I was lax about keeping tabs on things here, but that was only because I thought you had a handle on it. You sure knew how to make it seem that way. I bought your lie, Floyd, every single piece of it, hook, line, and sinker. If any of this is my fault, it's that I was too naive and too stupid and too trusting to look behind the pretty picture you painted to see the ugliness hiding behind it!"

I was standing at that point and shouting at him. Both men were looking up at me in alarm, but I had more to say, so I kept going.

"And what a brilliant plan too! Out here in Amish country, you knew this place could be run as an all-cash business with no eyebrows raised. You sent me a check every month to make me happy and e-mailed me your neat little financial statements to keep me away. Your books were perfect, Floyd, showing all sorts of logical, steady ins and outs. But they were fiction, all fiction! By creating purely bogus financial records, you were able to deposit your dirty cash into the bank with every penny 'justified,' at least on paper. You have customers staying at the B and B, paying in cash. Customers buying Amish-made goods, paying in cash. Guests splurging on fancy wine, paying in cash. You even made sure to file and pay taxes on all of that cash you were generating out here in Lancaster County. How very, very clever of you—especially when you look at the other column, the expenses that manage to keep this place just profitable enough to stay in business without going overboard. Housekeeping staff? You pay them in cash. Groceries to prepare breakfasts for the guests? You buy them with cash. The inventory of wine and quilts and toys? Purchased with cash. All cash, all the time, in and out. Amazing how that happens—and how there's always just enough left over at the end of the month to send me a little profit check."

I paused, leaning forward, hands on the table, lowering my voice in volume, if not intensity.

"But the books don't tell the real story, do they, Floyd? For that—for the truth—we would need a second set of books, wouldn't we? Those books would be the ones to tell where all that cash had really been coming from, of how this money had really been flowing in and out. Whose money is it, Floyd? Where has all of this cash been coming from?"

My words hung in the air, but he didn't answer.

"I'm guessing the mob has something to do with it," I added. "And Troy as well, of course."

"Of course," Floyd echoed. He hesitated, biting his lip, obviously weighing his words before he continued. "It was Troy's idea. He's the one who thought it all up in the first place."

I glanced at Heath, lowering myself into my chair. While I was glad that Floyd had finally decided to talk, I would take his words with a huge grain of salt. How easy to blame the dead man, the one who wasn't here to defend himself.

242 MINDY STARNS CLARK

"Go on," Heath said softly.

"Troy came up with this plan after your grandpa died," Floyd admitted, tugging nervously at his shirt collar. "Said he had the perfect solution to a very big problem. It would take some work, but he just might be able to pull it off."

"Really," I said, trying to keep my voice neutral.

"Yeah. Bottom line, he said *you* were going to be the key to everything."

THIRTY-TWO

"Troy said it all started with you," Floyd told me, relaxing against the back of his chair, "and some big myth about the Amish you were always griping about."

"Myth?"

"Yeah, how everybody thinks the Amish are so perfect and innocent and all?"

"Oh, you're talking about the 'myth of the pastoral,'" I said, taking a moment to explain to Heath what that was. I couldn't remember who first coined the phrase, but it had to do with the average person's tendency to see the Amish as some sort of unique race, one whose members lived in perfect harmony with each other and with nature, never had any serious problems or concerns, and spent their days in barefoot splendor, romping around their bountiful fields and embodying the very definition of peace, purity, and the simple life.

Because I was in advertising, I was particularly sensitive to how the tourism industry played on that ideal and worked to exploit it. Though this technique of idealization was often used to promote products to consumers, I was uncomfortable when I saw it being used to sell an entire people group, especially one so near and dear to my heart. In truth, though there was much to admire about the Amish, they were just people—flawed, normal people—who at their core were not all that different from the rest of us.

244 ✦ MINDY STARNS CLARK

"I hear what you're saying," Heath told me. "The more unique and special and different and perfect we all think the Amish are, the more likely we are to want to come out here and see it for ourselves…"

"And stay in the hotels and eat at the restaurants and buy the trinkets and on and on and on. And then we go home raving about everything we saw and heard, even if we never actually spoke to a real live Amish person, and thus we continue to perpetuate the myth."

Turning my attention back to Floyd, I asked him what that had to do with me and Troy. He said that when Troy and I had driven out here for my grandfather's funeral, I had gone on my usual rant about the whole myth thing, and as Troy was listening to me, the word that had stayed in his mind the longest was how everyone saw the Amish—and, by extension, this whole Amish-filled area—as "innocent." Right then, an idea had taken hold, the realization that he could capitalize on that "presumption of innocence" and use it to his advantage.

"See, you have to understand that Troy was the money man for a certain group of people who needed to, shall we say, legitimize some cash flow. Troy had been trying to think up some new ways to do that when your grandfather died. After listening to your myth thing, he decided that this region might just be the perfect location for some sort of cash-heavy business venture."

Floyd went on to say that all Troy had at that point were some vague ideas, nothing concrete. Then about a week later, after the reading of my grandfather's will, he and I had gone out to eat with my parents and brother, and we had all tossed around ideas for what we should do with our inheritance. As soon as Troy heard me mention opening a bed-and-breakfast, he knew that was it.

"It was perfect," Floyd said. "I mean, who would ever suspect a sweet little bed-and-breakfast in Amish country of doing anything seriously illegal?"

Floyd described how Troy had "worked" me after that, encouraging the notion of a bed-and-breakfast, coming up with solutions for financing, and generally ushering me down the path toward what would eventually become Harmony Grove Bed & Breakfast. The key to making Troy's plan succeed had rested in his assumption that once I had made it through all the thrill and excitement of planning and renovating and organizing and equipping this place that I would quickly lose interest in the far less exciting day-to-day workings of the inn. He had not been happy when he realized my parents were joining in on the venture with me, however, because he didn't know whether the same thing could be said of them or not.

"That's why your mother's illness was so perfect," Floyd said, "because it gave him the excuse to talk you into buying out your parents' share of this place."

Heath and I both gasped, startling Floyd.

"Oh, sorry. That didn't come out right. You know what I meant. Anyway, Troy felt better about things when he finally convinced you to hire me as your manager, and after you became the sole owner, he knew we were home free."

For the next few minutes, I sat there at the table listening as my feelings ranged from hurt to anger to embarrassment and back again. I couldn't tell if Floyd was being intentionally cruel or not, but it didn't really matter. In almost everything he said, there was at least a grain of truth.

In some cases, there was far more than merely a grain.

According to Floyd, Troy had always seen me as an excitement junkie, a strong starter who would shoot out of the gate at full speed, wow everybody with my gifts and intelligence and ideas, and give my all for as long as the situation felt new or exciting or challenging. Then, once the big and fabulous opening act was accomplished and it was time to move into the more mundane daily operations, I would quickly lose interest. Sometimes I would bail completely.

To make sure that wouldn't happen here, Troy had worked hard to come up with what he thought of as the perfect number: just enough of a monthly stipend to make the B and B worth the trouble for me to hang onto it, but not enough to cause any significant dip in the cash that was being laundered here.

"Wait, I don't understand," Heath interrupted. "Why on earth go to all of this trouble? Why not just buy his own B and B and not involve Sienna at all?"

Floyd pursed his lips disdainfully.

"That's how laundering works, man. The business has to look completely legitimate. It needs to be owned by someone who isn't connected to the people funneling cash through it."

He went on to say that sometimes the business owners knew what was going on and helped to facilitate in exchange for a payoff. But in my case, the less I knew about it, the better.

"The few times she asked questions," Floyd said to Heath, "even simple stuff, like what computer software would I like to use or what kind of check-in procedures was I going to have, I just did like Troy said and made my answer as dull and drawn out as possible, and pretty soon she would get bored with it and move on to something else."

It was miserable enough hearing all of these things about myself and having a flashlight shined on my very soul, but making the experience a thousand times worse was the fact that Heath was sitting here as well, hearing all of this. What was he thinking? Had he ever articulated to himself my shortcomings this way? If not, was he seeing me in a whole new light? Those were questions I knew I would have to deal with later. For now I forced myself to focus on the matter at hand.

Now that Floyd had admitted the truth about what had been going on, it was time to bring the police in on it as well. I said that to him, but much to my surprise he replied that he had already gone over all this with the police, and at great length.

"Well, not the police, exactly, but the FBI and the AG," Floyd admitted, suddenly rising from the table. "Now that you know that, maybe you'll stop trying to interrogate me yourself."

Before I could even tell him to sit down, he held out both palms as if to stop me and said that he was sorry, but he had already said way more than he was supposed to.

"I turned state's evidence," he added. "Now that I have a deal and I'm working closely with the FBI, I'm not supposed to be saying anything about all of this to anybody. And you can't tell a soul either, or you'll end up getting me killed."

Of course, I didn't believe him right away. But after verifying what he had told us with the FBI, I knew he really had turned state's evidence and was now working with the feds bring down the group of people behind the money laundering operation.

That turn of events created as many questions as it did answers, chief among them being whether or not I was still under suspicion for having some part in all of this. I also wanted to know if Troy had turned as well. If so, had the mob found out and killed him because of it? Hoping to find answers to my questions—and to clear my own name in the process—I got back on the phone and set up an appointment to meet with federal investigators tomorrow afternoon at their office in Lancaster. Thank goodness Liz would be here to go with me.

Once I hung up, Heath and I escorted Floyd to the door of his room, and I told him to pack his things and go.

"How 'bout we make a deal," he said, squinting his tired, red eyes. "You let me stay here tonight and leave tomorrow instead, and in exchange I'll let you in on a little gossip."

"Gossip?"

"Yeah," Floyd said, glancing left and right as if to make sure he wasn't being heard. "Not a big deal to me, but it might interest you quite a bit."

I studied his face for a moment and then accepted his offer.

"Thanks," he said, running a hand tiredly over his face. "Okay, well, when the cops brought me home tonight, the first thing I did was call Cap, a buddy of mine on the inside, to find out what he could tell me about Troy's death. He didn't know any more than I did, but he did say something very strange."

I waited, listening as Floyd lowered his voice.

"Like I said before, Troy owed lots of people lots of money, including a couple g's to Cap. For the past couple of weeks, Troy's been avoiding all his creditors, not answering his calls, and acting like a real deadbeat, you know? But the day he died, much to Cap's surprise, Troy actually answered the phone when he called. When Cap demanded the money Troy owed him, Troy said okay."

"Okay?"

"Well, not right away. What he said was that he was right on the verge of a huge windfall, and that if Cap could wait just a day or two more, he'd get back every penny and then some."

"Isn't that what gamblers always say?"

"Yeah, but Cap felt like this was different. Said Troy was on the trail of an actual *thing*, somethin' super valuable, and he even asked Cap if he could recommend a good fence for selling it once he had it in his hands."

I nodded, not all that surprised by this news. No doubt, Troy had been talking about the diamonds.

"Now I don't know about any windfall, or where Troy thought it was going to come from, but Cap says he sounded so earnest he was almost inclined to believe him."

"So how did your friend respond?"

Floyd shrugged.

"He said, 'Windfall, schmindfall, you got till Monday and then I'm breaking your kneecaps.'" Floyd grinned. "That's where he got his nick-name, you know? Anyway, Troy said no problem, that what he was looking for was right here at Harmony Grove and pretty soon it would be his. Said it was kind of like a treasure hunt and that he was getting close."

Troy had been talking about the diamonds all right. But those were *Emory's* diamonds, not Troy's. My anger surged.

"Anyway," Floyd said, slipping his hands in his pockets, "Cap said it sounds like Troy told the same thing to a couple of other creditors that day too, so if I were you, I'd be careful. Whatever 'treasure' Troy thought he was going to come up with here—even if he was just blowing smoke to buy himself some time—if word gets out and people think maybe he died before he found it, a couple of very curious treasure hunters just might come crawl-ing out of the woodwork."

I tried to process that thought, finally asking, "Guys with names like Cap? Bone Breaker? Slice and Dice?"

Floyd laughed.

"Something like that."

"So what do I do?" I asked, glancing over at Heath in alarm.

"You got me," Floyd said. "Why don't I sleep on it, and I'll let you know if I come up with any ideas by morning. Right now, I'm calling it a night."

With that, he stepped backward into his room and firmly shut the door in my face.

For almost a minute, I just stood there, frozen, reeling with astonishment. Would the surprises in this situation ever come to an end?

Finally, Heath and I returned to the dining room where we could speak more privately, both of us stumped by this last development. Were we in danger here? Would these shady-sounding people really come here in search of buried treasure? If so, once they didn't find it, would they come after us, thinking we could point the way? While the thought of that was certainly frightening, I doubted that anyone would show up immediately, not while the police and other officials still had such an obvious and frequent presence on the grounds. On the other hand, Heath and I both felt that as soon as the coast seemed clear, all bets just might be off. Thus, the race was on to find the diamonds for yet another reason.

We had to get to them before someone else did.

For the next hour, as we talked about how to proceed with all of the many issues that had been raised tonight, Heath seemed oddly distant and quiet. I didn't blame him. After the evening we'd had, especially after hearing my character assassinated like that, I had to wonder if he would still be around by morning

I wouldn't blame him one bit if he wasn't.

Beyond the personal attacks, the more I thought about all of Floyd's astonishing revelations, the more consumed I grew with anger and fear. As furious as I was with Floyd, I was even angrier at Troy. How could one man have done so much damage? Truly, Troy Griffin was in a class by himself. Now that he was dead, would we ever untangle the vast webs of lies he had spun?

Would we even survive to try?

After rehashing things several times over to no avail, Heath and I finally gave up for the night and headed to our rooms, too exhausted to think about anything more than sleep. After a perfunctory kiss goodnight at the door of Heath's suite, I headed down the hall to my own room.

There, I closed and locked the door and climbed under my sheets without even changing into my nightgown first. Clutching a quilted Amish pillow to my chest, I wept as quietly as possible, sobbing into the darkness until I had no more tears left to cry.

THIRTY-THREE

When I woke the next morning, I sat on the side of the bed for a while, aching from head to toe and trying not to rub my puffy eyes. Though I felt all cried out, the patter of rain tap-tap-tapping on the roof told me that the skies had taken over for me, weeping on my behalf.

The rain everyone had said was coming was finally here. My thoughts went to the poison in the grove, and I could only hope that the people from the EPA had managed to get it all cleaned up before the weather changed.

Slowly I stood. After last night's revelations, I needed to reframe everything I had learned in the past two days. Praying for clarity, I did a lot of thinking as I showered and dressed.

By the time I was ready to face the day—or as ready as I was ever going to be—my most urgent thought was of my boyfriend. I needed to find out if Heath was still around.

I hoped he was, but I wouldn't blame him if he wasn't.

Opening my bedroom door, I peered down the hall toward his room. Heath's door was closed, so I continued down the stairs, holding my breath until I heard his voice. His tones were oddly quiet and soothing, but I couldn't make out the words until I reached the bottom of the stairs and realized that he was with Floyd, doing the relaxation technique they had discussed last night.

Floyd was sitting on the couch in the main room. His eyes were closed as Heath spoke, telling him to relax muscle by muscle. I was a little nervous about seeing Heath, afraid that the uncomfortable strain from when we had said good night would still be between us this morning. He looked up at me with a finger to his lips.

So he was still in this thing. God bless him.

It sounded as though they were just getting started, so I didn't hang around to watch or listen. Instead, I tiptoed my way through the main room, down the hall, across the dining room, and into the side porch. If I couldn't go all the way outside, as per Mike, I decided this was the next best thing. I'd heard that the rains would bring cooler temperatures, and as I opened the door and stepped out onto the porch, I was glad I had put on a warm sweater for the day. Though it wasn't freezing outside, a definite chill was in the air.

I settled on the wicker couch, dialed my grandmother's number, and was greeted with her cheery "Hello." We chatted a bit first, and I was relieved to hear that she had already learned about some of the things going on out here—and she didn't seem interested in learning more. That was a relief, as I could focus on the questions I needed to ask her without having to take the time to bring her up to speed.

I decided to start by asking about Emory and the arrests from his youth. Not surprisingly, her answer was long and circuitous and started when the young Maureen Knickerbocker was hired by a friend of a friend named Abe Collins to care for his three-year-old son. Abe was a handsome and brooding young widower who lived in an old family home in the heart of Lancaster County, and he was in urgent need of childcare.

"That was at the end of my junior year in teacher's college, and I only took the job temporarily, for the summer, to help out while Abe looked for someone permanent. But the very first day I fell in love with little Emory, and within a few weeks I had fallen for his father as well. That fall, I put school on hold for a semester but eventually withdrew completely and married Abe instead. Your father was born a year later, when Emory was five."

She went on to say that they knew there was something wrong with Emory from a very early age, but whenever they tried to pursue treatment they were encouraged to institutionalize the boy, something neither wanted to do. They tried enrolling him in regular school, but at the end of the first week it was obvious to all sides that he didn't belong there. Hoping he would "grow out of it," Maureen kept him at home and tried to teach him as best she could, but not much ever seemed to get through. Meanwhile, marriage to the "handsome and brooding widower" wasn't turning out to be quite what she had expected. They were both dedicated to the children, but the gap between the two of them began to widen. It didn't help matters that Abe spent every spare minute working to create a grove as a living memorial to his deceased wife. Between his day job as a welder and his off-hours work in the grove, they barely saw each other. Meanwhile, Emory continued to falter.

"He and I were in the middle of a reading lesson one day when Harold interrupted us to give the answers himself. There he was, reading at five, and Emory still couldn't catch on at ten."

While they were relieved to know that Harold didn't share his older brother's limitations, they didn't know what to do about poor Emory.

"But then the decision was sort of made for us," she continued. "When Emory was eleven, he came home one day covered in blood, and he led us back to a place in the woods where a rabbit had been killed. He was hysterical, and he kept saying that he did it but he wouldn't or couldn't explain why. He just cried and cried. Of course, we had to follow up on it. Abe buried the rabbit, and then we took our son to the doctor. At that point he was taken away from us and put into a mental home. It just broke our hearts—especially when we would visit, and he would be sitting there drugged out of his mind, like a zombie. Doctors were so ignorant about mental illness back then! Oh, Sienna, you have no idea."

"I'm so sorry," I whispered, grieved to hear of such pain and sadness with my loved ones but glad at least to know that Emory had been remorseful about the rabbit.

"Like I said, things were already not so good between Abe and me," my grandmother continued, "and the stress of losing Emory was the icing on the cake. I left a month later, taking your father with me. I hated to do that to Abe, but at the time I felt I didn't have a choice. I just couldn't live that way anymore."

My grandmother then launched into the full story of her marriage and its issues, and I knew there would be no stopping her now.

"What was the basic problem?" I asked finally, trying to cut to the chase.

"Abe was fixated on his first wife," my grandmother replied. "I knew that going in, but I had convinced myself that over time he would learn to love me as much, and hopefully even more than he had ever loved Daphne. Of course, looking back now, I realize that more than anything the poor man probably had post-traumatic stress disorder from the war. He had been so traumatized—they all had—but even once the war was over and everyone was trying to pick up the pieces and start anew, he faced a second blow, the death of his young wife in childbirth. That had compounded his already damaged psyche greatly, I have no doubt."

I murmured in sympathy, shifting to a more comfortable position as she went on.

"My friend Bessie always said that if I had never become pregnant, Abe and I might have been able to make things work. But, you see, the day Abe learned we were expecting, it was almost as if someone flipped off a switch inside his heart. The man had never been one to easily share his feelings, but once I told him I was with child, he withdrew from me completely. Bessie said Abe's PTSD probably kicked into overdrive once he realized he might lose me just as he had lost Daphne. Whether he was conscious of it or not, the man cut me out purely from self-preservation."

"How sad."

"Yes, it was. Of course, we didn't know about things like PTSD back then. All I knew was that there were three people in our marriage, not two, and that the other woman, though long dead, was far more real and more important to my husband than I was."

She went on to explain that as Abe withdrew from her he began to obsess on the grove. Originally, it was supposed to have been similar to the one near Daphne's childhood home in Germany. But the closer they got to Harold's birth, the stranger and more obsessed Abe grew, expanding the original plan to encompass an entirely new section.

"It drove me nuts, Sienna, but how could I compete with a dead woman? I couldn't even try! The grove was her living memorial, and the more the trees grew, it was like Daphne was coming back to life as well. With every tree Abe planted, what he was really doing was burying his grief."

Hearing her tale, I looked through the screen at the grove in the distance. She was right. The entire place, though lovely, was really all about pain and grief.

"I shouldn't have left him, but I did. And life went on."

"I'm sorry, Grandma," I said, wishing she were here in person so that I could give her a hug. "I knew the basic story, but I never really understood it before. Thanks for sharing it with me."

"You're welcome."

"I'm just sorry that you went through so much pain and suffering yourself."

"Don't feel bad, honey. Once we left Lancaster County, Harold and I did okay. I finished my degree, as you know, and worked as a teacher. I've had a happy life, despite some painful bumps along the way."

That seemed like a good point to end our conversation, but there were still a few questions I needed to ask her.

"Grandma, what happened the second time, when Emory was again caught with a dead animal?"

"I wasn't directly involved that time, but I'll tell you what I know."

"Okay."

"Abe was never happy with the care Emory got at the home, but in the late sixties he found out something that just infuriated him. The doctors there were using 'behavioral treatment techniques' that were abusive to the patients. To make matters worse, they were also experimenting on them with various drugs, including LSD of all things. When Emory was in his early twenties, Abe had finally seen enough and took him out of there and brought him home."

"I don't blame him."

"At first, from what I understand, Emory seemed to do well, responding to his father's kindnesses much better than he had the cruelties at the home. They kept pretty much to themselves, but the two men got along. I think Emory had been back with Abe about a year when the police knocked on the door one night and told them that one of the Newtons' dogs had been found in the grove, killed in the same manner as the rabbit all those years before. Emory was arrested, but this time Abe got on top of things right away. Instead of taking his son to an 'expert' who would only institutionalize him again, Abe did everything he could to keep Emory at home and care for him himself. He paid off the Newtons, agreed to medicate and better supervise Emory, and even arranged for in-home care through a county program. It took all of that, but finally the charges were dropped. Abe had managed to keep his son out of jail or the mental home."

She said that that was pretty much how things had stayed for the rest of Abe's life. The two men lived together, Abe kept Emory on a close rein, and no other animal-related problems had ever surfaced.

"As Abe got older of course, he hired that young woman from across the street to work as an aide for both him and Emory." My grandmother talked about Nina for a while, stressing how very fond Abe had grown of her and how Nina had become the daughter he'd never had.

Changing the subject, I brought up my grandfather's will, asking if she remembered the part about Emory's mother's assets. "At the time you said you thought Grandpa was talking about some diamonds. Were there really diamonds, or could that have been just some figment of his imagination?"

"Oh, at some point there were definitely diamonds," Grandma Maureen assured me. "Daphne inherited them before she died, but I don't know what happened to them after that. I always assumed Abe had brought them to the states in secret and kept them hidden away, saving them for Emory. But once Abe died and no diamonds were produced, I wasn't sure what to think."

"How do you know that at some point diamonds actually existed? Did Grandpa tell you?"

"No, no. Haven't you been listening? Abe never told me anything, dear, except maybe 'pass the ketchup.'"

"Right..."

"I read it."

"You read it? What do you mean?"

"Oh, Sienna, when my marriage was falling apart, I did something I'm not proud of. Abe had an old journal of Daphne's, one she had kept when she was alive. It was written in German, which I don't speak, so I guess he figured I wouldn't ever bother trying to read it. He kept it tucked away in his top drawer. Anyway, when I couldn't take it anymore I stole that journal and had a German-speaking friend translate it into English for me. I just wanted to know more about the "other woman," as crazy as that sounds, to know what I was up against. The little journal had been given to her as a wedding present, so it only spanned a short time, about a year, from the day she and Abe were married until just before Emory was born. But in its sparse pages I learned a lot, far more than I ever wanted to know."

THIRTY-FOUR

Startled, I leaned forward, with one elbow on my knee, listening intently as my grandmother went on with her story.

"The only reason I took Daphne's journal in the first place was because I hoped that learning more about her might help me save my marriage. In the end I'm afraid it did quite the opposite. After reading her words, I understood the extent of the hold she had on Abe, and I was able to see Daphne as a real person and not just some ghost determined to cling to my husband from the grave."

I shivered at the very image.

"Sienna, Daphne was such a deep thinker, a poet of sorts, and her sadness and loss after the war were simply palpable. It sounds absurd, I know, but the poor woman had already lost so much that I almost felt guilty about taking Abe from her, even if she was already dead."

"What happened to the journal?"

"I threw it out, dear," she said, but when I gasped she quickly added, "No, not the original journal, of course. The translated pages were what I threw out. I didn't want your grandfather to discover them and figure out what I had done."

"Do you know what happened to the journal after that?" I asked, wondering if it could have been among the old documents of my grandfather's that Troy had found.

"I don't know, dear. I put it back in the drawer where he kept it and never looked at it again."

"Was it a special drawer, with a secret compartment in it or a false bottom or something?"

"Goodness no, dear. Just a regular drawer. Abe kept the journal under his socks."

My heart sank, but I was glad at least that Grandma Maureen still had all of her faculties. We may not have had the journal, but at least she had been able to tell me about the parts she remembered.

"Wait a minute, you know what?" said suddenly. "Now that I think about it, there were a couple of poems from the translation that I hung on to, just because they were so lovely and haunting I couldn't bear to part with them."

"Where are they now?"

"I'll have to think about that. I remember hiding them in the bottom of my sewing basket, at least until I left your grandfather. After that, they probably went into a file or a scrapbook or something. I can take a look around for them, if you want."

Yes, I did want, and we decided that if she was able to find them she would fax them over from the machine down at her community center.

"Text me first," I urged her, "just to let me know they are on the way."

Texting was a newly acquired skill for her, one my brother had patiently taught her several months before. We all loved Grandma Maureen, but she was so long winded that the entire family had been grateful for Scott's idea—though I probably used it far more often with her than I should, just because I was always so busy.

After giving her the fax number here at the B and B, I brought up one last topic, asking if the journal had said anything at all about a Fishing Tree.

"A Fishing Tree? Yes, it did. How did you know that?"

"It's a long story. I'll have to share it with you some other time. For now, can you just tell me what that is or what it meant?"

"It was just a tree. I don't know why it had that particular name, but that's how Daphne referred to it in the journal, as the Fishing Tree."

"What was its significance? It was an actual tree? In the grove?"

SECRETS of HARMONY GROVE ❦ 259

"Yes. In her family's grove in Germany."

According to my grandmother, Daphne Kahn was just a child in the 1930s when the German government began to create restrictions for its Jewish citizens. As their rights were slowly stripped away—the right to own land, serve in the military, belong to certain professions, and more—life for Jews in Germany grew steadily more difficult.

Though some Jews remained optimistic, hoping the anti-Semitic mood of the reigning Nazi party would soon pass, others were afraid they could see the writing on the wall, and it made them very, very nervous. Daphne's father was one of the nervous ones.

In early 1938 rumors began to circulate that soon Jews would be required to register all of their assets. Mr. Kahn knew if that happened it would only be a matter of time before they would be forced to surrender those assets as well. As a preemptive measure, he and his brother liquidated everything they could and used the money to buy diamonds. Their plan was to hide those jewels where they would be safe through whatever might happen next.

They managed to accomplish this just in the nick of time. On a dark night in early 1938, the two brothers buried their cache of diamonds deep in the ground beside a tree in the grove, the one they called the Fishing Tree. One week later, the Nazis announced that Jews were now required to register all of their wealth and property.

About six months later, Daphne's father was rounded up by the SS with other Jewish males in his community and taken to a concentration camp. Later, Daphne's older brother, who was handicapped because of a childhood case of polio, was taken to Bradenburg and gassed as a part of Hitler's secret T-4 euthanasia program.

"Eventually, of course," my grandmother continued, "Daphne and her mother and sister were also sent to a concentration camp—several actually, including Auschwitz, if I remember correctly, finally ending up in a subcamp of Buchenwald. Of the three women, Daphne was the only one who survived."

"Wow."

Grandma Maureen went on to say that as Hitler's regime began to crumble in 1945 and Allied troops were advancing across Europe, the Nazis forced their prisoners on death marches to other camps, where thousands froze, starved, or were shot along the way. By then Daphne was terribly ill from typhus, so to escape the inevitable death march from her camp, she hid among a pile of corpses, hoping to be taken for dead herself. The next day, the camp was liberated and she was saved.

"According to her journal, when Daphne was carried into one of the treatment areas that had been set up by the Americans, she was triaged by a handsome young medic who didn't speak much but had 'said volumes with his eyes,' or something like that. I knew she was talking about Abe. He always had such beautiful eyes."

As an army medic, Abe had helped to nurse Daphne back from death's door, though at first that had required him to feed her with an eyedropper. With his Amish heritage, he was able to speak German, and something about the connection they made in those first few touch-and-go days stayed with them both. Once Daphne was transferred to a nearby hospital, Abe began to visit, ostensibly to monitor her progress.

The two were falling in love. On the day that Daphne was finally released by the doctors, Abe asked her to marry him. She accepted, but because of the U.S. military's ban on marriages between American servicemen and German women, it had to be done in secret. The journal had been her only wedding present, given to her by the wife of the kind *Standesbeamte* who performed the private civil ceremony. Upon receiving the little blank book, Daphne had immediately begun filling it with the history of her family and all that they had been through since the Third Reich had first come into power.

After the ceremony, Abe and Daphne had traveled to her hometown of Erftberg, in the Westphalia region of Germany, to search for any surviving relatives. Daphne had received word on many who were dead, but she had held out hope that at least one or two of those rumors had been false. Sadly, that was not to be.

"That whole section of the journal is so very sad," Grandma Maureen said now. "It ends with her and Abe going out into the grove in the middle of the night and digging at the base of the Fishing Tree. When they found the diamonds, still there, Daphne knew that was the final proof that she was the only member of her entire family to have survived the Holocaust. She wrote that she would have traded every single one of those diamonds for just one more day with her parents or siblings. Oh, I tear up just thinking about it. Excuse me a moment."

As my grandmother fumbled for tissue on her end of the line, I thought about poor Daphne and all she had gone through before, during, and after the war. Suddenly, the diamonds had been given a whole new perspective. No matter how valuable they were, those diamonds would never be worth as much as a single human life.

"The journal didn't say much about the diamonds after that, beyond mentioning that they put the beautiful stones 'somewhere safe' once they wrapped up their trip and Abe reported to his new postwar position in Aachen."

"How much longer did Daphne live?" I asked.

"Uh, let's see…She became pregnant soon after they married, much to her dismay, and then, of course, she died when Emory was born. So no more than a year, I would say."

"And there's no mention of the diamonds in that time?"

"Not that I recall. She seemed to realize she wasn't strong enough to be carrying a child, and she felt certain throughout much of her pregnancy that she wasn't going to survive. She was right. Her last entry was dated just a few weeks before Emory's birth date. It's one of the poems I have, a lament about Abe and her fear that she loved him far more than he loved her."

"Sounds like you weren't the first wife he emotionally abandoned."

My grandmother was quiet for a long moment and then spoke.

"You know what, Sienna? I never thought of it that way before. But I think you're right. Even back then, with her, the man didn't know how to open himself up to love."

My grandmother and I concluded our call soon after that, and before I went back inside I forced myself to sit there on the wicker couch and process everything I had learned and how that applied to the situation with Troy.

Daphne's journal described finding diamonds.

Troy had obviously read Daphne's journal.

He had already known that the grove here was created as a replica of the one in Germany. My guess was that after reading the journal he had assumed Abe would have used the same hiding place over here that Daphne's father had used over there. Following that logic, it made perfect sense for Troy to conclude that the diamonds were buried at the base of the Fishing Tree. So had he found that tree? More important, had he found the diamonds?

I still couldn't know for sure, but at least after speaking with my grandmother I had a far better idea about the diamonds' original source. I was also more determined than ever to hunt them down myself.

And suddenly I had a really good idea about where to start.

Moving through the house, I was surprised to realize that Heath and Floyd were still at it. As I came up the hall and once again was given the "shhh" sign by Heath, I continued on through to the stairs and up to my room. Quickly slipping on my shoes and grabbing my keys, I came back down as quietly as possible, hesitating on the bottom step.

Floyd was looking very relaxed, his eyes still closed, and he was saying something about the smell of stale swimming pool water.

"Good," Heath told him in a soft voice. "Can you smell anything else?"

Floyd hesitated, then he replied, "Rust. I smell rust. But I'm thinking that must be all the blood."

If Floyd was actually remembering smells from the other night, the guided relaxation session must really be working. Now, if my little errand was successful, we might end up making progress on several fronts.

Catching Heath's eye, I held up my keys without jingling them, pointed at the back door, and mouthed the words "I'll be back." He nodded, so I eased open the door and slipped outside.

The rain had become a fine mist, so I didn't bother with an umbrella or raincoat. I simply made a quick dash to my car and slipped inside as quickly as possible.

Not wanting to get in trouble with the law for walking around outside, I started up my car, turned around in the widened parking area, and drove up the long driveway to the road. There I made a right and then a quick left, turning into the driveway of the home where Nina lived across the street from my inn. She was still in the hospital as far as I knew, but I hoped her mother might be home to help me.

As it turned out, the woman was just coming out of her side door as I pulled in. Turning to see who it was, she peered through the mist until recognition lit up her face.

"Sienna! So you've heard?" she cried, opening her umbrella and stepping toward my car.

"Heard what?" I replied, rolling down the window even as the mist was blown inside the car.

"It's Nina! She's awake!"

That was good news indeed. Finally, with a second witness to the incidents of Wednesday night, we might actually obtain some clarity regarding the chain of events. For a moment I thought about driving down to the hospital to see Nina myself, but when her mother said the doctors were only allowing one visitor at a time, for five minutes each hour, I decided to wait. I felt sure the police were already questioning her, and maybe Mike would let me know what she'd had to say—if he was speaking to me at all, that is.

Trying not to think about that, I told Nina's mother I had come in search of some documents that had belonged to my grandfather, documents I had a feeling Nina might have been storing at her place for safekeeping. Fortunately for me, the woman was so eager to get down to the hospital that she didn't ask any questions but simply invited me to take a look for myself.

"Her apartment's up over the garage, as I'm sure you know," she said, "and the extra key is on the molding above the door. Just be sure to lock it back up before you go."

I couldn't believe it was going to be this easy.

Soon, Mrs. Zane was gone and I was inside Nina's apartment, free to root around to my heart's content. I started with a quick, cursory search but didn't come up with anything, so then I focused on more subtle hiding places. Standing on one side of the rustic studio apartment, I slowly turned my head from left to right, looking for clever hiding spots or anything in the tidy place that might seem askew.

It didn't take long to find what I was looking for.

On the left side of the bed the dust ruffle was messed up, its hem caught between mattress and box spring. Moving over there, I reached down and lifted up the mattress, revealing a fat brown envelope hidden underneath.

On the front, in my grandfather's handwriting, was a single word: Daphne.

THIRTY-FIVE

Back at the B and B, I dashed from my car to the door through the mist, the envelope safely tucked underneath my shirt so it wouldn't get wet. Stepping inside, I was immediately greeted by Heath, who had a smile on his face.

"Sienna, big news! We may have discovered an important clue to this mystery!"

I eagerly listened as Heath explained what they had figured out. According to him, as Floyd had recalled each step of Wednesday night's events, he had recovered from his muddy memory one new piece of information, that he had felt some sort of pain in his leg following the flash of fire.

Armed with his new knowledge, Heath had taken it upon himself to examine Floyd, and what he had spotted, on the front of Floyd's right thigh, was a small, circular bruise at the center of which was an even smaller puncture mark.

Before I could even begin to guess what this meant, Floyd blurted it out.

"Doc thinks maybe I got shot by a tranquilizer dart," he said triumphantly. "Probably Nina did too, we bet."

Before I could respond, we were interrupted by the ping of a text message. It was from my grandmother: *Success! Found poems, will fax in just a bit!*

After sending back a "thank you" with some exclamation points of my own, I returned my attention to Heath and Floyd.

"Sorry about that," I said, asking Floyd to repeat what he'd just told me as I slid the phone into my pocket.

"Doc thinks I was shot by a tranquilizer dart."

"By accident?"

"No, on purpose," Floyd said, and when I looked at Heath, he explained the logic behind their reasoning.

"One shooting could have been accidental, but not both," Heath said. "Besides, the shooter disappeared and the darts themselves were removed from the scene after the fact. To me, trying to hide evidence shows intent."

None of us had any idea what this meant exactly or who might have pulled the trigger, but at least it gave us a starting point.

They each immediately began to pursue this information in his own way. While Heath spoke to the pathologist at the lab, Floyd called up his FBI contact. I thought about calling Mike as well, but I decided to leave all of that to the two men and focus on my own discovered secret, the packet of my grandfather's documents.

For some reason I didn't even tell Heath what I had found, not at first. Maybe I just wanted to have it all to myself for a while, to keep things between me and these ghosts of the past. As the rain began to drum more loudly against the eaves outside, I lit a fire in the fireplace, settled myself in the rocking chair, and held the packet in my hands for a long moment. Did the contents of this envelope contain answers to any of our questions?

I was just about to untwist the clasp and begin to find out when my phone began vibrating in my pocket. It was Grandma Maureen, calling to say she was faxing me the poems of Daphne's that she'd had translated from German to English.

Heading into the office, I thanked her profusely, but I didn't share my find with her, either. For the moment, it was still mine and mine alone. There would be time enough later to let others in on this treasure from the past.

Standing there, watching the pages feed through the fax machine that sat on top of the file cabinet, I wondered how Nina had ended up with the papers. Had they had been given to her long ago, by Abe, or much more recently, by Troy? Whether she had received them from one man or the other, I was just glad they had come into her hands somehow.

When the fax machine grew silent, its task complete, I lifted from its tray the pages of translated words. Between them and the brown packet, I had plenty to read and much to learn.

Back in the main room, I saw that Heath was off the phone and on his laptop instead, no doubt searching the web for information about tranquilizer guns and veterinary medicines and the like. From the sound—and the smell—of things, Floyd was in the kitchen cooking breakfast. Though I didn't relish eating food made by his hands—or even having to look at his lying, cheating, felonious face—I knew my stomach would win out. I was starving, and whatever he was making in there smelled incredible.

But for the moment I returned to the rocking chair beside the fireplace and sat, glancing at Heath, who was working from the couch.

"I'm finding some great stuff here," he said, looking up briefly before returning his eyes to the screen. "This all makes so much sense."

"Good," I said simply, wishing he wouldn't elaborate just now.

"Ready for this? Tranquilizer guns often contain a small explosive charge that flashes when detonated."

Lost in my own thoughts, it took me a moment to understand what he was saying. Once I got it, I gasped and said, "The creature's burst of fire!"

"Exactly."

We shared a triumphant smile, and then he concentrated again on his computer screen.

Feeling encouraged, I opened up the envelope to see what treasures it held. Inside were numerous loose sheets of paper as well as a small, leather-bound book, its brown spine crumbled with age. Carefully opening the cover of the book, my heart leaped at the words that had been written by hand on the very first page:

Frau Daphne Kahn Coblentz
25. Mai 1945

Daphne's journal.

My heart pounding with excitement, I closed the journal and turned my attention to the loose papers from the envelope, gently flipping through them. Most were yellowed with age and covered with sketches and notes, some in German and some in English, all in my grandfather's distinctive handwriting. Then came pages and pages of newer-looking lined paper, covered with a completely different handwriting, one that was softer and more feminine than my grandfather's. The words on the pages were dated, just like journal entries, so I compared those dates with those in the journal itself. Sure enough, they matched.

Next, I compared the pages with those faxed from my grandmother, but it was obvious that the handwriting was completely different. This was a newer translation, one by someone other than my grandma's old friend. Perhaps Nina had done this? Having grown up in this area, it wouldn't have been unusual for her to know at least some German.

Flipping through this embarrassment of riches, I decided first to go through the poems my grandmother had sent and then through the full translation. The poems were certainly interesting, and when I got to the third one, I did a double take, spotting amidst the verses the word "Werwolves."

Pulse surging, I read the entire poem, which said:

Not Our Final Home

I had but one wish to sustain me.
Now thwarted by Werwolves,
whose training casts long shadows from the castle.
The grove, it has betrayed me.
I shake off my sandal here
And will search for another,
One worthy
Of this final, sacred ash.

At the bottom of the page, in my grandmother's handwriting, was a note:

Sienna, I think the castle this poem refers to is Hülchrath,
near Erkelenz. Of course, the ashes would have been those of
her mother and sister.

I had no idea what she was talking about. Pulling out my phone, I googled both "Hülchrath" and "Erkelenz" and was astounded at what came back. I found article after article about an elite group of Nazi commandos who trained in Germany in the 1940s. They were called the Werwolves.

Composed primarily of Hitler Youth, the Werwolves had been created during the final months of World War II, even as the Allied forces advanced across Europe and it was clear to all that Germany would soon to be defeated. Werwolves were trained in various rural locations, including Hülchrath Castle, their mission to operate as guerrillas behind enemy lines, sabotage occupying forces, assassinate key allied commanders, and relay intelligence back to a centralized base. From what I could tell, during its brief existence the group had managed to carry out only one significant assassination, and otherwise their value lay more in propaganda and fear-mongering than it had in actual accomplishment. Finally defeated in the spring of 1945, the Werwolves had become, in the end, just another casualty of war.

Unbelievable.

I closed my eyes and tried to remember the words on the marker in the grove, the one in the German Gate section about werewolves. I wasn't positive, but I had a strong feeling that they had been taken directly from this exact poem.

My pulse surging, I suddenly wondered if all of the markers in that section had come not from some literary source but from poems written by Daphne herself. Looking for familiar stanzas, I flipped through the other pages faxed from my grandmother, spotting several lines that sounded very familiar. I recognized quite a few parts of one of the longer poems, and I read it now in its entirety. It was called "The Other Daphne."

The Other Daphne

She runs from love
From her Apollo
Though he follows fast behind
Racing onward
Arms upraised
Her one escape a leafy grave

I too am Daphne
Abe my Apollo
  Though our pursuit runs in reverse
I am the one
Who loves and yearns
  And he who always makes retreat

Oh, he is kind
And he is good
  He fed me water drop by drop!
He bound my wounds
And brought me home
  And in the dark created life

But still in Abe
I do not see
  The love my heart so deeply feels
Instead inside
That muscled chest
  Beats obligation, penance, shame

Worse, in his eyes
There pity lives
  And looks upon my tattooed skin
If only he
Showed love instead
  My heart would ache with one less wound

Yes, now I was certain that the poems in the German Gate section had come from Daphne's own words. How must that have been for Abe, to pull stanzas from his late wife's poetry to hammer into the small metal plates? Had he understood what this poem, "The Other Daphne," was saying, that he hadn't shown her enough love while she was still alive?

If so, how had that made him feel?

Blinking away sudden tears that filled my eyes, I saw that my grandmother had written a note at the bottom of the poem:

Sienna—how sad is this? Rereading it now, I realize you were
right. Abe was as absent with his first wife as he had been

with me. How heartbreaking—for both of us, me and her. I
just showed this to Bessie, and she said maybe that was part of
Abe's obsession with Daphne years later. He may have felt guilty
for not having loved the woman as much as she had loved
him while she was still alive. Who knows? Quite fascinating,
though. I'm glad you called today and asked about all of this.

So the story of Daphne and Apollo was more than just a fictional account of unrequited love. It also played out in the life of this Daphne and her "Apollo," Abe, though in her case Daphne was not the pursued but the pursuer.

How awful that must be, to love someone more than they loved you.

Running a hand through my hair, I looked over at Heath, who was still working away, immersed in whatever he was reading on his computer. Watching him there, his gorgeous blue eyes glued to the screen, his brow furrowed, his brilliant brain thinking, calculating, and gathering information, I felt a surge of tenderness toward him, one so strong that for a moment my heart felt too big for my chest.

I loved this man. I truly did.

So what was my problem? After watching him for a long moment unnoticed, I returned my attention to the poems in my lap. Sadly, I realized, in some ways I was more like my grandfather than I had ever imagined.

THIRTY-SIX

The menu for the brunch Floyd had prepared for us was a familiar one, and I realized that the luxurious spread of Belgian waffles, fresh berries, whipped cream, and crispy sausage was identical to the meal he had prepared for me the day he interviewed for the job as manager. As he served Heath and me at the dining table, I asked him if he was intentionally trying to rub in my face the fact that I had been stupid enough to hire him in the first place.

"No," he replied, sounding hurt. "It's just that this is the only breakfast I know how to make. Well, this and cereal. Troy made me learn how to prepare this and serve it before we met because he knew you would probably ask me to provide a sample meal as part of the interview process." Incredible, this pair, Floyd and Troy. They were like a sad, Lancaster County version of Paul Newman and Robert Redford in *The Sting*. I guess that made me Robert Shaw, the one who had been played for a fool.

The time had come, however, for Floyd to remove himself from the scene of the crime. I asked him how much longer he thought it would be before he was packed and could vacate the premises.

"Actually, I'll be out running errands most of the afternoon, but I was wondering if I could spend one more night here and leave for good first thing tomorrow morning. Do you think that would be okay?"

"Where will you go?" Heath asked kindly, as if that were of any importance whatsoever. As far as I was concerned, Floyd should be going directly to jail—without passing Go or collecting $200.

"I'm not sure, but my contact at the FBI is working something out for me with witness protection. Don't worry, I'll be fine. After they wrap up their big investigation, they'll probably relocate me somewhere sunny and sandy, with mango juice in my hand and babes in bikinis strolling past my reclining chair."

"Oh, that's great," I said, ready to punch Floyd—and Heath too, for that matter, just for being so kind to a man who had betrayed me so horribly. "So you play the tattletale and get off scott free, while I'm left here in financial ruin, possibly facing criminal charges, and my very life in danger."

"Yeah, you're in a big mess, aren't you?" Floyd said, as if he'd had nothing to do with my downfall himself whatsoever.

Rage coursing through my veins, I stood, hands on my hips, and told the man he had exactly one minute to get out of my sight or I would quite literally kick him out the back door myself.

"Okay, okay. I'm going," he said, holding out both palms. "No need to get violent. What do you think I am, Amish?" Laughing at his own joke, he explained that he had overheard some of the cops at the station talking about it. "But about staying the night tonight. That's okay, right? After tomorrow, I'll be out of your hair for good."

"Fine! Now go!"

I remained standing until I heard the back door close behind him.

"What did he mean by that?" Heath asked as I took my seat and spread my napkin on my lap. "The Amish remark?"

"Long story. I had a little run-in with an Amish guy yesterday. I kind of... gave him a black eye."

"You what?"

I told Heath the story of poor Jeremy Lantz and my right cross. The more I explained, the more distasteful the expression on his face grew.

"Don't judge me, Heath," I said suddenly, shaking my head. "It was an accident. Instinctive. I hit first and thought after. The same thing could have happened to anybody. He shouldn't have surprised me like that."

Irritated and afraid I might keep going and say something I shouldn't, I cut off a big piece of waffle, dipped it in syrup, and stuffed it in my mouth.

"That instinct is thanks to something called muscle memory, Sienna, which is used to train the U.S. military and one of the main reasons I lean toward pacifism."

Not wanting to have our usual argument, I didn't reply. Instead, once I had swallowed my giant bite of waffle, I changed the subject, asking him how he was progressing with his Internet research. He was about to reply when his cell phone rang and he excused himself to take the call.

While he was busy on the phone, I retrieved the documents and brought them back to the table. Before the food was ready, I had already gone through the various poems my grandmother had faxed, and now I was reading the translation of Daphne's journal that Nina had done.

What I read was fascinating, a first person account of the Jewish experience in the Holocaust. Daphne's story was so sad, so shocking, and so disturbing that it was hard to take it all in. But every time my eyes threatened to spill over with tears, she would shift gears on me, moving from the gruesome to the mundane, from the stacks of corpses piled ten feet high and left to rot to the metal spoon she traded for a stub of pencil and scrap of paper so she could sketch a bird.

Daphne's words would shift randomly from prose to poetry and back again, a style that made the journal both lyrical and jarring. One section told of the day her mother and sister were absent from roll call. Frantic, Daphne knew what that meant. They had been culled from the others as unfit and then they had been killed.

Daphne described the event from her perspective on her entry dated May 17, 1944.

> *Did not know until the night*
> *When I came in from the fields*
> *That my world, once five then three*
> *Had now been reduced to one*

From there, she went on to share an account of events so heartbreaking I had a hard time reading the entry through to the end. That night, in her

stupor of grief, Daphne decided to attempt an escape from the camp, knowing such an act would surely end with her own death. She didn't care. She
just knew she couldn't be there even one more minute without her family.

Creeping along the walls in the dark, past barrack after barrack, eyeing
the fences for a possible route of escape, she eventually found herself at the
crematorium. Realizing where she was, Daphne had stood there for a long
moment, one thought consuming her mind, that this was where the bodies
of her mother and sister had met their end.

In the light of a dim yellow bulb that hung in the brick archway between
chimneys, she spotted ash that had accumulated in a corner, on the ground.
Unable to stop herself, Daphne moved forward and fell to her knees, reaching out and scooping up two fistfuls of it. The very act seemed to snap her
from her stupor. Holding her ash-filled fists tightly against her chest, she
made a proclamation:

> *This is my mother, this is my sister, I said aloud, declaring for-*
> *ever that the ashes in my hands would represent both. If I could*
> *not join them in death, I would do what I could to give them the*
> *final resting place they deserved. I would bring these ashes home.*
> *Somehow, I made it back unseen, though not by my own*
> *doing. I stood up straight and simply walked from the cremato-*
> *rium all the way to my barracks. Perhaps Hashem laid a cloak of*
> *black around me as I went, blinding all who might have other-*
> *wise observed me.*

> *When the ash had cooled enough*
> *Slid it into sooty sock*
> *Stashed in flea-infested bunk*
> *Where none went except for lice*

> *I will take these to the grove,*
> *Long-beloved place of peace*
> *There will pour the ashes out*
> *Let their death give way to life*

"Sorry about that," Heath said, coming back into the room and sitting across from me. "That was the pathologist. Looks like our theory was correct."

He started to go on, but then he caught sight of my face and stopped. "Sienna, what is it? What's wrong?"

I shook my head, afraid to speak at that moment lest I cry.

"Honey?" he asked, rising from his seat to come closer.

Kneeling beside my chair, he brushed the hair from my face and tried to look into my eyes. I shook my head again, looking down, and then I held out the papers to him. He took them from me, flipped through several, and asked me if this was what he thought it was. I nodded.

"I had an idea earlier," I whispered, "that maybe Nina had the documents. So I went over there and got her mother to let me take a look around, and I found them."

"And?"

"And I don't know. It's complicated. I wanted them so I could learn about the diamonds, but so far I can't stop reading everything else too. There's just so much...this woman's story..."

"Oh, honey, come here," Heath said, wrapping his arms around me and pulling me toward him. I rested my head against his chest, wondering how Daphne could have survived. The poem that had hit me the hardest was also the one that validated my own experience with the darker side of man. Called "Denial," it railed not against Hitler or the Nazis but against regular German citizens, those who lived within the shadows of the concentration camps and knew what was going on but chose to look the other way. The last two stanzas read:

> Through the slats of inbound trains
> Proof stared back with hungry eyes
> Yet your heart remained untouched,
> More empty than the returning trains.

> Every time you turned away
> Though you think you bear no guilt
> Might as well have stoked the fires
> That turned each one to ash and smoke.

After comforting me for a while, Heath moved to the chair next to mine, sliding his plate over so we could sit and eat side by side as we studied the pages together. Skimming through, we were surprised to run across explanations for several different of the stranger markers in the German Gate section of the grove. "Singing Horses" were what the Nazis called prisoners they chained to four-wheeled carts and forced to sing as they pulled massively heavy loads of stones from a quarry. "Blood Street" was the name the prisoners had given to a long nearby road because so many thousands had died during the course of its construction. "Walking Skeletons" came from a poem of Daphne's and was simply her description of her emaciated fellow prisoners.

When Daphne had at last gone through the story of her experiences before and during the war, she moved into the present and began recording each day's events as they happened. After reading about her secret marriage to Abe and her adjustment to life outside the concentration camp and the hospital, we finally got to the part where the two of them had returned to her family home in Westphalia in search of living relatives. Daphne wrote:

> Success! We have found the diamonds, Abe and I, the whole bundle still there, untouched. The treasure was right where Mother had said it would be, in the grove, buried beneath the Fishing Tree.
>
> I am grateful, yes, but also dismayed, for deep inside I think I had held on to the hope that someone else besides me would have returned by now, some cousin who survived the camps and came back ahead of us to retrieve these family assets. Instead, the sealed and perfect package confirms everything I had already been told, that I am the only surviving member of my entire family. My father and his brother and their wives and all of their children are dead, the entire clan reduced to me, my husband, the baby in my womb, and four dozen perfect stones worth the combined wealth of both families. Oh, how I would give every single one of these diamonds back just for one more day with my siblings, one more hour with my parents!
>
> Holding the sparkling stones in my hands now, their smooth

sharpness numb against my burn-scarred palms, I can only thank Hashem that my father comprehended very early on, at least partially, the road that Germany was traveling down.

And yet I am angry as well. For how could he have understood well enough to preserve our wealth but not enough to preserve our lives? Though not as tiny as diamonds, we could all have hidden somehow, I know we could have! Each new day Abe and I learn of some neighbor or friend of a friend who endured the war while tucked safely away beneath houses, behind walls, in hidden chambers.

I would rather have been buried with the diamonds than lived through the horrors of the past seven years.

The next day's entry didn't say anything important about the diamonds, but it certainly spoke volumes about Abe and Daphne and their relationship.

We found my old flute buried at the base of the strawberry tree today, but it had not fared as well as the diamonds. Instead, its metal was rusted and its body invaded by some earthen creature that had long ago taken up residence inside. Unable to look, I told Abe that I was going into the house and for him to dispose of it while I was gone. But then, of course, I couldn't help but watch from the window. Bless him, he did not merely toss it onto the wood pile or bury it back in the ground. Instead, he gently wrapped it in a discarded blanket, placed it atop the pile of stony rubble, and lit it afire like a funeral pyre. He took a long time to come inside, and when he did his eyes were red.

Had he been weeping for the music I would never get to play, the music he would never have the chance to hear? Or were his eyes merely irritated from the smoke? Tonight I summoned my nerve and asked my stoic husband, but I should have known better. Abe carries his pain very deep inside and does not see the purpose in examining it as I do.

I watch
Smoke rising from my flute

Like notes on a page
If only Abe would speak to me
That song would be enough

Once we were finished eating, Heath and I took a break to clear the table and organize our thoughts. Thus far we had managed to confirm that the diamonds really had existed, and they were in Abe and Daphne's possession once they had dug them up from the base of the Fishing Tree.

We also now had a much better understanding of the markers in the German Gate section of the grove.

What we didn't yet know was what had happened to those diamonds.

THIRTY-SEVEN

Heath and I began to go through the other papers in the envelope. Though I recognized my grandfather's distinctive handwriting on most of them, it was hard to tell what, exactly, his scribblings and doodles were all about. We finally decided that many of the pages had to do with plans for the trees in the grove, with notes on everything from fertilizer mix to tree placement to marker diagrams.

Harder to figure out was a large, folded page that opened up to reveal what looked like building plans, though for what structure we could not imagine. Kind of like a studio apartment, the place would have been quite small, judging by the measurements on the diagram. Along one side of the page, Abe had written what looked like a grocery shopping list, but the quantities were odd: five cases of water bottles, twenty-five cans of tomatoes, ten jars of peanut butter. The list also included other nonfood items, such as lanterns, matches, candles, knives, batteries, tarps, and more.

"That sounds like camping gear. Maybe he was planning to build a hunting cabin somewhere," I said.

"How did he feel about the millennium?" Heath asked, reminding me how everyone had braced themselves for the shift from 1999 to 2000. "Maybe that's what this was about. Your grandfather was creating a stockpile against catastrophe."

"Would that have anything to do with these words here?" I asked, pointing to what my grandfather had written near the bottom of the page in capital letters, circled, and underlined: "FIRST TO GO!"

"'First to go,'" Heath read slowly. "I have no idea what that's about."

"Me either. But I can call my grandmother later and ask her if she knows."

In the end we were both disappointed that nothing else in the entire envelope seemed to have anything to do with Daphne's family diamonds. Whether Troy had discovered the envelope and its contents on his own, or if it had been given to him by Nina, it seemed to me that the only clue it contained about where those diamonds could possibly be buried was the single line in Daphne's journal indicating where they had originally been buried over in Europe for the duration of the war.

The final piece of paper in the pile was a letter dated just five years ago from a professor named Odette Moreau at East Pennsylvania University. The letter was a simple thank-you note to Abraham Collins for his participation in her department's Holocaust research project. I didn't know what that was about, but I had to assume that Abe had given them copies of Daphne's journal or at least her poems.

I made a mental note to follow up with that later, curious as to what it was about. Heath received a call just as we finished, so while he talked I returned everything to the envelope and took it to my room for safekeeping. By the time I came back down, he was just hanging up.

"Good news," he said, standing beside the couch. "That was the pathologist. Both Floyd and Nina tested positive for ketamine." He went on to explain that ketamine was an anesthetic used on both humans and animals, and it was often the drug of choice for tranquilizer darts.

"How do you think it happened? Shouldn't the humans have been shooting at the creatures and not the other way around?"

Heath was silent for a moment, rubbing his chin with his thumb.

"I don't know," he said finally. "Like I said earlier, I feel sure it was intentional, not accidental. People don't usually take pains to cover up accidents."

"Sometimes they do. What about hit-and-runs?"

He nodded, considering.

"Here, brainstorm with me," Heath said, walking over to the gift shop area and grabbing a little quilted beanbag. "This is how my roommate and

I used to toss ideas around in college. Whatever you do, don't let it hit the floor. It helps you focus." Positioning himself there, he threw the beanbag over to me.

Catching it easily and tossing it back, I said, "Okay, if he didn't do it on purpose, why would the person who shot Floyd with the tranquilizer dart want to hide the fact?"

He caught it and threw it back.

"It could have been someone who didn't want the police to know, for whatever reason."

"Why wouldn't someone want the police to know?"

"Maybe he got the ketamine illegally."

"Or maybe he had a lot of outstanding parking tickets."

"Or maybe he's just scared of cops in general."

That caused me to falter, nearly missing the beanbag as I thought of my uncle. Emory was scared of cops, that was for sure.

"Maybe it has to do with the animal itself," I said, finding my footing and tossing it back. "Maybe a big dog got loose and attacked Troy."

"A dog? What about the avian coccidiosis?"

"The dog ran through a chicken coop on the way and got the parasite on his fingernails."

"Dogs don't have fingernails."

"Tell that to Liz. She paints Mrs. Prickles' nails every week."

"Yes, but Mrs. Prickles isn't a dog. She's a human in dog form."

We were getting silly, but suddenly silly seemed to be the order of the day. Tossing the beanbag higher and harder, we still managed to keep it from hitting the floor—until I knocked over a lamp with my elbow. Scrambling to keep the lamp from falling, I tripped on the cord, lost my balance, and began to fall. The next thing I knew, Heath was diving toward me, trying to help but only making things worse. He and I ended up hitting the ground in a tangled pile of limbs, the lamp teetering over after us and landing on my head. Fortunately, at least, the lamp didn't break. Neither did my head, thanks to the fact that the thing had fallen lampshade first and had barely hurt me at all.

Catching our breath, we remained there together on the floor for a moment, our laughter fading to soft chuckles. Disentangling myself and rolling onto my side, I propped a head on my arm and looked at Heath, who was still sprawled facedown on the floor next to me.

"How's it going, Grace?" I quipped. "Did you have a nice fall?"

Turning his face toward me, smiling, Heath allowed his eyes to linger on mine. Then, reaching up with one hand, he slid his fingers under my hair and lightly smoothed it back from my face. Lingering there, he traced the line of my chin with one fingertip, ending at my lips.

Time seemed to stop. The world went away. Despite all the heartache of this day, in the moment all we had was this place and each other. Leaning forward, I touched my mouth to his.

The next thing I knew, we were locked in a fervent embrace, kissing passionately, holding on to each other tightly, as if to keep from falling from a cliff. At such an odd angle, pinned between him and the back of the couch, I would have expected to feel frightened and claustrophobic, panicked by a rush of memories. Instead, I wanted him to hold me even more closely, to lose himself in the moment and maybe even forget that we had boundaries and that we lived out what we believed.

But he didn't forget. Heath never forgot. He pulled away, sat up completely, and ran a hand through his hair as he let out a groan of frustration.

"You know," he told me in a low, gravelly voice, "if we were married..."

"I know," I whispered, wanting to continue even as I tried to catch my breath.

"With this big, beautiful place all to ourselves, we could spend hours... We could be together here, there, anywhere, anytime, Sienna, in every room of this inn if we wanted. You and me. Husband and wife. Think of the freedom in that."

"I know," I whispered again, wondering if this was his idea of a proposal or just some wishful thinking.

We were still sitting there, trying to get our passions under control, lost in our thoughts of what-if, when there was a knock at the back door and it swung open.

"Hello?" Mike called out, stepping inside and brushing the rain water from the vinyl case he was carrying.

He spotted the two of us on the floor before we had a chance to respond or get up. I wasn't sure how he would react, whether embarrassed or jealous or maybe just nonchalant. Instead, it was as if a steel door slammed shut behind his eyes. Looking away, he apologized for coming in like that, saying that he should have waited until someone came to the door.

"I wouldn't do this at a regular home," he added, "but since this is a B and B, I guess I wasn't thinking. It felt more like walking into a hotel."

"Please don't apologize," I told him, getting to my feet. "This isn't what it looks like. We had a little lamp mishap."

Heath stood as well, replacing the lamp on the table before stepping toward the door and holding out his hand to Mike for a shake. Though there seemed to be less macho posturing this time, I did notice the look that passed between them, a slight tilting of chins as if in challenge.

"So what's up?" I said, trying to make my tone light as I wondered why I kept letting myself get sidetracked by man issues when far more important things were going on.

"There are a couple of things I would like to discuss with you. Do you mind if we sit down and talk for a minute?"

I offered him coffee, which he accepted, so the three of us went into the kitchen together. While I worked behind the center island, putting a filter in the coffeemaker, scooping up ground beans, and pouring in the water, the two men seated themselves at the table. I wasn't sure if Mike had intended to include Heath in this conversation, but I could see that Heath wasn't going anywhere any time soon.

For a moment I looked from one man to the other, thinking how handsome each one was in his own way—Mike, with his strong features and muscular arms and crackling air of intensity, and Heath, with his chiseled cheekbones and intelligent blue eyes and sweet, gentle spirit. Given that the two men were so different, how was it I found myself attracted to both?

Trying to banish such thoughts from my mind, I was glad Mike didn't seem angry with me anymore, not like he was last night. Instead, as he began to explain why he was here, his demeanor was friendly but professional.

"First, I came by to give you an update on things. I thought you'd like to know that Burl Newton has been released. He'll still face charges for the cockfighting paraphernalia, but he's been cleared in the matter of Troy and his wound. We got more test results back. Turns out the avian coccidiosis wasn't the kind you find in chickens. The gash definitely didn't come from any of that cockfighting equipment."

Pulling three mugs from the cabinet, I braced myself for what I was afraid was coming next, that the evidence was pointing toward Emory's songbirds and, consequently, Emory himself.

"Instead, it's...hold on," Mike said, pulling his little notebook from his pocket. Flipping through the pages, he found what he was looking for and read it to us. "Okay, this coccidiosis can only be found in ratites, specifically those who are of the order Casuariiformes. Caz-u-air-ee-forms? Am I saying that right, Doc?"

"You got me," Heath replied.

"Well, anyway, that means the evidence in Troy's wound points to one of only two types of birds, genus *Casuarius* or genus *Dromaius*."

"In English, please?" I said, wishing he would get to the point.

"The first one, genus *Casuarius*, is what's more commonly known as a 'cassowary.' Cassowaries are the most dangerous bird alive. In fact, a cassowary can and will attack a human, and there have even been some fatalities."

"A bird that can kill a grown man?" Heath asked.

"I heard someone talking about this in the grove yesterday, but I thought they were exaggerating," I said.

"Nope, apparently it's true. A cassowary can kill a human, especially if its kick slices a major artery. But there are other ways the bird is dangerous. In the last recorded case of a fatality, a cassowary killed a teenager with a single kick to the neck."

"Wow," I said as Heath gave a low whistle.

"According to what the guy from the game commission told me, the birds are huge and incredibly aggressive, with probably a hundred and fifty documented attacks on humans per year. They're more commonly known for killing dogs or cows than humans, though."

"So Troy was attacked by a *cassowary*?" I asked, more confused than ever. "Where on earth—"

"Well, no, that's not likely. Yes, a cassowary is by far the more violent of our two choices here and could easily have made that gash, but while cassowaries live in the wild in places like Australia, the only ones you'll find in the U.S. are safely ensconced in zoos or on registered farms, neither of which are anywhere in our region. Which leaves the second species as the far more likely culprit."

"The one you called genus *Drominus*?"

"*Dromaius*," he corrected. "That's the only other Casuariiforme, the cassowary's closest cousin. Unlike the cassowary, birds of the genus *Dromaius* are fairly common in the U.S. and are, in fact, held in captivity in numerous places throughout Lancaster County."

Mike looked from me to Heath and back again, milking the moment, almost enjoying the suspense.

"Genus *Dromaius*, more commonly known as emu," he said at last. "Unless there's a cassowary running wild out here, Troy's leg was sliced by an emu. I'm sorry to be the one to tell you, Sienna, but we had to bring Jonah down to the station. As it turns out, this isn't the only evidence against him. In fact, I wouldn't be surprised if he ends up being officially charged with Troy's murder."

THIRTY-EIGHT

I refused to believe that my cousin had anything to do with Troy's murder. Jonah Coblentz was one of the kindest, gentlest souls I had ever known, not to mention a firm believer in nonresistance and turning the other cheek. I said as much to Mike now, but he countered by saying that not only was there evidence, but there was also motive. Troy and Jonah had had a very vocal falling out, one that dealt with racehorses, insider knowledge, and questionable betting practices.

"I already heard the story about that from Liesl," I told him. "That doesn't prove anything."

"Troy caused Jonah to lose a substantial part of his income. People have killed over less."

"But you have to remember that Jonah's Amish, Mike," I said, carrying two mugs of coffee to the table and setting them in front of the men. "He sees everything that happens, both good and bad, as God's will. He wouldn't have spent a moment plotting some sort of revenge. Instead, he would have been working on forgiveness. That's what the Amish do when they are wronged. Above all else, they forgive, instantly and completely—and over and over again, if necessary."

I put out cream and sugar and spoons, and then I grabbed my own cup and sat down with them.

"In theory," Mike said wryly.

Heath interjected to elaborate. "Didn't you see what happened after the Nickel Mines school shooting, when that man shot those Amish girls in their schoolhouse? Afterward, the Amish responded by almost instantly forgiving the killer. Gave the news media fits because they couldn't understand it."

"Seems weird to the rest of the world, but that's the Amish way," I added.

"Makes no sense to me," Mike said, shaking his head as he stirred a teaspoon of sugar into his coffee. "That's not the Jewish way."

I glanced at Heath, thinking about Daphne's saga and all the wrongs that had been done to her and to her people. For the Jews, forgiveness had to be a tough topic to handle indeed, as they had been wronged in ways that the rest of the world—myself included—could never understand.

"Jews believe that there shouldn't be forgiveness without repentance. Even then, as Rabbi Sackett says, forgiveness should never be spontaneous or instant. It comes slowly, through hard work and resolve and transformation of the self."

"But doesn't that just prolong the pain of having been wronged?" I asked.

Mike shrugged.

"People have to take responsibility for their actions," he replied. "If someone wrongs me, I'm not giving them a free pass. I need to see sorrow, repentance, and reparations. Troy offered none of that to Jonah."

"But, again, Jonah didn't need those things in order to forgive," Heath said. "As soon as it happened, I feel sure, he forgave and forgot and moved on. Forgive us our debts as we forgive our debtors. Not your typical profile of a murderer."

Sipping my coffee, I once again looked from Heath to Mike, from the peaceful pacifist to the crusader for justice. Both men had their points, but on the issue of forgiveness I stood firmly on the side of the Amish.

Choosing my words carefully, I explained to Mike my own position. I wasn't as quick to forgive as the Amish were, maybe, but my forgiveness didn't require anything of the one who had wronged me. To me, forgiveness wasn't a free pass at all. It was more like a "passing along" of the debt from me to God. When I forgave, all I was doing was giving up the right to be involved in a matter that was really between the one who had wronged me and the Creator who would ultimately hold him responsible on my behalf.

"As the Amish like to say, if I want God's grace, I have to give grace to others," I finished.

"Define grace," Mike replied, eyeing me curiously.

"Unmerited favor. I didn't earn it, but I have it anyway. I'm given it every day, all day long. Because of that, I have to give it to others."

The three of us were quiet for a moment, and I realized what a blessing this was, to be in a position to share my faith with someone in a nonthreatening way, and to see that he was hearing me without any knee-jerk defensiveness in response. In my experience, discussions like these were usually quite rare, regardless of the religious beliefs of the respective participants.

"So how do you explain the illegal gun purchase?" Mike asked. "You can't tell me that has anything to do with 'the Amish way.'"

Surprised, I admitted I didn't know what he was talking about. In response, Mike explained that several months ago, before Jonah and Troy had their falling out, the two men were involved in some sort of shady gun deal.

"Or rather, Troy bought a rifle, but he bought it for Jonah, at Jonah's request."

"How is that shady?" I asked, frowning.

Mike took a sip of his coffee before replying, taking his time with his answer. Then he said, "I can't give more details than that. Just believe me when I tell you that the two men were involved in the illegal purchase and transfer of a firearm."

Why Jonah might have wanted a firearm was beyond me, but that seemed beside the point. In my heart I knew, without a doubt, that Jonah could not have killed Troy.

"I'll have to ask Liesl about it," I said. "I'm sure there's a perfectly good explanation."

Thinking of Liesl, I realized that she must be beside herself right now. Her husband had been taken away and was being questioned as a potential murder suspect. Glancing at my watch, I wondered if I would have time to go over there and give her some comfort before my appointment with the FBI.

"Anyway," Mike said, obviously noticing my check on the time, "I need to get going. I just wanted to tell you about Jonah and also show you something. You want to walk me to my car? I'll explain on the way."

"It's pouring rain."

"Looks to me like it's stopped."

To his credit, Heath caught on immediately that Mike wanted to talk to me alone, and he didn't make a fuss. Instead, he stood when we did and excused himself, saying he had some calls he needed to make. Mike and I headed outside, where the rain had indeed stopped, though moisture still hung heavily in the air.

"I found something you'll be very interested in," Mike said as we walked across the spot where he and I had come perilously close to doing something we both would have regretted. "Found it late last night, and I couldn't wait to show you."

Mike was carrying a black vinyl case, and when we reached the car, he set it inside, on the seat, and pulled from it a heavy book. Standing there in the otherwise empty parking area, I waited as he flipped through the pages, maintaining a respectable distance as I did so, just in case Heath was watching from the window. He wasn't usually the jealous type, but in this situation his radar seemed to be on full alert. I wouldn't be surprised to know that he was keeping a close eye on us this very moment.

"Here it is," Mike said, holding out the book to me. "Told you I had seen it before."

Taking it from him, I looked down at the page and gasped. In vivid black and white was a photo of the German Gate—or at least of an identical version, though this one wasn't in a grove.

"What is this?" I whispered.

"Buchenwald," he replied. "That gate is at the entrance to Buchenwald concentration camp."

Stunned, I flipped several pages backward and forward, as the shocking, horrific images seared into my brain: emaciated prisoners, rotting bodies, mountains of confiscated possessions.

Buchenwald.

It made so much sense. The poems on the markers on that section were from Daphne, all dealing with her ordeal in the Holocaust. It stood to reason that my grandfather would have framed that entire part of the grove within its proper context.

"The word 'Buchenwald' actually means 'beech wood forest,'" Mike said. "Apparently, before the camp was built, that region was supposed to have been quite beautiful, a forest filled with beech trees."

He went on to explain a bit more about the camp, how its primary purpose had been to kill its prisoners through work, torture, starvation, or illness from lack of hygiene.

"After liberation, when Eisenhower saw for himself the conditions in the camps, he said that if America's soldiers hadn't known before what they were fighting for, at least now they knew what they were fighting against."

"Wow."

Flipping more slowly through the pages, I thought again of that section of the grove.

"So this explains the beech trees behind the gate in the grove, the ones that are so perfectly aligned, just like soldiers standing in a row. That must be exactly how he intended them to appear."

"No, actually, I think it's probably the opposite of that. I have a feeling your grandfather used those trees to represent the prisoners themselves. They were required to stand at attention for roll call every day, sometimes for hours on end, in the snow or rain or cold without food or water or shoes or proper clothing. Anyone who fell down or passed out was shot."

Overcome with emotion, I looked down at the book and tried to blink away my tears.

How could humans have done such horrible things to other humans? I couldn't understand it.

We were interrupted at that moment by the arrival of Floyd's car, which was probably a good thing. I needed to get ready to go downtown, not stand here and dwell on man's inhumanity to man. I would have to save that for later.

Floyd parked, said some quick, embarrassed hellos, and headed inside, and I told Mike I needed to get back in there as well so I could get ready for the meeting. He offered to let me borrow the book for a while, which I appreciated.

"See you later," he said, sliding into his car as I tucked the book under my arm and headed up the walk.

THIRTY-NINE

While I was getting ready to go, Liz called to say she was on her way but she needed to meet me at our appointment downtown rather than here at the inn. She asked if Heath would mind riding along with me and retrieving Mrs. Prickles, saying that it was just a little too chilly today to leave her precious baby in the car.

Heath didn't seem to mind at all, and in a way I was just as glad he wouldn't be in the meeting. I had no idea what was going to happen in there, but I sure didn't feel like a repeat of last night's humiliation.

I wasn't overly familiar with the city of Lancaster, so we gave ourselves a little extra time to get there. As it turned out, the building itself wasn't that hard to find, but we had to circle the block twice before securing a parking spot. After he turned off the car, Heath said he would text our location to Liz and they could do the doggie drop-off without me if I felt I needed to go on inside. The meeting was supposed to start in ten minutes, so I thanked him for helping, gave him a quick kiss, and told him I would see him later unless, of course, the feds decided to ship me off to Guantánamo Bay.

"I'll be praying for you the whole time," he said, taking my hand in his and giving it a squeeze. "You haven't done anything wrong, Sienna. You don't need to worry. Just be honest with them—and remember to do whatever Liz tells you to."

"Thanks," I said, giving him a hug and getting out of the car.

Inside, the building was set up like a doctor's office, including a waiting room complete with magazines. Instead of a receptionist, however, there was a sign on the wall, posted between the inner door and a doorbell, that said *Please press the button and then have a seat. We will be with you shortly.* According to my watch, I was still a few minutes early, so I decided to have a seat without buzzing and hoped that Liz would arrive before it was time.

I just wished I weren't so nervous! Sitting there alone on a cold vinyl chair, I couldn't help but wonder if a camera was pointed at me, and if somewhere in the bowels of the building federal agents were watching me.

Nonchalantly scanning the room for hidden lenses, I told myself to calm down and get a grip. After all, *I* was the one who had asked for this meeting, not them.

Four more minutes to wait for Liz.

Clasping my hands in my lap to keep them from trembling, I knew I should pray, but at the moment that was the last thing I felt like doing. Wasn't it just this morning that I had been wishing my boyfriend would have his way with me? It would take a lot of nerve to thumb my nose in God's face and then turn around and beg for his help in another matter just a few hours later.

No, for the moment I was going into this on my own strength and feeling pretty frightened and vulnerable. In light of my sin, the whole idea of God and his comfort seemed to be evaporating around me like mist in the grove. Despite what I had said earlier to Mike and Heath about the unmerited nature of God's grace, I was still finding it hard to believe that he was very happy with me today, or that he felt like granting me any special protection right now.

This wasn't just about my losing control with Heath. It was about the past week, the past month, maybe even the past year or two. What had God become to me? An obligation? A random thought? A candy machine dispenser?

Somewhere long ago in my past, God had been as real to me as if I were standing in his presence. He was holy and magnificent and revered, the Creator of the universe. These days, however, God seemed more like an idea than a Supreme Being, more like a lifestyle than the Alpha and Omega, the Maker of heaven and earth. I didn't know what had gone wrong. Perhaps, as Liesl liked to say, I had gotten myself on a "slippery slope," one of just enough affluence and compromise that I hadn't even realized it was happening.

The only thing I knew for sure in this moment was that I was tired of living in a strange netherworld, in this in-between place of foggy faith. Maybe it was time for me to examine my commitment to God, and get on with the rest of my life, either fully in or fully out. All I knew was that sitting on this particular fence was turning me into someone I didn't like very much, a hypocrite and an empty theology spouter.

Liz breezed into the room just in the nick of time, interrupting my melancholy thoughts. She looked stunning, as usual, her black hair pulled into a French twist, her elegant yet professional outfit straight off of a mannequin at Nordstrom's. After receiving a brief hug and a quick, instructional pep talk, I hit the buzzer, ready to roll. Somehow, just having her here beside me, the united front of Beauty and Cutie together again, was incredibly comforting.

As it turned out, our big meeting with the FBI was nothing to have worried about. I had been expecting an interrogation of sorts, probably by the same two men who had eyed me so strangely yesterday at Burl's place. Though I saw one of them in the hallway as we were being led to our meeting room, the person who ended up talking to us was an older man, a silver-haired fellow who treated me not as a suspect of some sort but rather as a source of helpful information. At first he was so nice I was afraid it was a trick. When he paused to go get Mike and bring him in on the discussion, I was doubly worried. But the mood remained cordial throughout, and it was clear from Mike's demeanor that he harbored no suspicions toward me of his own.

Liz was wonderfully impressive, listening intently to every word, speaking when necessary, advising and clarifying as needed. All in all, by the time we were finished, I felt like doing a couple of cartwheels. When the man told me that the U.S. attorney general's office was no longer considering me a person of interest in their particular investigation, I felt sure my sigh of relief could be heard all the way to Jon and Ric's office in Philadelphia.

Of course, this did nothing to solve the problem of Cap and his ilk showing up in search of the treasure. If that happened, I didn't know what we would do. At the very least, I knew we had to find those diamonds before anyone else did.

Then another person joined us, a thick-waisted woman in a frumpy brown suit and sensible shoes. She introduced herself as the liaison between the various organizations involved in the investigation, and after speaking with her for a few minutes, I understood why. She was obviously quite intelligent and fully informed. Best of all, she actually seemed to listen and hear what was said to her.

After gathering the information she wanted to get from us, she shared a little in return, though not nearly as much as I would have liked. She gave us a brief history of the case, saying that several different federal and state organizations had been looking into a certain group that was based in Atlantic City and had ties to organized crime. Gambling was legal in Atlantic City, of course, but there were certain kinds of gambling that were *not* legal—there or anywhere else in the United States. Without elaborating on exactly what she meant, she said that as this gambling ring grew larger and the stakes rose even higher, the various government agencies watching them had joined forces and mounted a full-scale investigation. It was through their monitoring of Troy Griffin that they had first become aware of Harmony Grove Bed & Breakfast.

"We probably wouldn't have given the inn a second thought if someone hadn't run the name of its manager through his database," she said, adding that not only had Floyd come up as having a prior conviction, but that he also had known ties to the group in question.

"The U.S. attorney's office came down hard on your place after that," the silver-haired man added, unapologetically. "When they ran a profile of you, they found enough to give them concern there as well."

"Like what?" I asked incredulously.

The woman looked down at the file she had brought in with her and flipped through several pages before answering.

"Like a forty-thousand-dollar bank deposit on August thirteenth, for starters; followed by the purchase of a brand-new condominium on the river.

This by a woman who had almost no tangible assets and a median checking account balance in the past year of less than a thousand dollars."

My mouth flew open as she even rattled off the condo's exact price tag.

"How do you know this stuff? Did you people monitor my bank account? My mortgage application?"

Mike put a hand on my arm and told me to relax. He explained that in an investigation with stakes this high, the feds were given a lot of leeway. Still reeling with that surprise, I was hit with another. The woman explained how they had then traced the source of that large deposit to an advertising agency in Philadelphia, one that just happened to be owned by two descendents of one of the most notorious crime bosses who ever lived.

Even Liz seemed flummoxed by that revelation.

"Are you telling us that Buzz has ties to organized crime?" she asked.

Both the man and the woman shook their heads.

"They do not, no," the man said. "But we had to make sure. Yesterday, both your name and theirs was removed from our suspect lists."

I wanted more information than that, but even after much cajoling from me and a veiled threat from Liz, they weren't willing to elaborate much. However, the woman finally told us that Ric and Jon's mother's maiden name was Capone.

At this news Mike burst out laughing, and even Liz cracked a smile. Personally, I didn't see what was so funny. Noticing the peevish look on my face, my lawyer broke form for a moment, poked me with her elbow, and told me to lighten up, that surely I of all people could see the irony here.

"I mean, no wonder they suspended you. If I had a name like Capone in my family tree, I'd be pretty skittish about this stuff too."

"They were probably scared," Mike added, still laughing, "especially if they ever spotted those guns of yours. Probably thought you took the job there just to do a hit on them or something."

Still laughing, Liz said to Mike, "Wouldn't you love to have been a fly on the wall the day they found out their new star player had possible ties to organized crime? What do you want to bet they were on the phone with their lawyer within seconds, trying to find out how fast they could terminate Sienna's employment?"

"No, the *second* call would have been to their lawyer," Mike replied. "The first was to their mother: 'Are you *sure* about this family tree business, Mom? Are you positive your cousin's cousin isn't holding some kind of grudge?'"

At that point, all four of the people in the room were having a good laugh. Not wanting to be a wet blanket, I joined in with a smile, but I still didn't think it was very funny.

In the end, what I most wanted to know was how Troy's death fit in with all of this. I asked them, straight out, if he had turned state's evidence, as Floyd had, but they said he had not. From the sound of things, he had been a key player with the group in question, a real wheeler and dealer who would have been slapped with a whole host of charges had he still been alive when the arrests went down.

"And when will that be?" Liz asked.

"Soon. Very soon."

"I would love to tell you how and why Troy Griffin died," the woman said, "but I don't know. At least Weissbaum here is the detective assigned to the case. If anyone can figure it out, Mike can."

Mike thanked her for the compliment, and as I listened to the two of them talking, I realized this wasn't the first time he'd overseen a case that had him rubbing elbows with the feds.

The meeting ended soon after that, with Mike giving us a wave and disappearing down the hall, the woman promising us that the overriding investigation would be coming to a close very soon, and the man repeating a stern warning about the confidentiality of all we had learned today.

As Liz and I walked down the hallway, my thoughts were distracted by that strange ripple effect that we used to call "the parting of the Red Sea." Back in college, everyone said that it was the combination of the two of us together that was so compelling, the light and dark, Beauty and Cutie. Though secretly I used to enjoy such moments, after the attack they only served to make me feel uncomfortable.

We had almost reached the door to the waiting room when we passed someone who knew Liz. Judging by their friendly greeting and ensuing conversation, they had at some point worked together, probably at a law firm or during an internship. Liz introduced me, of course, but as they continued to chat I found myself growing bored and wondered if Mike was still around. I really wanted to ask him about Nina. Telling Liz that I would be back in a few minutes, I caught the eye of our silver-haired interviewer and asked if he knew where I might find Detective Weissbaum. He directed me to the last door on the left, where he said Mike was sitting in on a training session.

"Oh, then I won't disturb him."

"It's not like that. You can go in there, no problem."

Taking the man at his word, I went down to the door and cracked it open to peek inside. The room looked like a small gymnasium. In the center of the shiny wooden floor was a large blue mat upon which stood two men, both in athletic wear, facing off in what looked like some sort of karate-type stance. Other people, both men and women, were hovering around the fringes of the mat, watching the two of them and cheering them on. At the very back of the room, not far from the door, I spotted Mike, who was leaning against the wall, arms folded across his chest.

Slipping inside, I tried to move toward him without attracting attention. I was looking right at him when he first noticed me, and I was startled by the expression of pleasure that filled his eyes for just an instant. He was genuinely happy to see me. But then that steel door slammed shut again, and I knew it didn't really matter.

Why *should* it matter? I had a boyfriend.

I was asking him my question about Nina when suddenly the whole group was looking our way and calling his name. From what I could tell, he was being summoned to the mat for his turn.

"Sorry, this is why they wanted me here," he said to me. "I'll call you later after I'm done."

"Can you tell me anything at all?" I asked, stepping back as he removed his jacket and shoes in preparation for his turn.

"Sure," he replied, placing his shoes against the wall. "I talked to Nina this morning. She's blaming you for everything, including Troy's death."

FORTY

Watching in stunned silence as Mike crossed the room to take his place on the mat, I decided that the man had a cruel streak. No decent person would tell someone a person was blaming her for another person's death when he wasn't in a position to follow up those words immediately. Did he enjoy tossing out bombshells and watching them explode? Or was this just some small way he could make a dig at me in retaliation for the rejection he felt I had given him?

Whatever this was about, it was a side of Mike I found very unattractive.

Pulling out my phone, I texted Liz to say that I was sorry, but I would be a few more minutes and for her to please wait for me. Then I put my phone away and focused my attention on the man in the center of the room. If I had to stand here until he was finished, I would. Now that he'd said what he said, I wasn't leaving without some answers, that was for sure.

It wasn't until then that I realized Mike had been invited here to demonstrate some kind of technique. The way he began to speak to the class, it almost sounded as though he was an expert on the topic.

"First of all, this is not the best place to train for Krav Maga, on a cushy mat inside a gym. Your workouts should be outside, on uneven terrain, and in more realistic conditions whenever possible."

Mike asked for a volunteer and then chose one from among the many raised hands. As the guy suited up with padding, Mike explained to the group just a little bit about the history and technique of Krav Maga. First designed for use by the Israeli army in the 1930s, this self-defense system pulled elements from a number of other martial arts, emphasizing close combat moves and fierce bursts of energy and aggression.

From the way he talked, it sounded brutally effective to me, and soon I was caught up in his lecture and had forgotten to be irritated with him. Facing his opponent, Mike handed the guy a rubber training knife and said to come at him full force and do whatever it took to stab him.

The action that followed was mesmerizing. No matter what the guy tried, he was no match for Mike, who seemed to be using karate blocks, judo throws, and even jujitsu disarming techniques. He hadn't been kidding when he said that Krav Maga incorporated elements from other martial arts. Soon, the opponent was on the floor on his back, the knife was in Mike's hand, and the match was over.

Mike stood, offering a hand to the guy to help him up. He asked for another volunteer, and though not as many hands shot up this time, he still had a few to choose from. As the second guy suited up, Mike asked the group if anyone could tell him what the most unique element of what they had just witnessed was.

No one seemed to give him the answer he wanted, so finally I raised my hand. With a bemused smile on his face, Mike called on me.

"You were blocking and striking at the same time," I said, and I was secretly thrilled when his expression immediately transitioned into one of respect.

"Exactly. Come on, people. She's a civilian, and she's the only one in this room who got it."

Feeling particularly proud of myself, I moved closer to stand among the others and get a better look at the action on the mat. From what I could see, the strength of Krav Maga was in the way it could be done in tight spaces, even where there wasn't any pullback room at all. Watching Mike easily defeat the second volunteer and then the third, I found myself wishing I had discovered this particular defense method sooner. Most of the techniques I had studied focused on protecting myself one-on-one against a single attacker, but Krav Maga seemed to offer techniques that would allow one person to ward off multiple opponents.

Of course, that spoke volumes to me.

To show this in action, Mike had everyone step onto the mat—everyone except for me.

"Sorry, Sienna. I can't let you participate for insurance purposes," Mike said. Glancing around to make sure that the others were distracted with putting on their gear, he added under his breath, "Not that I wouldn't enjoy it very, very much."

Adrenaline coursed through my veins as I looked away, stepping back to give them more room.

Over the next few minutes, as the class began to rush at Mike and he fought off every attacker in turn, things grew far more intense. At first, I found myself drawn to the violent spectacle, fascinated by it even. But the more I watched, the more things began to shift. Something about it began to feel disturbing to me. Maybe it was Mike's guttural yells or his fierce, blazing eyes, or the animal way in which he was so fully engaged in the fight.

Whatever it was, it rattled me. Suddenly, that ever-present element of danger in him was not so appealing, not at all. That intensity that always seemed to burn inside of him made me feel frightened and claustrophobic, as if it might burn me up completely.

My heart pounding in a familiar panic, I moved toward the door, opened it, and stepped into the hall. Taking a deep breath, I wondered if I would ever tell him what had just happened. Certainly, Mike understood panic attacks, as he had helped me through one very serious one in the grove. But this was a different kind of panic. This was about me and him and that strange dance of attraction we had been doing with each other since the moment we met.

As Liz and I drove toward the B and B, all I could think was that the dance was finally over.

Fortunately, Liz seemed to be in a pensive mood, and our drive was a quiet one, punctuated by my occasional directives to "turn left here" and "fork to the right." As we drew closer to the inn, she apologized for not being more talkative, saying that between a morning in court and an afternoon at an FBI interrogation, her brain was simply fried. I thanked her again for making the time to come, but she wouldn't even let me finish, waving away my words with her perfectly manicured hand.

We were just about to turn into the driveway of Harmony Grove Bed & Breakfast when I noticed movement in front of Nina's house. With a start, I realized she was home. Already?

Supported by a person on each side, Nina was being led not upstairs to her own apartment but straight into her mother's house. Hadn't she just recovered consciousness this morning? What on earth was she doing home so soon?

Remembering what Mike had said about Nina blaming me for Troy's death, I knew she and I needed to talk. If she genuinely blamed me for any part of this week's tragedies, then I wanted to hear that straight from her, and I wanted to know why. I would give her a little time to settle in, and then I would go over to her house for a chat. Our families had known each other far too long to let this matter rest—not to mention that I very much needed to know what had happened Wednesday night and why she thought I had had anything to do with it.

Turning left, Liz pulled slowly up my long driveway and came to a stop in the parking area between my car and Floyd's. Thinking about going inside to face him yet again, I couldn't believe I had agreed to let him stay one more night. As far as I was concerned, morning couldn't come soon enough if it meant getting rid of Floyd.

Mrs. Prickles met us at the car, with Heath following along behind. As Liz enthusiastically greeted her baby, I simply wrapped my arms around this man and held on tight, whispering a soft thank-you for having remained by my side thus far in this ordeal. Even the fact that he'd been willing to dog-sit back here at the B and B rather than insist he be allowed to attend the meeting spoke volumes about his character.

"Looks like Floyd may not be spending tonight here after all," Heath said as we headed up the walk. "He's waiting to hear from the witness protection people, who are trying to expedite things as much as possible."

Heath had pizza waiting for us inside, but Liz needed to hit the road, so she took her slice to go, promising she would keep me posted on any new developments as they arose. I had hoped she would be able to spend the night, but she asked for a rain check instead. Heath and I walked her out to her car, and as he settled Mrs. Prickles into the back seat, Liz gave me an extra long hug and told me to hang in there, that this would all be over soon.

After she was gone, Heath and I returned to the dining room and shared the pizza as I went through all that had happened, step-by-step, during my meeting with the feds. Of course, I omitted the part about Mike's Krav Maga class afterward. Half an hour later, as we were clearing the table, I looked out the front window to see that all of the cars were gone from across the street except for Nina's and her mother's. Whether she wanted to see me or not, it was time for me to pay my neighbor a visit.

Heath insisted on going with me. As we were walking out the back door, Floyd came out of his room and asked if there was anything he could do for us, if there was anything at all that we needed. His obsequiousness was more irritating than if he had chosen to ignore us completely.

"Just stay out of my sight, why don't you?" I told him as I stepped outside.

"That was pretty harsh," Heath said as he closed the door behind us and we headed down the walk.

"He deserves far worse," I replied, my jaw set stubbornly.

When Heath and I reached the driveway, we saw that another car had just pulled in next to mine, a black Buick with tinted windows. Discreetly, I reached for the gun at my waist, fearing this was the first of the underworld treasure hunters come to call. But when two men climbed out, neatly dressed and asking specifically for Floyd Underhill, I realized with relief that they must be the ones he'd been waiting for from the witness protection program. We told them they could find Floyd inside.

Then Heath and I drove to Nina's house together, but not wanting her to feel ambushed by the two of us, I suggested that he wait for me in the car and let me do this on my own. He had brought along the translation of Daphne's journal and said he would sit in the car and finish reading it while I talked with Nina inside the house.

I went to the door alone, afraid Nina's mother would be the one to answer it, but before I could even knock, it swung open to reveal Nina herself.

"What do you want?" she asked, bleary eyed and pale. At the moment, I

304 ❦ MINDY STARNS CLARK

couldn't imagine that anyone would call this girl "smoking hot." More than anything, she looked ill.

I started by asking her if she was okay and what she was doing home so soon.

"No health insurance," she replied, running a hand through her messy hair. "I couldn't afford to stick around the hospital any more than I absolutely had to. Is that all?"

She started to close the door, but I held out a hand to stop her, saying no, that was not all and that she and I needed to have a talk. Sighing heavily, she let me in but said her mom had just run to the store to get a few things and we had to be finished before she got back or we'd both be in trouble that she was out here talking instead of resting.

"Then I'll get right to the point," I said as she led us to twin rockers near the front window and we sat. "It's my understanding that you're holding me responsible for what happened Wednesday night."

"I sure am," she said softly, sitting in the creaky chair. "If it hadn't been for you, Troy never would have been out there trying to beat you to those diamonds."

I wondered if I had heard her correctly and asked what she meant.

As she talked it became apparent that the poor girl had been manipulated by Troy, who had fed her a bunch of lies. According to Nina, she had spotted Troy in the grove with a metal detector on Tuesday morning and had gone out to see what he was doing. They hadn't spoken in a month or two, and I had the feeling that mostly she just wanted an excuse to see him. He had acted odd, though, and after talking to him a little, it struck her that maybe he was out there looking for "Mr. Abe's diamonds."

"You knew about the diamonds?"

"Yeah, I've known about them for a long time," she replied, but she didn't elaborate. I could tell from her expression that there was more she wasn't saying.

She continued with her tale, explaining how she had asked Troy straight out if that was what he was doing. He finally admitted that yes, he was, but not so he could steal them. He wanted to find them for Emory's sake.

"Yeah, right," I scoffed.

"No, it's true. He told me he overheard you and your new boyfriend talking about how the two of you were going to come to the inn next week, find the diamonds, and keep them for yourselves. He said you were currently in Boston, but that as soon as you got back you were coming straight out here to find those jewels. He said he had only a couple of days to get out there and locate them ahead of you. Once he found them, he was going to take them straight to the authorities to make sure Emory got his full inheritance without you or anyone else stealing those diamonds out from under him."

Floyd was right. Troy *was* a pathological liar, and he had really pulled out all the stops on that one. My first reaction was one of disdain, wondering how Nina could possibly have been so naive as to fall for his lies. My second thought was that I lived in a glass house and had absolutely no business whatsoever throwing stones.

"You believed him, Nina? You weren't even willing to give me the benefit of the doubt?"

"I did! I called your office and asked for you, and they said you were in Boston. That was all the proof I needed that Troy was telling the truth."

FORTY-ONE

Knowing that Nina and I were just a pair of gullible fools, I hesitated, wondering how I would ever be able to make her understand that Troy had been lying about everything.

"The only reason Troy knew I was in Boston was because he called me on my cell phone Monday night to ask me about my grandfather's papers, and I mentioned it then," I said.

"You know about the papers?" she asked, casting a fleeting glance toward the door. I realized she didn't yet know I had been up to her apartment, found the envelope, and taken it away. Choosing not to bring that up now, I said yes and asked what she could tell me about them.

"Troy found them somewhere in your bed-and-breakfast," she replied. "He said that as soon as he saw the words *die diamanten*, he knew they had to do with Emory's inheritance and were worth reading. Once he did, he realized those documents held the key to where the diamonds were hidden, at the base of something called the Fishing Tree."

"Do you know, or did he know, which tree that was?"

She shook her head.

"I tried to help him figure it out. My German is better than his, so I took the pages and starting translating all of them, hoping to find more clues. Instead, I just learned a bunch of sad stuff about Emory's mother. I mean, Mr. Abe had told me about a lot of the stuff that was in there, but reading it for myself was really hard. Anyway, she barely mentioned the diamonds at all."

I kept going, asking Nina what happened Wednesday evening.

"Well, Troy searched for the diamonds all day Tuesday without any luck, and then he went back out there again on Wednesday. He had gotten rid of Floyd for a couple of days, you know, but when Floyd called and said he was heading home, Troy told me he needed my help. He knew Floyd was tight with you and your boyfriend, and as soon as he got back he was going to cause trouble. So Troy came up with a plan. He said we could put something in Floyd's drink, like a sedative of some kind that would knock him out for the rest of the evening. If it worked, we could do the same thing the next morning. We hoped that would buy enough time for Troy to keep working—without Floyd knowing—until he found the diamonds."

Glancing at Nina and seeing the sheepish expression on her face, I said simply, "The Ativan."

Looking out the window in the direction of Emory's house, she said she knew it was wrong to take Emory's pills, but in a way it was okay. "We were doing this for him, after all. Was it wrong to steal a few of his pills if, in the end, that was what got him the diamonds?"

We both rocked in silence for a long moment. Ignoring my own feelings about drugs being put into drinks, I kept thinking that by telling herself that lie, Nina had climbed onto a very slippery slope, one that couldn't lead anywhere but down.

I knew a thing or two about slippery slopes.

Nina went on to tell me how she had taken the pills out of the box while Emory was at his boss's house having dinner, and then she had gone into the grove to find Troy and give the pills to him. He was nowhere to be found, though, so she kept walking all the way to the inn. She was heading up the sidewalk toward the back door, just passing the open gate to the pool area, when she glanced inside and thought she saw something.

Pausing to look, she realized it was Troy, and he was floating facedown in the pool. Screaming for help, she immediately pushed open the gate, jumped into the water, and pulled him out. She tried to do CPR, but the next thing she knew Floyd was there, telling her that it was no use, that Troy

308 ❧ MINDY STARNS CLARK

was dead. Seeing the gun in his hand, she had immediately jumped to the conclusion that Floyd had shot and killed Troy.

"He kept denying it, but while we were arguing we heard a weird noise, like a strange, scary rumble, just beyond the far side of the fence. We turned to look, and then all of a sudden there was a big flash and Floyd collapsed on the ground."

"Did you see where the flash came from?"

She nodded, saying she knew it sounded stupid, but the flash had come from a big, black creature who had risen up from the bushes and shot Floyd with some sort of gun. I pressed her for a better description of the creature than the one Floyd had given, and she finally admitted that it had looked not unlike "the Michelin Man, all padded and lumpy, except that it was black instead of white, and it just had holes for eyes."

The Michelin Man? Padded and lumpy? I couldn't fathom what that could have been.

She went on with the little bit that was left of her tale, saying how she had run away as fast as she could, the beast in pursuit more slowly behind her. She had cut across the side lawn and around the front of the grove to Emory's driveway, and had made it almost as far as the covered bridge before she felt a sharp pain in her buttocks, "worse than a wasp—more like a big jellyfish."

That was all she remembered.

Again we sat in silence for a little while, rocking in our chairs, thinking about what she had just shared. As gently as I could, I gave her my defense, explaining how Troy had duped her and then explaining the much bigger way in which he had duped me as well.

"Yeah, that cute police detective already told me most of this," she said. Though she didn't seem fully convinced, I could tell that at least some cracks had been made in her certainty. Perhaps the more she thought about it, the more she would come around.

"Am I fired?" she asked suddenly, and I felt a deep surge of pity for this girl who had been through so much in her lifetime: the loss of a husband to divorce, the loss of a child to death. I didn't see any reason for her to lose her only job as well, and I told her so.

"But I stole Emory's pills," she said, her eyes filling with tears. "I've never done anything like that in my life."

I agreed that had been a serious lapse in judgment, but I told her I had a feeling it wouldn't ever happen again.

"No, never. I promise," she said emphatically, shaking her head from side to side. "Before he died, I told Mr. Abe not to worry. I said I would always look after Emory and keep him safe. I intend to keep that promise, whether I do that as an employee or as a friend."

"Our family appreciates how good you are with Emory."

"I try. Mr. Abe spent so many years obsessing about his son's welfare, you know, terrified that someday there could be another Holocaust and Emory's half-Jewish heritage would come back to haunt him. I just wish Mr. Abe could have found some peace about that."

"Me too."

We both stood, and though she was still weak and pale, I thought I could see a little spark inside of her now, no doubt the relief that came from confession and restoration.

"You really loved my grandfather, didn't you?"

She nodded, her eyes again filling with tears.

"My daddy passed away when I was so young, but Mr. Abe was like a second father to me. I loved him very much."

Stepping toward the door, I said I had never had much of a relationship with the man myself simply because he was always so quiet and remote.

"Yeah, he didn't talk often. But once in a while he would surprise me and come out with all sorts of stuff, especially when he got near the end."

I paused at the door, one hand on the knob.

"What sorts of things did he talk about?"

"Like how many mistakes he had made in his life. How he had hurt his first wife so deeply. How he had driven his second wife away entirely. He had a lot of guilt, you know. A *lot* of guilt. About the war. About the women he had loved. About the family he had hurt and the God he had disappointed."

"Did he ever talk about the diamonds?"

She studied my face for a moment before nodding, but she wouldn't elaborate. Rather than argue, I tried to come at it from a different way, posing other questions to her instead.

"You know," I said, "Abe was such a mystery. I've always wondered what it was that changed him so, back during the war. What made him regret his decision not to bear arms? Why did he do such a complete about-face on his stance of nonviolence? Did he ever talk about that with you?"

"Yes," Nina said, exhaling wearily, as if the very thought of explaining such a complicated transformation was almost too exhausting to comprehend. "He told me everything started to change when he first saw Buchenwald. Witnessing the horrors there, he realized what the war had really been about, and he felt that his choice to serve as a conscientious objector had been a mistake. He told me, 'I know Jesus said we're supposed to turn the other cheek, but what are we supposed to do when it isn't our own cheek we're talking about? What about when *others* are being hurt? Shouldn't we do whatever it takes to protect them from harm?' He couldn't figure that one out. All he knew for sure was that God never meant for anyone to suffer the way the Jews had suffered. If taking up a gun and fighting the evil of Hitler's regime was the only way to stop it, then he couldn't see how that could ever be wrong."

I thought about that, wondering if I dared share those sentiments with Heath, or if it would even make any difference if I did.

"I think the final clincher for him came a few days later," she continued, "when one of his patients asked him to do her a favor, a young woman named Daphne. She was nearly dead from typhus, but she wouldn't stop saying that she had to get the ashes, that she needed to bring her mother and sister home. If you ever read Daphne's journal, you'll know what I'm talking about. She had put some ashes in a sock and hidden it up under her mattress. When she begged Abe to go to her bunk in the empty barracks and find that sock and bring it back to her, he felt so sorry for her that he agreed to do it."

Nina looked so weak, I knew I shouldn't keep her any longer, but I couldn't walk away until I had all of my answers.

"When he went inside the barracks and looked under that mattress and found that sock, he said it was the saddest, most sickening moment of his entire life. Overwhelmed by the stench, the lice, the waste, he just stood there with that sock in his hand and wept. I think that's probably why he ended up marrying Daphne, at least at first—out of guilt and shame and obligation. It wasn't until later, until after she had passed away, that he realized he had actually loved her. But by then it was too late to let her know."

She went on to explain that by the time Abe felt strong enough to read the journal his late wife had left behind, he had already remarried and had another child on the way. Of course, he had been deeply affected by the whole journal, but especially by one of her poems, the one called "The Other Daphne," about how she loved Abe more than he loved her.

I sighed, thinking about that myself.

"Her poem just about broke his heart," Nina continued. "The first time he read it, he decided he would spend the rest of his life, if necessary, making that up to her. That's when he really got serious about finishing the grove. He still hadn't even sprinkled the ashes on it yet."

"What do you mean?"

"The ashes in the sock, plus Daphne's ashes too, from when she died—he still had all of them."

"You're kidding."

"No. See, when they went back to her home in Germany after the war, she was going to bury the ashes in the grove there. But then they found out that the Nazis had been using it as a training ground for some commando teams. She said the place had been spoiled for her forever and it didn't deserve those ashes. Abe promised her they would find another grove, but they never did and then she died."

"How sad."

"It gets worse. Believe it or not, some paranoid administrator at the hospital saw 'typhus' in Daphne's medical records and ordered that her body be cremated immediately."

"Isn't cremation against Jewish law?"

"Sure is, but the hospital people didn't even realize she was Jewish, especially with her being married to an American soldier. When Mr. Abe found out what had happened, he was devastated. Taking her ashes regardless, he promised himself that someday he would make the situation right. When he and Emory came back to America, he finally came up with a plan. He decided to recreate the grove here—her grove, exactly as it was—but without the taint of the Nazis. Then he would be able to bury everybody's ashes in there all at the same time, finally putting the matter to rest."

"Wow. I had no idea."

Nina looked as though she was just about finished, and though I felt guilty for pushing her much further, she still had one question to answer, so I tried again.

"What did he say to you about the diamonds, Nina? Did he bring them back to America with him when he came home?"

"Yes," she whispered.

"What did he do with them? Where are they now?"

Her cheeks began to flush, twin red circles on the pale skin of her face.

"I don't know. But they're real, Sienna. They do exist. I can tell you that for a fact."

"How can you be so sure? Did you ever see the diamonds yourself?"

She looked at me, eyes swimming with tears.

"Just one of them," she replied. And then she added, "The one your grandfather gave to me."

FORTY-TWO

This was too important to miss, but if we weren't careful, Nina was going to pass out soon. She leaned back against the wall, closed her eyes, and explained. She said that two and a half years ago, after her daughter's car accident and subsequent death, she had found herself in serious debt, with almost $40,000 in outstanding medical bills. When my grandfather found out about that, he had given her one massive, cut diamond that he said she should be able to sell for between $30,000 and $50,000. He wanted the proceeds to go toward her bills, no strings attached, as long as she promised to keep the source of the diamond confidential.

Nina had been shocked, of course, and though she tried to refuse, Abe had insisted. She finally relented once he told her that he had plenty more where that came from, that in fact he had an entire cache of diamonds tucked away for safekeeping. The diamonds had belonged to Emory's mother, and Abe had held on to them all of these years, intending them to be used for the cost of Emory's care and housing and other expenses once Abe was gone and could no longer provide for his son himself.

"I asked Mr. Abe if Emory knew about the diamonds, and he said yes but not where the diamonds were hidden. At one time, Emory *had* known where they were, but then Mr. Abe had caught him blabbing about it, so he chose a new hiding place, which he didn't share with anyone. He said that once he passed away that hiding place would be revealed. But it wasn't, and I've been wondering why ever since."

Nina was right: Whatever great revelation my grandfather had intended after his death had not taken place. Now it was anyone's guess where he had put the diamonds and if they were still there.

"Was his estimate of the value correct?" I asked, wondering how many diamonds there were altogether and what their total worth would be now.

Nina nodded, eyes shining.

"God bless him," she whispered, adding that she sold the stone to a private dealer for $46,000. "That covered every single one of my bills and then some."

That seemed an appropriate point for ending our conversation. Nina and I said our goodbyes, and I went to the car, deep in thought. Obviously, Abe had wanted Emory to be well cared for after he was gone, so what had he done wrong? Why hadn't the location of the diamonds ever been revealed? Was it possible that my grandfather's lawyer had lied, that the diamonds' hiding place had been specified in the will but that the man had somehow altered the document and stolen them for himself?

That didn't sound likely, but just in case I would ask Liz how to look into something like that. In the meantime, there were other avenues to pursue. Slipping into the car beside Heath, I gave him the high points of my conversation with Nina as we made the short drive back to the inn.

He, in turn, told me about the journal, insisting that I read the final entry, one in which she predicted her own death. Dated February 12, 1946, it had been written near the end of her pregnancy.

> *Abe won't let me talk about my fear that I will die giving birth to our child. Deep inside he must know I am not up to this. My health, sorely compromised in the camps, needs years yet to heal. But what can we do? Babies come whether we are ready or not. And so I go on. I pray for life, but I brace myself for death. Scribbling furiously every day, I have tried to write things down, every memory, every truth, wanting to leave something of myself behind for my child, who I fear will not otherwise know me.*
>
> *Is the tiny one inside my womb a boy or a girl? It matters not. What matters is that Abe keep his promise. No matter what, he will keep our child safe from harm always. Whatever it takes. Whatever the cost. This child must always have a place to hide.*

Daphne had been right about not surviving childbirth. Emory had barely survived himself, and during the birth he had been deprived of oxygen long enough to cause permanent brain damage. Perhaps one of the saddest elements of this tragedy wasn't just that Daphne had died, but that her mentally limited son would never have the capacity to understand or appreciate the treasure of the journal she had left behind.

I had to blink away tears as I read the last line. But before I could even begin to gather my thoughts, I realized that the two witness protection guys were coming our way. They looked as if they wanted to speak with us, so we put the papers away for now and got out of the car.

"Is something wrong?" Heath asked.

"Yes, there's something wrong. We thought you said Floyd was inside," one of them told us.

"He was."

"Not that we can see. We can't find him anywhere."

"Did you call out his name when you went in?" Heath asked.

"Called out his name, rang the bell, knocked, finally walked all over the entire place, inside and out, looking for him. He's nowhere to be found."

"That's odd," I said, certain there was a logical explanation. Floyd couldn't have left the house completely because the two men had been walking up as we were walking out, so one way or another one of us would have seen him. "Let me see if I can find him," I said, thinking maybe he had just gone down into the wine cellar or something and hadn't heard everyone calling him from upstairs.

Heath stayed outside with the two men while I went inside and began calling Floyd's name and walking from room to room. I checked the wine cellar, but it was empty. Thinking maybe he was out on the screen porch, I went there, but it was empty too, and the screen door was locked from the inside. After looking through the rest of the downstairs, I headed up to the second floor, checking the three rooms and their bathrooms in turn. There were no signs of Floyd anywhere.

This was so weird!

I came back downstairs, where Heath and the two men were just coming in the back door. I admitted that they were right. I couldn't find him either.

"We didn't see him outside," Heath said, "which means he could be hiding somewhere on purpose."

"That'd be my guess," one of the men replied, looking at his coworker and snorting derisively. "He musta seen us coming."

At Heath's suggestion, all four of us fanned out to look, this time in a more systematic fashion. My job was to check every door and window for evidence of an escape. When I had finished making my way through the whole house, I was more certain than ever that Floyd was here somewhere, because everything except the back door was locked from the inside.

So where was he?

"Well," I said as I met back up with the two men in the main room, "whatever part of the alphabet you guys come from—FBI, ATF, DOT, whatever—I guess the important question is, what do you do when your star witness goes missing?"

The two men looked at each other and then back at me.

"What do you mean?" one asked.

"I mean, how serious is this? I know Floyd turned state's evidence, but does that mean you need him to testify against the mob and all of that, or has it been enough just to have him as an informant?"

The men looked at each other in alarm and then at me.

"Floyd turned?"

"He's been talking to the FBI?"

"Yes. Of course. Isn't that why you're here?"

Suddenly, both men began edging toward the door.

"No, look, we gotta go," the first one said. "If you see Floyd, tell him we'll be in touch, would you? Just say some old friends came by to see him."

After that, the two men made a hasty retreat, practically running out the door and down the sidewalk. Once they were gone, it took me a minute to realize what had just happened. Those two hadn't been feds at all. They were criminals.

More than likely, they were the mob.

Reaching into the pack at my waist, I pulled out my gun, holding the grip firmly as I moved swiftly to the back door and flipped the deadbolt so that it was securely locked. I knew that Heath wouldn't be happy to see that I had the gun out, but that was his problem. Suddenly, I felt very, very violated.

Looking around me, the house was so quiet that for a moment I was ter-rified that Heath had disappeared too. Standing by the front door, I called out his name and was deeply relieved to hear a reply. It sounded as if he was in Floyd's room, so I went there now, gun in one hand, digging in my pocket for my phone with the other.

"Did you hear what just happened?" I asked, and when he said he had not, I explained.

"And that gun makes you feel safer now?" he asked, eyeing it warily. "Because it's not doing too much for me."

"Deal with it," I snapped, dialing with my other hand and waiting for Mike to pick up.

"Sienna? Hey, hold on a minute," Mike's voice said as he answered, and then I could hear him talking to someone else, just finishing up a conversa-tion. As I waited for him to come back on the line, the enormity of the situ-ation finally began to hit me. My stupid blunder had just clued in the mob that one of their own had been ratting them out to the federal government! Who knew what the fallout from that might be?

Beyond that, where was Floyd? Where on earth could he be hiding?

Suddenly, I thought of the final line from Daphne's journal: *This child must always have a place to hide.*

"Sorry, this is taking longer than I thought," Mike said suddenly through the phone. "Can I call you back in a few?"

My mind racing on this new possibility, I told Mike yes, adding that he should just come right over to the B and B because we had some important new developments to share.

"Will do," he said.

Hanging up, I looked at Heath, puzzle pieces clicking into place.

I thought of Abe's papers, of the plans for what looked like a small stu-dio apartment.

I thought of what Nina had said about Abe being obsessed with Emo-ry's Jewish heritage and the chance of some future Holocaust.

I thought of Abe's promise to Daphne to always keep their son safe, no matter what.

I thought of the words on those plans he had drawn, FIRST TO GO.

In Germany, the ones who were first to go weren't just random Jews.

They were what Hitler considered the most "defective" Jews of all: the mentally or physically handicapped.

"I think I know where Floyd is," I said. "Or at least I know how to find him."

Soon Heath and I were at the kitchen table, the drawing from my grandfather's papers spread out in front of us. And what a difference it made, to look at the drawing in the right context! Heath and I studied it together, considering the shape and dimensions, and it didn't take long for us to figure out that the hidden room had been built under a flight of stairs at one corner of the house. There were three staircases in this place, one on the main floor, one that led to the basement, and one that led to the wine cellar. Judging by the placement and shape of the room, we both felt like the wine cellar was the only logical choice.

Once we decided that, I gasped, a memory suddenly flooding into my brain. During the renovation, Troy and I had discovered something unusual about the stairs down there, but we hadn't really known what we were seeing. I doubt that we would have spotted it at all if we hadn't been working down there so much, faux-painting the newly walled-off corner of the basement to make it look like an old European wine cellar. When I was sanding the stairs for a coat of paint, I realized that the front of one stair, the part Troy had said was called the riser, was attached by hidden hinges, and it could be flipped open to reveal a secret cubby behind it. Checking each of the steps, we had found five in a row that had a false front and a hidden cubby. All five were empty except for the third one, which had a small latch on one side. We tried pulling the latch but it didn't seem to do anything. Finally, we lost interest and gave up—and the whole thing had completely slipped my mind until now.

"Follow me," I said, leading Heath down into the wine cellar as I explained. The space there was tight, about the size of an elevator, just enough for the wine racks and three or four people. Ignoring my claustrophobia, I held my gun at the ready while Heath pulled on the risers of each step, starting at the bottom and working his way up. When he got to the third one from the bottom, it popped open, just as I remembered.

"There's the latch," I whispered, pointing to the side of the cubby's interior, where a small wooden handle just waited to be pulled down.

Heart pounding, I held out the gun toward the stairs.

"Should we wait for the police?" Heath whispered.

"I'm not waiting another second," I replied.

Giving me a nod, he reached out and twisted the handle. Nothing happened at first, but I told him to keep trying, to push even harder. As he worked on that, I couldn't help but quickly check the other cubbies, flipping them open just to make sure they were all still empty.

They weren't.

Though the two bottom cubbies were empty, the top three were completely filled with cash—stacks and stacks of rubber-banded packets of bills.

"Whoa," I whispered, wanting to reach out and grab a packet, just to look at it more closely, but I didn't dare. Instead, we both just stood there and stared at all that money for a moment, and then we closed those cubby doors and returned our attention to the one with the latch. There would be time later to think about the cash, what it meant, and what to do about it.

Handing off the flashlight to me, Heath tried using both hands on the latch. Finally, with a big burst of strength, it gave, and with a metallic boing from somewhere deep inside, half of the staircase suddenly seemed to pop loose. Hinged at one side, it looked like the stairs were going to swing open like a door—a small, low door.

Taking what cover we could along one side of that door, Heath took back the flashlight and gave the stairs a single push open with his foot, both of us pulling back, cringing as the rusty hinges squealed in protest. As the crack widened, we were instantly enveloped in the musty stench of earth, loamy and stale. It was too dark to see anything inside. Holding my breath, I squinted into that darkness, but all I could make out were a few simple, wooden steps that descended into a deeper darkness below. Despite my trembling hands and wobbly knees, I knew we had no choice but to keep going.

The time for secrets was over.

FORTY-THREE

Moving in front of me protectively, Heath clicked on the flashlight and played its beam around the cavernous interior. Just as the plans had shown, it looked like a single room, with a toilet and sink in the far corner.

There was a minimum of furniture in here, just a bed and a chair and a table. In the middle of the room was a stack of boxes, piled about six feet high and four feet wide.

As I clutched the gun in both hands and Heath shined his light on those boxes, a head suddenly emerged from behind, two eyes staring back at us in fear.

Floyd.

"Are they gone?" he whispered.

It took both of us a moment to grasp the reality of the situation. Floyd was here, hiding in this secret room that had been created by my grandfather. My mind filled with questions, starting with what was he doing in here and how had he known about this place. I spat out every question that came to mind, saying that I wasn't going to budge until he gave me some solid answers.

So with our prisoner standing in the darkened room and Heath and I looking on from its entrance, Floyd launched into an explanation, starting with Troy's arrival here at the B and B on Monday evening. According to Floyd, he and Troy had found this room quite by accident that night.

"You're telling us that you and Troy 'just happened' to stumble on this room by accident? Heath and I almost couldn't find it on purpose—even with a blueprint in our hands! What were you doing poking around in the wine cellar anyway?"

As soon as the words were out of my mouth, I realized exactly what they had been doing: fooling with the cash in the cubbies, which was part of their little money-laundering operation. I asked Floyd if that was correct, and after a brief hesitation, he nodded.

"Okay, yeah, we've been using these stairs for stashing the money. But we never dreamed there was another whole room behind them! When we found it by accident on Monday night, we were shocked. Came in, took a good look around. Couldn't imagine what it was for. Then we thought maybe the boxes stacked here in the center contained some sort of hidden treasures. Why else would somebody build a secret room like this?" We didn't answer, so he continued, saying that together he and Troy had gone through every box, but to no avail. All they held were an assortment of non-perishable foods and some camping supplies, along with a packet of cash and an envelope full of old papers.

So this was where Troy had stumbled upon my grandfather's documents. No wonder none of us had ever seen them before! When Troy took a look at them, he must have seen a reference to 'die diamanten' in the journal, just as Nina had said, and decided to go on a treasure hunt—though obviously he didn't share his find, or his plans, with his partner in crime, Floyd.

"So why were you in here now?" Heath demanded.

"Because when you guys were leaving earlier, I spotted the Nightmare Twins coming up the walk, and I knew I'd better hide somewhere they would never find me."

"Why didn't you want them to find you?"

"'Cause I was afraid they were here to kill me!"

That led to a whole host of new questions, which we both threw out. Floyd listened, his eyes lingering on the barrel of my gun, and then continued.

"Okay, well, you already figured out that we were laundering cash here at the B and B, right? What you didn't know was that this wine cellar was all part of the original plan. Here was our idea: Once a month, Troy was going to bring the cash, check into his regular room—this room with the wine cellar—and stash the money in the stairs. It would be my job to come down here each week, pull out some of that cash, and deposit it in the bank. As long as my records showed receipts equal to the amounts of my deposits, we didn't think anybody would suspect a thing."

I glanced at Heath, once again feeling utterly humiliated by the lying and manipulative Troy.

"See, before the B and B actually opened for business," Floyd continued, "Troy and I thought we would need to have actual guests coming and staying once in a while to keep things looking legit. So that's when Troy came up with the idea of walling off that section of the basement and turning it into a wine cellar, one that could be reached only through the Bay Laurel room. As long as I never put anyone in that room except Troy, it didn't seem likely that our secret would ever be found out. As far as we knew, the only other person on the planet who was aware these cubbies existed was you. So all I had to do was remove the cash whenever I learned you were coming out, just in case. Lucky for me, you only came out once in a great while, and never for very long."

"And what happened to all of the 'actual guests'?" I asked.

Floyd shrugged.

"It didn't take long to figure out that wasn't going to be necessary. The whole cash in/cash out system worked great—you never showed up at all, and nobody was asking any questions, so it was just a lot easier not to fool with real guests."

"So you really have been collecting your paycheck as the B and B's manager for almost two years while all you've done is sit around in this big place all by yourself and take it easy."

Floyd grinned and said, "Pretty sweet deal, huh? Can you blame me?"

Ignoring the question—for which I had one very strong answer—Heath asked why they hadn't found the secret room before if they had been using the cubbyholes all along.

"We knew there was a lever in the third one, but Troy said it didn't do anything. I guess we just didn't pull on it hard enough to make the stairs pop open. I figured it was for an old furnace or a sump pump or something. Never thought about it again."

"So what was different this time?" I asked, the skepticism clear in my voice. Frankly, this man had been lying to me so much for so long I wasn't sure whether to believe anything that he was telling us now or not. That would be for the police to sort through.

Floyd asked if he could come out of the room into the wine cellar to demonstrate what happened that led them to discover the room. I stepped back, gripped the gun with both hands, and told him to come on out.

"Let me give you a little history first," he said as he stepped forward and gingerly climbed through the opening. "See, about a month ago, a little problem cropped up. Somewhere between my bosses' office in Atlantic City and here, some of the laundered cash started disappearing. At first, they accused me of skimming off the top, but it wasn't me, which meant it had to be Troy. We all knew his gambling was getting out of control, so it wasn't a big leap to assume that he had started helping himself to a little of the cash now and then." Floyd stood up and brushed the dust from his sleeves as he continued. "Last week, the bosses told me they'd had enough. Troy had to go, and I had to be the one to do him."

Heath and I looked at each other in alarm.

"I didn't want to, you understand. The man was my friend. Not to mention that killing isn't exactly my cup of tea, you know? I'll do the money stuff, no problem, but don't ask me to take a life. That's a line I don't like to cross."

We both stared at Floyd, astonished at the matter-of-fact way he spoke about killing another human being! Before either of us could speak, he continued.

"Anyway, I kind of didn't have a choice. They said if I didn't take care of Troy, they would send somebody to handle both of us. So when Troy got here Monday night, I confronted him, told him he'd been found out. I expected him to deny it, of course, and he did. Kept swearing that he had put every cent in the cubbies, that maybe the money had fallen down behind the steps through the cracks or something. He insisted on bringing me down here and making a big show of pushing on the backs of the cubbies, pointing out the places where the bills could have fallen through. Then it happened. Here, I'll show you."

Floyd opened one of the cubby doors and began removing stacks of cash, carelessly handing them off to us. Soon, both Heath and I were juggling gun and flashlight respectively as we cradled multiple packets of bills in our arms. I couldn't begin to imagine how much this would all add up to!

"Troy was pushing on this part here, like this," Floyd said, pressing against the back wall of the now-empty cubby, "saying that's where the cash must've slipped through, and all of a sudden, this board just popped off." With a final push, the piece of wood came loose, falling onto the floor of the hidden room inside with a muffled clatter. "Like that, see? We got a flashlight and took a look in this hole and realized there was a whole room back there. We thought for sure we'd discovered a secret treasure, like I said. It took a while to figure out how to get in, but by sticking a mirror up in there and shining the flashlight around, Troy figured out that was what the latch in the third cubby was for. Sure enough, he was right. This time, he just pulled and pulled until it actually worked."

Finished with his demonstration, Floyd brushed himself off as he explained what had happened next.

"See, Troy had been lying to me about not skimming the cash, and we both knew it. But once we found the room and went inside and discovered that packet of money in there, we figured out a way that he wouldn't have to die and I wouldn't have to kill him. We would simply use the same excuse with the boss that Troy had tried to use with me, saying that he hadn't taken any money after all but that it had been falling through a crack at the back of the stairs without either one of us realizing it. As long as I was able to produce the full amount of the missing cash—which we were able to do, thanks to the money we found in that envelope in there—they would believe me."

"Money that wasn't yours."

He laughed as if that were a mere technicality and kept going with his tale.

"After sleeping on it that night, Troy came to me Tuesday morning and said he'd been thinking that it might be better for both of us if I delivered the explanation, along with the cash, in person rather than on the phone. He offered to stay here and man the fort, so to speak—said I could even spend the night there if I wanted to and make a whole evening of it, maybe take in a show or something with the little bit that would be left over from the packet of money. Sounded like a plan to me, so I packed a bag and headed off to Atlantic City to meet with the boss, deliver the cash, and tell him our story, just like Troy said. After that, I had a great time, even caught the eight fifteen of Tony Orlando."

Floyd seemed to be speaking in earnest, which made me realize that Troy had even tricked his own partner in crime. Having seen the journal and its mention of diamonds on Monday night, Troy had figured out a way to get rid of Floyd by sending him on an errand Tuesday morning—one that had lasted all the way through to Wednesday night.

"So when you spoke to your bosses, they believed you?" Heath asked.

"I thought they did. In fact, everything seemed fine. It's strictly small time, this particular syndicate. They're a lot like me, more about the money than anything else. I figured they were just as glad I didn't have to off anybody to set things right, you know? By the time I left there, we were cool. Or so I thought. An old friend was even going to come with me to the show, but then he changed his mind once he heard Dawn wasn't going be there, just Tony. Anyway, things seemed great, but when I got back here on Wednesday evening, Troy was dead. I was shocked, figured they hadn't been as convinced as I had thought."

All of his talk about syndicates and groups and contracts made things sound more like a business network than a bunch of thugs. Then I realized it was both, really: After all, that's why it was called *organized* crime!

Floyd went on to say that the goons who had come into my inn this evening—at my own invitation, no less—were two of the most brutal hatchet men in the mob. In fact, he said, they were so tough they had only three real duties: bodyguarding the bigwigs, carrying out contract killings, and "all the C to B animal management stuff."

"*Animal* management?" I asked, pulse surging.

Suddenly, Floyd's face turned bright red, and from the look in his eyes I think he realized he had gone too far, saying something he shouldn't have.

"Sorry, I don't know a whole lot about that—C to B's an area I don't get into. Never mind."

"What is 'C to B'?" I asked evenly, thinking of all that had happened this week, of the creature we had been looking for, the gash in Troy's leg.

Face flushing an even brighter red, Floyd held up both hands and told us not to worry about it, that it didn't matter. With a burst of anger, I threw down the money I had been cradling in my arms, shifted my grip on the gun, and raised it to Floyd's face.

"Oh, but it does matter, Floyd," I said, ignoring the startled glance Heath shot my way. "You'd better keep talking, *now*. Or else."

FORTY-FOUR

"Okay, okay, but keep your voice down," Floyd whispered, real fear in his eyes. "I've been working with the feds on the money-laundering issue, but C to B is a whole 'nuther ball game—all of the wrong people involved, if you know what I mean, the kind of people that are very, very dangerous. If I spill on this, I'll be a dead man for sure."

"Looks like you lose either way. What does 'C to B' stand for, and what is it?" I asked slowly, my eyes and heart quick-freezing into ice. I had no idea if I would actually be able to pull the trigger or not if it came to that, but in that moment, it sure felt like a possibility. That must have shown on my face because after a beat Floyd continued, his voice nearly a whisper.

"Fine. 'C to B' stands for 'Canaries to Bears.' It's a kind of gambling, the kind that's not legal in the United States. I don't like it, never have, but I can't deny it brings in big bucks. That's the word on the street anyway."

I thought of the federal liaison Liz and I had met with earlier, the woman in the sensible brown shoes who had mentioned that there were certain types of gambling "that weren't ever legal in the U.S." This must have been what she was talking about.

"What does it involve?" Heath asked, his brow furrowed.

"Just what you'd think. C to B covers everything from canary fights to bear baiting and all sorts of other animals in between. Certain high rollers love it; they'll pay a fortune just to get the day and time and secret location of the next fight, which is always within a few hours' drive of Atlantic City but changes every month. The ones who come are loaded with cash—and not petty cash, either. I've heard that millions will change hands in a single night. Crazy, huh?"

Lowering the gun slightly, I tried to understand what he was telling us.

"You mean animals fighting animals?" Thinking of Burl Newton's father, I added, "Like cockfighting? These people watch the animals fight and bet on which ones will win?"

"Exactly."

"Did Troy participate in this stuff?" I asked in horror. Even with all I had learned about my ex-boyfriend in the past few days, this would have been the most shocking revelation of all.

"No way. He found it as disgusting as I did. But he knew about the C to B stuff. Everyone knows about it but nobody squeals, thanks in part to the Nightmare Twins. Word is, they'll handle and transport any kind of animal the bigwigs want to put on the docket, no matter how fierce. That should give you an idea of how tough those guys are. They don't give it a thought; they just go for it. Same thing when it's time to do a hit. There's no fear in either one of them. Not an ounce of humanity between the two either. Is it any wonder I came down here to hide when I saw them coming?"

Heath and I looked at each other, ignoring his question. All I could think of was the wound in Troy's leg, the one that had been made by an animal. I couldn't know for sure, not yet, but I had a strong feeling that wound had something to do with these C to B fights. Whatever got at Troy and cut him that way wasn't just some wild animal but one that had been raised and trained to kill. Maybe it really had been a bear after all, one that had been kept for a time in an emu's cage.

Before I could voice my thoughts out loud, Floyd offered to show us one more thing that might help us understand, a special feature of the hidden room they had also discovered down here on Monday night.

"Heath, do me a favor," Floyd said, turning toward the stairs. "Take hold of the banister there and push it upward. You gotta push hard, even harder than you did with the lever."

Doing as Floyd instructed, Heath set down the flashlight and the cash he'd been holding in order to put both hands on the shiny wooden banister and push it upward with all of his might. But nothing happened. I held my breath, watching as he tried again. Then, before I realized what was happening, Floyd had a gun—his own gun, which he had been concealing—pressed against my temple, and he was telling me to drop my weapon, nice and easy.

"Hands in the air, both of you," Floyd said as Heath spun around to see what was going on.

As I released the grip on my MK40 and listened to it hit the floor, I knew there was no other "special feature" they had discovered. Floyd had just been distracting us so he could gain the upper hand.

"Don't do this, Floyd," Heath replied, looking at Floyd's gun and slowly raising his hands as well.

"You think I want to?" Floyd asked, gripping my upper arm and moving me back from the stairs. "I got no beef with you folks. But my hands are tied, you understand? Open the door. And no quick moves, or she gets it."

Heath did as he was told, pulling the lever that popped the stairs loose and swinging them open to again reveal the hidden room inside. Floyd made both of us go in, where I felt sure he was about to finish us off, execution style. But then he simply kept the gun trained on us and told us to toss him our cell phones and car keys.

"Don't worry, you two," he said, trying to catch each item as it was tossed his way. "There's plenty of food and water in there. I'll give it a couple of days, and once the feds have honored their part of the deal and I'm on that beach with that mango juice, I'll give them your location and they'll come rescue you."

"And what's to stop us from coming out of here before then?" I asked, heart pounding in my throat, terrified of the prospect of being locked in this damp, dark space.

Floyd thought for a minute and then replied.

"Because I'm going to wire it up with a couple explosives before I leave. One bad move and this whole place goes kerflooey. Understand?"

Without waiting for an answer, he reached out and began to close the secret door. With a final, metallic ping as it clicked shut, Heath and I were engulfed in darkness.

Catching my breath, I stood there frozen for a long moment, blinking furiously, praying that this was just a dream and that I would soon wake up. But it was no use. The truth was staring me in the face, so to speak, a truth blacker than the darkness of this musty, smothering grave.

"You okay, Si?" Heath asked, the sound of his voice suddenly snapping me into action.

"We have to move fast, before he has a chance to set up the explosives," I said, thrusting out my hands as I blindly advanced toward the stairs.

He did the same, and though we both managed to reach the inside of the hidden door, it wouldn't budge no matter how hard we pushed. Feeling along the surface with our hands, neither one of us could find any sort of latch or knob that would open the door and get us out of there.

"Think!" I cried, on the verge of a total meltdown, hot tears streaking down my cheeks in the blackness. "Do you remember anything about this from the plans?"

"No, I was only worried about how to get in, not how to get out."

"What about the panel Floyd pushed loose?" I cried, pressing my hands against the back of the higher steps until I found the one that didn't have a back. "Here. It's here," I said, pushing my hand through to swing open the hinged, hidden front. Though the slight rush of fresher air from the wine cellar made me feel a little less trapped, the opening didn't let in any light. Obviously, Floyd had turned off the light and closed the door at the top of the stairs once he had finished doing whatever it was he had done out there.

"Any chance you could crawl through that opening?" Heath asked.

I thought I could give it a try, but it was so narrow even my head wouldn't fit through.

It was no use. We couldn't feel anything, couldn't see. The door's release had to be somewhere else in the room. For a little while, as I could hear Floyd clunking around above us, I tried to feel along the other walls, ignoring the sticky webs my fingers swiped through, the sensation of creatures crawling across my skin. But it was hopeless. The third time I clanged my shin sharply against something in the darkness, I finally gave in to my sobs.

"Whoa, whoa," Heath said from across the room, for the first time understanding the depth of my desperation. "Calm down, Sienna. We're okay. Do you honestly think Floyd would have wired this place for explosives?"

"I don't know," I whimpered.

"Even if he did, honey, we'll be okay. All we have to do is bide our time until Mike shows up."

"If he was really going to come," I said dismally, "he would have been here by now."

"Okay, but we know someone will show up eventually. Two people can't just disappear like this, especially given all that's been going on. Floyd was right, we've got food and water. We'll survive until help comes."

I couldn't stand the calmness in his voice, couldn't bear his rational, even-toned words.

"The supplies," I said, trying not to hyperventilate. "Can you remember the list? There were lamps in there, and knives. I know there was something about knives."

"Sienna! Get a grip, honey!"

"Don't you understand, Heath, I can't! I can't do this! I can't be trapped!"

I was screaming, trembling from head to toe, tears streaming down my cheeks. This was too much for me—didn't he understand that? If I didn't get out soon, I was going to die. I was literally going to die.

At last he finally seemed to understand.

Moving closer to me in the dark, Heath spoke in the same calm tones, only now I could tell he was completely focused on me.

"You're having a panic attack, Sienna, but you're going to be okay."

"No, I won't be okay!"

"How can I help you calm down?"

"You can't! You can't erase the past! This is who I am! This is what happens to me when someone holds me down!"

"No one's holding you down right now, honey. Nobody's touching you at all. There are no drunks here, no water, no pier. Nobody that would hurt you. Reach out your arms. Wave them in the air. See? You're not trapped, not really, not in that sense. We have a whole big room here, and I can give you plenty of space. You're free to move about all you want."

I knew what he was saying. Rationally, it made perfect sense. But the way I was feeling at that moment, mere logic wasn't going to make a difference. Even the smell—that horrid, musty smell—was reminiscent of the stench of the rotting wood of the dock.

"Get me out of here, Heath," I begged in a whisper. "Just get me out of here."

He was silent for a long moment, and in the void I realized that the sounds from above had ceased.

Floyd was gone.

"I think I can find a way to do this," Heath told me finally. "But if Floyd was telling the truth, if he really did set some sort of trip wire, you understand what's going to happen."

In theory, I understood: We would be blown to smithereens. In reality, I didn't care, and I told him so.

Standing there in place, still trembling violently, I listened as Heath went to work. Ripping through the boxes, searching their contents by feel, telling me what he was doing every step of the way, he couldn't find the lanterns or flashlights, but he did run into an axe. He was going to hack our way out.

"You're sure about this?" he asked one more time.

"I'm sure," I pleaded. "Get me out of here. Please."

At that, I heard him take a deep breath and then swing the first blow. With every strike, I waited for an explosion, knowing this was absurd. I was risking my very life just because of the panic that was driving me.

It wasn't until I heard the splintering of wood and knew he was making progress that I realized Heath was risking his life as well—for my sake.

FORTY-FIVE

From the sound of things, it didn't take Heath very long to break through, and no explosion happened—nothing beyond the crash of wood as he pounded it mercilessly with the axe.

Once the hole he had made was big enough to crawl through, I insisted on going first, though Heath kept telling me to watch for trip wires and wood shards. The wine cellar was dark, so as soon as I made it out I ran up the stairs and flipped on the light.

I knew Floyd had been lying about the explosives. He was only trying to buy himself some time. But that didn't mean we were home free.

"Sienna, wait!" Heath commanded, and I looked down to see him pulling himself through the opening.

But I couldn't wait. Instead, I flung open the door at the top of the stairs and fell out into Troy's room, taking in the deep, gasping breaths of freedom. We were out! We had made it!

But we weren't safe yet.

I ran to the phone on the nightstand and picked up the receiver, but it was dead. I was pushing the buttons, desperately trying to get a dial tone, when Heath emerged at the top of the stairs. Pausing there, face pale, he turned to study the doorframe, and it wasn't until that moment I realized why he had told me to wait: Afraid that the explosives had been wired to this door instead of to the stairs, he had wanted to go first, just in case. Again, he had been willing to risk his life for mine.

"The phone's dead," I said, clicking the button to no avail.

"Floyd must've cut the wire," Heath said.

Our eyes met for a long moment, and the emotion that passed between us was intense, far more intense than anything we had ever shared. That's when I knew the truth: Though Heath might not be willing to kill for me, he was certainly willing to die for me, and in that moment I realized that was far more than enough.

Together, we ran through the dark house, trying the other phones, but they were all dead. Our cell phones were nowhere in sight, nor were our car keys. Worst of all, Floyd had taken my revolver from the bedside table drawer where I had been keeping it. We would have to make a run for it without any protection at all.

The closest houses were directly across the street, at the end of my very long driveway. We decided to go out through the front door and run across the lawn, tree to tree, until we had made our way to the road and then across to whichever house had its lights on and people who seemed to be home. There were only a few trees on the front lawn for cover, but at least it was dark, and that might help to hide us a little bit if we encountered anyone we shouldn't. Heath would go first, and I would follow, staying one tree behind so that we both had cover.

Before we opened the door, I turned and placed my hands on each side of Heath's face, looking deeply into his eyes. I wanted to say something, but suddenly words failed me.

"You okay now?" he asked. "Feeling more in control?"

"Yes," I whispered, "but I'm sorry, Heath. I should never have asked that of you."

He studied my eyes, and then he surprised me by gripping my face as well and planting a long, fierce kiss on my mouth.

"Don't you get it, Si?" he whispered, his lips still at mine. "I may not be all dangerous and exciting and intense like your detective, but I'm a good man and I'm a safe man and I love you so much sometimes it takes my breath away."

He punctuated his words with another hard, passionate kiss, and at that moment he took my breath away as well.

Thus united, we opened the front door as quietly as possible and looked out at the dark, grassy lawn. Where was Mike? Why hadn't he come? Was he out there waiting somewhere, intending to do us harm? If not, then had some harm come to him instead?

There were no signs of activity near the house, at least not that we could see. Across the street, the two homes on the end seemed to have a lot of their lights on, so I pointed to them and Heath nodded.

He gave my hand a final squeeze, and then I watched, heart pounding, as he tiptoed down the steps of the front porch and darted as silently as possible across the grass to the first tree. Stopping there, he looked back at me, gestured for me to do the same, and darted on to the next.

As quietly as possible, I too moved down the steps and across the grass to the first tree. Once there I stopped, looking forward in the darkness to see if Heath had made it to the second. He had, but he was holding up one hand. I realized he wanted me to wait, probably because it sounded as if a car was about to pass on the road out front.

Careful to shield myself from sight behind the trunk, I waited, my senses taking in the night that surrounded me. Crickets chirped. A few fireflies still lit the air. Up ahead, the sound of the passing car reminded me that for some people life was going on as usual.

Finally, judging by the fading sound of the engine and the sweep of the headlights, the car was gone. Peering around the tree toward Heath, I saw him give me the all-clear signal and take off. But as I was about to make a run for it myself, a sudden burst of fire flashed brilliantly in the night air from somewhere off to the right.

I froze, swallowing the yell that threatened to emerge from my throat. Blinking furiously, I willed my eyes to adjust after that shock of light. When they did, I looked ahead toward Heath, only to see him stagger for a moment, grabbing at the back of his leg, and then collapse into a heap on the ground.

Before I could run to him or even call out his name, a hand clamped around my mouth from behind, and I was jerked backward against a solid wall of muscle, my arms pinned to my sides. Whoever had grabbed me held on tight, my struggles no match for his power, my feeble attempts at breaking free like a moth beating wings against glass. Finally, I felt hot breath against my ear. Even before he spoke, though, I knew who it was. I recognized the smell of aftershave, earth, and sweat.

Mike.

My mind reeling, I tried to break free, but he only gripped me more tightly, bracing us against the tree trunk, one hand still clamped across my mouth, the other firmly pinning my arms to my sides. I had no room to make a move at all, not even the most basic self-defense techniques, a kick to his instep or a pinch to the tender skin of his inner thigh. I was trapped.

"Sienna, don't fight it," Mike whispered into my ear. "Trust me. I'm trying to protect you."

Trust me.

Could I trust him?

Before I had the chance to decide, another burst of fire came out of nowhere, even closer this time. Hot breath shot against my neck with a loud grunt. Then slowly the arms that had been holding on so firmly relaxed, and Mike, too, simply fell onto the ground, unconscious.

Eyes wide, trembling violently, I looked up to see someone running toward me with what looked like an air rifle in his hand. As he neared me, he stopped, looking down at Mike's body and then up at me, meeting my eyes. It was Burl Newton, the man who just yesterday had been arrested and held overnight for possession of cockfighting paraphernalia.

"Sienna! Are you okay?"

I was shocked and disoriented, my mind trying to match what I was seeing with what I knew to be true. Looking down at Mike, I watched as Burl leaned over, set the gun on the ground, and carefully pulled from the detective's hip what looked like a large yellow plastic dart with an orange tip.

Burl had shot Mike—and Heath as well, obviously—with tranquilizer darts. What I had thought was an air rifle was actually a tranquilizer gun.

"Good thing I got here when I did," Burl said, pulling a small plastic case from his pocket and gingerly placing the dart inside. He acted as if nothing was wrong, as if it was perfectly normal for him to be kneeling here, doing this. My mind raced as I watched him.

I thought of his isolated, ramshackle farm, of the empty rooster houses out back, of the big, empty cages and coops in his yard. What a perfect place it would be for mobsters to hide wild animals from time to time—animals bred, raised, and trained for fighting. For blood sport.

Burl's father had raised gamecocks. Was it really that much of a leap? The son had simply taken things to the next level, to the world of C to B.

Canaries to Bears.

Animals killing animals for the entertainment of man.

I didn't know what kind of game Burl was playing, but obviously he thought I was stupid, or at least uninformed, and that as long as he acted innocent, I wouldn't know who the bad guy in this scenario really was. Before he made his next move—whatever that move was going to be—I had to overpower him and make my escape.

For an old guy, though, he was far more nimble than I would have expected. Suddenly, before I could do a thing, he had pulled Mike's gun from its holster and was pointing it straight at me.

"Hold it right there, Sienna," Burl said, standing, his beady little eyes fixed on mine. "Don't move."

"What do you want, Burl?" I asked. "Are you going to tranquilize me too?"

"Nah, that wouldn't do any good. I need you nice and awake."

With a surge of nausea, I held my breath, terrified of what he might say next. What horrible thing did he have in mind?

"Don't look at me like that," he said, shaking his head. "I just want you to take me to the diamonds. I know you know where they are."

I hesitated, blinking. That was not what I had expected to hear!

"The diamonds?"

"Yeah, the diamonds. Don't act all surprised and innocent. Let's go. To the grove."

For the next few minutes we walked toward the grove, me at gunpoint as I argued with him. From what I could tell, he had overheard the lies Troy had given to Nina, saying that Heath and I were planning to come here and steal Emory's diamonds to keep them for ourselves. I tried to tell Burl that Troy had been lying, and that I had no clue where the diamonds were, but he wouldn't believe me.

"Are you doing this for Emory's sake?" I asked, thinking of the friendship the two had shared over the years. Perhaps Burl's motives were more altruistic than they seemed.

That hope was dashed with the laugh that gurgled from Burl's throat.

"What does Emory care about diamonds?" he cried. "Talk about a waste! I've been trying to find those things for years, ever since he showed them to me when we were just kids."

I thought of my conversation with Nina, of what she had said about Emory and the diamonds. *At one time, Emory had known where they were, but then Mr. Abe had caught him blabbing about it, so he chose a new hiding place, which he didn't share with anyone.*

The person Emory had blabbed to was Burl.

Burl had known about the diamonds all along. He'd been looking for them for years. Then along came Troy on a diamond hunt of his own, and Burl wasn't going to let that happen.

"You killed Troy," I whispered.

"He was digging in the grove, trying to find the diamonds!" Burl said angrily, poking me in the back with the gun to get me moving again. "All I did was set things up a bit so he would end up killing himself. His own greed is what did him in."

Almost proudly, Burl explained how he first saw Troy out in the grove with a metal detector on Tuesday and knew immediately what was going on. That whole day, he had shadowed Troy, watching and listening, even hearing his exchange with Nina. That first evening, after Troy had given up for the night, Burl had set his traps. From doing odd jobs now and then, he knew that there were some old, hazardous chemicals in Emory's barn. All he'd had to do was dig some holes in the grove, fill them with one of the chemicals, throw something metal in the mix to set off the detector, and then cover it all up with some dirt. When Troy would go to scoop out that dirt the next day, he was going to get plenty of it on his hands, enough for a fatal dose of poison. Best of all, it would simply look like an accident, like Troy had stumbled upon some pesticide without realizing what it was.

"This grove is huge, Burl," I said, shaking my head. "How many holes did you dig and fill?"

"Just a few. But getting him to find those holes took a little finesse."

As we reached the outer path and headed toward the main gate, Burl told the story of how he had manipulated Troy.

"I came out into the grove on Wednesday afternoon—just walked right up to him and said hello. 'Is that you, Troy?' I called out, acting like I was all confused. "Cause for a minute, I thought I was seeing things, I thought you were Abe himself, come back from the grave.' Of course, Troy wasn't in the mood to chat, and he sure didn't want me to notice what he was doing and start asking questions. So I didn't hang around. I just wrapped things up real quick and said, 'The last time I saw Abe in here digging a hole, it was over in that section by the blackberry bushes.' That was all it took. I left, and what do you know? Within an hour, there was Troy, digging around by the blackberry bushes and getting all excited when his metal detector went off. Everything worked like a charm—at least until he got confused and started wandering off the wrong way. Unlocking latches, setting things free, it looked like it was gonna be a big disaster for a while, especially when those other two got into the mix. Thank goodness I had my tranq gun, or I don't know what I would've done."

"What was the animal, Burl? What kind of creature attacked Troy?"

He just laughed and said that it didn't matter now, that I didn't really want to know.

We reached the main gate, where I was planning to make my move. All the way here, I had tried to come up with something, and this was the best I could do. This was the gate about Cupid, the one with the ironwork that featured two arrows, one tipped with "lead" and one with "gold."

"All right, well, here we go," I said, trying to sound frustrated and dejected. "Believe it or not, the two arrows in the design of this gate are hollow. The diamonds are down inside."

It was a lie, but as I spoke I positioned myself behind the gate, telling Burl that there was a little latch somewhere along there that would pop the tip of the arrow off.

Glancing at Burl, I could tell that he wasn't sure whether to believe me or not. But I continued to act it out, running my fingers along the cold metal, much as I had run them along the wall inside the hidden room. Finally, when he had stepped close enough to take a look himself, I gripped the gate with both hands and swung it forward as hard as I could, knocking him to the ground.

He recovered quickly, too quickly for me to get the gun away from him. So I did the next best thing. I pulled a surprise leg sweep, kicking in a broad, sideways curve that knocked his legs out from under him again. As he hit the ground, I took off running into the grove, zigzagging in the darkness, diving for cover as bullets pinged into the trees around me.

At least I was younger than he was, and faster. When I got to the bridge at the center, I ran across it and kept going, around the Daphne tree and back onto the path. I wanted to run to Jonah and Liesl's house, but their open fields would provide no cover, making me an easy target. Instead, I ran to Emory's, an idea springing to mind as soon as I emerged from the grove and into his yard. Abe and his son had lived in this smaller house for thirteen years before he died. Surely, he had created a "safe room" for Emory here, just like the one at the B and B.

Running to the door, I didn't even knock but simply burst in, startling both Emory, who was sitting in his recliner eating popcorn and watching TV, and Liesl, who was folding a basket of his laundry nearby.

"Sienna! What—"

"Emory!" I cried, locking the door behind me, racing from window to window to check the locks. "We're in danger! Do you have a special place you're supposed to go if this happens—if you find yourself in danger?"

Emory stood, dropping the bowl of popcorn to the floor, his mouth open wide in shock.

"It's okay, I know your dad told you to keep it a secret, but you can trust me. I want to protect you. Liesl and I both do."

"What's going on?" she demanded.

"Emory, where is it?" I said, ignoring her for now. "Where is the entrance to your secret room?"

Liesl looked from me to him and back again.

"It has two entrances," he said finally. "The closest one is through my bedroom closet."

FORTY-SIX

Emory went through the opening first, a bit agitated but so far under control. Surely he and his father had practiced drills like this throughout his life in order for him to be ready for a moment such as this. As Liesl climbed down inside after him, she stared around in shock and awe. Later, when we were free to talk away from Emory, I would explain to her fully what this room was and why it was here.

I had no intention of going into the hidden room with them. My goal was simply to get the two of them to safety while I used Emory's phone to call for help and then keep myself out of sight elsewhere in the house until the police arrived. Right now, though, they still needed the light that was coming in through the open doorway, so I told them I would be right back and used the phone on Emory's nightstand. Fingers shaking, I dialed 911, feeling exposed and wishing this was a portable phone and that I could return to the closet to finish this call.

At least I connected with a 911 operator right away. This time, it was a woman, and she told me she was sending help immediately.

"Thank you," I gasped. "I won't hang up the phone, but I need to hide, so I'm just going to set the receiver down here on the nightstand. If the police come and they can't find us, tell them we're hiding in a safe room that can be accessed through a hidden panel in the back of the closet in the bedroom that has the bird posters in it." I added that on the front lawn of the

Harmony Grove Bed & Breakfast next door were two men who had been shot by Burl Newton with a tranquilizer gun and that one of them was a police officer.

"Roger that," she replied. "Now get yourself to safety."

Returning to the closet, I pulled its outer door tightly shut, wishing there was a way to lock it from the inside. Moving to the open panel, I sat, straddling the threshold of the hidden room, though why I found it less terrifying to sit like that than to commit to the room fully, I wasn't sure. Maybe the smell was what had frightened me before, though this one certainly had a different odor than the hidden room over at the B and B. That had been musty and stale, like a basement that had been closed up for decades—like the rotting wood of a pier. This hidden room didn't smell musty at all, though it did have other odors to it, hints of old fruit and dirty bathrooms.

I told Liesl that help was on its way. She was standing at the bottom of the steps, trying to light a propane lamp.

"But what is going on?" she whispered urgently in reply, glancing toward Emory. He was sitting in the nearest chair, rocking slightly, mumbling to himself.

Cupping my hands around my mouth and hoping Emory wouldn't hear, I whispered to Liesl that Burl was the one who killed Troy and now he was after me. Before she could even respond, I heard a loud crash from somewhere else in the house.

Now I had no choice but to move inside. Quickly, I used both hands to pull the panel shut behind me. As it clicked into place, we were engulfed in darkness. Thinking I heard another noise out there, I pressed my ear to the panel and listened. Much to my dismay, it sounded like the closet door had swung open. Sure enough, I could hear that someone was there, right on the other side of the panel!

Afraid that it might be Burl and that he was going to shoot through the door, I backed down the steps and crouched on the floor, pulling Liesl down with me, just in case, whispering an explanation to her as best I could. I hoped that Emory would stay put in his chair and not try to move around in the dark or, worse, go to open the door himself.

I held my breath. We listened and waited. Suddenly there was a thump at the panel, followed by the sound of Burl's voice.

"Not the smartest choice you ever made," he called loudly, chuckling. "If I knew about the diamonds, don't you think I'd know about the hidden room too? Gosh, I even make use of it myself now and then, as I'm sure you'll find out."

At his words, I felt like slapping myself on the forehead. Way to go, Sienna. Not the smartest choice indeed.

"Don't worry, I'm not coming in after you," Burl continued. "I don't need to. Just understand this: You're not gettin' out of there until those diamonds are in my hands. And trust me, you are *definitely* gonna want to get out of there."

I didn't know what he meant, but I knew the prudent thing was to remain silent regardless.

"Is that Burl?" Emory asked in a loud whisper.

"Shhh," I replied softly. "Stay where you are, Emory. He's up to no good, but he'll go away in a minute."

Except for more clunking in the closet, all was quiet for a long moment, as we waited to hear the sounds of sirens outside. This whole waiting scene was far too reminiscent of the other night beside the pool with Floyd and Troy.

"He's up to no good a lot of times," Emory commented in the understatement of the year.

Then we heard the rumble, a low, guttural sound that was like a cross between the staccato vibrato of a machine and the throaty growl of a monster. We could almost feel the vibrations as much as hear them.

And they were coming from within this room.

"What is that?" Liesl screamed.

I told her to get that lantern lit. Heart pounding, all I knew for sure was that this was the noise that had preceded Troy's death.

"Emory, what is that sound?" I demanded. "Do you know? Does it have something to do with you?"

"No, it's not mine," he said, "but I think I know what that is."

"What?"

He was quiet for a moment and then from his own throat came an imitation of the rumble. He made the sound again, better that time, and in response came the real rumble from across the room.

"I think that's a cassowary," he said in astonishment. "I've seen them on TV, but I never saw one for real."

A *cassowary*.

The most dangerous bird in the world, one that was big and aggressive and capable of killing a grown man with a single kick.

"Got it!" Liesl cried as the flame finally flared into life. Turning it up as high as it would go, she stood and held it out, illuminating every corner of the room.

At the far wall, just standing there looking back at us, was one of the biggest birds I had ever seen. The size of an ostrich, it had shiny black feathers and a vivid blue and red neck. On its head was a solid ridge of what look like cartilage or bone, like a peaked helmet. Its scaly gray feet had three big toes, the middle one huge and elongated—five inches at least—with a thick black nail at the tip.

Judging by the mess around it on the floor, the animal had been here for a few days. The stench of the room was a mixture of animal waste and old fruit.

I had no doubt that this was the beast that had attacked Troy, and I said as much to Liesl and Emory now. Though I didn't want to scare them, they needed to understand the seriousness of the threat.

"You said there were two entrances to this room," I whispered to Emory. "Where is the other entrance?"

"Over there," he replied, gesturing beyond the bird. "It goes up to the springhouse."

The springhouse. Of course. That was why Burl had been there the other day, doing all of that noisy construction. With cops and feds swarming all over the property, he needed to be on hand in case the cassowary he had stashed underground starting making rumbles and ended up giving its presence away.

"The supplies," I said, gesturing toward the boxes that were piled in the center of the room. "We can build a wall with the boxes of supplies. Just don't make any sudden moves."

Slowly and quietly, the three of us began stacking the boxes around us like a fence. All we had to do was hold off the animal for a short while and then help would arrive.

But there weren't enough boxes for our plan to work. As I frantically looked at the pile, trying to figure out how we could make it wider or higher, I heard a new sound coming from the bird, one that sounded sort of like a sneeze.

"Uh oh," Emory said.

"Is it sick?" Liesl asked.

"No. That's the sound it makes before it starts to charge," Emory replied.

Looking at my uncle and cousin, I knew that I had done this, had done it to both of them, had brought them here.

It was my job to protect them now.

I glanced around frantically, hoping to find something that I could use as protection from the bird, a pipe or a stick. Spotting a broom behind me, I grabbed it and raised it up over my shoulder like a baseball bat, moving forward. The thing was, as I stood there facing off with this massive, beautiful bird, I realized that even if it attacked me I wasn't sure that I could bring myself to strike back.

It wasn't its fault that it was trapped down here or that we had come upon it this way. It didn't deserve to be hurt by me, not even in the name of self-protection. It snorted again, and shifted its weight, and my mind raced, praying for help to get here soon, for my family to be protected from this powerful beast.

"We could go up," Emory said from behind me. "Cassowaries can jump but they can't fly."

I thought he was just speaking hypothetically, but when I looked at him I saw that he was pointing toward a huge oil tank on the side of the room, one that was mounted on a raised platform. Looking at it, I decided there was probably enough space between the top of that tank and the ceiling for us to squeeze in to safety. And if cassowaries couldn't fly, the creature would have no way to get up there to hurt us.

"Get up there!" I cried. "Use the boxes! Stack them like stairs! Go!"

Liesl and Emory did as I directed, shifting the boxes and using them to half-climb, half-pull their way on top of the tank. Emory was taller, so first he helped Liesl. She climbed up and was making room for him when the cassowary finally made its move.

Wham!

Slamming into my chest, the bird's feet knocked the wind out of me, sending me skittering across the room, landing on my bottom. Gasping as I tried to catch my breath, I looked down at my chest, expecting to see blood. There was none. It had gotten in a good punch but no cut. Getting to my feet, I immediately went into my boxer's stance, knees bent, arms raised, trying to breathe, knowing that I was no match for this beast but hoping that at the very least it wouldn't kill me.

From what I could remember of Mike's timeline, on Wednesday night when I had called 911 from the pool area, the emergency response time had been about nine minutes. It stood to reason that the timing would be similar here. If four or five minutes had already passed since I called, that meant I only needed to hold my own for about that many more. Trying not to picture the gash in Troy's thigh, I braced myself for what I feared would be the longest four or five minutes of my life.

Across the room, Emory tried making the rumble sound of the cassowary again, this time from atop the tank, but the creature was no longer interested in anything except getting in another kick at me.

"Please don't hurt it," Emory called to me.

"Sienna!" Liesl cried. "Come on, climb up here with us!"

"Had enough yet?" Burl yelled through the door at the top of the steps.

"I can't help you, Burl!" I yelled. "I don't know where the diamonds are! I don't!"

"Troy told Nina they were buried at the base of something called the Fishing Tree. You must know what that is!"

Wham!

The bird hit me again, but this time I saw it coming and was able to sidestep and deflect most of the blow. What I didn't expect was a second, follow-up kick, which again sent me sprawling in the other direction. This time, however, I didn't land on the cold, hard floor but on something softer and cushier. Afraid to take my eyes off of the charging bird even for an instant, I took the risk, glancing down to see that whatever it was, it was soft and puffy and black.

Getting to my feet, I pulled it up and held it in front of me for protection, realizing as I did that it *was* protection, that what I was holding up was a padded suit of some kind, like a goalie outfit for a really brutal hockey team. I wasn't in a position to suit up fully, but even just slipping my arms through the sleeves made a world of difference. Thus protected, I was able to deflect far more blows than I caught.

"Sienna!" Liesl cried. "Look where you are!"

Turning, I realized that I had made it across the room to the springhouse entrance. Backing up the steps, I pushed at the door, but it wouldn't budge. Burl must have stacked his heavy toolbox and other equipment against the opening on the other side as an added measure of protection.

Turning back toward the room, I saw the bird charging toward me at full speed, but it was too late for me to do anything about it. I screamed, curling into a ball right there on the steps, praying the end would come quickly.

Suddenly, the other door burst open and a flash of fire erupted into the room.

Just before the bird leapt for its final blow, it was hit. It faltered, staggering once and then righted itself and came to a stop. Wobbling unsteadily, it finally collapsed into a seated position. There it remained, blinking its eyes, head bobbing slightly, looking very much like a fellow who'd simply had a little too much to drink, one in a vivid red and blue scarf.

Heart pounding, I looked across the room to see the authorities spilling in through the doorway. After securing the animal, some of them helped Emory and Liesl get down from the tank, while others came over to tend to me, telling me that I would be okay, that an ambulance was on the way. Only then did I realize I was bleeding in several different places on my arms and legs. None of the cuts were anything like Troy's, though they hurt pretty bad, nonetheless.

Handing over the black padding, I realized that at least we had solved the mystery of the Michelin Man. What Floyd and Nina had seen by the pool that night was a glimpse of the cassowary followed by the sight of Burl in his protective suit, shooting at them with the tranquilizer gun. No won-der they hadn't understood what they were seeing.

Soon the springhouse entrance was cleared from the other side, and we were able to move out onto the lawn. Despite my injuries, I immediately went looking for Heath. He wasn't there; I was told he was already on his way to the hospital, as was Mike.

I wanted to go after them, to be there when Heath awoke from the tran-quilizer, but first they said I should be examined by the paramedics myself. Waiting beside an open ambulance as directed, I observed the throngs of officials who were once again descending on the scene. There were so many uniforms here that I was concerned for Emory, but right now he didn't seem to be too worked up. Instead, it sounded as though he was being celebrated as a hero, with Liesl telling everyone that his quick thinking about climbing up on the tank had helped to save both of their lives.

Watching my uncle's grinning, innocent face, it suddenly struck me that he hadn't killed those animals so many years ago. A far more likely scenario was that both the rabbit and the dog had been casualties of the Newtons' gaming cocks, perhaps when they wandered too close and were unexpect-edly attacked. I wasn't sure if a really fierce rooster could kill a dog or not, but with a razor-sharp scythe strapped to each ankle, I had no doubt it could.

As Liesl and Jonah were tearfully reunited, Emory came to stand next to me. I looked at him, thinking of how clearheaded and helpful he had been, and I told him so.

"When you were younger and people said you hurt those animals, you didn't really do it, did you?" I added.

"I didn't hurt Burl's dog," he replied.

"What about the rabbit?"

"I don't know. I was in the woods, just playing, and I found it. Then all of a sudden Burl was there, saying, 'Look at what you did, Emory. Just look at what you did!' So I guess I did, and I just didn't remember."

I looked out at the black night, at the swarm of law enforcement officers, at the sight of Burl being put into a police car and driven away.

"Burl was lying, Emory," I said, shaking my head sadly, ashamed even at myself for doubting this gentle man who could never hurt a soul.

"Is that why the police are taking him away?"

"Yep. Also because he killed Troy, and I think he did a lot of other bad things too."

Emory nodded, thinking about that.

"What was he saying in there about the Fishing Tree?" he asked. "I hope he didn't hurt it. The birds love all those worms."

Startled, I turned to my uncle, his face the very picture of innocence.

"You know which tree is the Fishing Tree?" I asked incredulously.

"Sure," he replied. "It's the Southern Catawba. Everybody knows that. Some people call 'em 'fishing trees' or 'fish bait trees.' That's because they attract worms."

"And there's one of those in the grove?" I asked, a grin spreading across my face.

"Sure is," he replied. "Hey, maybe when you're better and your cuts and everything have healed, I can show it to you."

Shaking my head in wonder, I replied that I would like that very much.

FORTY-SEVEN

Once they finally evaluated me, the paramedics said that two of my cuts were deep enough to need stitches. So after I made sure Liesl was okay and Emory was all set and I was free to leave the scene, I accepted Georgia's offer of a ride to the hospital. We went in her patrol car, and the whole way to Lancaster I was so exhausted and punchy that I was tempted to reach out and flip on the lights and siren, just for fun. Good thing I wasn't a cop myself or I might end up terrorizing entire neighborhoods.

As we neared the hospital, I realized that she wasn't just making casual conversation, she was trying to find out how I felt about Mike. From the way she talked, it was obvious she had a lot of respect for the man, both personally and professionally, and she didn't want to see him get hurt. I appreciated her candor and was honest in return, telling her that while Mike was certainly a catch, he wasn't the one for me. I had decided I wouldn't be pursuing any relationship with him except friendship.

"Fair enough," she replied as we reached the hospital and turned in. After pulling up to the door of the emergency room and coming to a stop, she added, "If you end up sticking around, maybe you and I could be friends too."

I smiled, agreeing, saying how much I would like that.

But all through registration and treatment, and even as an intern deadened the cut on my knee and began to sew it up, I kept thinking about one thing Georgia had just said: *If you end up sticking around.*

That was exactly what I had been thinking about doing.

In my whole life, I had never thought of Lancaster County as a place I might live. It had been my father's childhood home and a great place to visit during my own childhood, but I had always considered myself to be a city girl at heart.

Yet if I had learned anything over the past few days, it was that maybe the city wasn't the best place for me after all. That had nothing to do with Philadelphia itself and everything to do with me, with my competitive nature, with my tendencies toward ambition and material wealth, and that ever-present need for excitement that any city would feed.

Those were the elements that had led me to Troy in the first place, that had brought me down a number of paths I probably shouldn't have gone down. Now, after all that had happened here, I had to wonder if I ought to start over again in this place where I already had family and friends and the accountability those people would bring.

Of course, that would mean having to quit my job at Buzz, but I had a feeling that was one resignation I wouldn't mind turning in at all. At least my skills and experience in advertising wouldn't go to waste. I could simply channel them differently, focusing on the marketing and running of my very own inn.

"You doing okay?" the intern asked as he finished off the short, tidy row of stitches at my knee.

"I'm fine. Can't feel a thing," I assured him. Pleased, he moved on to the cut at my shoulder, numbed it, and went to work there as I returned to my thoughts.

There was definitely something satisfying about the thought of living on land that had once been owned by my great-grandfather. I only wished Grandpa Abe could have found peace and contentment there in his lifetime. I understood now that he had never really recovered from the atrocities of the war. Obsessed with the fact that he hadn't carried a gun and fought against the evil that was Hitler and his regime, Grandpa Abe had ended up pulling away from everyone, including the women who loved him. Even from God.

If I asked Liesl or Jonah to defend the Amish stance on nonviolence, even in light of the Holocaust, they would probably say that if everyone practiced nonviolence, there would be no Holocausts, no Nazis to fight, no Hitlers, no persecution at all. Which was a valid point. At least after the past few days, when so much violence had swirled around us, I would be more respectful of Heath's position, glad at least that he was a man of conviction.

As for me, I would continue to maintain that Christians should turn the other cheek in situations of retaliation, but when it came to persecution, not only were we free to protect ourselves and others, but it was our Christian responsibility to do so. Fortunately, I had finally come to understand that on this issue Heath and I really could agree to disagree.

By the next morning I ached in every fiber of my being—not just from my run-in with the bird but also because I had spent much of the night sleeping in a chair beside Heath's hospital bed. He had gone in and out of consciousness all night, talking gibberish and tossing and turning, but now he seemed to be in a good, deep sleep.

Seizing the opportunity to freshen up, I decided to go for a walk as well and check on Mike, who was in a room down the hall. Much to my surprise, he was fully awake and back to his normal self again.

Pulling up a chair beside his bed, I sat while we talked about the events of the night, the status of the case, and his own brush with ketamine. He said he felt as though he had a bad hangover but otherwise would survive. He was more concerned about my injuries, but I assured him that I'd had worse, and that this too would pass.

We were quiet for a bit after that. I wanted to say that I appreciated more than he would ever know all he had done for me, and that I had tremendous respect for him and would always be grateful he had been the detective assigned to my case. But as soon as I launched in, he interrupted me, cutting to the chase.

"So there's no chance for us, Collins? We'd make quite a pair, you know."

Smiling sadly, I reached out and took his hand, giving it a squeeze.

"Yes, we would. I have no doubt we'd light up the sky like fireworks."

We shared a smile. Then I tried to let go of his hand, but he squeezed mine harder, holding on.

"What's wrong with fireworks?" he pressed, leaning toward me.

Again I met his eyes, wondering how I could make him understand.

"Nothing," I whispered. "This may not make sense to you, Mike, and I'm sorry. But these days what I find myself most wanting instead are fireflies—the quiet, gentle glow of a million fireflies, lighting up the night."

Heading back up the hall to Heath's room, I was surprised to run into Nina—and even more surprised to learn she was there to see Mike.

"He and I don't know each other that well," she told me, her cheeks flushing, "but I wanted to make sure he was okay, and to thank him for everything he did to solve the case."

"I'm sure he would appreciate that."

After expressing concern about my own injuries and Heath's condition, Nina tried to apologize for not having believed me about Troy, but I wouldn't let her finish. Instead, I told her that I understood, that she wasn't the first woman to buy into the lies of a handsome and exciting man.

"That's why we need friends and family and community around us, so we can get input and accountability and make wiser decisions," I explained, adding that this was something the Amish had always understood well.

Nina nodded, thinking.

"So what are your thoughts on…the detective?" she asked, her cheeks again flushing as she glanced toward Mike's room.

I smiled, telling her that I endorsed him wholeheartedly, that I thought it was about time she set her sights on such a good man, the kind of man she deserved.

Nina and I parted ways for the time being, and as I stepped back inside Heath's room, I stood there and looked down at his sleeping form, wondering if I deserved him. He, too, was a good man, one who would love and care for me the rest of my life.

The one who would be the string to my kite.

But didn't he deserve better? Didn't he need someone equally solid, who wasn't so impulsive, so easily led astray, so prone to wandering down all the wrong paths?

Slowly he opened his eyes, and when he saw me, the first thing he did was open his arms as well. Moving into those arms and burying my face against his shoulder and holding on as tightly as I could, I said a silent prayer, asking God for guidance in this relationship and in my life.

"I love you," Heath whispered, stroking my hair with his hands as he held me close.

I needed to bring him up to speed, to tell him why he was here in the hospital and explain about everything that had happened since he'd been taken out by one of Burl's tranquilizer darts. Instead, I remained silent as he went on to list qualities of mine that he loved the most. As he spoke, describing me as "spontaneous" rather than "impulsive" and "adventurous" rather than "foolhardy," I suddenly realized something that not only made me feel better about myself as a person but also reaffirmed our relationship as well.

To fly without flying away, the kite needed the string, yes. But just as important, the string needed the kite—to lift it up, to keep it always aiming toward the sky.

EPILOGUE

Three Weeks Later

We gathered the first Saturday of November, a beautiful, crisp fall day. The colorful autumn leaves had faded to duller yellows and browns, but in the grove there were so many different kinds of trees that everything always seemed vivid anyway.

Only a few of us would be at this morning's private ceremony, but this afternoon was going to be a different story. This afternoon, we would fling open the gates and welcome anyone who wanted to come. That would be a happy time.

This morning was a far more solemn occasion. In attendance was only a handful of people: my uncle Emory, my parents, my grandmother, my brother, and me. We had also invited Nina, as Abe's honorary daughter, but she had declined, saying this was a time for "real" relatives only.

This small, private ceremony had been a long time in coming, and every single person gathered felt guilty about that. There was no excuse for not having done this sooner. The man had now been dead for two years and four months! It was high time we honored his last wishes and sprinkled his ashes on the grove.

My father had brought the ashes and the instructions from the lawyer, and once we were all together at the main gate, he opened the envelope and read my grandfather's final directive: that his body be cremated after death,

356 ⊕ MINDY STARNS CLARK

that his ashes be buried in Harmony Grove, and that once we had done this, we were also to bury here the ashes of his first wife, Daphne, and those of her mother and sister.

When we heard that, my brother and I looked at each other in surprise. *Hadn't Grandpa Abe already done that himself at some point?*

"There's a personal note written at the bottom," my father added, reading it aloud to us:

"I'm sorry to burden all of you with the matter of these other ashes when it involves people you never even knew. In this and so many other ways I have failed in my lifetime. Unable to bring myself to bury their ashes, I ask humbly that you bury them on my behalf once I am dead and gone. In many ways I was a coward in life, but in this most of all—that I could not bear to carry out myself the one final wish that had been asked of me. It was too hard. The pain was too raw."

Nina was right. My grandfather had been a man who carried a lot of guilt. Even after death, he was apologizing!

"And that's it," my dad said, folding the page and sliding it back into the envelope. "As he didn't specify any particular place where he wanted his ashes to go, Emory and I have taken the liberty of choosing several different spots in the grove where we think his ashes could appropriately be buried. If anyone else wants to add to the ones we have chosen, by all means speak up and we'll do that too."

As I watched my dad address our little group, I was amazed, as always, by his mellifluous voice and "pastorly" ways. Before we started out, he led us in prayer, and his words to the Father sounded as sweet and simple as the prayers of the angels.

When he was finished, we all gave a rousing "Amen," and then we began, pausing first at the Main Gate. There, Emory dug a shallow hole at the base of the first tree Abe had planted, the very genesis of the grove. My father sprinkled some of the ashes in the hole, and Emory used the shovel to cover them up with the freshly turned earth. Walking to the next site, which was a row of weeping willows along the creek where Abe had first taught Emory to fish, my grandmother Maureen sang out the chorus of a beloved hymn, and we all joined in as well. It felt good to sing as we walked, to support my dad and his brother as they sprinkled the ashes, and to memorialize once and for all the man who had long ago looked out on this wide patch of land and envisioned something altogether profound and lovely.

As we passed by the Fishing Tree, the Southern Catawba near the Peace Gate, we all grew silent, sharing the same frustrated thoughts, I felt sure. Despite lots of digging and probing and even consultations by experts, we had never found any diamonds buried there. Wherever my grandfather had hidden them, he hadn't replicated their original hiding place in Germany after all. Perhaps we would never know what had become of poor Emory's diamonds!

As we reached the final place my father wanted us to see, I was surprised by his choice, a marker with a brief quote from *The Metamorphoses* that read, *I who am chasing you am not your enemy.*

I didn't understand its significance, but as my father spoke for a bit, I realized he was using it as an opportunity to share with us some closing thoughts about Abe and his life.

"These things we run from," my dad told us, "don't always need to be feared so strongly. Sometimes we need to stop and remember that which is chasing us is not our enemy. My dad let guilt and shame dog him throughout his life, always nipping at his heels. My prayer for all of us is that we take time now and then to turn and face those things that are chasing us, acknowledge them, and accept the fact that they're a part of who we are. If possible, maybe we can even embrace them for the good that has come out of the bad. If my father had been able to do that, he would have ended his days as a far, far happier man."

Wanting to end things on a more upbeat note, my dad went on to list the many qualities Abe Collins had that were admirable: integrity, bravery, loyalty, creativity, and more.

"He wasn't the best husband," he said, smiling sympathetically toward Grandma Maureen, "but he was a darn good father. He would've done anything for the two of us, and he always made sure we knew that. Right, Emory?"

"You betcha!" Emory replied, and we all chuckled as he grinned, pleased with himself.

We closed our little ceremony with a prayer, this one while standing in a circle, our hands joined. After the amen, we lingered that way, singing together a chorus of "Blest Be the Tie That Binds." As our voices rose and blended among the trees, fresh tears filled my eyes. I realized in that moment that this truly was "harmony" grove.

Lunch would be served back at the B and B, a special meal provided by our many Amish cousins. Liesl had coordinated the meal, and as we walked back to the inn I was pleased to see the driveway now filling up not just with cars but also buggies. There was something about the blending of the Plain community with the rest of us, the Amish cousins with the English, that felt healing and right, given Abe's long-ago break from the faith. I knew the Amish would always keep themselves "apart," following their own ideology, but that didn't mean we couldn't support each other or show love to each other. I would always treasure the Amish friendships I had, especially my relationship with Jonah and Liesl.

Since all of the mess three weeks before, I had learned the truth about the gun charge that had gotten Jonah in trouble. Apparently, Pennsylvania regulations required a photo ID for the purchase of new firearms, with no religious exemptions. Like most other Amish, Jonah refused to have a photo ID, so he had been forced to ask a friend to buy a hunting rifle for him. The problem in this case was that the "friend" happened to be Troy, back before they'd had their falling out over the horses. Once that whole matter was cleared up with the authorities, Jonah repented of the matter to his bishops and church community, and the whole thing had been forgiven and forgotten.

Burl wouldn't be getting off so easily. Charged with all sorts of crimes from murder to animal cruelty to environmental endangerment and more, we knew he would be behind bars for many, many years to come.

I was glad to have a few more of my questions answered, including the whole matter of the latch that Troy had unlocked that night while on the phone with me. According to Burl, who had watched events unfold while hiding nearby, once Troy had contaminated himself with the poison and had begun to get confused, he had wandered in completely the wrong direction, ending up at the back of Burl's property. Facing the big wire cage that sat half concealed in the bushes, he had opened the latch, realized that the cage door led nowhere, and turned around and tried going in another direction.

What Troy hadn't noticed, thanks to the overgrown bushes and weeds and trees that surrounded the cage, was the big, black bird with the vivid blue neck and red wattle resting silently in the far corner. Once the door was open and Troy had left, the cassowary followed, and Burl had had no choice but to run into his house, don his protective gear, grab his tranquilizer gun, and try to subdue the bird without revealing himself to Troy.

It hadn't been easy. When the bird attacked Troy, knocking him down and gashing his leg, Burl had taken his first shot but had missed. Troy managed to get up and run away, finally climbing over the fence into the pool area. The cassowary followed as far as the fence, where Burl's second shot finally hit its mark. As the bird had sat down there in the bushes, tranquilized and docile, Troy had proceeded to drown in the pool, right on the other side of the fence—mission accomplished, as far as Burl was concerned.

The threat to the diamonds had been eliminated.

After that, Burl was just getting a rope around the bird's neck to lead it home when Nina showed up, spotted Troy's dead body, and started screaming. Crouching down in the bushes not far from the resting bird, Burl had hoped he could wait things out and at some point slip away from the scene, bird in tow, unnoticed.

Unfortunately, the cassowary had had a different idea. Just as Floyd and Nina were arguing beside the pool, it had tried to stand, letting out its signature rumble. When they both turned to see what was going on, Burl had no choice but to rise up from his hiding spot nearby and take down first Floyd and then Nina. After retrieving the darts from their sleeping bodies, he had made the decision to bring the cassowary not back to its cage, where officials might see it and put together what had happened, but instead to the hidden room at Emory's house, which Burl had used occasionally in the past to hide some of his animal fighting paraphernalia. Thanks to the second entrance through the springhouse, Emory had never known, and Burl had hoped he wouldn't learn about the creature being in there either.

After that, Burl had put out a call for help to the C to B syndicate, asking that the animal wranglers come and remove the cassowary as soon as possible, at least until the heat was off. Apparently, the evening that the Nightmare Twins had shown up at the B and B looking for Floyd, they hadn't intended him any harm. They had simply wanted some help getting Emory to leave his home for a while so they could remove the animal unobserved.

I was glad to learn that Floyd really had been telling the truth about not having much involvement with the C to B gambling ring. He was aware of its activities and its key players, but he hadn't been a party to any of their dealings, nor had he had anything to do with Burl's ties to the group.

Troy, on the other hand, had been the one who first established those ties, getting Burl connected to the men who ran the whole C to B gambling syndicate in the first place. Having seen Burl's isolated farm and empty animal housing, Troy had spotted yet another opportunity to milk the "myth of the pastoral," and had managed to make the connection between the retired chicken farmer who could use some extra cash and the animal wranglers who were always on the lookout for places to stash their animals between fights. After all, who would ever suspect such nefarious dealings here in the heart of perfect, innocent Amish country?

At least this whole mess had helped authorities crack a case that had been dragging on for years. Like dominoes toppling, once they had arrested Burl and persuaded him to talk, they had been able to make more arrests, apply more pressure to those people, and eventually shut down a vast network of C to B-related activities. Though I still couldn't fathom how animals could be used for blood sport, I knew the darker side of man allowed for some pretty evil things.

Learning about Daphne's experience in the Holocaust had been an even more somber reminder of that.

As for Floyd, we weren't sure what happened to him, and the authorities weren't saying, though I had a feeling he had finally made it to some distant beach where he was now taking it easy, sipping mango juice and no doubt cooking up more trouble. Floyd was just one of those people who knew how to work things to his advantage—and, when he couldn't, somehow landing on his feet anyway.

My thoughts were interrupted by the appearance of my cousin Lucy emerging from the side porch, coming out to give us all hugs. Daniel was with her, his sister Annie propped on his hip, though when she saw me she smiled and held out her arms and leaned forward until I was holding her instead.

"Si-na," she said, pointing at my face.

"That's right," I laughed, smiling at this little blond-haired angel in my arms. "Si-en-na."

"Si-nen-na," she echoed, and we all shared a chuckle.

After visiting with everyone for a while, sampling the delicious food, and reveling in the compliments about my beautiful inn, I was glad when my father announced to the small crowd that he and Emory were going next door to retrieve the other ashes and would then head to the Daphne tree so we could honor Abe's request. Anyone who would like to join the family was welcome to meet there in about twenty minutes.

When it was time to go, Liesl and I were deep in conversation, so we walked together, talking as we went. There was plenty to discuss now that I was seriously considering moving out here to Lancaster County and taking over the running of the inn myself. That couldn't happen until I sold the condo, which could take a few months, but at least I knew now what I wanted and where I belonged. My experiences here just three short weeks ago had taught me that.

In the meantime, the B and B was sitting vacant, though Jonah and Liesl were keeping an eye on it for me until I got all of my ducks in a row. They were also making some changes to it, removing the wine racks and rebuilding the stairs. Though the hidden room was no longer a secret, I thought someday I might turn it into a memorial of sorts, perhaps using the unique space to educate people about the Holocaust and as a display area for some of Daphne's poetry.

"You know," Liesl said now, tucking a hand in my arm as we walked, "I have to tell you something I have been thinking about for a long time, ever since Uncle Abe died."

"Yes?"

"I notice that the English are always saying 'I'm sorry for your loss, so sorry for your loss.' It is an appropriate expression, I suppose."

I nodded, wondering where she was going with this.

"But for me," she continued, "what I realized is that at other times when things are going well and a person is finding herself to be quite successful and affluent, earning and achieving and expanding, what I would like to say is 'I am sorry for your gain.'"

I couldn't help but laugh, asking what on earth she meant.

"Just that the ways of God's people are not the ways of this world. Success and money and achievement can be a terrible hindrance to one's spiritual life. At least at times of loss, we are reminded of our priorities, of our many blessings. In times of gain, we can so often lose our way. This is why the Amish stress simplicity in all things at all times, because nothing should ever be allowed to turn our eyes away from what is truly important, from the cross."

I nodded, surprised as tears suddenly filled my eyes.

"You're right, Liesl. That's exactly what happened to me. In the midst of my biggest successes, I lost my way for a while."

She simply nodded, putting an arm around my shoulders and walking alongside me the rest of the way through the grove. In our comfortable silence, I found myself turning to prayer, as I had done often these past few weeks. I didn't know what the future held in store, but I did know one thing, that being fully committed to God was a far, far better place to be than sitting on a fence, imagining the view on both sides.

"And what of your young man?" Liesl teased as we neared the bridge. "Any decisions in that area?"

Reaching the bridge and waiting our turn to file across, I smiled, telling her that I had come a long way in that regard as well. Now that I was fully committed, and Heath was looking for a new position with one of the hospitals out here in Lancaster County, I couldn't imagine why I had ever hesitated with regard to this man at all. He was everything I had ever dreamed of in a future husband and more. Glancing at my watch, I wondered how much longer it would be before he arrived. As we assembled around the tree at the center of the grove, I glanced back toward the path at the final stragglers, pleased to see that the crowd now included Mike, who was talking animatedly to Nina, and the cops Rip and Charlie, who had taken a sort of fatherly interest in things around here and had begun advising me on the care and tending of the many trees in the grove.

At last, Heath finally arrived as well. As he stood at the end of the line, waiting for his turn to cross the narrow bridge, our eyes met. In the smile we shared, I saw everything: my past, this present, our future. We hoped to marry in the spring and make Harmony Grove Bed & Breakfast our permanent home.

I couldn't imagine a better way to live happily ever after.

"Welcome, everyone," my father said, standing with Emory at the base of the Daphne tree. "Thanks for coming out here and sharing this special moment with us."

He went on to explain about my grandfather's directive and what we were doing, whose ashes these were, and why this moment was important. As he spoke, he held in his hands the decorative box that had long sat on the mantel at Emory's house. I had always known it once contained Daphne's ashes, but I had assumed that they had been sprinkled out here long before now.

"As you know," my father continued, "thanks to the generous donation of my mother, Maureen, this afternoon at three the grove will officially open to the public as the newest addition to the Lancaster County parks system. But for the next few hours, it still belongs only to us, and in the intimacy of this moment we are pleased to put to rest, finally, these ashes that have come here from halfway around the world."

With that, Emory held out the box as my father opened the lid and removed two small containers, tiny metal jars that had been labeled with the names of Daphne's mother and sister. As he opened each jar and sprinkled its meager contents at the base of a fig tree, we all looked on in respectful silence.

Next, he removed from the decorative box the larger container that held Daphne's cremated remains. Opening the bag, he held it out toward Emory, who set the box down on the ground, took the ashes from my dad, and walked in a circle around the tree, carefully pouring out his mother's ashes onto the ground. When he was finished, I doubted there was a dry eye in the whole group.

My father picked up the box and was closing the lid when he spied something in the bottom: a bulky manila envelope, on the outside of which Abe had written *"Open after sprinkling ashes."*

I looked at Heath, who slipped a warm hand in mine and gave it a tight squeeze. Before my father even looked inside the envelope, we both knew what he would find there: the diamonds, the sum total of Daphne's family fortune, and the final assurance that Emory's needs would be covered for the rest of his life.

Sure enough, we were correct. As my father offered a glimpse of the sparkling stones to the crowd, and everyone looked on in awe, I watched Emory, who was excited as well but quickly lost interest in the stones, his attention caught by the sight of a beautiful red bird who had landed on a branch nearby, its song suddenly filling the trees of the grove with music. At least Emory knew how to focus on what was really important. And that was a lesson I had recently learned myself.

With the help of my loved ones, it was one I hoped to remember for the rest of my life.

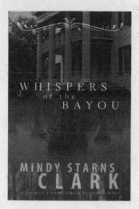

WHISPERS OF THE BAYOU
What Mysteries Lie Hidden
Beside the Dark Water of the Bayou?

Swept away from Louisiana bayou country as a child, Miranda Miller is a woman without a past. She has a husband and child of her own and a fulfilling job in a Manhattan museum, but she also has questions—about the tragedy that cut her off from family and caused her to be sent away, and about those first five years that were erased from her memory entirely.

Summoned to the bedside of Willy Pedreaux, the old caretaker of her grandparents' antebellum estate, Miranda goes back for the first time, hoping to learn the truths of her past and receive her rightful inheritance. But Willy's premature death plunges Miranda into a nightmare of buried secrets, priceless treasure, and unknown enemies.

Follow one woman's search through the hidden rooms of a bayou mansion, the enigmatic snares of an ancient myth, and the all-consuming quest for a heart open enough for love—and for God.

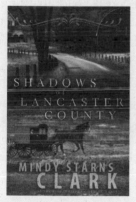

SHADOWS OF LANCASTER COUNTY
What Shadows Darken the
Quiet Valleys of Amish Country?

Anna Bailey thought she left the tragedies of the past behind when she took on a new identity and moved from Pennsylvania to California. But now that her brother has vanished and his wife is crying out for help, Anna knows she has no choice but to come out of hiding, go home, and find him. Back in Lancaster County, Anna follows the high-tech trail her brother left behind, a trail that leads from the simple world of Amish farming to the cutting edge of DNA research and gene therapy.

During the course of her pursuit, Anna soon realizes that she has something others want, something worth killing for. In a world where nothing is as it seems, Anna seeks to protect herself, find her brother, and keep a rein on her heart despite the sudden reappearance of Reed Thornton, the only man she has ever loved.

Following up on her extremely popular gothic thriller, *Whispers of the Bayou*, Mindy Starns Clark offers another suspenseful standalone mystery, one full of Amish simplicity, dark shadows, and the light of God's amazing grace.

UNDER THE CAJUN MOON

*What Secrets Can Be Found
by the Light of the Cajun Moon?*

New Orleans may be the "Big Easy," but nothing about it was ever easy for international business etiquette expert Chloe Ledet. She moved away years ago, leaving her parents and their famous French Quarter restaurant behind. But when she hears that her father has been shot, she races home to be by his side and to handle his affairs—only to learn a long-hidden secret that changes everything she knew to be true about herself and her family.

Framed for murder, Chloe and a handsome Cajun stranger must search for a priceless treasure, one whose roots weave through the very history of Louisiana itself. But can Chloe depend on the mysterious man leading her on this cat-and-mouse chase into the heart of Cajun country? Or by trusting him, has she gone from the frying pan into the fire?

Following up on her bestselling Gothic thriller, *Whispers of the Bayou*, and Amish romantic suspense, *Shadows of Lancaster County*, Mindy Starns Clark offers another exciting standalone novel, one full of Cajun mystery, hidden dangers, and the glow of God's unending grace.

ABOUT THE AUTHOR

Secrets of Harmony Grove is Mindy's fourteenth book with Harvest House Publishers. Previous books include the bestselling *Whispers of the Bayou, Shadows of Lancaster County,* and *Under the Cajun Moon* as well as the well-loved Million Dollar Mysteries.

Mindy is also a playwright, a singer, and a former stand-up comedian. A popular inspirational speaker and conference teacher, Mindy lives with her husband, John, and two daughters near Valley Forge, Pennsylvania.

In any story, where facts are used to mold and shape fiction, sometimes it becomes hard for readers to tell the two apart, particularly when learning about a history or culture that isn't overly familiar to them. For more information and to find out which elements of this story are fictional and which are based on fact, visit Mindy's website at

www.mindystarnsclark.com

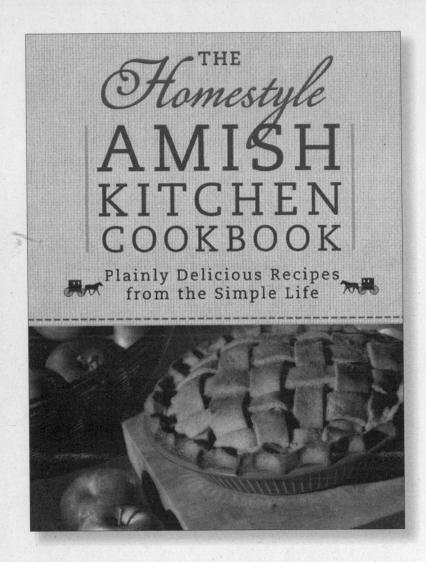

THE Homestyle AMISH KITCHEN COOKBOOK

Plainly Delicious Recipes from the Simple Life

"What a delightful and authentic cookbook! Not only is my family enjoying the recipes from *The Homestyle Amish Kitchen Cookbook*, but so are my characters, because I consult its pages whenever I'm writing Amish fiction."

—MINDY STARNS CLARK